Warwickshire County Council

SN	W H I	12/20	
0 9 SEP 2019			
11/2/20 PMB			
3/3/20			

This item is to be returned or renewed before the latest date above. It may be borrowed for a further period if not in demand. **To renew your books:**

- **Phone the 24/7 Renewal Line 01926 499273 or**
- **Visit www.warwickshire.gov.uk/libraries**

    Discover ● Imagine

D1352541

Also by Julie Miller

Also by Addison Fox

Discover more at millsandboon.co.uk

PERSONAL PROTECTION

JULIE MILLER

THE COLTON SHERIFF

ADDISON FOX

MILLS & BOON

First Published in Great Britain 2019
by Mills & Boon, an imprint of HarperCollins*Publishers*
1 London Bridge Street, London, SE1 9GF

Personal Protection © 2019 Julie Miller
The Colton Sheriff © 2019 Harlequin Books S.A.

Special thanks and acknowledgement are given to Addison Fox for her contribution to *The Coltons of Roaring Springs* series.

ISBN: 978-0-263-27432-5

0819

Printed and bound in Spain
by CPI, Barcelona

PERSONAL PROTECTION

JULIE MILLER

For Jana Boyll Thompson, my singing buddy.

I so enjoy hanging out with you at City Singers
and doing a show together every now and then.
We'll try not to get into too much trouble.

Prologue

May 1—Lukinburg Day in St. Feodor,
on the steps of the historic palace square

"In three months, St. Feodor will play host to a group
of dignitaries from our sister city in the United States.
We will introduce the Americans to the charm of our
country and show them that they need us as much as
we need them. They need our rugged mountains, our
beautiful beaches, our vast supply of natural resources,
the skills and grace of our people."

Cameras flashed in the crowd, and the low white
noise of television and radio commentators from across
Europe and the United States, speaking a dozen different languages, buzzed in the background beneath static
from the old broadcasting system. The world was waiting for tiny, mountainous Lukinburg in Eastern Europe
to blossom after decades of oppression to take its rightful place on the world stage once more.

A black-haired woman in a cream-colored suit moved
in behind the prince at the podium and tapped him on
the shoulder. "Do not forget to mention the city's name,
Your Highness," she reminded him.

"Thank you, Galina," the prince whispered before

turning back to the microphone. "Kansas City, Missouri, our sister city, will become Lukinburg's partner in worldwide respect and future prosperity. We shall be great friends."

The crowd erupted in applause. He adjusted his glasses at his temple and scanned the throng of onlookers through the bulletproof glass surrounding the podium. He looked past the placards here to support the new regime to the handful of scowling doubters with their own less supportive signs, waiting for the opportune moment to voice a protest.

A public gathering of this size in the capital on one of the country's biggest holidays once would have been a prime target for dissidents. Change was hard for any citizen. Change was the enemy to those who'd once held positions of power, who were now either imprisoned or being asked to embrace what was good for the country over what was lucrative for themselves. But the prince had reached out to those dissidents, had listened to their complaints and fears, had formed alliances and reached compromises with many of them. Yet, some of the most die-hard rebels hadn't given up the fight, and they would always see the new monarchy as their enemy.

Lukinburg's army had some of the finest trained soldiers in the world, and the plainclothes security force that now surrounded the country's leaders at every venue were on constant guard against any threat that would topple the fragile new government. He looked at his friends and former military comrades flanking him on the podium. They were doing this. They were making Lukinburg great again. Their hard work and dedication had given the country reason to celebrate today.

Ivan Mostek, the crown prince of Lukinburg, was

nearing the end of his long fight to replace the corrupt government of this country. A hardworking regency government and brave voters had replaced the corrupt dictator and mafia-like power brokers who had made Lukinburg a haven for criminals and arms trafficking. Part of electing a new Parliament and reestablishing the democratic monarchy this picturesque country had enjoyed before World War II was locating a true heir to the Lukinburg throne. As a distant cousin of the last legitimate king's late grandnephew, that dubious honor fell to Ivan. Plucked from graduate school where he'd been earning his MBA, he'd accepted the position. Patriotism and DNA had left him with no other choice but to say yes, and accept that within the next year, he would be crowned king.

With the discovery of gold and mica deep beneath the mountains east of Lake Feodor, Lukinburg now had raw materials that countries in the West and Far East were clamoring to build their electronics and develop new computer technologies. The prince had implemented environmentally safe mining practices to sustain the new resources. From his newfound position of power, he was jump-starting the country's economy, feeding the poor, capitalizing on new industries and putting people to work—all while paying tribute to Lukinburg's traditional culture and storied history.

Public appearances were necessary to assure the citizens of the solidity of the new government. And public appearances meant crowds of people and noisy fanfare and making speeches. After the cheers had died down, he continued, "Kansas City's manufacturing, agricultural and business leaders will be in our beautiful country, in this fair city, in three weeks. A carefully chosen delegation of representatives from Lukinburg will negotiate trade agreements and cultural exchanges that will benefit both our countries."

He spied movement in the shadows of the pointed Gothic archways in the cathedral across from the palace steps where he stood. He looked across the podium to his friend Konrad Pavluk. They exchanged a nod of awareness. Konrad had spotted the movement, too. The other man drifted across the dais to stand beside Galina. Anyone less observant would have missed the hidden squeeze of hands, the subtle whisper of a warning. She nodded and moved up behind the prince again to relay a message.

The military marksmen stationed in decorative ramparts atop the stone buildings surrounding the public square didn't seem concerned by the hooded man in the long coat making his way through the crowd of bystanders. Maybe they didn't see him. Or perhaps, as the prince had confided to his best friend only days earlier, someone within his inner circle was still working with the extremists. Did the uniformed guards' lack of response mean they were unobservant? Traitors? Was he overly paranoid about the prince's safety because an attempt had already been made on his life?

Although that sniper had been captured and taken into custody, the threats against Ivan's life continued. It had been random gunfire that had wounded his driver and ignited the engine of the car they'd taken to an ore refinement facility being built outside the city. Were the extremists here today? Mingling with this crowd of innocent civilians? Would they strike again, regardless of the casualties a group this big might sustain? Was the man in the hooded coat one of them?

He glanced over to the security chief, Filip Milevski. Although the dark glasses he wore made the direction of his gaze unreadable, the stocky man with salt-and-pepper hair was on the radio pinned to his wrist, no doubt asking for a situation update from his men and hopefully sounding a potential alert to stop the man who was now circling the fountain in the middle of the square.

The prince's voice was slightly less composed, tinged with a bit of anger, when he continued. "I promise to make Lukinburg great again. We will move past the shame of our former leaders. We will return to the democratic monarchy of our ancestors. I will work closely with the new prime minister and your votes will count. All your votes," he added, perhaps emphasizing to the extremists in the audience that they were not excluded from the new government.

Another round of cheers from the crowd nearly drowned out a lone dissenter who booed him. "You're selling us out, Ivan!"

Security Chief Milevski sidled closer to the prince. "Wrap it up, Your Highness." He moved Konrad and another one of his men farther down the granite steps in front of the podium. "There are too many of us exposed here. We're all in danger."

His gaze zeroed in on the hooded man. He'd sat on the edge of the fountain and was unbuttoning his long coat. The prince kept talking into the microphone, keeping the crowd engaged while members of the security team made their way through the onlookers to reach the suspect. "We need free trade. Our people need food."

"Our people need a leader they can respect!" The protest came from another corner of the audience.

"I agree. For too long, we have been led by men our people fear. Fear doesn't put food in people's bellies. Our people are working again. They aren't afraid to leave their homes and share their opinions and vote however they please."

A tall man, with hair as black at the prince's himself, moved in beside him with a whispered warning. "Your Highness. We need to go."

The security team converged on the fountain as the hooded man stood. "End Ivan!"

"Bomb!"

There were too many screams to make out the words that followed. The crowd split and ran like a tidal surge away from the fountain.

"Stop him!"

"Save the prince!"

Armed men in suits ran forward.

A sniper guarding the gathering from a turret high above the street raised his rifle and took aim at the insurgent. But he was too late.

"Save yourselves!" Prince Ivan warned. His bodyguards swarmed around him and shoved him to the stone steps behind the podium. The square erupted with light and the deafening roar of an explosion.

The prince's cheek scraped against stone as the black-haired man covered his body with his. His ears were stopped up by the concussive blast. But he heard the screams of his people, the stampede of running feet, gunfire, as if the violence was all happening far in the distance instead of a mere few yards beyond the podium.

He spotted blood on the steps a split second before something sharp and hot seared his skin, cutting through the invisible target on his back.

The prince's public rallying speech in the heart of Lukinburg's capital left him wounded. Landmarks had been damaged. People were injured, dead.

The dignitaries from Kansas City wouldn't be coming.

Chapter One

August—Kansas City, Missouri

After the explosion in the palace square, the business-people and government officials Ivan Mostek needed to talk to in Kansas City had refused to travel to Lukinburg. They were concerned for their safety, and rightly so. The shrapnel scars on his back were still pink and tender from that attack.

But he wouldn't give up on the new government's vision to reform his country.

So, the prince had come to Kansas City. These negotiations were going to happen, no matter what a few leftovers from the old regime thought of him. They'd lost their power and weren't above using an assassination to get it back. Perhaps the threats he faced were coming from loyalists who believed the modernization of their country would irrevocably change it, and they'd lose their cultural identity. What they'd lose was any kind of standing as a first world country. Their economy was dying, and the old ways didn't feed his people.

Ivan Mostek, Crown Prince of Lukinburg, the symbolic leader of his country and heir to the throne, had no intention of giving power back to the thugs that had nearly ruined their country, nor did he intend to destroy any of the things that made Lukinburg so uniquely special. The plan was a good one. But he had to survive first. Survive this trip to the States. Survive until his coronation and hopefully live a long and healthy life afterward as the leader of Lukinburg.

The first step in that plan meant leaving his country and traveling to Kansas City for a week. The second step meant surrounding himself with people he trusted. That was proving more of a challenge than he'd expected since it seemed that no matter what security measures his team put into place, the threats kept coming. So, he'd put in a call to KCPD to ask for help from strangers. The local police had no ties to Lukinburg. He was counting on them to provide a layer of protection that couldn't be influenced by politics, fear of change or revenge.

Striding up the steps from his limousine, Ivan followed his chief of security, Filip Milevski, into the lobby of Fourth Precinct headquarters. His trusted adviser and good friend, Aleksandr Petrovic, followed right behind him, while another bodyguard, Danya Pavluk, brought up the rear. His third bodyguard and new driver, Eduard Nagy, would park the car and wait for them to finish their respective meetings.

After lining up their visitor badges, Filip, a tall, beefy man with graying sideburns, punched the button to call the elevator. "I will escort you to your meeting with Captain Hendricks. Then Danya and I will meet with the SWAT captain and senior patrol officer to coordinate security at your public appearances."

Ivan smoothed the knot of his tie and nodded. "Do not forget to have them set up extra officers outside the

Lukinburg embassy on Saturday. Your team can work
with embassy security inside, but the ball will dramati-
cally increase traffic and bring many wealthy and important local and state people to that part of town."

"I forget nothing," Filip huffed, as though it was an
insult to remind him. The elevator doors opened, and
he waited for the car to empty before leading them inside. "I do not understand why you could not stay at the
hotel and let me handle the police department. This Joe
Hendricks you are meeting with is not on my list of contacts." No, but Chief of Police Taylor had recommended
the precinct captain when Ivan had called to ask for the
secret favor. "I cannot control your safety when you surprise me with meetings that are not on your agenda."

Ah, yes. Filip loved his routines. If he had any idea
what Ivan was planning behind his back, he'd be livid.

"I told you, this is personal. You do not need to be
involved."

"But it is my responsibility—"

"I am inside a police station. I will be fine without
you hovering over me." He grinned at Aleks, who was
people watching the comings and goings of officers,
detectives, visitors and staff through the lobby check-
point and service counters. He flicked his friend's arm
to get his attention. "You should have brought a camera," he teased.

Aleks's grin formed a bright crescent of white in his
long black beard. "Did you see that plaque on the wall?
They have created a memorial to a little girl—"

"Aleks…" Ivan urged his friend to join them. "Business first. Sightseeing later. You know we must—"

"Hold that elevator!"

Ivan's sentence trailed off and he instinctively

grabbed the door as a woman with a dirty, soot-streaked blond ponytail darted onto the elevator. She pulled in an equally grimy, handcuffed man by his upper arm and guided him to the corner farthest away from Ivan and his staff, ordering her captive to face the wall. Filip cursed under his breath as he and Danya quickly positioned themselves between Ivan and their guests and allowed the doors to close.

"Thanks." He saw the woman wore fingerless gloves when she pushed some flyaway strands of hair off her face. He also saw the badge hanging from a chain around her neck. Ivan's senses tingled with an alertness he had to hide. "Sorry. I didn't relish dragging this dirtbag up the stairs or waiting for the next elevator."

She wore a long, dusty man's coat over jeans and worn leather boots that were nearly as big as his own feet. Gloves? Coat? Boots?

In August?

No wonder there was a sheen of perspiration on her pink cheeks.

As intrigued by her apparent toughness as he was curious about her ratty, overheated appearance, he offered her a succinct nod. "We are happy to oblige the local constabulary."

Her prisoner glanced over his shoulder at Ivan. "What's that mean?"

"Quiet." The officer nodded toward the keypad and asked Filip to push the button for her. "Third floor, please."

"We should not share an elevator, Your High—"

"This is fine," Ivan insisted, reaching around his security chief to press the number three button himself. It was probably best not to advertise his real identity just yet. Not until all his security was in place. "We are here to make friends with the people of Kansas City, not make their lives more difficult."

"You talk funny," the handcuffed man slurred, laughing at their accents.

And he smelled funny. Dreadful, actually, as Ivan crinkled his nose up against the odors of urine, body odor and smoke filling the confined space. At least, he hoped it was the criminal and not the female officer escorting him who reeked of the streets. Ivan had been trained to keep such negative observations to himself and be a polite gentleman at all times. "English is not my first language."

"Your English is better than mine, pal."

"Dougie. Sorry about that, sir." The woman jerked on the handcuffs, warning her prisoner to be quiet again. Apparently, standing still and keeping his mouth shut was an ongoing battle for the twitchy bum. "I am already in a mood. Don't push it."

Even though the woman wasn't terribly chatty, Ivan noted that she was extremely observant. She marked their number and position on the elevator as it began its ascent. She sized up the flak vest and guns Filip and Danya wore beneath their suit jackets and pulled back the front of her coat to keep her gun within easy reach. Although he wanted to reassure the woman that they meant her no harm, backing up that claim would mean that he'd have to identify himself and his entourage. And Ivan wasn't ready to reveal anything when he had this much of an audience surrounding him.

His training in the Lukin military had made him observant, too. The woman had an ordinary face. She was of average height and indeterminate shape, thanks to the bulky coat she wore. In addition to a stylist, she needed a comb and a shower and a much more cooperative prisoner. Ivan curled his fingers into his palms, fighting back the urge to push Filip and Danya aside and assist her with the recalcitrant man who muttered and fidgeted instead of obeying her authority. Maybe a good twenty years older and hundred pounds heavier than her, the man seemed familiar with handcuffs and causing trouble. No wonder she'd been anxious to get him into a jail cell or interview room and off her hands.

He also noticed she had green eyes.

And lips. Ivan averted his gaze as if he'd uttered that ridiculous observation out loud. Of course, she had lips. But they had drawn his attention to the middle of her flushed face. Despite her determined lack of femininity, her lips were pink and asymmetrical, sleekly defined on top and decadently full on the bottom. She had a mouth that reminded him just how delightful it was to kiss a willing woman, and just how long he'd denied himself that pleasure.

"Y'all ain't cops, are ya?" Her prisoner twisted around again, ignoring her order to face the wall. "With your fancy suits and fancy accents. Damn foreigners."

"Douglas Freeland," she warned. "You be nice to these people."

"I ain't been nothin' but nice this morning. I got a sickness and you know it. You set me up." He called her a crude name that fisted Ivan's hands with the need to shut him up and make him apologize. He was embarrassed to see his bodyguards ignoring the verbal abuse and staring fixedly at the elevator doors as they slowed to a stop. "I ain't goin' back in."

The moment the doors slid open, the prisoner twisted

out of her grasp. In the next second, he spun around and butted his fat, bald head against her more delicate skull.

The urge to intervene jolted through Ivan's legs as she tumbled to the floor. But Filip and Danya pushed him against the railing, blocking him from the scuffle. "Protect the prince!"

Not that the officer apparently needed his or anyone's help. Before the man got both feet off the elevator, her legs shot out and she tripped him. Then she was on top of the guy with a feral yell as she smushed her attacker's face to the floor. Several other officers from the third floor had rushed to help, but they stopped in their tracks, backing up a step as she hauled the prisoner to his feet. The big man wasn't muttering anymore. She pushed him against the seam between the wall and the elevator, using him to prop the door open while she checked his cuffs and evened out her breathing.

Filip took Ivan by the arm to lead him off the elevator. But Ivan didn't need to be sandwiched between his bodyguards. The woman, despite the blow to the head, seemed to have the situation under control.

Still, he knew the toll hand-to-hand combat like that could take on a person. There would be bruises, and her head would be throbbing. He shrugged free of Filip's grip. "Are you all right, miss?"

"Officer. Officer Valentine." Her green eyes widened with a message that could be understood in any language. *Get off the damn elevator already and let me do my job.*

"Very well. Gentlemen." They all exited the elevator and headed to the sergeant's desk for directions to the captain's office.

With a nod to the officers who'd come to her aid, Officer Valentine pushed a long tendril of caramel-colored hair off her face and walked her prisoner through the maze of desks on the main floor. Her dialogue trailed off as they went their separate ways. "That was your big plan? Escape onto a floor filled with cops? Now I get to add a second assault charge…"

Relief that Officer Valentine was all right, as well as admiration at how she'd handled the situation herself, eased the tension inside him. Ivan wondered at the rush of adrenaline he felt ebbing from his system and chalked it up to jet lag finally catching up with him.

"THIS IS EVERYTHING on my schedule while I am here in Kansas City." Ivan forwarded the text from his chief of staff, Galina Honchar, to Captain Hendricks's phone. In turn, Joe Hendricks, the captain of the Fourth Precinct, copied the list of events and locations to his administrative assistant in the adjoining office and asked her to make a printout. "Occasionally, a meeting runs long or something unexpected comes up…"

"Last-minute changes could be handled by the liaison officer you're asking for," the captain finished. "She'll be able to keep me in loop, so I can have whatever assistance is needed on standby."

That was part of his plan, Ivan conceded. "That would be a benefit to your department." But he was asking for something more than a communications liaison with the local police.

After sending Filip and Danya off to their respective meetings, the only person from Lukinburg here with Ivan on the third floor was Aleksandr Petrovic. Last he'd seen, Aleks was cooling his heels in Captain Hendricks's outer office, chatting up the captain's administrative assistant. Even though the woman wore a wedding ring and was obviously pregnant, flirting and having a good time seemed to be hardwired into Aleks's DNA. He had survived the mines and poverty of Moravska, relying on hard work and sheer determination to leave his past behind him. His friend had been a city kid, raised in a modest neighborhood in St. Feodor, and had used that innate charm to impress the right people and negotiate one successful business deal after another. To look at them now, with their tailored suits and limousines, Ivan and Aleks seemed to be cut from the same cloth, but their personalities and backgrounds couldn't be more different. Still, Aleks was the one confidant the prince had trusted with the real goal of this meeting, and, if he wasn't too distracted by the woman out there, was keeping an eye out for when Milevski and the rest of the security team returned.

Ivan was learning that secrecy was practically impossible for royalty. But that secrecy was necessary. The crumpled note sitting like a fishing weight in his pocket warned him that keeping his secrets was a matter of life-and-death. "I told my security chief that I have reconnected with an old flame in the US from my military days, when we did joint operations with other countries. That is why I am making this request privately. They believe I am being discreet for romance's sake, not because I suspect a breach among the members of my entourage."

The black man with the weathered face and receding hairline nodded. "I can help you with your request to place an undercover operative inside your delegation for the duration of your visit. I've lined up a couple of candidates of the appropriate age for you to meet."

Ivan reminded him why he sought him out for assistance. "Finding a woman who served in the military is the only plausible way I could think of for me to have met an American and have had the time to develop a relationship with her. I worked with several American soldiers when I was in the military police."

"I haven't told them why they've been summoned to my office yet. I have to admit, this feels a bit like I'm playing matchmaker."

"I assure you, that is not the case, Captain." A tinge of awkwardness heated his skin. "I do not like that I have been forced into this situation. But I must choose a woman today, before I leave this building. My people must get used to seeing her with me. Masquerading as my…paramour…is the only way I can guarantee that we will have time alone to discuss who wants to kill me and devise strategy to unmask the traitor or traitors before they do me or anyone else harm. If I simply take on an American bodyguard, my security team will expect to be working together with that person. Since I do not know who I can trust, I require an ally who reports only to me, one who can convincingly play the role of consort to a prince, and whose qualities meet the needs of this very delicate investigation. I do not care what she looks like or if she fits some profile I would put on a dating site. She only needs to be good at her job."

"That's what I needed to hear." Hendricks pressed a sturdy index finger into the blotter on his desk, the gesture making Ivan think that warning finger would be pressed against his chest—royalty or not—if he dared to misuse one of Hendricks's officers. "If I hear that anything freaky happens to my officer while she's working with you, I promise I will bring the full force of this department down on your head."

"Understood. A good officer protects his troops. I respect that. And I will respect her."

Hendricks nodded. "Then let's do this, Your Highness."

Ignoring the urge to rub at the tension cording the back of his neck, Ivan nodded his appreciation. He was still getting used to answering to *prince* and *Your Highness*, although the proud posture and cautious, controlled movements that had been drilled into him during his stint in the military and on a UN coalition team in Bosnia served him well in conveying the air of authority he needed to project. The suit and tie he wore were better fitted and more expensive than the clothes he'd worn when he'd been a happy, anonymous commoner. He'd put on the hand-me-downs he'd worn growing up in the poor mountain village where his aunt and uncle had raised him if it meant he could go back to being an ordinary guy without the death threats and suspicions about the people closest to him churning inside his brain. He'd trade his penthouse suite for his old studio apartment in Moravska if it meant he'd no longer have the future of an entire country resting on his shoulders.

But those shoulders were broad and strong from the years he'd worked in the mines. The military had disciplined him, and a technology degree had given him a better life. He would do whatever was necessary to save the fledgling monarchy and put the discontents who would bring their country to its knees again out of business forever. Saving his own skin would be an added bonus.

He adjusted the glasses that pinched his nose and

looked across the desk into Joe Hendricks's golden-brown eyes. "You understand my need for secrecy?"

"I do." The man with the salt-and-pepper hair that receded into twin points atop his coffee-colored skin leaned back in his chair. "The fewer people who know about this charade, the better. Only you, me and the officer you select will know exactly what's going on. I'll serve as her undercover handler on this assignment." He rose from his chair and crossed to a set of blinds and opened them, revealing a bank of windows that overlooked a hallway and a beehive of desks and cubicle walls beyond that where uniformed officers, detectives, administrative staff and even a couple of criminals handcuffed to their chairs—including the lowlife who had attacked Officer Valentine—worked or waited. "If there's any chance the threat is legit, and one of those people—what did you call them?"

"They call themselves Lukin Loyalists. I call them the remnants of the mafia thugs who used to control our government. Lukin is a nickname we gave the citizens who were part of the underground resistance during World War II. These people are nothing like those brave souls."

"I thought I heard on the news a while back that the Loyalist situation had been resolved."

"So we thought." Ivan inhaled a deep breath and slowly released his frustration with the entire situation. "There are still some philosophical disagreements, but we've given them a voice in the new government. The minority whip in our Parliament is a Loyalist. He denounced the assassination attempt in the capital."

"There could be some fringe members of the party who feel their leadership has sold them out."

"Seven people died in that blast in St. Feodor, including a friend of mine. Whoever these people are, I take their threats seriously."

Hendricks agreed. "If one or more of these Loyalists are in Kansas City, planning an assassination attempt, then I want to know about it. I want to prevent any attack if possible and minimalize casualties—including you and my officer."

He pointed through the blinds to two female officers, one wearing a crisp blue uniform. She was engaged in an animated conversation with Aleks. Ivan grinned. Leave it to his friend to find someone new to practice his charms on. It was hard to remember a time when he'd been that carefree and able to stay squarely in a happy moment to enjoy it to the fullest.

The two of them looked very much alike, both with jet-black hair and blue eyes behind the glasses they each wore. Although Ivan stood half an inch taller, Aleks packed more muscle onto his frame. As the prince, he wore his hair cropped military short and kept his beard trimmed close to the angles of his jawline while his friend took his curly facial hair to a shaggy professor look. They'd done their requisite two-year stint in the army after university, where they'd met and become friends. After that, their paths had diverged—one remaining in the military, and the other going back to graduate school—until they'd come together again in service to the new government. They shared looks, history, pride in their country. And yet, the prince's world was vastly different from that of Aleksandr Petrovic. The orphan and the prince. The charmer and the disciplined soldier. Ivan's jaw clenched as his smile faded. Had he sentenced himself to a life of loneliness by answering the call of duty and giving himself over to the needs of his country and its people?

Ivan studied the female officer as she laughed at something Aleks said, and he felt a stab of envy at the normalcy of their interaction. But he reminded himself of the reason why he was here—to find a bodyguard he could trust without question, and an investigator who could help him identify the traitor in his inner circle. Knowing Filip Milevski and the rest of his security detail would be returning in the next fifteen to twenty minutes, Ivan rose, buttoned his jacket and joined Captain Hendricks at the window. He needed to evaluate the officers' suitability for the assignment before selecting his undercover partner.

The uniformed officer sat in one of the chairs lining the hallway, while Aleks stood beside her holding a paper cup of coffee. She touched her hair and ate up Aleks's attention. She was light, fun, perhaps not a strong enough presence to portray a convincing royal consort.

Meanwhile, the other woman, probably a detective, judging by her gray slacks and jacket, was plugged into her earbuds, and was scrolling through information on her phone as she paced the hallway outside the office's glass windows. Her expression remained stern as the uniformed officer caught her attention and tried to share the joke with her. The detective shook her head and continued her pacing. The woman's gravitas would certainly come through as they made their public appearances. She'd be a beauty if she smiled. But the tight lock of her mouth indicated a rigidity that might make it hard for her to adapt to the spontaneous opportunities for secret conversations he expected to arise as the investigation unfolded. And thus far, not much about being a prince was going according to any organized plan.

Captain Hendricks buried his hands in his pockets. "Either one of those women would make a fine liaison officer between you and KCPD."

They were both no doubt competent law enforcement officers, although neither type initially appealed to him. Not the way Officer Valentine's earthy vitality and tempting mouth had switched on his male radar. However, he wasn't here to meet the love of his life. If the woman could act her part as half of a convincing couple, then so could he. His life and the future of his country might depend on making the right choice here. A lightweight or a hard case. "They both have undercover experience?"

"Yes. Detective Wardyn is a few years past her last UC assignment, but she's a seasoned investigator. Officer Rangel is fairly new, but she has a higher marksmanship score."

Brains or brawn? He needed both.

"Then I suppose we should bring them in for a conversation. I don't want to reveal too much to either of them. The fewer people who know the specific details…"

And then a dusty ponytail and long black coat came into view as Officer Valentine shot up from her chair and circled her desk to point her finger in the face of the fat man who was mouthing off at her.

"Tell me more about her." Ivan nodded toward the argument that was not ending well for the handcuffed man. The grungy woman slapped a photograph on the desk in front of the man and forced him to look at it.

"Officer Valentine?" The captain chuckled at something Ivan failed to understand. "Looks like she's brought in a perp for processing."

Perp. Perpetrator. Ivan quickly translated the American slang and determined that Officer Valentine was a brave woman. The man she'd handcuffed made two of her, even with the heavy coat she wore. And yet she...

Ivan felt the hint of a smile relaxing the tight lines beside his mouth. "What about her? Does she have a military background? Earlier, she used a move on her prisoner that I learned during hand-to-hand combat training. Skills like that might be more useful than marksmanship when it comes to a protection detail."

"Carly Valentine? You think *she* can be your princess? Or, you know, personal bodyguard?" Hendricks didn't seem to be a man who was used to stuttering over his words, and he quickly shook off his surprise at Ivan's interest in the woman. "Valentine does a lot of UC work for us. She's a natural on the streets but—"

"Can she look professional when she is not in that costume?" Ivan paused for a moment, wondering if he should trust logic over what his instincts were telling him. "That *is* a costume, yes?"

"Let's hope so. You want to meet her?"

"Yes. There is something about her that seems like we could have worked together before. Under different circumstances. It might make our cover story more believable."

"It's your call." The captain crossed to his desk and picked up the phone to call his assistant. "Brooke? I need to see Carly Valentine in my office ASAP. And pull up her personnel file for me, please. Thanks."

Ivan was still at the window, watching as Carly Valentine answered the phone at her desk. Her shoulders sagged before she glanced back toward the captain's office. She spoke to the man sitting at the desk across from hers. After he nodded, she unlocked the perp from his chair and handed him off to the other officer, who led the prisoner out of sight down a long hallway.

Officer Valentine brushed off the sleeves of the oversize coat she wore, sending up a puff of gray dust in a cloud around her. The shake of her head told Ivan she was nervous about being summoned to the captain's office. She tried to tuck the loose waves back into her ponytail but stopped to inspect her hands. Another officer pointed to her face and Ivan could read the curse on her lips at the streak of soot her fingers had left there. She peeled off her fingerless gloves, quickly wiped her hands and face on a wad of tissues, and then steeled her shoulders before crossing to the captain's outer office. Her coat billowed out around her like the dusters cowboys wore in the American Western movies he loved to watch.

Joe Hendricks stood at his desk, reading information off the computer screen. "I've got Valentine's file here. She did have MP training in the National Guard. Looks like her stint with them ended earlier this year about the same time she earned her associate degree in criminal justice studies. She's been with the department four years. That's not as much experience as either of those officers in the hallway."

Didn't matter. "What does she do for you?"

"Right now, she's working an undercover assignment. She's attached to our human trafficking task force."

"Human trafficking? As in prostitution? Sex slavery?"

Hendricks nodded. "She's on the streets, identifying runaways and at-risk individuals."

Ivan turned back to the window. "And the man she brought in?"

"I'm not sure. But with Valentine, I'm guessing she caught him with his hands on the wrong person. She's a natural-born protector. Can't imagine what kind of fierce mama bear she'd make if she ever decides to have kids."

"Fierce mama bear?" She was in the hallway right outside the office now. Her gaze met and held his through the window. Her eyes were green like the mountain meadows of his homeland—and narrowed with suspicion.

"That's our Valentine."

She blinked, breaking the momentary connection between them. Oblivious to Aleks's curious interest as she walked past him and the other two female officers, she tossed her long ponytail down the center of her back and strode into the assistant's office.

Grimy. Plain. Fierce. Intriguing. Very good at playing her part.

A woman he just might have something in common with.

Chapter Two

"Hey, Brooke." Carly Valentine closed the door behind her and crossed the small office over to her friend's desk. Her pulse thrummed in her ears with more nerves than the adrenaline charge that had raised her heart rate when Dougie Freeland had whacked her in the temple with his big, bulbous head. "Can you give me a clue? What did I do?" She thumbed over her shoulder to the bull pen where the detectives and uniforms worked when they were in the office. "Did those guys in the elevator complain about me or my gruesome twin out there? I swear I didn't let Dougie touch them."

"You didn't do anything wrong." Brooke Kincaid looked up from her computer and smiled. The gesture was meant to reassure her, but that smile shifted into an apologetic frown, leaving Carly feeling anything but. "I'm still not sure what's going on, other than I've pulled service records and promised that anything I see or hear can't leave this office. By the way, are you okay?"

"Nothing that an ibuprofen won't cure. I've been hurt worse wrestling with Frank and Jesse." Although, unlike the man she'd brought in for booking, her older brothers hadn't meant her any real harm. They'd simply been picking on her for getting in their space or being the annoying little sister who'd done her best to keep them fed and dressed in clean clothes after their mother had died. Carly nodded toward the hallway where she'd passed the other two female officers and the geeky-looking guy who'd been flirting with Emily Rangel. "Does it have something to do with them? Am I getting transferred? A reprimand in my file?"

"I don't think it's anything bad." Brooke stood, resting a hand on her pregnant belly as she circled the desk to get close enough to whisper. "The guy in there with Joe is an honest to gosh prince from a little European country called Lukinburg."

"Lukinburg?"

"I looked it up. There's a delegation here from his country negotiating trade agreements. They're even hosting a ball, a fund-raiser for scientific research, while they're here in the US."

"A ball? Like dancing and sparkly gowns? Men in tuxedos?"

"The same."

"What's he doing here at the precinct?"

Brooke crinkled up her nose and sat back on the edge of her desk before answering. "Everything's all hush-hush. The prince called early this morning and asked to see Captain Hendricks as soon as I could fit him into the schedule. You should have seen it when he arrived—he has bodyguards."

"I met them in the elevator. That explains why they said, 'Save the prince' when Dougie went wacko on me."

"He called me *madam* and he bowed when he introduced himself—Ivan Mostek. He's no Atticus…" Brooke smiled, referring to her husband, the detective who oversaw the task force Carly was assigned to. "But he's hot. He's not soft underneath that suit and those manners. I think he could take care of himself if he had to."

Hearing Brooke refer to anyone besides her husband as hot was something new. Bowing and madam-ing certainly didn't sound like the visitors they usually got around here, either. Carly's heart rate wasn't slowing down. "He runs his own country? And he wants to see me?"

She glanced down at her dirty clothes and ruined steel-toed boots that she'd borrowed from her older brother Frank, who ran a construction business. It was already ninety degrees at lunchtime, and she'd been out most of the morning working her contacts. Dougie had taken exception to her interfering with his gross habit of flashing and had peed on her. The fact that there had been so much traffic through the old burned-out Morton & Sons Tile Works warehouse near the Missouri River had been reason enough to follow Freeland inside. But when she found him strutting his wares with a young prostitute she was certain was underage, Carly had broken her cover and placed him under arrest. Tackling him in a pile of charred debris from the fire and rolling in dust and ash that had been there for four years had turned her disguise from homeless to filthy.

She held up her hands, admitting the obvious. "I'm hardly looking my best."

"Or smelling it." The phone buzzed on Brooke's desk and she pushed to her feet. "That's Joe. He said there's a time crunch on whatever Prince Ivan needs. You'd better get in there." Brooke's nose crinkled up again and she clapped her fingers over her mouth, looking as if she might be sick. "You're a little ripe."

Carly instinctively retreated a step. "Sorry about that. Dougie didn't come quietly when I arrested him."

"The baby seems to make me really sensitive to smells right now." She turned her head to the side to inhale a deep breath, then reached out to Carly. "Better let me take your coat, at least."

Nodding her thanks, Carly quickly shed her brother Jesse's old duster coat from his cowboy days. That phase had lasted about two months, once he realized that a real working cowboy got a lot dirtier and smelled a lot worse than the ones he'd seen in the movies. Not all that different than what she was smelling like right now. She didn't have to be pregnant to know how Dougie's crude attempt to scare her off had left its mark on her.

She plucked the white T-shirt she wore away from skin that was damp with perspiration and tucked it beneath the belt and holster on her jeans with the holes in the knees. Then she adjusted the chain that held her badge around her neck as if it was a piece of jewelry that could dress up her poor girl from the streets look and gave Brooke a hopeful smile. "I don't look too scary?"

"It'll have to do."

Brooke turned her toward the captain's office just as Joe Hendricks opened the connecting door with an impatient whoosh of air. "Valentine. Good. You're here." He shifted his attention to Brooke while Carly sidled past him into his office. "We're not to be disturbed. Not even if his men call."

"Yes, sir."

The door closed behind her and Carly stopped in her tracks as the man with coal-black hair that she'd seen through the windows rose to greet her. The tailoring of his suit emphasized the width of his shoulders and tapered waist, making him appear taller, though she guessed he was about six feet in height. He practically clicked his heels together and offered her a curt nod. *Bowing*. Wow. Had any man ever been so formal about meeting her before? "Officer Valentine. I am pleased to meet you."

"Hey." Was she supposed to say something more? Shake his hand? No. Not in the shape she was currently in. "Nice to meet you."

The captain gestured to one of the two guest chairs while he circled around to his side of the desk. "Take a seat, Valentine."

With a nod, Carly tore her gaze from their guest and perched on the edge of her chair. Partly because it helped her sit up straight and gave her a stronger posture, and partly because she was painfully self-conscious about her soiled clothes leaving a stain on the beige fabric. "Will this take long, sir? I promised Gina Cutler that I'd cover her citizen self-defense training class after work, so she and Mike can go to birthing class." It seemed that several of her friends were well beyond her in the get-married-and-start-a-family department. "I'd like to grab a shower before then. I think the class would like me to, as well."

Her attempt at humor fell on deaf ears. "This will take as long as it needs to." The captain loosened the tie that cinched his collar and gestured to the man seated beside her. "I'd like to introduce you to His Royal Highness, Prince Ivan Mostek of Lukinburg."

Carly pushed to her feet. "Wait. Should I have curtsied?" She skimmed her hands over the hips of her frayed jeans and frowned at the stains on her boots. "I'm so sorry. I would have changed into my uniform if I'd known I was meeting a dignitary. I just came in off an undercover assignment. I had to blend in with the homeless community in No-Man's Land. I…" She threw her hands up, helpless to deny the truth. "I'm dirty and I stink."

The prince stood when she had risen from her chair. With a perfectly straight face, he said, "All I smell is the smoke from a fire. I trust you were not hurt."

"Aren't you a gentleman?" A nervous laugh snorted through her nose, and embarrassment warmed her face. "Of course, you're a gentleman. You're a prince. I'll be okay. I mean, my pride is shot to…" Carly bit down on that word and the heat in her skin intensified. She was pretty sure that one didn't curse in front of royalty. "I'll have a few bruises, but nothing serious. Thanks for asking." She turned to the captain, silently begging for backup. "Sir, tell me to shut up."

Now the captain chuckled. Great. Way to impress the boss and visiting royalty.

"At ease, Valentine," Hendricks ordered. As he had before, the prince waited for her to sit before he took his seat. She didn't deserve that kind of chivalry with the impression she was making, but his patience with her had a surprisingly calming effect on her nerves, enabling her to concentrate more on what the captain was saying rather than the humiliation she was feeling. "Lukinburg's capital city, St. Feodor, is the sister city of Kansas City. Prince Ivan and his delegation are here for a week to negotiate trade agreements, do a cultural exchange with the Nelson-Atkins Art Museum, meet with local and state officials, host a charity ball at their embassy—you get the idea."

"Uh-huh. What does that have to do with me?"

"The prince has a proposition for you."

Carly turned her attention to the man beside her. Good grief, his eyes were as blue as she'd imagined when she glimpsed them through the office window a few minutes earlier. The lenses in his glasses didn't dim their intensity one bit. Whatever this guy had in mind, it wouldn't be the worst offer she'd ever gotten from a man. Brooke was right, Ivan Mostek was attractive in a polished, faintly arrogant sort of way. In fact, if she met him in a bar, she'd be…lusting after him from afar because she had no clue how to come on to a guy, especially one who looked like he'd stepped out of the self-made CEO section of *Forbes* magazine and was way out of her league. But she'd definitely enjoy her beer and appreciate the scenery from a distance. Still, she knew Captain Hendricks wasn't setting her up on a date. She broke the connection with those penetrating blue eyes and looked to her captain. "What sort of proposition?"

"Captain, if I may?" The prince leaned onto the arm of his chair, close enough to catch a whiff of a scent that was much more pleasant than her own. Something clean, all business, masculine. "Due to instability in my country, as we transfer from a corrupt dictatorship to a democratic society, I am required to step up security. Not every Lukinburger is eager to support the new government."

Ivan articulated every word and avoided contractions. He'd practiced that delivery, so his English would be clearly understood. His tone was less guttural than German, more articulate than Russian, deep in pitch and seductive like fancy poetry. She wondered what that voice sounded like in his native language, whatever language a Lukinburger spoke. Lukinburger? The urge to laugh tickled her thoughts. That made her think of a hamburger. And this guy was nothing but prime steak.

"You find something amusing, Miss Valentine?"

That tone was a little less mesmerizing and a little more *His Imperial Majesty*, and she shook off the inappropriate detour of her thoughts. "Uh, no. No, sir. But I saw your geeky science guy and bodyguards on the elevator. That's not security enough?"

"Geeky science guy?" He repeated the phrase, a question in his eyes. Right. Language barrier.

"You know, nerdy? Thick glasses? Needs a haircut? I bet if he trimmed that mountain man beard and got the bangs out of his eyes, he'd clean up as good as you."

"I assure you he has showered."

He hadn't understood the slang she'd used. "Clean up as in he'd be attractive if he, you know, took care of himself a little more. Like you." The blue eyes narrowed. Great. She'd just admitted she thought the prince was attractive. Or had she just insulted his friend? "No offense. Clearly, the guy's a charmer. Making a woman laugh is a good thing." Heat crept into her cheeks again. "I'm rambling again. I'm a little self-conscious right now. I don't know the etiquette…am I allowed to have a regular conversation with you?"

"No matter the etiquette, it has not stopped you yet."

Her blush intensified. "Sorry."

"Do not apologize. You are very observant, Officer Valentine. A good soldier should be. I understand that you served in the military before joining the police force?"

"That's right. Army National Guard. That's how I paid my way through school."

"I, too, served in the army of my country. I admire that sense of duty." His compliment altered the heat she felt into a bud of self-confidence. As he went on, steering the conversation toward work further distracted her from her embarrassment. "The man in the hallway is my friend, Aleksandr Petrovic. He is a trusted adviser to me. He has, as you Americans say, a nose for business."

"You mean a head for business? It's a nose for news, a head for business," she pointed out. When his eyes narrowed, she pressed her fingers against her lips and apologized, "I'm sorry. I shouldn't interrupt."

"No. I must use your language correctly." His fingers spanned her wrist, pulling her hand away from her mouth. The light touch sent tendrils of warmth skittering beneath her skin before he released her. She was just as sensitive to the calluses on his manicured fingers, and surprising strength of his hand that she'd associate more with a working man like her father and brothers than a fairy-tale prince. But the charm was certainly there as he bowed his head to her again. "Thank you for the correction."

"You're welcome. You were saying?" Man, was she blowing it in the public relations department. "Your Highness?"

"Ivan will do fine when we are in private like this."

She was supposed to call a prince by his first name? In what universe? Had she taken a harder hit to the head from Dougie than she realized?

"Just as with our embassies in Washington and now Kansas City, we are coordinating with the Department of State and local law enforcement to ensure that our visit here is a safe one—both for ourselves and for your people. Your captain is indulging a personal request while my chief of royal security and his team are meeting with others in your department."

"That makes sense." Carly turned to Captain Hendricks again. "Are you looking for volunteers to work extra duty shifts?"

"Not exactly."

"Then what? Why the private meeting?"

Prince Ivan touched the arm of her chair to recapture her attention. "I need a personal bodyguard. An American who can assist with my understanding of local idioms, someone who knows the city and can provide security specifically for me while I am here."

"You mean a liaison officer between your men and KCPD?"

The men exchanged a look. This time she bit down on the urge to keep talking and waited for one of them to explain why she was here.

Captain Hendricks steepled his fingers together on top of his desk. "The prince believes there is someone inside his delegation who is feeding intel to the dissidents who tried to kill him in Lukinburg. He doesn't know who it is. He's not sure who he can trust."

Carly nodded as understanding dawned. "You're looking for an outsider. Someone who isn't a part of your inner circle." The captain and the prince were looking for a cop who could convincingly portray a member of his security team. Maybe a reporter covering his visit. Or even waitstaff or a maid at their hotel. "You want me to sniff around, see if I can find out anything. I can probably get in and out of your functions without drawing any attention to myself. I'm pretty good at blending in."

"You misunderstand. I want you to be my escort at those functions."

Carly realized her jaw was hanging open, and quickly snapped it shut. "What?"

"His girlfriend," the captain clarified. "He's looking for a female police officer who can be his date at public events. The cover story is that he has an old friend who works at KCPD, someone he met during a military training exercise, and a romance blossomed. His trip to the States has reunited you. She'll provide a level of security no one will question. Someone who can be seen with him, or even stay the night in his hotel room without anyone questioning why you're there."

"Undercover girlfriend? Stay the night?" She snorted a laugh when she heard what the captain was proposing. Then she saw the look in his dark eyes and stopped abruptly. "You're serious? No. No, sir. Do you see what I'm wearing? Do you see how I look?" She pointed to the bull pen. "I'm in the middle of another case. Emily or Detective Wardyn or any other number of female officers would be a better candidate for that kind of assignment than I would."

"Valentine—there were two attempts on the prince's life in Lukinburg."

"The last one was three months ago," the prince added. "I have fresh scars from that explosion. Seven people, including a member of the Royal Guard and the bomber himself were killed that day. I felt that coming to Kansas City would ensure the safety of my delegation, and of your people. By distancing myself from the threat."

Scars? Seven dead? Her panic ebbed at the sobering news. "They tried to kill you?"

"Twice. The bullet missed. The bomb did not."

"And the threat followed you here to the US."

"I believe so." He pulled a note from his pocket and handed it to her.

"You dusted this for prints?"

"There are none," Ivan answered. "At least, not according to my chief of security, Filip Milevski."

"One of the guys you're not sure you can trust?"

"It appeared in my attaché case on the plane during the flight. I do not recall seeing it there when I left St. Feodor."

With a nod from both the prince and Captain Hendricks, Carly unfolded the typewritten note.

Prince Ivan. The false prince.
We won't let you sell our country to the Americans.
We will stop you. Dead.
Lukin Loyalists will rule.

Carly let out a low whistle. "Does Homeland Security know about this? The terrorists may be yours, but they're on our soil." She folded the note and handed it back to the prince. "No offense, pal, but you need to go home."

"Valentine—" the captain chided.

The prince waved off his defense and leaned toward her again. "It is all right, Joe. I appreciate her frankness. Miss Valentine—I cannot tell you for certain that the threats are politically motivated. Perhaps they come from criminals seeking revenge for what the new government has taken from them. It could even be something personal I do not yet understand."

"Personal?"

"Perhaps. This is why I need your help. Whoever is behind this will try again. I want to stop him before any of your people get hurt."

"Prevent collateral damage."

"These trade negotiations must happen to ensure the economic success of my country. I need a strong Kansas City police officer, one who knows undercover work. I need a woman to fulfill this role, one who can handle herself as I saw you handle that criminal out there. I need someone I can trust, who is not influenced by the crown, someone who is there to watch *me* and help *me*. Lukinburg's security contingent are trained Special Forces soldiers. If one of them is against me…" He sat back, lifting his shoulders in a weary sigh. "I would like to have an ally in my corner. I would like it to be you."

She paused a moment to consider what these men were asking of her. "I won't fit in with royalty. I'm working class right down to my dad's plumber's truck. I don't even own a dress."

"We'll get you the right clothes, the right hairstyle, to play the role we need you to. You'd be working straight through the week he's here in Missouri. We'll comp you the time, give you a vacation once the assignment is done."

Prince Ivan nodded. "I will pay for all of these expenses. You will keep anything I purchase for you as a thank-you gift."

"Dressing me up won't make me a lady."

Hendricks rolled his chair back, looking as if this meeting was over and the decision had been made. "You'd be protecting Kansas City by preventing anything from happening to him. You can do this."

"Are you ordering me to?"

"Do I need to make it an order?"

"No, sir. I took an oath to serve and protect my city. That includes its visitors." She stood when the captain did. She was okay with the cop part, investigating and protecting, and with keeping a secret. But the rest of this assignment? She only hoped these men understood what kind of magic it would take to turn her into a woman who would date a prince. "When do I start?"

His Royal Blue Eyes rose and buttoned his jacket. "I need you to start the job now. Right here. Before my people return to the captain's office. I worked as military police when I was in the army, so it is plausible that we are acquainted."

"How long ago did we allegedly meet?" She'd better start prepping for this part if she was to have any chance of pulling it off.

"Two? Three years ago?"

Carly nodded. "I was deployed to Bosnia two years ago. Guarded the base near Tuzla."

"I took part in a training exercise in Sarajevo."

She recognized the city southwest of the base where she'd been stationed. "Then it's believable that we could have met. If the dates coincide."

Captain Hendricks circled his desk. "I'll prep your cover file to make sure they do, in case anyone runs a background check."

Carly inhaled a deep breath. "Then I guess we're doing this."

The prince crossed to the door leading into Brooke's office. "My first public appearance is tomorrow. I am in meetings throughout the day, but I will have lunch with you to go over the information I have on these threats in more detail, and to discuss the protocols my countrymen would expect from a woman I am with. That will give you until tomorrow morning to get whatever you need to look the part. Aleks will set up an account you may use to buy anything you need."

At least she didn't snort this time when she laughed. "I'm gonna need more than a day to make that kind of transformation."

"Make it work, Valentine." Captain Hendricks was done with any more excuses. "You'll be reporting directly to me."

"I hope you don't live to regret this, sir."

"I hope I don't, either."

When she opened the door, Brooke was pouring coffee for the armed men from the elevator. A glimpse of a wire curling beneath their collars reminded her that this was Ivan's security contingent.

"Your Highness." The man with slicked-back dark hair striped by silver sideburns stepped forward. "Coordination with the local police, providing traffic clearance and venue security is in place. They have your schedule and have assured me they have the manpower to provide the backup my team and embassy security will need. I will coordinate the joint agency security team, of course."

"Of course." Ivan laced his fingers through hers, and Carly startled at the unexpected touch. He pulled her up beside him, ashes, grime, stink and all. He hadn't been kidding. The charade was starting right now. "I want to introduce you to my good friend. Miss Carly Valentine. My valued chief of security, Filip Milevski."

Um, uh… *Think, Carly!* Not homeless, not hooker, not task force cop. *Girlfriend.* She summoned a smile. "Hi."

Brilliant. Convincing. Not.

The security chief's dark eyes bored through her with a different sort of intensity than the electricity that charged Ivan's blue eyes. Yep. That was less of a *nice to meet you* and more of a *what the hell?* expression on his clean-shaven face. "This is the woman from the elevator. Why did you not acknowledge her at that time if she is your friend?"

"She was working," Ivan explained, spewing out lies as if they were second nature to him. "Besides, it has been so long since I last saw her—her hair is much longer now and we are both older—I was not sure it was her."

Carly could play the lying game, too. "And I wasn't— I'm not—exactly looking my best. I was a little embarrassed for him to see me like this."

"Nonsense, *дорогой*. You know I love to see a woman in action." What did he say? Huh? Was she going to have to learn a new language for this assignment? Learning to be a proper lady would be hard enough.

Filip Milevski didn't bother to mask his disapproval of her—although whether it was the idea of his boss having a girlfriend or her, in particular, he disliked— and he acknowledged her with a nod and dismissed her at the same time. "I contacted Eduard. Our car is waiting for us out front to take us to the embassy to meet Ambassador Poveda. The rest of the delegation has gone on to the hotel. Galina is discussing protocol with the hotel staff. She will meet us at the embassy."

Ivan's grip tightened around hers, and she got the idea that Milevski's reaction hadn't pleased him. "I will finish introductions first, as you will be seeing more of Miss Valentine throughout the week." He gestured to the sour-faced man with the reddish-brown buzz cut and blotchy skin. "Danya Pavluk. He has worked palace security for years. The Eduard whom Filip mentioned is Eduard Nagy, another bodyguard, specifically, my driver. You will meet him later."

"I look forward to it."

Danya Pavluk looked like making polite conversation pained him. All he said was, "Madam."

"How do you do?"

Danya drank his coffee. Apparently, that conversation was over.

Ivan squeezed her hand again, and she was reminded of the strength and heat of even that casual, deceptively possessive touch. He called to his friend in the hallway. "Aleks, are you ready to leave?"

The nerdy numbers guy said his goodbye to Officer Rangel and came to the doorway. Without waiting for an introduction, he crossed the room to take Carly's free hand. He kissed her knuckles before stepping back and straightening his glasses on the bridge of his nose. "I am Aleksandr Petrovic. It is my pleasure to meet you."

She couldn't help but smile at the way his natural geekiness softened his effusive charm. "Carly Valentine." He looked like a shaggier, softer version of Ivan. His nose was straighter, his shoulders slightly less imposing. And so far, he seemed to be the friendliest Lukinburger she'd met. "The pleasure is mine."

So these were some of the suspects Ivan thought might betray him to the Lukin Loyalists who wanted to kill him. She'd need to run background checks and spend some time observing and conversing with all the delegation members to get a better read on who was trustworthy and who hated the prince enough to send a death threat.

She made a mental note to make sure she carried a gun or Taser with her at all times. The security men were armed. Pavluk was built like a tank, and though Milevski was older and had more paunch, she suspected he would be equally hard to take down if she had to protect the prince from one of them. And geek didn't necessarily mean defenseless, so she couldn't count Aleks out as a threat, either.

But investigating would have to wait. Sizing up her odds in a physical altercation slipped to the back of her mind, too, when Ivan moved to stand in front of her. With his back to the others, his blue eyes locked on to hers, sending a silent message of gratitude for her alone. Or no, that was a warning. Warning her about what?

Her eyes widened as he dipped his face toward hers and kissed her. Not some fake air-kiss or polite European cheek-to-cheek greeting, either. His firm mouth pressed against the seam of her lips, warmed the spot with moist heat, lingered. His beard and mustache tickled, and she was curious enough about the texture of the dark spiky silk teasing the skin around her mouth that she lifted her free hand to stroke her fingertips across his jaw. The lines of his face were strong, unyielding. She discovered the firm ridge of a scar hidden near his ear when she stroked against the grain of his beard. From his time in the army? A previous attempt on his life?

A blush of feminine interest in his controlled, masculine touch heated her skin as much as self-conscious embarrassment had warmed it earlier. Every instinct inside her wanted to push her mouth more fully against his. She wanted to part her lips and feel that ticklish heat on the tender skin inside. The kiss was easily the most potent she'd ever received, certainly the most unexpected. Ivan's touch was mesmerizing, magical...

Fake, Valentine! The kiss is fake.

A pair of invisible fingers snapped beside her ear, waking her from the momentary spell she'd been under. She quickly curled her inquisitive fingers into the palm of her hand and stepped back. She needed a shower and some nice clothes and a seriously intense lesson in royal etiquette before anyone would believe the prince's interest in her was real.

"I will see you tomorrow," he promised.

"Right. Oh." Before he turned, she pulled a card from the wallet behind her badge and tucked it into his jacket pocket. "That has all my numbers on it. If you need to call."

He laid his hand over his heart as if she'd given him a treasure. He looked to Brooke, who stood with one hand curved around her belly, the other clutching the back of her chair, as if she was too shocked by what she'd just seen to stand on her own. Ivan bowed his head. "Mrs. Kincaid. Thank you for your hospitality—and your discretion."

Brooke cleared her throat before she spoke. "Of course, sir. My pleasure."

"Captain Hendricks," he acknowledged. Then Ivan bowed to Carly. "I look forward to our next meeting, *дорогой*."

There it was again. The foreign word rhymed with *the frog boy*. Only it sounded secretive, sensual, anything but insulting, in his deep, accented voice. She wished she had anything half as clever to say. "Me, too."

Ivan and his entourage left, closing the door behind them and heading past a dozen curious glances from the main room to the elevators before Carly released the breath she'd been holding and turned to Brooke. "*Dorogoy*. What's that?"

Brooke typed the word into her computer and pulled up a translation program. "Darling. Sweetheart. It's an endearment."

An endearment. She should have guessed as much simply from the tone of his voice. Oh, he was good at this. Carly seriously needed to step up her game if they had any chance of making this undercover mission work. She also had to remember that the charm and kisses would be fake. She was no fairy-tale princess, and he wasn't really her prince. But he was just shy enough of handsome to make him really interesting to look at. He treated her like a lady, even when she reeked of the streets. And he needed her. It was a potent combination guaranteed to turn her head.

Right then and there she sent her heart a warning that she couldn't have real feelings for Prince Ivan Mostek of Lukinburg. This was a job.

Joe Hendricks's gruff voice sent the same message. "Valentine, you're done for the day. Process your perp and get out of here. Brooke? We need to arrange a leave of absence for Carly. Dismiss Rangel and Wardyn and meet me in my office."

"Yes, sir."

He went back into his office and Brooke grabbed a notepad and pen from her desk. She handed Carly her coat and stood there, searching for the right thing to say. "You're going to explain this to me?"

Of course, she was. Just as soon as she figured out

what to say. "Ivan and I go way back. To my army days. I didn't put it all together when you said Lukinburg earlier. I had no idea he was in town. In the country, even." Rambling was never a convincing way to establish a solid cover story. She was supposed to be a better liar than this. "Meeting him…again…was definitely a surprise."

Brooke nodded, still looking confused. "For all of us."

She hated lying to her friend. Not that she didn't trust Brooke completely. But orders were orders. The truth couldn't leave Hendricks's office. Still, she needed a friend who had some relationship experience right about now. "Do you have a place you go to get manis and pedis?"

"Sure. I can get you the number."

"And where exactly does one purchase a ball gown?"

Brooke frowned as if she'd spoken gibberish. "Why?"

"Apparently, for the next week… I'm dating a prince."

Chapter Three

Carly folded her cotton socks down over the tops of the worn leather boots she'd just tied off. She was happy to be in shoes that fit again, happy to be in a tank top and cutoffs instead of a coat that was way too hot for August, happy to be showered and clean and back in the comfort of the home she shared with her father.

Her room, bathroom and the laundry room were down in the basement, while her dad lived on the second floor where her two older brothers had stayed before leaving home to get their own places. Carly didn't mind the low ceilings and cold concrete beneath the carpeted floor. She had enough windows to bring in the summer sunlight, and walls thick enough to give her privacy and quiet from when her brothers and their friends stopped by for a visit. Plus, the freedom to decorate everything down here as she wanted—from the antique oak furniture to the turquoise paint on the walls to the bookshelves crammed with cookbooks, travelogues, romances and fantasy novels that had entertained her for countless hours and were too dear to part with— allowed her to create her own haven from the dangers and stress of her job and the loneliness of her misfit life.

She crossed to the oval mirror above the dresser

and pulled a comb through her hair, plaiting the damp waves into a loose braid and securing it with a band. She dabbed some lip balm on her mouth and hurried up the stairs, anxious to get to the kitchen to start dinner before her dad discovered the cherry pie she'd put in the oven. Carly and her father, whom she'd been named after, shared a love of sports, books and sweet things. But while Carly included regular exercise in her daily routine to counteract those sugar indulgences, Carl Valentine was more of an armchair athlete as the back issues he'd struggled with since a work accident some time ago affected him more and more with each passing year. If he got to the pie first, he'd fill up on that and skip dinner. It was a nice compliment to her baking abilities, but hardly the healthy diet she wanted for a man who needed to watch his weight.

Besides, she deserved a piece of that pie and a scoop of ice cream herself after a very long, very weird, very unsettling day.

"Dad? Did you get the grill started?" She hurried through the living room into the kitchen, stopping to pull a pair of hot mitts from a drawer as the timer went off on the oven. "Dad?"

She heard a high-pitched whir of machinery coming from the backyard and paused, cradling the hot plate in her hands. Was that a power saw? That meant company. The odds of getting a slice of cherry pie after dinner just diminished.

The back door leading onto the deck smacked shut as she set the pie on the cooling rack. "Hey, Carly Barley."

With a mock groan, she tilted her face to the muscular man with the wheat-colored crew cut. Her big brother. "Frank. What are you doing here?"

"I had some free time. Thought I'd come over and make those repairs on the deck that Dad's been whining about all summer. He's out back watching the charcoal, making sure we don't burn down the house."

Carly eyed the sawdust sprinkled across his forearms, sticking to the perspiration there. When he reached for the piping hot dish, she nudged him back onto the rug in front of the door, ordering him to brush himself off and wash his hands before he touched any of her food. "Invited yourself to dinner, did you?" She opened the refrigerator to pull out a five-pound package of thawed hamburger and an armload of veggies and condiments.

"Invited myself to find out what's going on with you." When she set everything on the counter beside the stove, Frank was leaning his hip against the lower cabinets, drying his hands. He tucked the towel around the handle of the oven door before crossing his thick arms in front of the Valentine Construction T-shirt he wore. "Are you still available to play on our coed softball team this Saturday? We need you at second base."

Was she free this weekend? She hadn't been informed of Prince Ivan's schedule yet. Was she supposed to forgo her normal life, as well as her regular work hours, to be available for his protection detail 24/7? She was guessing a community league softball game wasn't on his itinerary. She opened the pantry to pull out the spices she needed. "I don't know. I'll have to get back to you."

"I knew it. There *is* a guy." Frank pounded his fist on the counter. "Damn it, I just lost a bet."

"What are you talking about? What bet?"

"Jesse texted that some fancy dude came by the pre-

cinct offices to see you." Jesse would be her other big
brother, a jack-of-all-trades with an ear for secrets and
a mouth that often got him into trouble. His current job
as a bartender at the Shamrock Bar, an establishment
frequented by several of her colleagues, put him in the
perfect place to fine-tune those gossiping skills. "Some
officers were in the bar after their shift, talking about
this guy. They say he kissed you in front of everybody.
I bet ten bucks Jesse was makin' up a story."

"You bet against me?" Embarrassed that her own
brother didn't believe in her feminine appeal, she channeled her frustrated anger into the onion she was chop-
ping. "You don't think a 'fancy dude' would want to
kiss me?"

"I didn't think any guy would…" He seemed to suddenly realize that the woman glaring at him held a sharp
knife in her hand. He wisely backed off a step. "You
know how Jesse's always… I mean, the fact that some
guy is hittin' on you at all…" His cheeks flushed brick
red above the golden scruff on his square jaw. "Jesse
also said you were cooking dinner tonight. That you
called him to bring beer for the sauce. I've never eaten
anyone's food better than yours. That's why I'm here.
To eat."

"Pretty weak save, Frank." She split the onion between a saucepan and a sheet tray before pushing him
aside to wash her hands. "Now tell me again why you
can't keep a girlfriend?"

"I'm sorry." He followed her to the bag of potatoes and back to her cutting board, still trying to make
amends for his jab at her ego. She came by her question-
able social skills honestly. Although, whether a lack of
tact was imprinted in the Valentine DNA, or a by-prod-

uct of being raised in a motherless household, it was a mystery for the ages. "Do you need me to check this guy out? He's not messin' with you, is he? Those cops said they could tell he had money. He had guys opening doors for him. Drove off in a limo. Guys like that think they can throw around some cash, and girls will—"

"Stop before you stick that big foot of yours any farther into your mouth." Carly didn't consider herself a diminutive woman, but next to Frank, she was downright delicate. That had never stopped her from standing up to him, though. "One, I am a woman, not a girl. I can kiss whoever I damn well please. And two, why is it so far-fetched that a man might like me?"

Despite the square jaw and workingman's build, Frank could still pull off that sweet little boy expression that had gotten her to do more than her fair share of chores growing up and made her forgive him just about anything. "I love you, sis."

Carly shooed him out the back door. "Get out of my kitchen. Make sure there are no power tools on the picnic table and the deck doesn't collapse by the time dinner is ready. And try to have a little more faith in me, okay?"

Then maybe she'd have a little more faith in herself that she could pull off this assignment.

IVAN STEPPED OUT of the limousine onto the sidewalk. He buttoned his jacket and straightened his tie before sliding his hand into the pocket of his slacks, burning his fingers against the latest gift that had been left for him in his hotel suite. Unlike the flowers, gift baskets and bottles of wine, this one had no color, no wrapping, no welcoming message. It had no words at all on it. Just a set of numbers scrawled across an old black-and-white photograph.

Another death threat.

Carly needed to see it. Someone he trusted needed to know the danger he was facing—the danger a lot of innocent people might be facing if he couldn't unmask who was behind this terror campaign. Who wanted the Prince of Lukinburg dead?

A startled gasp tore him from his thoughts. He took a deep breath that expanded his chest. He nodded to an elderly woman with hair that was as curly and white as the small dog she held by its leash. "Madam."

With her eyes wide and the poodle dancing back and forth across the sidewalk, she eyed him and the black car behind him. "Are you a movie star?" With a squeak of excitement that made the dog yip at her feet, she pressed her hand to her chest. "Did Carl win one of those lottery giveaways?"

He arched an eyebrow at the question he did not understand and smiled. "I am here for Miss Valentine."

Other car doors opened and shut as advisers and security gathered around him. "For Carly? All of you?" The woman scooped the dog up into her arms and stepped closer, dropping her voice to a whisper. "Is this one of those television shows where you pull a prank on somebody? Am I on TV?"

"Why? Have you seen any cameras?" Aleks teased, climbing out of the limousine behind him. Like Ivan, his gaze swept the neighboring houses. Just a normal evening in American suburbia, it seemed. But while Ivan's gaze continued to study their surroundings, Aleks straightened his tie and grinned at the older woman. "How do I look?"

Ivan allowed them their laughter before he made proper introductions. "I am Prince Ivan of Lukinburg."

Her eyes widened with recognition. "I saw you on the news, getting off your plane at KCI."

"We are visiting your beautiful city." He extended his hand. "And you are…?"

"Gretchen Pischnotte. You're really a prince?" He nodded. "What are you doing in this part of town? I've known the Valentines for years. Carl moved in with Carly and the boys right after their mama died."

Carly's mother was deceased? Yet another unfortunate detail they had in common.

Schooling his curiosity to ask for more information about the woman who would be his secret weapon against the traitors who wanted him dead, Ivan fixed a smile on his face. He lightly clasped the older woman's fingers as she gave him a little curtsy. But before she released him, her dog nuzzled against Ivan's hand and licked him. His smile turned genuine. When was the last time he'd been able to run with a dog, or simply pet one? He scratched his fingers over the dog's head. "Who is this little guy?"

A shadow loomed up beside him. "Madam, I need you to move away from the vehicles. Now." Filip Milevski's stern tone made Ivan's stilted conversation sound suave and charming, by comparison. With Filip's right arm blocking Ivan across the chest, pushing him back toward the car, the chief of security pointed up the street. His jacket gaped open, revealing the gun holstered beneath his left arm.

The older woman's skin blanched. "Did I do something wrong?"

"No—"

Filip inched his bulk in front of Ivan. "He is not signing autographs or taking pictures this evening. Move along."

"It was nice to meet you, Mrs. Pischnotte." Ivan bristled at the curt dismissal. With a fearful glance up at Filip, the woman dropped her dog to the ground, and they hurried along the sidewalk that circled the end of the street. She stopped to chat with a man wearing some sort of workman's uniform. He was digging holes in his front lawn. Perhaps not his lawn, since there was a white van in the driveway with a company logo on the side panel. But he seemed to know Mrs. Pischnotte. With a tired sigh he leaned against his shovel as she took his arm in a fearful grasp, pointing at them in an animated conversation. Ivan pushed Filip's arm away, his glare conveying his displeasure at the needless bullying. "Was that necessary? The idea of this visit is to build a good rapport with our sister city, not show them we are a bunch of thugs like the previous regime. I hardly think an elderly woman is a threat to the throne."

"Is it necessary to be here at all, Your Highness? What about the man she's talking to now? The family next door? I haven't vetted any of these people to see if they're on any kind of watch list. We do not know if the Loyalists' threats have followed us from home." The photograph burned a hole in Ivan's pocket. Perhaps he'd been wrong to keep his security team out of the loop. But a member of that team was as good a suspect as any other passenger who'd been on the plane with him. At least the note confirmed his suspicion that there was a traitor among the royal delegation, someone feeding inside information to the dissidents. No one else would have access to his briefcase. No one else could have taped the photo on the mirror in his penthouse bathroom. "You are not the first leader I have served. I am responsible for your protection. Deviating from your schedule and leaving the hotel to visit your mistress on a whim—"

"You will not refer to Miss Valentine as my mistress, and certainly not in that condescending tone." He waited for Filip to lower his gaze and bow his head slightly. The big man needed the reminder of the hierarchy and just who worked for whom. The fact that Ivan didn't know exactly how this relationship between him and Carly was going to work made him hesitate. All he knew was that she was doing him a favor, and he would not tolerate the snide subtext in Milevski's words. "She is to be treated as an honored guest to the throne."

"As you wish, sir." Filip snapped his fingers for the other bodyguards to split up to do a reconnaissance of the tree-lined street. He made a show of buttoning his jacket, his shoulders bristling with irritation at not being in control of the situation or location. "This is an uncharted part of the city. There are no police officers patrolling the area."

"There is a police officer inside that house." Ivan pointed to the white columns and soft yellow siding on the porch in front of the Valentine home before gesturing to the other houses. "It is a fine neighborhood. The homes and yards are well taken care of." He nodded to the couple in the driveway next door, who'd paused in the middle of loading two boys and bags of baseball equipment into the back of their minivan to watch the interchange between the delegation and their neighbor. "It is hardly the mean streets of the inner city."

"Springing surprises like this on me makes it difficult to plan safe travel routes and make sure my men have time to scout ahead for potential security breaches." Filip waved his hand toward the curve of houses at the top of the street. "This is a dead end. Hardly a street I would have chosen in case we have to make a quick getaway."

It was no surprise that Aleks made a joke to diffuse the tension in the air. "Yes, because that killer poodle was an assassin in disguise. It's a veritable hotbed of terrorist activity here on—" he craned his neck to read the road sign at the corner "—Maple Street."

"Aleks…" Ivan chided, even as he welcomed the levity. Filip didn't share his friend's sense of humor. He wondered if he'd heard Milevski laugh even once since being put in charge of the royal security detail. Still, a growly chief of security with an obsessive need to control Ivan's every movement meant negotiating time alone with Carly would be practically impossible. He desperately needed the normalcy of an informal conversation with someone he knew didn't want him dead just as much as he needed private time to discuss suspects and expand the cover story between them so that no one in the prince's inner circle would suspect the ruse. He smoothed things over with Filip as best he could without surrendering the opportunity at hand. "I will endeavor to give you more warning in the future. But understand that I wish to see Miss Valentine as frequently as possible while I am here in the United States. We have a lot of catching up to do. And my schedule, as you well know, is incredibly busy. Since I have this evening free, I thought it would be fun to surprise her at home."

"Fun?" the security chief growled.

"Honestly, Filip." A woman's cultured, melodic voice chided the man as Galina Honchar stepped out of the opposite side of the limo. The scent of her expensive perfume reached Ivan a few seconds before she did. "Has it been so long since you've been with a woman that you've forgotten all the juicy bits about being in love?"

Filip glared daggers at the raven-haired beauty, but Galina deflected the silent accusation as though flicking away a raindrop. Filip stepped aside as she approached, avoiding a verbal sparring match he had no hope of winning.

She reported on the phone call she'd been finishing up in the car. "I cleared two hours on your schedule for lunch and sightseeing Wednesday, Your Highness. But you will need to be ready for cocktails with the May-weathers at five thirty. They'll be cohosting the fund-raiser ball at the embassy on Saturday. I've noted which suits are to be worn at each event on your phone."

Still in mourning over the death of her fiancé, Kon-rad, black was her color of choice. Galina had lost a little weight since that fateful day in St. Feodor. But some-thing about losing the man she loved in that bombing had galvanized her into becoming more than Ivan's ad-ministrative chief of staff. She would not allow for Kon-rad's death to be without meaning. Now, Galina guarded the prince's interests as well as his time, serving as an extension of his royal hand. She'd become his emo-tional protector as well as his personal planner, as they neared his coronation at the first of the new year. She had been efficient before, but now Ivan suspected she could run the palace and even Parliament without him.

Her black suit remained wrinkle-free, despite the

long hours of traveling they'd been through today. "Filip does make a point. Why haven't we heard of Miss Valentine before now? An 'old friend' from your army days?" Galina, a mix of efficiency and deportment, would have made an ideal consort for a prince.

Yet despite her classic beauty and flair for social networking, she did absolutely nothing for Ivan. Even if she didn't still wear her late fiancé's engagement ring, she didn't stir his hormones. Didn't stimulate his curiosity to get to know her on a more personal level. Didn't engender trust with the calculating sharpness of her dark brown eyes and knack for getting things done behind the scenes, handling details he never knew about. He wasn't chauvinistic enough to eliminate her as the traitor in his inner circle simply because she was a woman. He watched everything he said or did around her. Galina, perhaps more than anyone else in this delegation, would be able to spot a charade. Whether or not she was the mole leaking information to his enemies, she would be a hard one to fool. Even if she was innocent, her suspicions would most likely put the real traitor on alert about his relationship with Carly.

Ivan had carefully considered the lies he needed to tell. Ones based on a truth would be the easiest to remember. "I do not say much about my military service and the people I worked with or missions I took part in. And I certainly do not discuss my love life. With anyone," he added for emphasis.

A bright grin appeared in the middle of Aleks's curly black beard. "You never thought you were going to see her again, did you? Now you cannot stand to be this close—in the same country, the same city—and be away from her for a moment longer." He flashed that smile at Galina. "It's called passion, darling. Perhaps yours died with poor Konrad."

"Aleks," Ivan scolded. "You take your teasing too far."

"I am fine, Your Highness." Galina arched one perfectly sculpted eyebrow upward at Aleks, silently informing them both that she was perfectly capable of taking care of herself. "I have not forgotten what love is like. Nor have I forgotten the cause that Kon died for. As long as the indulgence of this affair doesn't distract the prince from the goals at hand, I will support it."

Eduard and Danya returned from their reconnaissance of the nearby homes in the cul-de-sac. Eduard Nagy, Ivan's personal driver, the more sedate of the two, peeled off the sunglasses he no longer needed on the shady street. "Everything looks secure. Almost every house has eyes on us, though. I talked to the man digging up that yard, a Bill Furness. He's the caretaker. The retired couple who lives there is away on a mission trip to Central America for several months. He said the only new residents in the neighborhood are the moles destroying his lawn. He hasn't seen anything unusual." He turned his gaze, scanning the entire neighborhood. "I'll need to pull up the city map on my laptop and mark the through streets and potential bottlenecks in this area if we're going to be frequent visitors."

"We will be," Ivan insisted.

Filip grunted his acceptance before firing off another command to his staff. "Run that watch list of names Homeland Security gave us, too. Make sure there are no potential enemies nearby."

Danya seemed irritated that they hadn't found anyone who seemed an obvious threat. "Your lady friend is cooking on a grill in the backyard, and a man is doing construction work there."

"A man?" Ivan asked. Surely, Carly would have mentioned if she had a boyfriend or fiancé who'd throw a wrench into their pretend relationship.

Danya muttered a word of frustration in their native language. "I didn't take names. I was looking for weapons, not checking out your competition."

Ivan wondered at the anticipation quickening his pulse. It was probably just relief that he'd get to share his suspicions with Carly sooner rather than later. "Just do the job you are paid to do, Danya. And do not use language like that in front of Miss Valentine."

"She speaks Lukin?"

"She understands the tone, if not the words."

Aleks rubbed his hands together in a different sort of anticipation. "You said grilling? I have read that Kansas City is famous for this cuisine. We will be staying for dinner, yes?" He climbed back inside the limo to retrieve the basket of fruit and one of the bouquets that had been delivered to Ivan's hotel room to welcome him. "Perhaps we will bargain for a bite to eat?"

Ivan hated the idea of regifting the items, but he hated to show up empty-handed as well as unannounced even more. He patted the chest pocket where Carly's card rested against his heart. He'd considered calling first, to see if they could meet. But he worried she'd make up an excuse to say no. Plus, upsetting the schedule with this impromptu detour might just put the traitor off his or her game long enough for him to pick up on a clue that might reveal their identity.

Appreciating Aleks's ability to defuse a tense situation, Ivan moved up the sloped driveway to the concrete steps. "We can ask."

Filip lengthened his stride to move ahead of Ivan. "Eduard, stay with the vehicles. Find out what you can online. Danya, you're with me. I'll lead the way. I want to do a sweep inside the house, as well."

Ivan jogged up the second tier of steps onto the raised porch. "I remind you, we are knocking on the front door, not invading a neighboring country."

He bit back the same Lukin curse Danya had used as Filip pressed the doorbell before Ivan could reach it. "Indulge me, sir. I don't have my full team with me in the States. That means I must be more vigilant than ever."

And yet someone had managed to get around that vigilance and send him a death threat. Twice.

Ignoring the urge to point out the failure, Ivan smoothed his fingers over the angle of his beard. "Fine." Flanked by Aleks and Galina, with Danya watching the street from the steps behind them, Ivan motioned Filip to stand aside. "I speak first. I do not want you frightening anyone else."

The inner door swung open, revealing a stocky man with a royal blue and white ball cap pushed back past the receding points of his graying blond crew cut. Although the face was older and male, the green eyes were the same as Carly's. "Mr. Valentine?"

The older man looked at the entourage on his front porch and frowned. "Yeah?"

"I am Ivan Mostek of Lukinburg."

"I'm Carl Valentine of Kansas City," he echoed with sarcasm, raising his voice to be heard over the whir of an electric saw from somewhere in the back of the house. "I ain't interested in anything you're sellin'."

"I am not selling anything."

"Then what do you want?"

"To see your daughter."

Carl Valentine laughed.

Chapter Four

Ivan didn't get the joke.

Apparently, Carly hadn't mentioned him to her father. While it was not allowable for her to share the details of her new assignment, she might have at least prepared her family for the new man who would temporarily be a part of her life. "Is she at home?"

"Is this KCPD business?"

The lies came more easily as he grew impatient. "This is a social call."

His thin eyebrows arched toward the brim of his ball cap. The grinding noise of the saw stopped abruptly, leaving the shock of Carl Valentine's incredulous words filling the room. "Like a date?"

Carl's obvious surprise at meeting the man who'd come to call on his daughter was hardly the kind of reaction that lent believability to this relationship. "Sir, Carly and I—"

"Dad, if that's Jesse, tell him I need one of those beers right away." He was relieved to hear Carly's voice shouting from the kitchen. "Then he can be a lazy butt and watch the game."

"You got company, Carls." Her father stepped back from the door and invited Ivan and the others onto the landing that opened into the living room and split into stairs going up and down to his left. "Better get in here, girl."

"What are you talking about?" Carly strolled into the main room, drying her hands on a towel. "I still have to finish the potato salad... Ivan?"

She stopped in her tracks when she saw the prince and his entourage. It took a split second for her startled expression to soften into a smile, and in that moment, he breathed a sigh of relief. Yes, she'd be able to play this undercover role. Even on the fly like this.

But relief wasn't the only thing he was feeling. She had on no makeup, but that only revealed that her skin was tanned and smooth, glowing with a sheen of perspiration. Her hair was a rich mix of caramel and wheat, and it hung in a loose braid over her shoulder. Even the black leather boots with the thick soles and scuffed, gray toes looked sexy on her, their heft balancing the athletic curve of her legs and making them look impossibly long in those raggedy denim shorts. His body hummed with an awareness that was as invigorating as it was foreign, since he'd purposefully shut down any male needs months ago when he'd agreed to take this position. Carly was no conventional beauty. But she was unique. Intriguing. He suddenly wished he knew her as well as he pretended to.

Their gazes locked for several moments before he realized she was struggling with the protocol of the unexpected meeting. "Should I have said, Your Highness?"

He put up a hand, urging her, and reminding himself, to relax. "Ivan will do fine."

When he took a step toward her, her father put out his hand to stop him. "Wait a minute. You're a prince?

Like, you're going to be a king one day? In my house? For my girl?"

The moment Carl's hand touched Ivan's shoulder, Filip was there. With a sweep of his hand, he sent Danya up the stairs and poked his finger in the middle of Carl's chest, knocking him back a step. "No touching."

Carl swatted the offending finger away. "What are you doing? Where is he going? This is my house."

"Filip!" Ivan grabbed the security chief himself and dragged him back to his side. "We are guests."

He needn't have bothered. Carly moved in front of her father, her eyes locked on to Filip like a lioness siting her prey. "It's okay, Dad. This is Prince Ivan's security team. They're checking the house. Your man will find my father's hunting rifle locked in a gun cabinet in his bedroom closet. My badge and service weapon are in a lockbox downstairs beside my bed. My brother is out back using power tools. Otherwise, we're unarmed." Although her demeanor remained calm, there was no mistaking the warning in her tone. "If you ever touch my father like that again, I will break that finger."

Ivan swallowed a grin as she faced off against the man who was twice her size. Either deciding a confrontation wasn't good for international relations, or perhaps wondering if she could make good on that threat, Filip offered the Valentines a curt nod and hurried down the stairs. "My apologies."

After tucking the towel into the back pocket of her shorts, she tilted her eyes up to Ivan, sending a silent look that was filled with frantic questions. *Why are you here? Did something happen?*

When we're alone, he wanted to answer.

Her words came out in a surprisingly casual tone. "I thought we were meeting tomorrow. For lunch."

"I could not wait that long to see you again. Is it rude if I invite myself to dinner?" He sniffed the sweet, spicy smells coming from the kitchen and wafting around her. "It smells delicious."

He was as aware of everyone in the room watching them as he was of her transformed appearance. If they were alone, this meeting might go very differently. But with an audience, he took her hand and played the attentive suitor. He leaned in to press a kiss to her cheek, lingering longer than he intended because he couldn't resist inhaling the essence of something tasty on her warm skin. Although he still detected a faint wisp of smoke clinging to her, her scent was cinnamon-y, with a hint of onion and something warm, like molasses or brown sugar, just like the food he smelled from the kitchen. Carly's homey, natural scent was much more appealing than the stain of body odors that had wafted about her at their meeting earlier in the day. He pulled away, stroking his fingertip across her cheek to remind her to blink instead of looking so stunned by his attention.

Her voice was a breathless whisper, for his ears alone. "Are you going to kiss me every time we meet?"

He answered just as quietly. "Are you going to blush every time I kiss you?"

If anything, the rosy tone on her cheeks intensified and she pulled away. She cleared her throat before addressing him in a normal voice. "I swear I don't always smell like ashes. I've been wrestling with the grill out back." She smiled up at her father. "Somebody left the bag of charcoal out in the rain."

"I said I was sorry." Blushing much like his daughter, Carl quickly changed the conversation. "You might as well stay. Carly's been fussin' over a big dinner. Plenty of food. You folks like baseball?" he asked, gesturing into the living room where the television was broadcasting a sporting event. "The game's about to start."

Ivan gave him an honest answer. "It is not a sport we play often in Lukinburg. I follow football, er, soccer. But I wish to learn more about your country."

Aleks stepped up beside Ivan, hugging the flowers and fruit basket against his chest. "I understand your team is called the Royals? That seems to be a fortuitous sign with the prince here. I would like to watch."

Carl nodded. "They're actually named after the American Royal livestock show that's been around since we had stockyards and cattle drives in KC. But it sounds like good luck to me. Come on in and sit."

"Thank you." Needing no other invitation, Aleks pushed the flowers and basket into Carly's arms and followed her father to the sectional sofa.

Galina took his place at Ivan's side, extending her hand. "We have not had the pleasure to meet. I am Galina Honchar, His Royal Highness's chief of staff. I coordinate his appearances and manage his schedule."

Juggling the gifts she held into one arm, Carly reached out to shake the other woman's hand. "Carly Valentine. Nice to meet you. I…date him."

"Whatever you are cooking smells amazing." Ever an icon for etiquette, Galina asked the question Ivan should have. "Are you sure we are not imposing?"

"It's not fine dining, but you're welcome to stay." The basket and flowers teetered over the edge of Carly's arm, and Ivan reached out to grab the cellophane-wrapped basket of apples and oranges before they hit the floor, forgetting for a moment that the future leader of Lukinburg did not haul anything, especially when there was staff there to do it for him. "Thanks. I'm grilling burgers." She grinned. "For Lukinburgers." As quickly as she'd smiled, she frowned. "Wait. That's not an insult, is it?"

Galina laughed politely as Ivan hastened to reassure Carly. "Not if the food tastes as good as it smells."

Or as good as Carly smelled.

Her smile reappeared, and Ivan suddenly felt as successful as he would once the Kansas City agriculture and trade officials signed the new business contracts with his government.

But any feeling of victory was short-lived when the front door burst open behind him. A young man with shaggy brown hair, wearing a T-shirt and a leather vest entered with a bellow. "What the hell are those cars doing out front? I had to park way… Whoa."

The security team returned in a blur and shoved the young man up against the wall. He lifted the six-pack of bottled beer he carried out of Danya's way when the bodyguard felt beneath his leather vest and patted down the sides of his jeans. "Hey, pal, you ought to buy me dinner first."

"Danya." Ivan ground the order between clenched teeth. "Retreat."

The bodyguard pushed to his feet. "He is not armed."

Green eyes. Square jaw. Another Valentine. Great. He was scoring zero points in the public relations department with this family. But the young man didn't seem to mind the rude greeting once his gaze landed on Galina. Instead of complaining about the welcome, he smiled. "Nice. Wish you'd have frisked me."

"Jesse!" Carly chided. Including the young man and Danya in her glare, she slid between the two of them, motioning for Danya to back away. "This is my brother Jesse. If you try to frisk my brother Frank, he'll punch you."

She linked her arm with her brother's in protective solidarity. Her smile tightened into a grim line as she went through the introductions. "His Royal Highness, Prince Ivan. The prince's friend, Aleksandr Petrovic. His chief of staff, Galina Honchar. Chief of security Filip Milevski. And Danya… I'm sorry, I didn't catch your last name."

"Pavluk."

"Have the Russians invaded?" Jesse asked.

Danya stepped forward, taking the joking remark as an insult. "We are not Russian. We are proud citizens of Lukinburg."

"Oh, hell. It's true. Hey, Frankie! You here? You owe me ten bucks." The rhythmic pop of a nail gun that had underscored the entire conversation stopped as the young man extended his hand. "Nice to meet you, Ivan. What's your business with my sister?"

Before he could answer the question, another Valentine entered through the kitchen. This one was bigger, blonder, but the family resemblance was the same. "What are you on about now, Jess?" He pulled a ball cap off his head to mop at the sweat on his brow and pointed the cap at Danya. "You're that guy I saw lurking around the Fitzes' yard. What are you doin' in our house? With guns? The kids don't need to see those."

"It's okay, Frank. My older brother." Carly made the

round of introductions again, and Ivan shook his hand. He didn't like admitting the relief he felt to learn this was her brother, and not a potential rival for her time and attention.

Frank Valentine appeared to be about the same age as Ivan, in his early to midthirties. He crossed his brawny arms over his chest. "You really a prince?"

"Are you really her brother?"

Jesse, clearly the more outgoing of the two, laughed. "A wiseass, huh?"

Carly pinched his arm. "You don't say things like that in front of—"

"It is fine." Apparently, plain speaking was a Valentine family trait. Ivan could appreciate that. In fact, he envied their openness. He didn't have to second-guess what they were thinking and if they were plotting against him. "Before I had to bow to royal protocol, I, too, had a penchant for sarcasm. It still slips out every now and then."

"I'll take this off your hands." Galina plucked the fruit basket from Ivan's grip and moved forward to take Frank Valentine's arm. "It is time for us to leave the prince to the reason for his visit. Spending time with Miss Valentine. Filip, Danya—perhaps you should check with Eduard to see what information he has discovered?" After the security team exited onto the porch, Galina's smile included an invitation for Jesse to join her and Frank. Both men seemed eager to oblige. "Teach me about this baseball."

While the others settled in front of the television, Ivan followed Carly into the kitchen. "Does no one help you prepare the meals?"

"I like to cook. This is my therapy when I need to

think." After setting the flowers on the counter, Carly stirred beer into the pot bubbling on the stove. Then she opened the refrigerator and took out a tray of hamburger patties. She peeked into the living room, confirming that everyone was busy with the game or engrossed in conversation, then dropped her voice to a whisper and hurried to the back door. "Does that jacket come off?" she asked when he moved in beside her to hold the door open. "You might want to roll up your sleeves and loosen your tie. It's hot out here."

Sensing the urgency in this sudden shift in behavior, Ivan shrugged out of his jacket and draped it over the back of one of the kitchen chairs before following her down the steps into the backyard. He joined her at the grill. "I need to speak with you privately."

"I didn't think you were here for a booty call."

He folded the crisp white cuffs of his sleeves. "I do not understand."

"You know, when a guy calls or drops by to…" Her cheeks blushed bright pink and she shoved the tray into his hands, asking him to hold it while she added the extra burgers to the grill and slipped ones that were already cooked to a warming bin.

"Carly, I need you to speak always so I understand you. What is *booty call*?"

"A quickie. Sex." She patted her backside. "It's slang for this. That guys want to… Women, too…" Her cheeks heated with another blush that he doubted could be attributed to the hot coals or humid summer weather, and she went back to flipping burgers. "That's why your friends think you're here, isn't it? Why you want to see me? Only you and I know the truth."

Ivan's gaze had settled on the curve of her denim

shorts the moment she'd touched herself there. What was wrong with him? Why did this earthy woman make him forget every bit of protocol that had been trained into him? Why did he care if she blushed adorably when he paid attention to her or feel a knife-hot urge to defend her when anyone said something demeaning or took advantage of her? But he remembered the photo, he remembered his duty to his country, he remembered the promise he'd made to her police captain, and politely raised his focus to her eyes. "I will remember this slang. Because you have a memorable booty."

"Um… Thank you?" She took the empty tray and set it on the shelf beside the grill. "Tell me why you're here. We weren't supposed to meet until tomorrow, so something must have happened."

Ivan nodded. His shoulder brushed against hers as he turned, keeping his back to the living room windows, in case there were curious eyes on them, and pulled out the mutilated photograph. "I did not know who else to trust with this."

She closed the grill and took the photo from him. "It looks old."

"I am afraid its meaning is new." He pointed to the rectangular image, in shades of gray and black, centered in the picture. "It is the flag of Lukinburg, draped over a coffin. It is an historic picture. The last rightful king was assassinated shortly after the Second World War. A bomb went off at his summer house on Lake Feodor. He lay in state in the palace. A few months later, while the government was in transitional chaos, there was a coup. Our democratic government as we knew it was over."

"Until you stepped in?" Carly tilted worried eyes up to his, keeping her arm flush against his so she could return the photograph without being seen. "It's dated this upcoming Saturday."

"It is the night of the embassy ball." The message might be symbolic, but the meaning was clear. If he didn't step down, *he'd* be the next head of state lying in a coffin. And his death would happen on Saturday. "It was left in my hotel suite. Anyone in my delegation could have put it there. We held a meeting there this afternoon."

"Someone on the hotel staff, or pretending to be, could have left it."

He shook his head as he folded the photo and stuffed it back into his pocket. "Filip has limited the staff who has access to my suite. He personally ran background checks on each of them and cleared them."

"He could have cleared someone with ties to the Lukin Loyalist movement. You think he's your mole?"

"I do not know." The heat and humidity of the summer evening burned through Ivan's skin, reminding him of the pressure building inside him since he'd agreed to take this job. If he had a clear enemy, he'd know how to handle this. But the mind games, the threats, the collateral damage that could result if he made a mistake—how was he supposed to fight that?

Carly bumped her shoulder against his, drawing him from the dark turn of his thoughts. "The obvious question is—can you cancel the ball?"

"No."

"Right. Too important to you and your country." She glanced behind her, then laced her fingers with his down between them. "How many messages like this have you gotten?"

Was her touch for comfort? Or for show? Was someone watching them? Ivan decided he didn't care. He liked the sure grip of her hand in his as much as he liked everything else about her. He tightened his fingers around hers, absorbing some of that strength. "Two since I've touched down here in the US. Several more back in Lukinburg. I believe they are trying to scare the prince into abdicating the throne, letting someone more malleable lead the new government."

"The prince?" She laughed softly. "You just referred to yourself in the third person."

"Did I?" Perhaps jet lag was getting the better of him. Or stress. No wonder he couldn't keep his thoughts straight. He needed to be on point every waking moment if he was going to accomplish all he'd set out to do. Who was he kidding? He couldn't even afford to sleep without being on guard for his life.

"It's probably easier to think the threats and attempts on your life are happening to someone else."

"Perhaps." The marks of the injuries peppering his neck and back burned with the enormity of the challenge he faced. "Yet I am the one with the scars. If they cannot frighten me from my duty, then they will kill me."

"No pressure, hmm?" She released his hand to reach up and trace her fingertip against the scar that cut through his beard. Although it was meant to be a comforting gesture, every nerve ending seemed to rush to the spot, pulsing beneath her touch. The moment he thought the contact might mean something more to her, too, she pulled away and went back to work, opening the grill and flipping the hamburgers. The hiss and pop of the moisture hitting the coals masked her words as much as the steam and smoke hid their expressions from any curious onlookers. "All right. I'll talk to Captain Hendricks, and we'll try to get as many people undercover next Saturday to beef up security as we can. We can put SWAT teams on alert and lock the embassy down as tightly as possible without alerting your traitor. You and I will have an emergency evac plan in place that Milevski doesn't know about. In case it's him."

"I will make sure you have an opportunity to tour the embassy this week."

"In the meantime, I'll do everything I can to identify whoever is behind the threats and get him out of the way before Saturday night."

"*We* will do this. We will work together."

"We're a team. The prince and the commoner. The European and the American. The uptown leader of his own country and the downtown nobody." She closed the grill before pulling the towel from her back pocket and wiping her hands. "Are you sure your people are buying this between you and me? A few kisses and holding hands are one thing, but somebody's still going to have to teach me how to dance."

"I would be honored to do this." She thought of herself as a nobody? How could any man miss her vibrant energy and brave spirit? There were beautiful green eyes in that ordinary face. And, judging by the awareness still fizzing through his blood, he was extremely glad that he'd added the word *booty* to his English vocabulary. "It would not be a lie to say I find you attractive. Perhaps you are not the typical royal consort, but that part, I do not have to pretend. Thank you for helping me."

"Nobody's blowing up anyone in Kansas City on my

watch." She tilted a smile up to him. "And nobody's blowing up our most honored guest."

Answering that smile with one of his own, he turned her into his arms. "First lesson." Her forearms flattened against his chest and she was suddenly stiff, as if bracing herself for something unpleasant. He placed her left hand on his shoulder and folded her right fingers into his palm before settling his hand at her waist. "A simple waltz is three steps. Right, left, right. Left, right, left. Your feet move the same direction as mine, like a reflection in a mirror."

One boot came down on the toe of his polished oxford. "Sorry. Clearly, these aren't the right shoes for this."

"Again. Right, left, right. Left, right, left. Feel my hands pull you with me when we turn."

"There's a turn?" She froze. Stomp. Ivan gritted his teeth at the pain stabbing through his little toe. "Sorry."

When she tried to push away, he tightened his hold on her waist. "Carly, do you practice any kind of martial arts or fight training?"

"Of course, I do. It's required to maintain my badge. I run, kickbox, do yoga once a week to take a break from working out."

"This is no different than learning an attack sequence or exercise routine. Memorize the pattern. Then feel your way through it." He shifted her in his arms, pulling her hips against his. "Do you feel the rhythm when I move?" She nodded, still trying to peek over his arm down at the patio. "Look in my eyes, not at our feet. My arms and thighs will lead you in the direction you need to go."

Those pretty green eyes fixed on to his. Ivan

hummed a strain from Strauss, emphasizing each downbeat. Gradually, she relaxed against his arm at her waist and she eased the death grip on his shoulder. This time, she spun with him in a dramatic turn. "I'm doing this."

There were only a few more stumbles of her boots knocking against his shoes before he swept her into a turn. She laughed until a snort made her pull up with embarrassment. He pressed a kiss to the bridge of her nose, enjoying the genuine sound of delight before pulling her into step again and waltzing across the patio with her.

She was humming *The Tales of the Vienna Woods* with him when the back door burst open and her brother Jesse ran out onto the deck. "Carly! Get in here. Something's wrong with Frank."

Her smile vanished. The music stopped. The grill was forgotten. She charged up the stairs. "Frank?" Ivan ran into the living room behind her. He paused in the archway, taking in the convulsions of the big man writhing on the floor. "Frank!" Carly dropped to her knees beside her brother, grabbing at his stiff arm. "He's having a seizure. What happened?"

"Is he epileptic?" Ivan asked.

"No."

He spotted the cellophane ripped off the fruit basket. Galina was picking up fruit that had spilled out and rolled across the carpet. Frank crushed the remains of an apple core in his fist. This was familiar somehow. But how did he help?

Carl Valentine was on the phone to 9-1-1. "My son—"

"Tell dispatch I'm with KCPD," Carly shouted, giving her badge number. "Get a bus here now." Carly turned Frank onto his side as her father continued the call. Ivan knelt beside her, helping her position the big man as his back arched and he became harder to control. "Don't let him hit the fireplace."

Jesse knelt opposite her, the three of them fighting to keep Frank in a position where he could still breathe and not knock into any furniture. "He said he couldn't wait until dinner. First, I thought he was choking. I tried to give him the Heimlich. Then he started doing this."

Carly slipped a pillow beneath her brother's head and held it in place. "He's burning up."

Ivan had never witnessed a fit like this himself, but he'd seen pictures, training films when his unit had been briefed on nerve gases and other toxins that had been hidden and forgotten in eroding bunkers and old army bases from World War II. One of his earliest assignments had been with a team sent in to destroy any weapons that could leech into the environment or be accidentally triggered by an innocent explorer who happened upon them.

Aleks tiptoed past him and squeezed his shoulder. "We need to get you out of here. This is not the kind of publicity—"

"No!" Ivan shrugged off his touch. "I know this. It was a torture from the old days. Strychnine." He pried the smushed apple from Frank's hand and sniffed the bitter chemical smell of the pulp. Galina was reaching for an orange that had rolled over by the brick hearth. "Do not touch that!" The startled woman snatched her hand back. "He has been poisoned. We must get him to a hospital right away."

"Ambulance is on its way," Carl reported, kneeling

beside Jesse. "They said he only has a couple of hours before the internal damage becomes irreversible. Son?"

But Frank couldn't respond.

Ivan didn't bother stating the obvious, not when another man's life hung in the balance. Not when Carly could lose her brother.

That fruit had been a gift to him.

He was the one who should be dying.

Chapter Five

Ivan stood the moment the door to Frank Valentine's room opened. Saint Luke's Hospital was quiet, yet surprisingly busy for this time of night. His eyes burned with fatigue after being up for over twenty-four hours, but he didn't intend to sleep until he knew for certain that he hadn't gotten Carly's brother killed, and that there wouldn't be lasting effects from the poison.

So many lives were impacted by every choice he made. But he didn't intend for his desperation, his utter isolation from people he could trust, to ruin the life of the woman he was foolishly learning to care for in a very short time. Carly Valentine felt like salvation to him, like something real despite the charade of their relationship. She was the touch of humanity he'd been missing from the pomp and circumstance of his life as the crown prince.

The doctor came out first, chatting with Joe Hendricks, who'd been called in to take the official report for the police department. Carly followed next, with her father and Jesse right behind her.

Still in her tank top, cutoffs and boots, Carly now wore her gun holstered on her belt and her badge hanging around her neck. Despite the tough facade, there was something vulnerable about the way she ran her hands up and down her bare arms and hugged herself. There were small divots of shadow beneath her eyes now, indicating fatigue and stress, even as she hung on to every word exchanged between the doctor, the captain and her father.

"Give me a few minutes with Miss Valentine." He paused when Filip shot to his feet, preparing to follow. Ivan put up his hand, warning him that he didn't need any help walking across the room. "Send the others back to the hotel. A few of us, at least, should get some sleep before the meetings tomorrow morning. I plan to stay until I get a full report on Frank Valentine, and I know Carly is all right."

"As you wish. I will also be staying."

Ivan tipped his head to the sterile ceiling, his nostrils flaring with a measured breath. He admired Filip's dedication to his job even as he found his need to hover irritating. Or was his attentiveness something more purposeful? Like keeping his prey in sight? An instinctive male need to call him on his behavior had to be squelched. "You have been up longer than I have. Leave Danya or Eduard and get some rest. I will have Captain Hendricks with me. I am perfectly safe."

Filip adjusted the flak vest he wore beneath his shirt and jacket, as if the protective armor didn't quite fit his muscular bulk. Maybe he didn't feel comfortable wearing it, if his next words were any indication. "I failed to protect you this evening. I should have checked every delivery myself. I will not fail again. I am staying."

Ivan nodded. He wished he could trust this longtime servant to the crown without hesitation. Right now, he could only act as if he did. "Very well. But, privacy? Please?"

Filip gestured to the end of the hallway. "I have secured a room for you, just around the corner. I anticipated you would wish to speak to Miss Valentine. You will not be disturbed. I will dismiss the nonessential personnel and wait for you here."

"Thank you."

With a sharp nod, Filip crossed the waiting area to speak to his team, plus Aleks and Galina and a pair of uniformed officers who had accompanied Captain Hendricks to stand watch and keep a trio of local reporters away from the family and the royal entourage. Ivan shrugged off his suit jacket and went to join Carly the moment the doctor excused himself.

Up close, Ivan could see the goose bumps dotting Carly's skin. He hadn't imagined the chill she felt. He draped his jacket around her and squeezed her shoulders in a subtle show of support before moving in beside her to join the circle of hushed conversation. "Is Frank all right?"

She clutched the jacket together at her neck, offering him a weak smile of thanks. "Dr. McBride said Frank probably feels like he's been hit by a train with the severity of those muscle spasms and pumping his stomach. He's on pain meds. Stimuli might trigger new seizures until it's completely out of his system, so they're keeping him mildly sedated in a quiet, dark room."

"Barring any complications, the doc says he's going to pull through." Carly's father looked as if he'd aged since they'd first met earlier that evening.

Even her smart-mouthed brother seemed subdued by the close call. "I've always looked up to Frank. He's the strong one. Seeing him hooked up to all those IVs and beeping machines freaks me out as much as seeing him writhing on the floor did."

Carly linked her arm through Jesse's and rested her head on his shoulder. "Dr. McBride said everyone's quick actions, including yours, saved him. Frank *is* strong. He's too stubborn to die. Focus on that."

Jesse leaned over to press a kiss to her temple. "Nice pep talk, Carls. But we all know this was no accident. Are you gonna get this guy for us?"

"Of course, she will." Carl winked at his daughter. "That's her job."

Not for the first time, Ivan wondered at the balance in this family. Was Carly a strong woman by nature? Or was she forced to be that way because her brothers and father needed her to take care of them? "Mr. Valentine, I am sorry that your son was hurt, when clearly, I was the target. I wish to pay for any medical expenses—"

"Did you poison Frankie?"

"Of course not."

"I didn't think so. So don't apologize. And don't think you gotta throw your money around to make up for what happened to my boy. You've got enemies, Your Royalness. And if you're going to be dating my daughter, that means we have enemies, too. But you're not one of them. Of course, you hurt my little girl and all that changes."

How was he supposed to respond to that? He would never intentionally hurt Carly. And yet, he feared he already had. "Sir—"

"Dad…" Carly began.

Carl removed his ball cap and waved off both of their protests. He rubbed the top of his head down to his nape, sighing as if that burst of anger had drained whatever stores of energy he had left. He clapped Captain Hendricks on the shoulder. "Joe, you get the bastards who did this."

The police captain nodded. "I will."

The other man's promise seemed good enough for Carl. "I'd better sort through that insurance mess."

There was nothing subtle about Carly widening her eyes at Jesse and pointing toward their father as he walked away. It took a split second for him to catch on before he snapped his fingers. "Wait up, Dad. I'll come with you."

He hurried to catch up to Carl and squeezed a hand around his shoulder, offering his support so that none of them would be alone.

Captain Hendricks waited for Carl and Jesse to move out of earshot before he leaned in. "We need to talk. Your Highness?"

Ivan inclined his head toward the bodyguard pacing the waiting area. "There are ears here." Placing his hand at the small of Carly's back, he led them into the private room around the corner. "I wish to hear anything you have to say."

It was no secret that Carly was a cop and that Joe was her precinct commander, so no one questioned why an officer of his authority was on the scene when a crime like attempted murder occurred in the company of a visiting dignitary. But the real gist of their conversation needed to remain between the three of them.

As soon as the door closed behind him, Joe pulled a notepad from the pocket of his jacket. "Since this is such a high-profile case, I expedited the tox results on that fruit basket through the crime lab. Every apple was injected with strychnine."

"Just the apples?" Carly ran her hands up and down the silk-lined jacket that hung around her, as if Ivan's coat alone wasn't enough to chase away the chill she felt. "Why not the oranges?"

Ivan had the answer to that. "The prince does not like oranges."

Her eyes darted up to his, and a tiny frown mark dimpled her forehead. Great. He'd just referred to himself in the third person again. But when Joe didn't mention the odd phrasing, Carly didn't ask the question stamped on her face. She crossed to the minibar that held a steaming pot of coffee but didn't pour herself a cup. "That would narrow down the possibility of the wrong person eating the poison. If it's common knowledge."

"Most of Lukinburg knows this. There was an embarrassing news report during the last orange harvest about how difficult it is to peel an orange. I did not take the time on camera to eat one presented to me. The reporter suggested I hire someone to peel oranges for me. It became a jab at increasing government spending on what some consider to be frivolous programs." That attempt at humor had given the Loyalists some unnecessary ammunition against the new government.

"Are they?" Carly asked, facing him again. "Frivolous? It could be motive for the threats."

"I do not consider bringing in agricultural consultants to reclaim our overtaxed land and increase crop production to feed my people to be a frivolous expense." Ivan bristled at how the old guard resented change, even if it was to their own benefit. "We spend a fortune importing grain and meat. One of our goals during this visit is to negotiate more equal trade with your farmers, as well as meet potential consultants. In the long run, we will save money by doing this."

Joe tucked his notepad back into his jacket. "Save the political speeches for your official appearances. Right now, I'm looking to narrow down our list of suspects. The forensics report wasn't much help." He included both Ivan and Carly in his dark gaze. "The lab dusted the basket and remaining fruit for fingerprints. Somebody wiped it clean."

Carly pushed away from the counter and paced to the door. "I didn't think to secure it right away. I was worried about Frank."

"Actually, it narrows down our suspect list," Joe said. "By the time the lab got a hold of it, the plastic wrap was completely missing. Whoever did it had to be someone at your house, covering his or her tracks."

Carly stopped in front of Ivan, tilting her face to his. "Could he or she have wiped the prints to protect you from being a suspect? You handled the basket."

"So did you. And Galina and Aleks."

"Dad and Frank, too." She shook her head and continued to pace. "There should be a ton of prints."

The rest of Joe's report wasn't much more enlightening. "The lab also matched that first note you showed me to the printer on your airplane. I think we can safely confirm that this is an inside job."

"But is it one person? Or is that inside man the representative of an entire rebel faction? Could there be others from the Lukin Loyalist movement here in Kansas City?"

"If there are, we'll find them. Hopefully, before they

make their move." The captain buttoned his collar and straightened the knot of his tie. "In the meantime, I'll have a lab team go through everything in your suite with a fine-tooth comb to see if there are any other threats there."

"You will have to go through Filip for security clearance."

Grinning, Joe buttoned his jacket and headed for the door. "It's a Kansas City hotel, not embassy property. All I need is to wake up a judge and get a search warrant." He turned his dark eyes to Carly. "Sorry about your brother. You okay, Valentine?"

She nodded. "Yes, sir."

"Good. You're going to need sharp eyes and a clear head. I need you with the prince as much as possible until we figure out who the mole is and what his ultimate plan might be. You're our first line of defense and our main source of intel. I want to get ahead of this guy."

"So do I."

Ivan extended his hand. "Thank you, Joe."

They shook hands. "This may have started out as a courtesy to a visiting dignitary. But now they've threatened my town. They've hurt one of my citizens. It's personal."

After Hendricks left, Carly resumed her pacing from the untouched coffee to the door and back again. "Do you recognize the handwriting on that photograph with Saturday's date?"

Ivan propped his hands at his waist, anchoring the center of the small room as she moved past him. "There is not enough to tell, no."

"And the fruit? Who gave you the fruit?"

"There was no card. I assumed it had come with

something else. The welcome gifts were all from local officials, companies I am meeting with, the embassy."

"Someone either snuck them in or doctored them after delivery." Her gaze flickered up to his as she walked by again. "Is there a log of every single person who enters your suite at the hotel?"

"Filip would have that."

"And we don't know if he would tell us the truth. If *any* of your people would tell us the truth." She caught the edges of his jacket and hugged herself more tightly inside it. "Have you at least run a background check on everyone in your entourage? Would any of them have a connection to these Loyalists? A family member? A lover?"

He regretted that he couldn't guarantee the answer to that question, either. "Filip—"

"Filip is in charge of that, too." She exhaled on a stuttering breath, and for a split second, he thought she was crying. But there were no tears, only a white-knuckle grip on his jacket and shoulders that were visibly shaking. "It's so damn cold in this hospital."

He caught her by the arm when she walked past and drew her up against his chest. Ignoring the token protest of her hands bracing between them, he wound his arms around her, rubbing large circles against her back. He wrapped her up, jacket and all, absorbing every shiver, warming her with the heat of his hands and body, standing strong for her when she was ready to crumble. He rested his cheek against her temple, tangling strands of her hair in his beard as he whispered into her ear. "Take a deep breath, *dorogoy*. It is the adrenaline crash after so much stress and worry. You have had a long day and are very tired. You will get through this."

Seconds, maybe minutes, passed before she moved. Then her arms snaked around his waist. He felt the imprint of ten fingers fisting into his shirt and pressing into the skin underneath as she burrowed into him, snugging the crown of her head beneath his chin. Ivan widened his stance, letting her move as close as she wanted to be. Comforting this woman—warming her, calming her—seemed like the most useful thing he'd done in the past few months. Feeling capable again, like he was the right man for this particular job, soothed some of the tension he carried inside. He treasured Carly's faith in him and prayed that her trust wouldn't be misplaced. "I am sorry that your brother—"

"Shh. Dad's right. No apologies. It's ninety degrees outside tonight, and I can't get warm. Just hold me a little longer."

He smiled against her hair, liking that she told him what to do, completely ignoring royal decorum and the fact he was about to lead an entire country into the twenty-first century. She didn't need him for who he was supposed to be—she just needed him. "If you insist."

Ivan held Carly until the shivering stopped and comfort changed into a subtle awareness of her sleek, athletic body relaxing against his. Her small breasts pebbled beneath the nubby friction of his jacket catching between them. The scent of her hair reminded him of the laughter they'd shared beside the grill, dancing on her patio. The clutch of her fingers in the back of his shirt eased their grip and flattened against his spine, mimicking the stroke of his hands on her.

A warm sensation pooled around his heart that had nothing to do with the exchange of body heat. He was falling for this woman. He wished he could simply be a man and not a prince, that, like at this moment, her needs were more important than his responsibilities. They were both creatures of duty, both accustomed to hiding any weakness, both isolated by the need to keep their true mission a secret. She had beautiful green eyes, those crazy, sexy legs and a penchant for speaking her mind that made him want to discuss all kinds of topics with her, from politics to what she liked to cook best to how she'd react if he kissed her. A real kiss. Not for show, not for anybody but the two of them. Would she blush again? Would she take charge, or would he have the pleasure of training her how to do that, too?

Carly took a deep breath and pushed away from him, cutting off his errant thoughts. "Where does strychnine come from? Who'd have access to it?"

It took a second for him to switch topics with her. The woman wanted to work.

Ivan retreated a step, tamping down the nerve endings that were prickling with disappointment at not being in contact with her anymore. "There are remote stashes of chemical weapons in my country that contain this poison. We are in the process of disassembling them. If one has the proper clearance, you could access them."

"How would you get it into the United States?"

"On a jet with diplomatic clearance," he was embarrassed to say. "In small quantities, it could pass for powder in a toiletry bag."

Her eyes narrowed as she considered another option. "Strychnine is the deadly ingredient in rat poison. That'd be easy enough to purchase stateside. You could liquefy it and turn it into an injectable liquid."

Rat poison? Those sensitized nerves went on alert again, but this time for a different reason. "Would it be used for killing moles, as well?"

"They're similar critters. I imagine the poisons would have the same ingredients. I'd have to do some research. Why?"

Ivan replayed a conversation from the evening before. "One of your neighbors, an older gentleman—my bodyguard Eduard talked to him—said he was baiting traps to kill moles when we arrived."

"Mr. Furness?" She shrugged. "I don't know him all that well. He couldn't have poisoned my brother, though. That fruit went straight from you to me to Frank. It never left the house."

"You do not know Mr. Furness as well as say, Mrs. Pischnotte?"

"Mrs. Pischnotte has lived across the street for years. I've known her since I was a little girl, back when her husband was still alive. Mr. Furness isn't really our neighbor. He works for a company that's house-sitting for the Abshers. Sometimes, he shows up. Sometimes it's another guy. I've met a couple of them when I go running."

A full-blown alarm raised the hairs at the nape of his neck. "Then Furness lied. He told Eduard that everyone on your street has lived there for years. Including him." He shook his head, searching for a more hopeful answer. "Maybe it was a language problem and Eduard misunderstood."

"Or your bodyguard lied."

"Why would he…?" Of course. What did he truly know about anyone in his inner circle? Before that bomb had gone off in St. Feodor, he'd trusted every one of them. Now he trusted no one. He was glad to have a fresh set of eyes to look at them as suspects instead of employees or friends. "Eduard is new to my security team. Filip thought we needed some younger blood. I confess I do not know him as well as Filip or Danya."

Carly snorted through her nose. "You mean Mr. Personality?"

He frowned at the nickname. "Sarcasm?"

"Oh, yeah." She paced the room again, but this time he could see the thoughts running through her head, energizing her, instead of the stress leaking through her pores and sapping her resilience. "What Danya Pavluk lacks in charm, he makes up for in grouchy negativity. He has a big chip on his shoulder. He's not friendly. He's really unhappy about something for him to be so grumpy."

"Unhappy about the changes happening in Lukinburg?"

"Or it's personal. Somebody really hates your guts. Enough to kill you in a dozen different ways. Poison. You said someone shot at you. Bombs." She stopped in front of him again, her hand finding his where it rested at his waist. She squeezed his fingers, emphasizing the dire turn of her suspicions. "Maybe there's a team of would-be assassins, each with his or her own specialty. Different members of these Lukin Loyalists." She closed her eyes and shook her head as if the possibilities were overwhelming. "Or one person wants us to think it's a group of individuals who are after you by varying the means of their attacks." Her eyes popped open. "Since there are a lot of suspects with motive, maybe we should focus on the means—how these crimes are being committed. We should look at anyone who has experience with explosives, as well as anyone with access to poison, syringes, that kind of medical or chemical expertise."

"More than one assassin?" He muttered Danya's favorite curse. "Every able-bodied citizen in Lukinburg is required to serve at least two years in our military. Not everyone sees combat, but theoretically, any of my people could have knowledge of explosives. Or poison."

"We should check their service records, then. Maybe someone worked as a medic? Nurse? An exterminator? Can you do that? Do you know how to do research? Or does someone always do that for you?" She released his hand, frowning as if the idea of him using a computer or analyzing data was foreign to him. "If you give me access to that information, I could look it up for you."

"Not easily. All but the most basic personnel information is encrypted for security reasons. Filip changes the codes regularly."

"So, that's a dead end. How are we ever supposed to get an upper hand on this predator?"

He caught her hand before she pulled away. This time he was instilling some clarity into her. "I have not always been the prince. Once upon a time, I worked in my uncle's business. Growing up, I worked in a mine. I was a soldier for six years. I know how to get information. I know how to get a job done." He paused when he realized he was defending his manhood, at least a little bit. He released her hand to rake his fingers through his short hair. "Filip would be suspicious if you make inquiries. I will do this. I do not want the threats against me to become threats against you."

"Just tell me where to look and I can—"

"This job is more impossible than I could have imagined." He wasn't going to argue about this. As much as he needed an ally, he didn't want to see her hurt. Or crashing into an emotional catharsis again. "I never meant for anyone in your family to get hurt. I will speak to Captain Hendricks to remove you from the investigation and find another way to deal with the threats."

"I'm not going anywhere."

"I have asked too much of you. Too much of anyone who is not a part of the Lukin—"

"I agree with the captain. It's personal now." She crossed her arms beneath his jacket, looking up at him with the same grit he'd seen when she'd taken down that pervert at the police station. "Even if this Loyalist group didn't intend to hurt my family, they did. I made a deal with you. You didn't ask me to help because I look pretty in a party dress and can dance in high heels—which, incidentally, I don't know that I can. You needed a cop. You needed someone who could find answers without it looking like an official investigation. If I quit, who's going to have your back?"

A smile spread slowly across his face.

That faint pink blush crept into her cheeks as she pulled back a step. "Why are you smiling? What did I say?"

He reached out to capture a lock of caramel-blond hair that had fallen over one eye and tucked it into place behind her ear. "Usually, people are not allowed to lecture the crown prince. You may advise me, but I make the decisions."

"What are you deciding?"

"I like how you talk to me, like you are talking to the man—not the crown. Although, you should not do this in public. It undermines royal authority."

"My badge is the authority I answer to. If I think you're doing something wrong, something that might endanger you or anyone else, I have to speak up."

He pulled his fingers from her silky hair and curled them into his palm. "Very well. I can see you are a stubborn woman. But I am a stubborn man. You may have my backside if you wish." He knew his English phrasing wasn't quite right. He'd find a translator if she didn't understand. "But you will also allow me to have yours."

"You can't risk your life for me. I won't—"

"Those are my terms. I cannot carry a gun, but there are things I can do to protect you and your family. I will not have you fighting this assassin, maybe an entire rebel faction, on your own."

"I can call KCPD for backup."

"Your booty is mine."

Ivan felt the heat creeping up his own neck when a giggle snorted through her nose.

"Is that not the right word for your backside? I have yours as you have mine."

"It's okay, Ivan. I like keeping an eye on your booty, too."

He didn't need a translator to understand that. She'd just admitted that the attraction he felt wasn't one-sided. Good to know. The timing and situation stank, but the possibility of something impossible between them smoothed the raw edges off his embarrassment and protective anger. "Then, despite my reservations, we shall continue working together. You are not alone."

"You aren't, either." There was neither flirtation nor argument in her tone when she spoke again. The police officer was back. "Is there anyone in your delegation you trust without hesitation?"

His choices were limited. His bunk mate from basic training was the only one he'd reveal a secret to. "Aleksandr."

"Then we need to enlist his help."

Ivan scrubbed at the tension cording the back of his neck. "I would rather not."

"You need every ally you can get."

If he'd believed teaming up with Aleks had been a real option for this covert mission, he wouldn't have needed to go to KCPD for help. "Aleks…is smart and has great vision for the future of our country. But he is also…how do you say it? His mind is absent."

"Absentminded? He gets distracted?"

"Yes." She should understand how preoccupied Aleks could get when he focused on his work—or on whatever pretty face or passing scenery caught his eye. "I do not know if he could handle himself in a dangerous situation. I would not want to put him in that position."

"Then you have to let me investigate. You have to let me talk to your people, search through your records. I need answers, Ivan. Someone nearly killed my brother. They keep trying to kill you, and the more I get to know you, the more I don't like that." She fingered the badge that hung around her neck, perhaps reminding him of her oath to protect and serve, perhaps reminding herself. "They're threatening to kill a lot of innocent people next Saturday. I need to stop them."

He'd taken a similar vow when he'd agreed to become the crown prince. "*We* need to stop them. I will do what I can to get the information you require."

"Don't get caught, okay?"

He smiled at her persistence. "I will do my best."

"I imagine your best is pretty good." He followed her to the exit, reaching around her to open the door. She paused in the open doorway and tilted her face up to his. "Thank you."

"I believe I am the one who should be thanking you, Carly." He caught the end of her braid and rolled its dark golden weight in the palm of his hand. "Does your name mean lioness, by any chance?"

She glanced down at the strands he held, then back into his eyes. "No."

"Surely you are named for your bravery and determination."

She tugged the braid from his hand. One of those endearing blushes heated the apples of her cheeks. "It's the feminine version of Carl."

"It is not short for something else? Carlotta?"

She shook her head. "Carly Rae Valentine. What you see is what you get."

"I like what I see."

She leaned back against the door frame, keeping her gaze locked on to his. She might not be used to intimacy with a prince, but she wasn't afraid of it. "Are you trying to charm me, Your Highness?"

He braced his hand on the metal frame above her head, drifting in to maintain the closeness between them. "Is it working?"

She captured the end of his tie and examined it the same way he had studied her hair. "Thank you for caring about my family, about me. I know you have a lot on your mind."

"At this moment, you are the only thing on my mind." His voice had dropped to a husky whisper.

When she tilted her gaze back up to his, she tugged

on his tie and stretched onto her toes. She kept coming until her mouth pressed against his. Her lips were tentative, perhaps unsure of their welcome, but the fingers curling into the front of his shirt and sliding against his jaw to hold his mouth against hers told a different story. Ivan was powerless to resist the sweet thank-you and eager invitation. Leaving one hand above her head, he slipped the other beneath the jacket, curving his fingers around her waist. His knuckles brushed against the gun she carried, but all he could feel was soft cotton and cool skin and the sinewy flex of the muscles running from her flank over the flare of her hip. Her kiss seemed to be an exploration, and Ivan seized the opportunity to learn the taste of her mouth, as well. Running his tongue against the seam of her lips, he coaxed her to open for him and swept his tongue into the soft heat of her mouth.

Her throaty squeak of surprise muted into a hum of pleasure as she welcomed and returned the need in his kiss. Her fingertips clung to the skin beneath his beard as her tongue darted into his mouth. They danced together in a new way, advancing, retreating. A gentle stroke here, firmer pressure there. A nip, a suckle. His body caught fire with the electricity surging between them. The slow build of heat burst into flame and he longed to back her into the door and sandwich her body against his. He wanted to learn her curves, match her strength to his. He wanted to get drunk on the scents of smoke and spice that clung to her skin and hair. When her hand slid around the collar of his shirt to dig into the tension he carried there, he was the one growling a hungry approval in his throat.

"Carly…" He tried to retreat. He wanted too much,

too soon. "We are tired." He kissed her. "I want you." He kissed her again. "The hour is late." He couldn't seem to stop.

She dragged her teeth across his bottom lip and desire arced straight down to his groin, erasing any of the restraint he'd tried to grab onto. "Please tell me this isn't part of the charade. It feels convincing to me."

"Are you pretending?" he whispered against her lips. "No."

"Neither am I." Claiming her mouth in a kiss that was anything but pretend, he drifted closer, sliding his hand down over the curve of her rump and squeezing its beautiful shape as he pulled her thighs into the arousal straining behind his zipper. His brain burned with the fever to have all of her. His heart pounded against his ribs. His pulse thundered in his ears.

A bright light flashed in the corner of his vision, shocking him back to common sense.

"The prince and his local Cinderella," a man's voice said. Ivan swore as a second flash went off from the hallway, capturing them in the open door. "Readers are going to eat this up."

Ivan lifted his gaze to drill the reporter taking pictures of the embrace, even as he moved to stand between Carly and the unwelcome interruption. "I ask you to leave, sir. This is a private moment."

"Obviously. Could I get a name, miss?" the reporter asked.

Ivan's hand fisted at his side. A smaller, surprisingly strong hand curved around his, and Carly moved up beside him. "It's all right." She pulled back the front of the jacket to reveal the gun and badge she wore. She glanced at the man's press credentials hanging around his neck. "Listen, Mr. Decker. I'm armed and dangerous. If I see that picture in the paper with any kind of crude story or suggestive headline, my boss at KCPD will be calling your boss."

If her voice hadn't started in that breathless tone, he might have thought she was unaffected by that mini make-out session. Still, Ivan wasn't sure if he should admire her self-possession or feel offended that she could get over his kiss so easily. He shouldn't have let things get out of hand. Losing focus like that was all on him. It was up to him to make this right.

He turned and called down to the waiting room. What the hell was security for if they didn't do their job? "Filip!" He eyed the name badge and credentials hanging around the reporter's neck. Ralph Decker. *Kansas City Journal*. Ivan didn't recognize the man's name from the press packet he'd reviewed on the plane. "I trust you will be as diligent about reporting on the fundraising efforts my people are working on for your city this week, Mr. Decker?"

"You give me an invitation to that embassy ball, and you're damn straight I'll cover it. Unless you've got something a little meatier you'd like me to write about?" Decker had been fishing for an inside scoop all along. But he winked at Carly. "You never gave me your name, Miss…?"

"*Officer* Valentine."

Decker nodded and reached for his phone to type in the name. "Gettin' a little personal protection, eh, Princie?"

Filip Milevski's bulk rushed past them in a blur. "I am sorry, Your Highness." He clamped his hand around the reporter's arm and dragged him down the hallway. "You lied to me. You said you were going to—"

"Hey, if I'm getting stuck with this lousy story, then I'm going to make sure I have something to write about."

"You go. Now."

Decker raised his free hand in surrender, and Filip released him, staying right by the reporter's shoulder as he walked to the elevator under his own power. The rest of their conversation became inconsequential.

Carly shrugged out of Ivan's jacket and pushed it into his arms. "I need to check with Dad and Jesse. Find out what you can. I'll call the crime lab later to see if they can tell me anything else."

He caught her by the arm before she sprinted away. "That kiss was not a charade," he articulated as clearly as he could. "Not for me."

"It makes our cover look authentic, though, doesn't it?" Her brusque dismissal left him thinking she might not believe him. "Good night, Ivan." She twisted away before he could stop her, nearly plowing into Aleks as he turned the corner. "Mr. Petrovic."

"Miss Valentine." And then she was gone. Beyond Ivan's reach, beyond his line of sight. Beyond any chance to talk about that kiss and the potential fallout she might endure from the press. Aleks's dark brows arched above the rim of his glasses as he ambled up. "That should have been 'Good night, Your Highness.'"

Ivan shook his head, torn between duty and doing the right thing by Carly. "Don't start with me, Aleks," he muttered in their native language.

"A late-night rendezvous?" Aleks glanced toward the elevators where Filip waited with the photographer to escort him out of the hospital. He spoke purpose-ful English, as they'd agreed to while they were in the States. "I cannot wait for that headline."

"It was one kiss." One hell of a kiss. A kiss that could have led to something more if the world would just leave him the hell alone. He pulled on his jacket, unable to ignore the faint essence of grill smoke and cooking spices clinging to the wool from Carly's skin and hair. "I thought you left with Galina."

"Temper, temper, my friend. You are forgetting your-self. And the promise you made to me, to our entire country." Aleks's amusement faded as he circled around Ivan into the private room. "May I talk to you for a mo-ment? As your friend?"

Ivan exhaled a deep sigh of frustration before closing the door behind him. Weariness dogged at his heels, so he dropped onto the room's love seat, crossed his right foot over his left knee and leaned back into the stiff cushions. "Go ahead."

"I know you have not been the prince for that long." Aleks poured himself a cup of coffee. Ivan refused the offer for a cup of his own. He was already exhausted and didn't need caffeine to disrupt the two or three hours of sleep he'd be getting. "You cannot be seen in an embrace like that with someone like—"

"Like what? Be very careful what you say next, Aleks." His friend wisely chose not to complete that sentence. "You are the one who seems to be treating this trip as if it was some grand adventure. Am I not allowed to have a few moments where I do not have to be *on* for meetings or the public or press? Carly means something to me."

"Does she?" Aleks challenged. "You and I both know she is not your old friend from the army."

"That does not mean the feelings are not real." Ivan pulled off his glasses and rubbed at the bridge of his nose.

Aleks sipped his coffee, made a face at the taste and dumped it down the sink before tossing the paper cup into the trash. All a stall for time, and the opportunity to come up with the right words, Ivan suspected. "I do not begrudge you this relationship. But there are expectations. We need our trade partners to know we are serious, and not think we are in Kansas City for you to fool around…" He took a seat across from Ivan and leaned in. "She is delightful to converse with, but she seems…coarse. Tell her to wear a dress. Tell her to at least hide that gun. It looks as though you are consorting with a gangster. Like someone from the old regime."

Ivan shot to his feet, towering over his friend. "She is an honored police officer. A military veteran."

"Even if she was in uniform, it would be an improvement." They'd known each other for too long for Aleks to be truly intimidated by him. He slowly rose to his feet to face him. "Put body armor on her and she could be one of the Lukin rebels. Please, if you must have this affair…" He put up his hands when Ivan started to protest. "I remember a prince's speech saying that we must earn the respect of the world again to save our people. I am only telling you this because I know you want the best for our country. I know you have been lonely since taking on the responsibilities you have, that you have not had time to pursue any kind of personal life. But fraternizing with Miss Valentine in public is not the image that will earn that respect."

Only his best friend could talk to him like this—could insult Carly like that—and not find himself flat on the floor. "You want me to dress her up in public and keep my feelings for her private?"

"Yes. If you must have her with you."

"I must." Ivan's hand went to the tension at the back of his neck, which Carly's grasping fingers had temporarily dispelled. "Aleks, she reminds me of where I came from. Where *we* came from and what we have overcome. She reminds me of the strength that lies within me, which I will need to complete this job. I need her. Plus, I will not abandon her when she is dealing with this attack on her family."

"That attack was meant for you."

"That mistake does not lessen the impact of nearly losing her brother."

"So, this is guilt?"

"This is the way I say it will be." Ivan buttoned his collar and straightened his tie, putting on his princely facade once more. "Now, we have bigger concerns than my love life." He headed out of the room, waiting for Aleks to fall into step beside him. "Tell Filip to bring the car around. Have Galina prepare a short statement to release to the press regarding this unfortunate incident. And Aleks? Find me a laptop."

He'd made a promise to Carly. There was work to be done.

Chapter Six

"Brooke? Help me."

Carly got the zipper of the sleeveless polka-dot dress partway down. But no matter how she twisted and stretched, there was no way to reach the little tab to pull it down the rest of the way unless she dislocated her shoulder to do it.

Yesterday's luncheon and shopping on her own had been an absolute disaster. Carly had picked out a little black dress that apparently wasn't the universally chichi thing the magazine she'd read through had indicated. Her father had asked what funeral she was going to. Galina Honchar had tsk-tsked at her before ushering her to her seat. Ivan had been a compelling speaker, and if she was a farmer, she'd certainly be willing to talk more about selling her beef and soybeans to Lukinburg. But during the mingling with the guests afterward, someone had mistaken her for one of the servers and asked her for a refill of coffee.

About the only thing useful that had happened was the chance to stand back from the group and observe Ivan's staff. Aleks was a natural-born salesman, probably Ivan's greatest asset when it came to discussing facts and figures, as well as entertaining guests around the conference room. Galina carried her computer tablet with her everywhere, and seemed to either be whispering into Ivan's ear, making introductions, or steering someone away from Ivan if their conversation ran on too long. Danya stood inside one set of conference room doors, avoiding all conversation, keeping his eyes on Ivan as he moved about the room. Eduard stood at the other set of doors and acknowledged her with a friendly salute. Although his earpiece and concealed gun indicated he was security, he interacted with guests who came and went, even laughing with some of them. Filip moved through the crowd with Ivan, never two or three feet away from the prince.

Ivan had been kind enough to pull her to his side and introduce her to the Lukin ambassador and the president of the American agri-business group. Both men made her feel welcome enough, but she'd been more interested in why Filip had put more distance between himself and Ivan when she was at his side, and who he was talking to on his cell phone when he did slip away. And what had Galina and Eduard been arguing about before she sent the young bodyguard out of the room to do her bidding.

Afterward, Carly had been dropped off with no time for debriefing or goodbyes beyond a quick kiss. And though he said that he'd rather spend the rest of the day with her watching a ball game and eating the barbecue he'd missed out on the night before, Galina had tapped him on his shoulder and reminded him that they needed to get to the TV station to tape an interview for the evening news. Ivan had brushed his finger across Carly's cheek, whispered something in Lukin that sounded like a promise and climbed inside his limo to drive away with the rest of his delegation.

She was beginning to understand time alone, time away from being the prince and representing his country was a rare, precious thing for him. Carly vowed then and there to make the most of the time they'd have alone—to go over answers together and give him a break from the heavy responsibilities he carried on those broad shoulders.

But so far, today hadn't been much of a success. She hadn't been able to find more than basic public info about the suspects who might be threatening Ivan, and she was stuck in this stupid dress.

Carly flexed all ten fingers out straight, eyeing the strange spots of pale pink polish where her plain, stubby nails used to be. Then she took a deep breath and contorted herself in the dressing room's three-way mirror in an effort to reach the back of the dress. "My toes and fingernails feel claustrophobic. Can nail polish numb them?"

"Really?" Her friend's pregnant belly appeared in the mirror a split second before her gentle smile did. "You're a tomboy, not a shut-in. You said you enjoyed the foot scrub. They're beautiful. Tastefully done without looking flashy." Brooke reached in and unzipped the back of the dress. "You're just not used to seeing yourself all spiffed up."

"How do you girlie-girls put up with this stuff? I wouldn't have been able to use my hands at all if the manicurist had put those tips on the way she wanted to. I don't remember the last time I wore pink." Carly pushed the dress off her shoulders and let it fall to the floor before stepping out of it. "I'd say this one's a no. If I can't even undress myself..."

"You can't wear the navy pantsuit all week." She held out her hand for Carly to pick up the dress and returned it to its hanger. "Ms. Honchar's note said you'd specifically need a dress for the university reception tomorrow. I think we've determined that black is not your color. It's either this or that cream floral with the short sleeves."

"I think Ms. Honchar would prefer that I dress in something that makes me invisible." She eyed the floral dress. "You're sure it's proper for a university reception?"

"It's flattering and has a little color without being over the top. Besides, you can get in and out of it all by yourself. That's a plus."

"Ha ha," Carly deadpanned. She eyed the open boxes of shoes on the dressing room floor. "What do I wear with it? The sandals?"

"I'd go with the beige heels with the bows on them."

"The ones that pinch my toes?"

Brooke laughed. "You've survived on the streets working undercover in No-Man's Land. You can survive dressing up and going to a party."

With a mock groan, Carly reached for her friend's hand and squeezed it. "Thank you for doing this. I wasn't sure who to call for this wannabe princess makeover."

"I'm a regular fairy godmother." A bit on the shy side of things, Brooke Kincaid was quite possibly the kindest soul Carly had ever met. She didn't know if their friendship stemmed from their opposite personalities drawing them together, or from being the two awkward outcasts at the Fourth Precinct offices who'd found themselves on the sidelines at more than one social event. Brooke hung the dress behind the vintage-looking floral with the easy-to-reach buttons. "I think you should get this one. After this week, you could wear it to church or out on a date."

Carly snorted. "I've never worn anything but jeans on a date."

"When was the last time you went out with a man? And I don't mean out with the guys to a bar after your shift." Brooke dropped her voice to a conspiratorial whisper. "You know, the kind of evening that ends with intimate conversation and a good-night kiss?"

A brush of electricity skittered across Carly's lips at the memory of the kiss she'd shared with Ivan at the hospital. Even though she'd initiated the kiss, he'd quickly made himself an equal partner, inviting her to do whatever she liked with his handsome mouth, so long as he got to have his way with hers, as well. She thought he'd given her a glimpse of the man behind the crown. He'd called her a lioness, like she was brave and golden, a woman to be admired. If he'd called her sexy or beautiful, she'd have been less turned on, less likely to believe the connection growing between them.

Yesterday's goodbye kiss had been a perfunctory farewell, kept necessarily short because of too little time and too much of an audience. But even that simple touch had crackled with electricity, reminding Carly of those private moments they'd shared in the hospital.

That kiss had been heady and decadent, the most grown-up, intense kiss she'd ever shared with a man. Despite his genteel facade, Ivan was all sharp angles and hard edges. His beard tickled her fingers, lips and palms. His jaw was warm, unbending, saved from perfection by the ridge of scar tissue that bisected it near his ear. But even more than the draw of his lips, she'd loved it when he'd held her in his arms before that kiss. She'd been on the verge of breaking down with fatigue and stress and self-doubts about being the right woman to pull off this job. She hadn't been able to protect her brother, much less a visiting prince and the whole of Kansas City. Ivan had been rock-solid, more so than she'd expect from a man who filled his days with business meetings and press conferences, and she'd treasured the unfamiliar sensations of warmth and strength surrounding her. She was always the strong one in her family—on the emotional front, at any rate. She'd never dropped her guard and melted into a man's chest before, trusting, for a few moments, at least, that someone could protect her for a change.

But Monday night hadn't been a date. She wasn't even sure it counted as a real kiss, despite yesterday's picture in the society pages of the *Kansas City Journal*. Local Connection to Visiting Prince? hardly described whatever stars had aligned between them that night. Somewhere along the way, she'd lost track of everything except Ivan and the way his hand and mouth and heat had made her feel. He could have deepened that kiss for the reporter's benefit, or to seal the believability of their cover story as reunited lovers for the curious eyes of Aleks Petrovic and suspicious glares from Filip Milevski. She didn't have enough experience to read real passion versus a guy who was pretending he was into her. She only knew what she herself had felt. She was probably lucky they'd been interrupted before she followed the urge to climb right up the prince's body and wrap herself around him.

"You're thinking about *him*, aren't you?" Brooke smiled, politely ignoring Carly's deer-in-the-headlights expression in the mirror. "Who'd have thought my best friend would be dating a prince?"

"For a week, Brooke. And it's not dating so much as…" She almost ended the sentence with *work*. But remembering the need for secrecy, knowing that even a well-meaning friend could accidentally let it slip that she'd only known Ivan for a couple of days, that she was more bodyguard than girlfriend, Carly blinked her eyes and looked away. "Ivan wasn't a prince when I knew him…before. I'm hardly going to get serious with a man who's about to go off and run his own country in a week."

"But that kiss…" Brooke had the good grace to blush at the photograph that might as well have been on the front page from all the teasing and comments she'd gotten from her brothers and coworkers. "It looked so romantic."

Romantic wasn't the half of it. Carly shrugged off the visceral memory, reminding herself not to make too much of the bond she felt to Ivan. This was a job. A responsibility. Not a happily-ever-after in the making. "I'd never fit into that world. My life is here. My job? Dad and the bros? They need me."

Brooke seemed disappointed by her answer. "What about what you need?" Then she smiled again, as if she thought Carly needed cheering up. "That doesn't mean you won't find someone else after Ivan's gone back to Europe."

Carly silently thanked her for the unknowing save.

"Point taken. Maybe the wardrobe upgrade will help in the romance department. Maybe there's an Atticus out there for me, too." The fact that Brooke's husband, a protective, by-the-book detective, doted on her gave Carly hope that one day she, too, would find a guy who'd either look past her lack of feminine charms or who'd embrace her awkward, kick-ass self for who she was. Princes with stellar kissing abilities need not apply. Time to change the conversation. "I'm lucky Captain Hendricks gave you today off to help with my makeover. Clearly, I wasn't making the magic happen yesterday on my own."

"I was already scheduled off this morning for my OB appointment." Brooke dug through her purse and pulled out a bag of crackers and nibbled on one. Carly frowned, wondering if she'd been pushing her friend too hard today. Those crackers had been Brooke's constant companion for the past eight months. "It gave me the opportunity for some last-minute pampering before the baby arrives."

Carly hugged the discarded dresses to her chest and urged Brooke back out to the waiting area to hand them off to the clerk who'd been waiting on her. "You are not having that baby on my watch. I've got enough on my plate right now."

Brooke laughed, rubbing her belly as she sat. "Relax. She's not due for another three weeks." She waved Carly back behind the curtain, reminding her that, even though this was the women's department, she'd come out in her bra and a half-slip.

"You found out she's a girl?" Carly tugged off the slip and added it to the pile of clothes she wanted to purchase.

"We didn't want to know." Brooke raised her voice to be heard through the curtain. "That's what Atticus is hoping for, though. I guess with all his brothers, he's tired of having so much testosterone in the family."

Carly smiled at her friend's humility. "He's probably looking forward to a daughter who's as sweet and pretty as her mama."

"As long as she or he is healthy, that's all I care about."

"Are you sure you're holding up okay? We've been at this for hours. I'm exhausted, and I'm not pregnant." She poked her head out around the curtain. "Do you need to take a break?"

"Are you kidding? I wouldn't miss seeing Carly Valentine in a dress and high heels for anything. I plan to take a picture, by the way. No one will believe me, otherwise." She swallowed the last of her cracker. "You'd better start on the gowns. It's after twelve thirty. Isn't Prince Ivan meeting you at one?"

"I guess I can't put it off any longer." Carly groaned at the thought of all the lace, sequins and spiky heels waiting for her.

Twenty minutes later, with five of them spent trying to get a pair of strappy silver sandals cinched around her ankles before giving up on shoes altogether, she'd modeled lavender, champagne and blue gowns. Any one of them would do, as far as Carly was concerned, although Brooke had pointed out faults in too much skirt, showing too much skin, or looking like one of her spinster aunts.

Carly opened the curtain and stepped out in a pale turquoise gown with a beaded bodice and a simple, flowing skirt. "This is the last of them," she announced. "Which one should I get?"

"That one," a deep, accented voice answered.

Carly curled her toes into the carpet, lamenting the heat that crept into her cheeks the moment she realized Brooke wasn't alone. Ivan was perched on the back of the couch, chatting with her friend. But he stood when Carly appeared, tucking his handkerchief into his pocket and sliding the glasses he'd been cleaning back over his gorgeous blue eyes. Hungry eyes, she thought, as he raked his gaze up and down her body. Happy to see her. Liking what he saw—if she could read a man correctly, and if this man's expression actually conveyed the truth. Not everything was as it should be in royalty land, though, judging by the lines of fatigue framing those piercing blue eyes. Carly's heart squeezed in concern over whatever stress was worrying him now. Had there been another threat? Another attempt on his life? A long, difficult meeting that hadn't gone his way? Ivan revealed nothing but a smile.

"That color is stunning on you." He pointed to her bare toes. "Although I do recommend shoes. There will be a lot of dancing at the ball."

Carly backtracked from her initial worry. She was the bodyguard here, not his girlfriend. She looked beyond his shoulders, quickly scanning the store out to the double front doors, spotting Milevski waiting just outside. Reminding herself that she shouldn't let her feelings get real for this man, she distanced herself with a joke. "I didn't think my boots went with the look." There was no one else in the shop save the clerk at the counter who'd paused in the middle of hanging up the dresses Carly had discarded to gawk at the handsome, raven-haired man who'd strolled into her department. "Where's your security team?"

"Filip and the police are outside keeping anyone else

from coming in. Danya and Eduard are clearing the floor of any other customers and staff."

"Can you do that? Close down a store?" Carly asked, perhaps understanding for the first time the level of security necessary to allow a prince to be out in public. She saw Danya herding a group of employees into the break room. She traded scowls with the surly bodyguard before he closed the door and raised his arm to report into the radio he wore on his wrist. Then she saw Eduard chatting with a trio of young women as he opened the glass doors and walked them outside. "Of course, you can. You've already done it." She dragged her gaze back to Ivan, hiking up her skirt and retreating to the dressing rooms. "I don't want to hold you up. I'll get changed and be ready ASAP."

"ASAP?" Ivan asked.

"As soon as possible," Carly and Brooke echoed together.

"I see. No rush," he assured them, signaling Eduard stay by the front doors. "I am yours for the next two hours." He bent to kiss Brooke's hand. "Mrs. Kincaid. You are looking radiant today. Will you be joining us for lunch?"

"No, thank you. I wouldn't dream of intruding. Besides, I'm meeting my husband." Flustered by the prince's attention, Brooke quickly excused herself. She looped her purse over her shoulder and picked up the large Doc Martens shoebox on the seat beside her. "I've worked all the miracles I can. She's coiffed, painted and dressed for success. Don't let her buy the boots." She placed the box in Ivan's hands. "They're the only thing she picked out on her own."

"Traitor." Carly watched Ivan peek at the thick-soled boots that had caught her eye.

He laughed. "They would certainly make a fashion statement with that dress."

Carly grabbed the box from him, finding it impossible not to smile as the tension around his eyes eased. "At least they're in better shape than the ones I usually wear. I was going to pay for them myself."

Brooke reclaimed the burgundy boots. "Ms. Honchar said princess, not goth chick or biker babe. I'm putting them back for your own good. You know I love ya, Carly."

"Love you, too." Carly hugged her from the side, carefully avoiding her pregnant belly. "Thanks for everything. Tell Atticus hi."

"I will. Good luck. With everything," she whispered the last bit into Carly's ear, reminding her that Brooke thought this relationship was real. Brooke carried the boots over to the clerk before pulling out her phone. Carly could hear how her friend's tone softened as she called her husband to let him know she was ready to be picked up. Eduard pushed the door open for her and exchanged a nod as she left the store.

Carly touched the stack of clothing and unmentionables that Brooke had deemed were necessary for this week's public appearances. "Are you sure this isn't too much? I got something for every event on Galina's list. Brooke made sure they were appropriate."

Ivan gathered up the items from the couch and snapped his fingers for Eduard to handle the purchase. "She can be a stickler for details."

"That's why Brooke gets to run the captain's office.

Captain Hendricks thinks he's in charge, but we all know who keeps the precinct running."

"I meant Galina. She's planned my days down to the minute. She's asked that any changes go through her." Right. Different taskmaster. "I am sure your friend is very good at what she does. I apologize for being late, but my meeting with the mayor ran longer than planned."

Carly headed back into the dressing room to change into the blue pantsuit. "Did everything go okay?"

"I spent longer than I wanted talking about Ralph Decker's photograph of us in the paper. It was not my intention to make you the center of local gossip."

"No one will question whether you and I are the real deal or not now. That's one good thing about being caught off guard like that." A mortifying thought made her stick her head back out through the curtain. "It didn't cause trouble at the meeting, did it?"

Ivan shook his head and touched his watch to remind her of the time before waving her back inside to finish changing. "Actually, everyone seemed to think it was positive publicity for my visit. They likened it to a royal wedding. Although I am not sure I like my new nickname—Prince Charming. How will anyone take me seriously?"

"Prince Charming?" Carly groaned on Ivan's behalf. "Have any of them actually talked to you?" she teased.

"Very funny, Officer Cinderella," he teased right back.

Her groan was legit this time. "Is that *my* nickname?"

Ivan laughed. "When we got down to business, the new mayor was very welcoming, and amenable to

moving forward with our proposed research and agri-
business deals."

"That's good, right?"

"That is very good."

Carly pulled the jacket on over her new pink blouse
and slipped her feet into the ballet flats Brooke had
chosen for her. She tucked her gun into the holster at
the back of her belt. Then she picked up the package
of baby blankets in shades of green, yellow and peach
and draped the evening gown over her arm before re-
joining Ivan. "Is this okay? It feels a little like I'm in
uniform—without the sturdy footwear."

"To be honest…" He leaned in to kiss her cheek and
whisper beyond curious ears and prying eyes. "I like
the shorts better." He brushed the tip of his finger across
the cheek he'd kissed, seeming amused by the heat she
could feel coloring her skin before he pulled away. "But
this is more flattering than the black dress. Perfect for
a luncheon with a prince."

Idly, Carly wondered if any man's attention would
make her blush like a girlie-girl, or if it was Ivan Mostek's superpower to make her react to every intimate
word or touch they shared. And since she had no words
to ask him if he meant half the compliments he gave
her, she headed to the checkout counter. "I want to buy
these baby blankets Brooke was admiring. To thank her
for helping me out. I'll be just a few minutes."

Ivan plucked the package from the baby department
out of her hands and gave it to the clerk with a smile
that made the other woman press her hand to her heart.
"We will take these, as well. Put them on my account
and have them delivered to Miss Valentine's home with
everything else."

"Yes, sir," the clerk answered, looking equally flustered when Eduard joined them.

"Shall I bring the car from the parking garage, Your Highness?" Eduard asked. His wink to the clerk left her scurrying to do her work.

"I thought we could do something different," Carly suggested. "We're only a couple of city blocks from a really good, yet casual, authentic Kansas City barbecue restaurant. Since you didn't get to try any of mine Monday night."

Ivan looked pleased by the suggestion. "It is a warm, sunny day. I believe we will walk. The fresh air will do me good." He scanned the store before fixing his gaze on Eduard again. "Notify Filip of the change in plans. And tell Danya to release those people to do their jobs. We are not holding prisoners."

"Very good, sir."

While Eduard radioed the security team to do the prince's bidding, Ivan settled his hand at the small of Carly's back to walk her to the door. They were barely out of earshot before his fingers tightened around the bulge of her Glock beneath her jacket. "Is that necessary?"

Carly kept her voice equally low. "Have you figured out who's sending those death threats yet?"

He shook his head.

"Then yes, it's necessary. Still not sure where it's going Saturday night, though."

His tired smile didn't reach his eyes. "I have no doubt you will figure out an interesting solution."

Once he'd opened the break room door and dismissed the staff, Danya strode through the store, his eyes drilling holes through Carly. Did he blame her for the change in security protocol? Or was the man simply incapable of smiling? Maybe he had a thing against cops. Or women. Or Americans. Maybe he resented how closely Ivan wanted to tie their country to the United States. Wasn't that the reason the rebel Lukins had protested the new government? The surly bodyguard was definitely on Carly's suspect list.

Ignoring every cautionary instinct that warned her she shouldn't care what Ivan was feeling, she faced him. "Are you going to tell me what's wrong now?" She touched one of the lines creasing his temple. "You didn't have these yesterday."

He covered her hand with his for a moment before pulling it down and lacing their fingers together. "Not here."

Something *had* happened. But before she could press him for details, she realized Ivan was slipping a small rectangular object into her palm. A flash drive. Carly tightened her grip around the tiny device and slipped it into the pocket of her jacket. "I assume there's something you want me to read on here?"

"Personnel histories and notes from Filip's investigation into the threats and bombing in St. Feodor," he whispered. "I finally had a chance to download them last night."

"You said Filip encrypted his files. How did you get past his security codes?"

"I am good with a computer." He glanced beyond her, no doubt making sure their exchange remained private. "May I stop by tonight after the cocktail party I am attending to discuss anything you find on it?"

"Of course."

"I accessed Filip's files using Aleks's laptop but had

time to do little more than make a copy. I translated as much as I had time to do so into English. But some of it is still in Lukin. We can go over that together. I am not sure what is on there. It is hard to be alone. I deleted the browser history afterward. Hopefully, Filip will not know you have these."

"Or that someone's been snooping in his records." She reached for Ivan's hand again and squeezed it with a promise. "I'll keep them safe, use my computer at home so that no one knows what we're doing."

The chatter of the employees coming back out onto the floor ended the hushed conversation. Still, she startled at the grumble of Danya's voice behind her. "Are you ready to depart, Your Highness? I will follow you and Miss Valentine since you insist on walking. The police and Filip will make sure your path is clear." Carly hadn't realized how icy the bodyguard's pale gray eyes were until they zeroed in on her. "If you would be so good as to give me the name of your destination?"

Carly had seen the same distrust in the gazes of homeless and trafficking victims she worked with on the streets. But there was a mean streak rather than fear lurking behind that distrust. Still, she wasn't going to give him the satisfaction of thinking he could intimidate her with either his bearing or his disapproval. "The barbecue restaurant on Wyandotte Street." She tugged on Ivan's hand and started for the front doors. "I thought you might enjoy a sampler of authentic Kansas City burnt ends."

Danya's hand clamped over her arm, stopping her, forcing her to face him again. "You're taking the prince to eat burnt food? That is beneath him. *You* are beneath him." His fingers dug painfully into her arm as he shook her. "This whole affair distracts him from what needs to be done. You are not royal. You are not Lukin. I should not have to put up with you."

Chapter Seven

"Danya!" Just as Carly was twisting away from the bodyguard's rough grip, with her free hand poised to strike his bulbous nose, Ivan palmed the center of the bodyguard's chest and shoved him back. With a precise turn of his wrist, Ivan had the bodyguard's arm pinned behind his back and his face planted on a display table. "You overstep your duties, Danya. You are not to touch Miss Valentine again."

His warning was as crisp and concise as an officer commanding his troops.

"Are we clear on this?" Ivan prompted when he got no response beyond Danya's heavy breathing.

Carly stayed back, mindlessly massaging the five future bruises on her upper arm. She had nothing against chivalry, but what the hell? Where did a prince learn a move like that?

Allowing time for his anger to ebb, Danya finally nodded. "Yes, sir. We are clear."

Only then did Ivan release the stocky man and back away. His glance across the store to Eduard and the wide-eyed clerk dared either one of them to utter a word about what they'd just seen. Eduard nodded and turned his attention back to the clerk to reassure her that everything would be okay. Ivan straightened his cuffs and the front of his jacket, keeping his body positioned between her and Danya. "You will apologize to Miss Valentine."

"My apologies." Danya straightened his own clothes and made a token effort to stack the piles of scattered T-shirts back into place. "I am too loyal a patriot who has had too little sleep. I was not…thinking clearly… when I touched you."

"A change in plans messes with your routine. I get it. No harm, no foul." Both men looked at her with a quizzical expression. "Basketball? The phrase comes from when referees call too many fouls for little infractions…" She was the one who needed answers about what had just happened. "You didn't do any serious damage, so there's no penalty. Apology accepted."

Ivan's eyes narrowed. "I will have to learn more about this sport. It sounds violent."

As good as their English might be, apparently, they didn't teach American idioms in Lukinburg schools. She was guessing they didn't teach that hand-to-hand combat suppression trick, either. "How long ago were you in the army?"

Ivan smoothed his hands over his short hair and adjusted his glasses instead of answering.

"I could have handled Danya myself," she insisted, stating a fact, not bragging. "You shouldn't put yourself at risk like that."

"I saw you do something very similar at the precinct office to the last man who assaulted you."

Carly shook her head at his faulty reasoning. "I'm not about to be crowned leader of my own country.

You have responsibilities. There are precautions you need to take."

Danya cleared his throat. "That is the point I was trying to make. I am only concerned for your safety and your reputation, Your Highness. I feared you were being reckless."

"And you thought insulting my companion was the way to express yourself?" Ivan challenged. "I will not allow this."

"Of course not." Danya's head remained bowed. "I was merely concerned about you taking a stroll through Kansas City on this woman's invitation. It deviates from the plan Filip and Galina agreed to for the day. You are to be in the car at all times and dine at specific locations we have already scouted out. Walking through a public neighborhood such as this without barricades and proper crowd management creates security variables that we cannot control. At least, let Eduard drive you."

"Make it work," Ivan ordered, dismissing Danya's plea. "I have two hours of time free of diplomatic obligations. I wish to see and sample more of this city first-hand. I wish to meet the people. Miss Valentine will be my guide. You are the one who will adapt to *my* wishes. Not the other way around."

"Yes, sir." Danya took a step back.

"What exactly are burnt ends?" Ivan asked, perhaps trying to relieve the sting of Danya's attack, or perhaps genuinely curious.

"Smoked and glazed little nuggets of barbecue heaven." Carly smiled up at Danya, making more of an effort to make him feel welcome than he had done for her. "Would you like to join us?"

"He would not," Ivan answered for his underling,

nudging the store's front door open. "It is hard to be romantic with that face glaring at us."

Danya grunted at the teasing and led the way outside. "I will make sure your path is clear. Eduard will follow in the car."

"Not in this traffic, he won't." Once they reached the sidewalk, Carly tilted her face to Ivan's, squinting against the hot August sunshine. "The Plaza is full of tourists in the summer. He won't get anywhere very fast if there's an emergency." She dropped her gaze to their surroundings, assessing the crowds gathered at crosswalks and popular stores, gauging the flow of traffic and determining the most direct route to the restaurant. "We should talk to KCPD, ask them to block off the streets."

"And draw even more attention to my movements?" He studied their surroundings over the top of her head. "Having a rigid schedule makes it too easy to find me and plan an attack. An impromptu walk and smaller security presence should make me harder to find."

"But if there's an inside man—"

He clasped her hand, silencing that argument. "Then he will not have time to readjust to the changes. His plan will be scraped."

"You mean scrapped?"

"Thank goodness you and I can communicate in other ways." He dipped his head toward hers, and for a moment, she thought he would kiss her again. She shocked herself with just how much she wanted him to put his lips against hers. Instead, perhaps because of the audience of bodyguards and bystanders, he brushed his fingertip across the apple of her cheek. Who was she kidding? She didn't need Ivan's kiss, not when she reacted to even that simple caress with an instant, answering heat.

"Thank goodness," she whispered, her voice dropping to a husky pitch. Had she been foolish to think, for any moment, that this connection between them had been pretend? The history between them might be a fiction, but everything she felt for Ivan Mostek was real.

She inhaled deeply and pulled away as another thought struck her. She was going to get her heart broken, wasn't she? In a matter of days, she was already halfway in love with Ivan. But days were all they had, all they could ever have. There was no commitment to this relationship, not when it was built on lies and danger and political intrigue. Was this her life? That she would give her heart to the one man she could never have?

Sealing up her heart against caring too much, Carly relayed the route she planned to take through the Plaza to Filip. She was here to be a cop, to be a secret protector. Ivan wasn't really her Prince Charming, she wasn't any stinkin' Cinderella and she had no business falling in love with him.

While the security team moved out, Carly stayed by Ivan's side and pulled out her phone. "I'm going to call the captain and let him know our location. He can put some officers on standby. Just in case."

"Already done," Filip declared, tucking his phone into his jacket pocket. He jogged up to join them. "Maybe you're right, and you can blend in with the tourists."

After Filip headed out, Carly reluctantly put her phone away. "How far do you think someone like Danya would go to maintain his standards of honor and Lukin tradition? Clearly, he doesn't think I'm worthy. Would he go after a prince who is modernizing and maybe even Americanizing his country?"

"Everyone around me is suspect," Ivan confessed. "Danya might feel he is putting country before king by sending those threats."

"No more gallant moves to defend me, okay?"

"I make no guarantees." Despite the distance she tried to keep, Ivan gripped her hand and they set out side by side. Although his team cleared the area immediately surrounding them, there were a few pointing fingers and whispers about a TV appearance that morning from the people they passed. One brave soul asked if she could take a picture with Ivan, and he obliged. Carly was aware of a few more phones capturing a snapshot or video, of bodyguards warning onlookers to keep their distance and of friendly questions from pedestrians they passed.

Ivan answered each request with a wave and a smile and something complimentary to say about Kansas City. No one spoke to Carly directly, although she was certain she was included in some of those informal photographs.

Lunch was a yummy mix of brisket, scalloped potatoes and conversation with a man who was both funny and endearing. Who was she kidding with the whole this-is-a-charade-don't-let-your-heart-get-involved vow? Carly was already involved.

She didn't think she'd ever tire of looking into that polished, angular face that was more interesting than handsome. And she didn't think she'd tire of listening to Ivan's sexy accent—whether he was discussing food, the Lukin economy or the dribble of barbecue sauce he dabbed from the corner of her mouth. The more time she spent with Ivan, the less she thought of him as a prince and the more she thought of him as a man. An attractive man. An attractive man who made her feel feminine, and yet who respected, or perhaps was even fascinated by her independent spirit.

The more time she spent with Ivan, the more the lines blurred between charade and reality. She might not fully trust that his kisses and flirtations were real, that he was falling for her the same way she was falling for him, but she could think of him as a friend. And she liked that. She liked that a lot.

They polished off the crème brûlée he'd insisted they share for dessert while Ivan told her about his childhood in the poor mining town of Moravska, nestled in the mountains near the Lukinburg border. Including their military service and working-class upbringing, they had more in common than two people raised on different continents with such different futures might expect.

"What happened to your parents?" Carly asked since he'd only mentioned the aunt and uncle who'd raised him. "Sorry. That was a little abrupt." She cushioned the blow of the forward question by revealing her own loss. "My mom died in a freak accident. She was carrying laundry down to the basement, fell on the stairs and hit her head on the concrete floor. Dad was at work. Frank and Jesse were at school. I had half day kindergarten. I called 9-1-1 when I heard the crash. We'd just learned that at school—what to do if there's an emergency."

His eyes narrowed behind his glasses, and it was becoming less and less of a surprise when he reached across the table to take her hand. "You found your mother?"

Carly was touched by his concern, but then shrugged it away with a smile. Her mother's death was a tragedy that had impacted her entire life. But she'd also come to terms with the loss. "The ME said she died almost immediately. Not that I would have known how to help her. I just held her hand until the paramedics came."

Ivan's thumb rubbed against the pulse point of her wrist. "You have always been a brave woman."

She wondered if he could feel the blood hammering through her veins at the subtle caress that was as arousing as it was comforting. "I was five years old. Hardly a woman."

"You took action. You did what needed to be done at a very difficult time. Even so young. I am sorry for your loss."

"Losing her so young also explains why I'm better at taking down bad guys than I am at dressing up and playing princess. As you might imagine, Dad and my brothers were never very good at that girlie-girl stuff."

He smiled at the joke for a moment before the laugh lines disappeared and he leaned into the table. "My parents were murdered by Vasily Gordeeva. He was head of a crime family who had great influence on the previous leaders of Lukinburg. Mother and Father took exception to having their wages garnished at the munitions factory where they worked to pad his bank account. They protested working conditions in general. When they led the movement to unionize laborers, there was a car bomb. My uncle whisked me away right after the funeral."

"Oh, my God. How awful. I'm so sorry." She switched their grip to capture his hand with both of hers. Then she leaned in as a frightening possibility turned her compassion to suspicion. "Ivan. A car bomb? The bombing at St. Feodor? The king who was blown up? Couldn't the incidents be related? Could what's happening now be a part of the protests your parents were involved with?"

"Of course not. Mother and Father were never…" He released her and sat back in the booth, pulling off his glasses and rubbing at the dimples on either side of his nose left by the frames as if he was plagued by a sudden headache. He set his glasses on top of the table and focused those blue eyes at her. "Gordeeva died in 2012, after serving time in prison. His influence on the former government's regime died when he did. The king's assassination happened when my parents were children. They are not related."

But Carly couldn't ignore the obvious similarities between the crimes. "Ivan, we can't dismiss any possibility right now. Even something that happened years ago. When you're investigating a case, you look at all the facts and then come up with a theory. You don't force the facts to fit into whatever theory you might have."

"Their murders are not related to any of the threats against the crown." On that royal dictate, he slid out of the booth and buttoned his jacket, preparing to leave.

But she was neither a Lukinburg citizen, subject to his will, nor ready to give up on the potential source for the threats against him. "Crime families are known for exacting their revenge. If your parents' murders are the reason he went to prison—"

"My parents' deaths have nothing to do with the threats now," he snapped in a hushed tone. End of discussion.

For him, maybe. "You forgot these, Bossy Boots. Excuse me, Your *Royal* Bossy Boots." She scooped up his glasses from the table as she stood, refusing to ignore what he'd told her. "Did Gordeeva have family? People who feel they've been wronged have long memories."

"Bossy Boots? The words make no sense to me. But I understand by your attitude that I was rude. No better than Danya." He inclined his head in a brief bow. "I apologize for my tone. We should go." He slipped his glasses on and headed for the front door.

Once they reached the lobby, Filip stepped in to handle the bill and tip. Carly pulled Ivan into a relatively private corner of the foyer. "What's wrong? What aren't you telling me?"

His chest expanded with a deep breath before he captured her face between his hands and touched his forehead to hers. "I have been as honest with you as the dictates of this position allow me to be." His fingers slipped into her hair and tightened around her skull as he pressed a hard kiss to her lips. She felt the stamp of his mouth like a brand against her skin. Her blood quickened in her veins and pooled in places that made her feverish with desire. But he ended the kiss before she could fully respond. "Please do not hold this against me. I cannot tell you how important your trust is to me."

Carly wound her fingers around his wrists to keep him from pulling away. "Do you really think keeping secrets right now is the smartest way to go? How can I protect you if I don't know everything I need to?"

"I have said too much already. You…" He smoothed her hair into place as his mouth twisted with a wry smile. "You distract me. You are a breath of fresh air in a life that has not been my own for these long past months. But I cannot forget my duty to my country."

He pulled away, capturing the braid that hung in front of her shoulder before releasing that, too. "I am sorry, *dorogoy*."

She studied him intently, on the verge of understanding something she couldn't quite put her finger on. Maybe after all these years, her feminine intuition was finally kicking in, and she was recognizing the genuineness of his interest in her, along with the regret he felt at starting something that couldn't last. She stretched up on tiptoe to capture his mouth in a quick kiss that didn't convey half of what she was thinking or feeling, only that she was thinking about and feeling more for this troubled prince and this impossible relationship than a street-smart survivor like her should.

"We're still partners in this. Even if you can't tell me everything. Right now." She hinted that maybe he would before this week was over, although he gave no indication that he might. With her undercover work, she understood about keeping secrets better than most. Still, when it came to her personal life, she wasn't a big fan of holding back the truth. With a mental slap to the back of the head, she reminded herself that her relationship with Ivan *was* an undercover assignment, not the real deal, no matter what her blossoming feminine intuition might say. "We'd better get going. I won't have Danya accusing me of making you late for your next appointment in addition to forcing you to eat burnt American food."

He laughed at that, his expression relaxing into a more natural smile. "Do you know how many people are afraid to stand up for what they honestly think if it differs from my opinion? Other than the threats, they kowtow to the crown and tell me what they think I want to hear. Never be that person."

"Mouthy? Pushy?"

"Honest."

The irony that he wasn't being completely honest with her wasn't lost on either of them. She could read the regret in his eyes. Maybe that was a hazard of politics. There were always secrets to keep.

Filip nudged Ivan from behind before she could decide how to respond to that compliment. "We are ready, Your Highness."

Ivan linked his hand with hers and they walked out the door together. This time, in addition to the suffocating envelope of humid air pressing around them, a group of pedestrians had gathered on the sidewalk outside the restaurant, blocking their path.

"He was on TV."

"I saw him in the paper."

"I thought he was single."

"He's cute."

"Prince Ivan!"

Cars stopped on the street beyond them, too, the drivers curious about why people were congregating there. And although a few pedestrians walked on by, most of them stopped, growing the size of the crowd in either direction. Almost all of them raised their phones to snap pictures and videos, and call or text their friends to share this brush with fame. Others held out pens and various items like notebooks and coffee cups for an autograph.

Ivan pulled up, smiling and waving for a few pictures. A school-age girl handed Carly a flower and asked if she was a princess.

But there was no place for them to go without walking into the crowd.

Danya grumbled behind them. "I believe the tourists are now aware that there is royalty among them. We should go back inside and wait for the car to pick you up."

Filip stepped toward the crowd, pushing them back as he gave Danya an order. "Get them moving toward the parking garage." He turned to their audience. "Ladies and gentlemen, please. Prince Ivan is grateful for your interest and support, but he must get to his next engagement."

Carly wondered how anyone could possibly get used to this kind of attention when she saw a white van pulling up on the other side of the median. A man scrambled out from behind the wheel and hefted a camera onto his shoulder. She recognized the dark-haired woman from a local news station scurrying after him with a microphone. "A TV crew is here, too." Someone in the crowd called her Blondie, told her to smile and snapped a picture. She was certain she'd looked more startled than photogenic. "Is this normal?"

Ivan managed to speak under his breath without losing his smile. "Not spur-of-the-moment like this. There are other public appearances planned, with larger venues to accommodate this many people. This is unexpected. Someone must have posted to social media that I was at the restaurant."

Not anyone who wished him well. "This could turn

ugly fast." She tugged on Ivan's hand, pulling him with her a few steps. "Someone could get hurt."

But it seemed that for every square foot of pavement Filip cleared in their forward route, the curious onlookers who'd spotted the visiting celebrity pushed in that much closer behind them. Soon, Carly's and Ivan's backs were against the stucco walls and storefront windows, and their path to the next cross street was blocked. Traffic was quickly backing up beyond that. It didn't help that Ivan was being his cordial, diplomatic self and answering questions on everything from "What did you have to eat?" and "Do you have a crown?" to "How much gold is in Lukinburg?"

"We have plenty of gold now that we have developed new mining practices," he explained. But either she tugged, or he nudged with each answer to keep them moving toward the street. "Our real treasure is quartz, which is used in high-tech applications, such as circuit boards and computer components here in your country." He planted his feet and stared into the crowd as people jostled for position to see and hear him. Carly understood now that he was trying to control the crowd, to keep them from stampeding or stumbling off a curb or getting pushed in front of a moving vehicle. The crowd pulsed like a living, breathing thing. And while Carly searched for a clear path, Ivan raised his voice to be heard. "Please. I am happy to answer your questions. Perhaps if we all take a deep breath."

Carly turned her face to his shoulder. "I'm sorry I got you into this mess. But we need to get out of here."

The click of cameras and phones and whispered conversations sounded like the buzzing of bees. "Any ideas?"

"I'm thinking." She scanned up and down the street, looked past the crowd, glimpsed everyone's reflection in the display window behind them. Something wasn't right. She turned, trying to make eye contact with every face in the crowd.

Ivan answered a question about the upcoming ball. Maybe if he kept talking, they would stand still and listen. "We are hosting a joint fund-raiser with one of your local universities to develop clean technology that will use our natural resources. I will be meeting with Dr. Ian Lombard and his team tomorrow to discuss this exciting new research."

"Is it true that someone tried to kill you?" someone shouted.

Ivan's smooth facade slipped for a moment. His grip tightened on Carly's hand and the crowd fell silent. Like Carly, he skimmed the faces in the crowd to see who had asked that. "I am sorry. Who…?"

The chatter started up as suddenly as it had stopped, growing louder as people shouted questions and turned to each other to voice curiosity about Ivan's well-being and concern about the threat of danger to themselves.

"Have those threats followed you to Kansas City?" The television camera caught them in a spotlight as the female reporter thrust her microphone toward Ivan. "I heard that someone tried to poison you."

Ivan shielded his eyes and muttered under his breath to Carly. "I did not publicize—"

"That reporter at the hospital," Carly seethed beneath her breath. "He wasn't after a scandal. He wanted to know what happened to Frank. He must know about the threats."

"If I get my hands on Ralph Decker—"

"Please. Ladies and gentlemen." Filip moved in front of them, his sheer bulk forcing the crowd back a couple of feet. "Prince Ivan's security and that of your people is our top priority. As you can see, he is perfectly fine." The camera's bright light swung toward him. "We are working very closely with the local police to ensure everyone's safety throughout our visit to your lovely city."

Danya cursed ahead of them. "Where are all your police friends now?"

Good question. Lunch had lasted over an hour. Hendricks should have had officers on the scene long before now. "Did you call for backup?"

Filip bought them two more steps. "Of course I did."

Did he? Did he really?

"Where are they?" Carly glared at him. There should be bicycle cops, patrol cars. She should have followed her instincts and called Hendricks herself.

But this wasn't the time for placing blame. Maybe the traitor had countermanded Milevski's order. Maybe Milevski had seen an opportunity to create chaos to mask an attempt on Ivan's life, and had never called for local reinforcements at all.

Danya shouted to them from the corner. "This way!" But the path he'd made to the crosswalk filled in before they could reach it. "Eduard! Get the car. Now!"

"Yes, sir!" The younger bodyguard pushed his way through the mass of people. When he reached the relative opening of the boulevard, Eduard put up his hand to stop traffic, running across to the median and onto the next block.

"Go." Filip looked over his shoulder and used his head to point them toward Danya. "I will handle this." He turned back to the reporter. "If you want specific details about the poisoning incident, you should contact Galina Honchar at—"

"Your Highness!" Danya moved a pair of teenagers aside and waved Ivan closer.

They weren't going to make it. Ivan bumped into Carly's back when she stopped abruptly.

Ivan's hands clamped around her shoulders. "Carly?"

Something wasn't right here. This was no ordinary gathering of fans and curiosity-seekers. "Do you feel like you're being herded to a particular place? In a particular direction?"

Ivan considered her assessment. His fingers tightened in a silent yes. "We have no other way to go."

The crowd had become a living, pulsing entity, pushing forward, nearly encircling them, as if someone was egging them on in pursuit of the prince. All it needed was a spark of panic to flash over into a mob. Carly glanced up at the second-story windows and rooftops. They had no advantage here if things went south. Everyone's eyes were on Ivan. Who knew how many more people she couldn't see might be watching them right now? Maybe if she removed the star attraction, the crowd would disband. Carly looked back at Filip. "Where's the car?"

"Parking garage across from the bookstore. Lower level." Filip had one hand on Ivan's shoulder and his other arm extended to keep anyone from coming any closer.

And then she saw a reflection in the display window. A man who didn't fit with the rest of the fans. He wore a hooded coat, masking most of his face. He wasn't asking questions, wasn't taking pictures. And the shadowy maw inside that hood was focused squarely on them.

Chapter Eight

"Why is he wearing a coat?" Carly murmured, feeling the threat rising like the heat on her skin.

Ivan had seen him, too. "That is him."

"Him who?"

"End Ivan!" someone shouted. The hooded man?

To Carly's surprise, Ivan lunged toward the threat. She caught his arm and pulled him back. "Are you crazy?"

"That is the same threat the bomber yelled before the explosion in St. Feodor. These people are not safe."

When she scanned the crowd again, the hooded man was nowhere to be seen. "The best thing you can do for these innocent bystanders is leave. You're the target. If he loses his target, he'll move on." She pushed Ivan back the way they'd come, knocking Filip out of the way. "Cover us. Get these people out of here."

"What? It is my responsibility to—"

"I've got an idea." Carly grabbed Ivan's hand and opened the door of the nearest shop, pushing her way through the staff gathered at the windows. She pulled her badge from her pocket and thrust it into the face of a startled clerk. "You got a back door?"

The woman nodded and pointed to the back of the shop as two other people snapped pictures.

"Don't follow us," Carly warned. They ran through the store into the storage room, distance dulling the noise of the crowd outside.

"This way." Ivan spotted the rear exit. Understanding the gist of her plan, he pushed open the door that opened onto a loading dock in the alley behind the store.

Carly slipped in front of him, ensuring the alley was clear before leading him down the ramp and past the trash cans and power poles to the sidewalk that ran perpendicular to the one in front of the store. The blare of honking horns and sound of an approaching siren raised the decibel level again.

"Which way?" Ivan asked, scanning the parked cars and bumper-to-bumper traffic ahead of them.

She pulled him into the street, flashing her badge again to stop approaching vehicles as they jogged across to the center median and onto the opposite side of the street. Carly shrugged out of her jacket and tied the sleeves around her waist to keep her gun masked. "Lose the tie and roll up your sleeves." Ivan had already fallen into step beside her as he shed his jacket and transformed his look into something more casual, so they blended in with the businesspeople hurrying back to work after lunch meetings and shoppers who hadn't yet picked up on the mob scene just a couple of blocks away. Carly lengthened her stride to match Ivan's. They turned the corner and spotted the bookstore. "The parking garage is this way."

Ivan dipped his head close to her ear, never taking his eyes off the people around them, never breaking stride. "What if there is a bomb back there? Those people could be in danger."

"Those people are safer now that you're not there. You're safer."

"I do not want to be responsible for any more deaths."

"If we figure this out, you won't be." She caught his arm to stop him as a delivery van pulled out of the driveway in front of them. "Did you notice that the guy in the coat disappeared?"

"I was momentarily blinded by the television camera. I thought I had lost him in the crowd."

Carly glanced over her shoulder to see if the man was following them. But there were too many people, too many buildings and streets and cars to focus in on just one of them. "It might be a coincidence. A lot of the homeless people wear all their clothes, coats included. It could be nothing."

"It is not. He was there for a reason." Ivan sounded certain. "Perhaps you were right, and he set a trap for us. He was using the crowd to move us toward it."

"Moving toward what, though? And where is he now?" She had her gaze on continuous scan now. "And where are Filip and Danya? Shouldn't we be running into your security team?"

"Perhaps they stayed back to help with the crowd." He tilted his head toward the man running down the entrance ramp into the parking garage just half a block ahead of them. "There's Eduard." He urged her into a jog. "Come on. When we get to the car, we will be safe. We can compare notes of what we saw back there."

Carly spotted two bicycle officers maneuvering through the gridlock of vehicles. A black-and-white was coming down the hill from downtown. Good. Backup was arriving. Hopefully, soon enough to keep all those people safe. She could focus solely on Ivan now.

They hit the gated entrance into the parking garage. She saw Eduard Nagy racing down the ramp to the lower level.

The clerk in the booth waved to them. "Hey, you're that prince on TV."

"Prince Ivan?" a voice from the sidewalk called to them. "Get his picture."

"He's not as handsome as those British princes."

"I can't believe I'm this close to a real prince."

It was starting again. People milling together at the entrance to the garage. They couldn't get trapped by another mob. "Ivan?" Carly prompted.

"Eduard!" Ivan pointed out their escape and pulled her into a run beside him. "Start the car!"

Because of its length, the limousine was parked off by itself across two spaces against the far wall.

Carly's nostrils flared to draw in more oxygen as they raced toward the safety of the polished black car. They were thirty yards away. Twenty. Eduard climbed in behind the wheel. The headlights came on as he inserted the key and started the engine.

A bright light flashed beneath the car's black hood and Carly skidded to a stop. It was too late to retreat.

"Get down!" she yelled, shoving Ivan toward a concrete pillar.

Strong arms snapped around her, pulling her with him as the limo exploded with a deafening roar. A concussive wave of heat swept over them, carrying them several feet through the air before they hit the concrete and rolled to a stop against the wheel of a truck. Every point of her body was bruised or numb from the crashing fall. Knuckles, elbows, knees, heels. Ivan's full weight on top of her made it hard to breathe. But even as her lungs protested and her vision spun in circles, Carly clamped her hands around his biceps, trying to reverse their positions and drag him behind the shelter of the pillar.

But in the next second, Ivan shifted, bracing his elbows on either side of her and palming her head, tucking her face against his chest and shielding her body with his as flying metal and burning car parts rained down around them.

A heavy chunk of twisted fender clanged down beside them. Carly shoved at his chest, hating the vulnerability of his position. Instead of budging, his hold on her tightened. "Damn it, Ivan. *I* protect *you*!"

He jerked once, and she knew he'd been hit.

"Ivan!"

"Shh. Shh." He brushed his lips against her ear, calming her fears and anger, stilling the fists drumming against his chest, shielding her until the flying pieces of car parts grew smaller and ended with a staccato of tiny fragments of metal and plastic landing on the concrete around them.

The mini crashes of settling debris gave way to people screaming and the crackling whoosh of the fire burning through the remnants of the car. The telltale warning of a car horn followed by the crunch of metal on metal told her there'd been an accident on the street at the top of the ramp. At least one of those drivers had been paying more attention to the crowds and explosion than to traffic. She wasn't sure what else could go wrong.

And then she knew. "Eduard?"

When Ivan inhaled a deep breath, Carly released the death grip she had on the front of his shirt and rolled him off her. They sat up and Carly pushed to her feet. But orange-and-gold flames swirled through her vision and she stumbled against the pillar. She felt the icy cold concrete warming beneath her hand from the heat of the fire fifteen yards away as she circled around to the other side to see if there was any chance of saving the driver.

But there was no saving the bodyguard, no chance of pulling him from the flames that engulfed the car. Carly's eyes stung with tears. He'd died in the line of duty. "Poor man."

What a waste of a good, loyal man. That could have been them. It was supposed to be them.

"He is gone!" Ivan shouted in her ear.

She startled and spun around to see him on his feet, leaning against the pillar behind her. The force of the blast must have impacted Ivan's hearing. She reached up to cup his jaw, turning his face from one side to the other, checking for pupil dilation and head injuries. She didn't see anything beyond the charred bits of debris in his hair, which she brushed away.

"The blast must have hurt your ears. You're shouting."

"What? I can't hear you."

Carly smiled at the unintended humor of that tragic moment so that she wouldn't burst into tears. She'd like to blame the fumes from burning oil and gasoline on this uncharacteristic urge to cry, but she knew the emotional letdown had more to do with the shock wearing off than it did the sting of chemicals in the air. Shutting off her emotions and relying on her training, she ran her hands over Ivan's shoulders and down his arms, gently pulling away the shredded material at his elbow to see the oozing skin that had been scraped away in their tumble across the concrete.

But it was hard to check for anything more serious because Ivan's hands were on her, too, framing her face, feeling up and down her arms. "Are you hurt?"

"I need to call this in." Was her phone even working? She pulled it from her pocket. Thank goodness. Everything lit up as she swiped her thumb across the screen. She'd lost a shoe in that tumble. She needed to find it and get moving. "And make sure there are no other casualties."

The man at the gate booth was on his phone already, calling 9-1-1. She gave him a thumbs-up when he asked if they were okay, and he returned to his call, alternately yelling at bystanders to stay back and reporting the situation to the dispatcher. A second man in a maintenance uniform had run up to the blaze with a fire extinguisher, but he was fighting a hopeless battle and had to back away from the heat.

"Carly, are you hurt?" Ivan's tone had returned to its normal volume. He captured her hand to inspect her scraped knuckles, then caught her chin between his thumb and fingers. "Are you dizzy? Nauseous?"

"I was dizzy at first. It passed. I'm okay." Her gaze landed on the smear of blood on the pillar and her heart dropped to her stomach. "You're not." She moved behind him to inspect the blood-soaked tear in his shirt. There was a one-inch spike of metal protruding from the back of his shoulder. "That shrapnel needs to come out."

"I've been hurt worse."

That was supposed to reassure her? "Do you have

a handkerchief? Something I can stanch the bleeding with?"

He picked up his soiled jacket from the floor and pulled out a handkerchief. He muttered a curse when she pulled the shard from the wound and pressed the cloth against his skin. "You need a doctor."

"One travels with my entourage. He is at the hotel."

"Then that's where we need to go."

Ivan braced his fist against the pillar and watched the car burn while she fashioned a makeshift bandage with the handkerchief and her belt around his neck and beneath his arm to keep it in place. Although his breathing was measured and deep, there were no more curses as she doctored his injury. His entire focus was on the burning limo, the people on the other side of the flames and the man he'd lost. "Poor Eduard. I do not even know if he has family. Those files. We need to read them."

"The flash drive!" Carly fumbled with the jacket still tied at her waist. The material was dusty and splotched with a smear of oil from the concrete, but the flash drive was still there. It was intact. "It's okay. I don't see any damage."

Despite the sirens she could hear in the distance, more people were gathering in the sunlight outside the parking garage entrance. "The man from the ticket gate needs our help to keep everyone away from the fire. I need to find Filip. Where is he?"

After spotting a uniformed officer jogging down the ramp to help secure the scene, Carly punched in Joe Hendricks's number on her phone. Then she pulled Ivan deeper into the garage. She'd already spotted the basement level entrance to one of the shops above them.

"I'm sorry, *dorogoy*, but we can't wait for Filip. And KCPD doesn't need our help. We have to go."

He tugged her to a stop. "What did you call me?"

"Didn't I use the nickname right?"

"Your Lukin was perfect." He leaned down and pressed a quick, hard kiss to her mouth. They traded several emotions in that one brief kiss—caring, relief, worry, a sense of urgency, desire that time and circumstances allowed for nothing more to pass between them. "I might like it if you call me that." Pulling away, he shrugged into his suit jacket to hide his wounds, wincing at the pain. He took her arm and followed her through the empty part of the garage. "Lead the way. Talk to Joe, and then I will call Filip. If I may borrow your phone."

"You don't have a phone?"

He reached into his pocket and showed her his. The cover had fractured like a spiderweb and the screen was dark. "Not anymore."

"I thought maybe you couldn't. Because you're a prince."

"My country is not so backward that we do not have cells."

"But security? Couldn't someone call in a threat or track you? I know some countries don't allow royalty—"

Her call picked up and Joe Hendricks's voice boomed over the line. "Valentine? I've got 9-1-1 calls overloading dispatch at your location. What's going on?"

"Bomb in the Forty-Seventh Street garage. Somebody blew up Ivan's limo. Killed the driver." Ivan tore the remnants of his phone apart and tossed it in a trash can as they hurried past, perhaps taking her tracking concern to heart. "Looks like traffic is bottlenecking. You'll need a tow truck to clear a fender bender at the Forty-Seventh Street entrance before KCPD can get a truck in here. About the only good thing is the limo was parked away from other vehicles, so I don't think the fire will spread."

She pulled her badge from her pocket and looped it around her neck as they entered the store. She paused a moment to ask the staff and customers watching from the door if they'd seen anything or anyone suspicious in the garage. The general response was no help. They'd heard the blast and had come to look after the fact.

Warning everyone to stay back and let the first responders work the scene, she and Ivan headed for the escalator that would take them up to street level. "I have the prince with me," she reported to Captain Hendricks. "Ivan is okay. We're separated from his team."

"Securing Ivan is priority one. Get him someplace safe."

"Will do." She eyed the stalled line of traffic outside the front doors and crossed the street to the opposite side where the cars were at least crawling along. A patrol officer was diverting traffic off onto a side street to help get a fire engine through the intersection. Ivan stayed right at her side. He flipped up his collar and kept his head down to avoid recognition, but she was aware that his eyes were studying every face they passed as thoroughly as she did. She wasn't sure where she was leading him, other than as far away from the Plaza as they could get. Did she take him into the nearby residential neighborhood, where there was no hope of finding transportation? Head for Saint Luke's Hospital that was only a few blocks to the north? He wouldn't want the kind of attention that came with a wounded celebrity walking through their doors would bring. Maybe, they could at least catch a bus to get them out of the congested area. But why exactly *was* it so congested? This wasn't rush hour. And yes, there were tourist attractions and stores and offices in this historic area, but the chaos had gotten crazy fast, *before* that bomb had gone off. "Sir? We had a mob scene about five blocks from here. Did Milevski call in for backup down at the Plaza?"

"Backup is on its way."

"I mean about eighty minutes ago, before the explosion."

She heard the suspicion creeping into the captain's tone. "I'll have to check with his department contact. SWAT Team Two just left the building and are en route. But there was no tactical team dispatched before that. I'll see what patrol officers were sent in."

"Check social media, too. That crowd got big and rowdy awfully fast. Without enough security on the scene, we had no choice but to hit some back alleys and make a run for Ivan's limo. We're lucky more people weren't hurt."

"You think this was a setup?"

"That bomb was no accident." They reached the next intersection where another officer was directing traffic and hurried on across. As more police reached the area, pedestrians were being funneled away from the parking garage to the same side of the street they were on, packing the sidewalk with the crowds she'd been trying to avoid. "We had no other place to escape to besides the limo."

"Is the prince safe?" Joe Hendricks asked.

Carly looked up at Ivan, who was doing his best to

avoid bumping into anyone and aggravating his wound. She knew he needed medical attention. Still, he was moving like a soldier advancing through enemy territory, his hand on her back moving her forward as much as she was leading him. "He's hurt."

"A minor injury, Joe," Ivan insisted, dipping his head close to her phone. "I am fine."

"He will be as soon as I can get him out of here."

"My hotel," Ivan suggested while Captain Hendricks ended the call with a demand to keep him posted. He steered her around the next clump of pedestrians. "It is downtown. Do you have your car?"

She shook her head. "It's at the precinct. Brooke's husband dropped us off. I'd planned to be riding with you."

He punched in Filip Milevski's number and gave his security chief a sit-rep about losing Eduard, the name of the cross streets where they were now and that he was with her. She didn't need the phone on speaker to hear Filip's tirade about running off and getting so close to the bomb—or to hear the warning about staying put and letting Filip and Danya come to them. "Do you have a car?" Ivan challenged, cutting him off when she heard her name among the angry words. "Then you are not driving me anywhere. You deal with the police, and I want someone to stay with Eduard's body."

A glimpse of stillness among the rush of activity filling the streets and sidewalks drew her attention and slowed her pace. A chill skittered down her back, despite the heat and humidity and man standing so close beside her. "Ivan?"

"You do not think a man shouting, 'End Ivan!' is threat enough? Call the hotel and make sure that Aleks,

Galina and the others are safe." He ended the call and slipped the phone back into Carly's pocket. "What is it?"

"Ten o'clock. On the other side of those parked cars."

When she stepped toward the curb, Ivan's arm folded around her waist and pulled her back against his chest. She was certain the curse he muttered in his native language was something blue and damning.

The man in the hood had reappeared. Despite the material shading his face, there was no mistaking the "I'm watching you" signal he sent, gesturing with two fingers to where his eyes would be before pointing at them. Carly reached behind her back, nudging Ivan aside to pull her gun. But when she blinked, he'd disappeared. Moving west, she thought. But she didn't have eyes on him anymore. "Damn it. I can't leave you to pursue him."

She felt Ivan's fingers on her wrist, keeping her gun in its holster. "There are too many people here to draw your weapon."

True. She'd probably cause more panic if she did pull her gun and race after the suspect. Plus, going after him meant leaving Ivan completely unprotected. Or worse, he'd insist on coming with her, putting himself in the line of fire. "Did you see where he went?"

He pointed to the west. "That way. But I lost him behind the cars. He had a backpack. He probably stuffed his coat inside and blended into the crowd."

Being out of uniform with no radio, she turned back to the officer directing traffic and identified herself. She gave the officer a general description of height and build, plus the hooded coat and backpack, and asked him to put out an APB on the suspect. Although she guessed that Ivan was right about the man changing his outfit and clearing the area.

"Let's keep moving." She reached back to lace her fingers together with Ivan's. "How are you doing? You're not bleeding out on me, are you?"

"If you will not complain about the scratches on your hands and face, then I will not complain about my injuries."

She halted again, lifting her hands to see the black-and-violet bruising and raw skin on her knuckles. "I hadn't even noticed."

"I notice everything about you." He touched the tip of his finger to a tender spot on her jawline. "My doctor will be treating you as well, when we reach the hotel."

Suddenly, she realized how much her body ached after flying across the concrete, and just how much worse her injuries might be if Ivan hadn't shielded her with his body when the bomb had gone off. "Thank you for protecting me." She sensed she was due for a physical and emotional crash once the adrenaline of these past several minutes wore off. But that time wasn't now. And Prince Blue Eyes needed a stern reminder about the rules of this charade. "I'm the bodyguard, remember? The relationship is for show, but the gun and the badge and my job are real. If you ever do anything like that again, I will—"

A car spun around the corner and screeched to a halt in front of them. The passenger side window went down and Ralph Decker, the reporter who'd photographed them at the hospital leaned across the front seat. "Need a ride?"

"What do you want?" Carly asked, suspicious of his timely arrival.

"To do you a favor." Decker pulled his hands from the steering wheel and shrugged. "Unless you want to fight your way through this crowd and get stuck in traffic for another hour."

Carly spotted Filip on the far side of the street, doing just that, fighting to get through the crowd. Ivan had seen him, too. He opened the back door for Carly and nudged her to get in. "We accept your offer, Mr. Decker."

Carly braced her hands against the door frame. "We don't really know this guy."

"Please, Carly. We need to see the doctor." She shivered at the whisper of Ivan's lips against her hair and responded to the plea in that accented tone. Although she suspected this was more about getting her away from the danger than getting himself to his physician, Carly relented, climbing in and sliding across the back seat. If she was far from any threat, then he would be, too. Ivan slid in beside her. Clearly, he believed now, more than ever, that the person behind the threats was getting help from someone inside his delegation. Perhaps it was easier to trust this relative stranger than someone he knew had the means to betray him to his enemies. "This does not mean I am giving you an exclusive, Mr. Decker. Nor do I give you permission to take any photos of Carly and me today."

"Understood. But you can't tell me there's not a real news story here. Something a lot bigger than this affair you're having. An explosion and an attempted assassination? I can't help but ask a few questions."

"This was a mistake." Ivan reached for the door handle.

Carly stopped him. This time he had no argument

when she unholstered her gun and held it up for Decker to see in the rearview mirror. "He'll behave himself."

Decker grinned and shifted his car into gear. "You make a convincing argument, Officer."

She gave him the name of Ivan's hotel. "Go."

As they drove up the hill toward downtown, she saw Filip break free from the mass of pedestrians and run across the street to the spot they'd just vacated. He was joined by Danya now. Both men were breathing hard from exertion, both watching the car as it sped away. Filip dabbed at the perspiration on his forehead with a bright white handkerchief. When he pulled the cloth from his face, he looked pissed. Danya's hands were fisted at his sides. She didn't have to read lips to know he was cursing.

But were they angry that she'd taken over their job to keep the prince safe? That a coworker had been murdered?

Or that Ivan had survived the blast?

Chapter Nine

Carly thanked the doctor who had bandaged her left hand and cleaned the scrapes on her jaw and elbows. While Ivan washed up in the adjoining bathroom of his hotel suite, the doctor packed his bag and exited the bedroom where she'd peeled off her ruined blouse for him to check her injuries.

With the door propped open, the white noise of heated conversation she'd heard from the main room sharpened into words she could understand. Most of them, anyway, since some of the arguing seemed to be in Lukin. Seizing the opportunity to eavesdrop on potential suspects, she clutched the torn blouse to her chest, ducked behind the door to keep it from fully closing and listened.

Galina's shrill voice reprimanded someone. "We should be thanking God or fate or whatever you believe in that the prince was not in that car."

Filip didn't like to be lectured. "He should have stayed with me!"

"And been trampled? Shot?" Galina countered. "It's unfortunate enough we lost Eduard. But if Ivan had been killed, this entire trade mission would have been ruined—maybe even our alliance with the United

States, our sister city status with Kansas City. It could have thrown Lukinburg into chaos."

Aleks couldn't resist diving into the thick of the argument. "Our relationships with any foreign nation would be at risk. They'd all be saying, 'Keep your political troubles and unhappy citizens at home in Lukinburg.'"

"This is not my fault," Filip argued. "*She* altered the prince's schedule."

"And if she hadn't, the prince would have been in that car when it blew up, too."

"You don't know that," Danya Pavluk grumbled. "Maybe the bomber wouldn't have had the chance to plant the device if we'd stuck to our plan."

"What plan would that be?" an American voice asked. Ralph Decker had hung around to eavesdrop, too. The reporter had a knack for showing up when least expected. Was that luck on his part? Good reporting? A source inside Ivan's delegation feeding him intel? Could he have any agenda beyond covering a story?

"Mr. Decker," Galina snapped, then softened her tone to polite decorum. "Once again, I will ask you to leave. We thank you for your assistance today."

"The prince said he wanted to thank me personally. I'm curious to find out what he meant by that."

Danya muttered a curse, as if Decker had just made a point for him. "See? There are too many loose ends. Filip, you need to run a tighter ship."

Filip didn't bother to mutter. "Are you questioning my authority?"

Carly smelled a hint of icy fresh soap a split second before Ivan reached around her to close the door. "Learn anything new?"

More than not sensing his approach, Carly was startled to turn and discover a shirtless prince. Was that allowed? Showing off broad shoulders? Drawing her attention to a muscled chest dusted with a V of crisp, dark hair that trailed in a line over his flat stomach down to the button of the black dress slacks he wore?

A split second of heated admiration passed before she realized that he'd asked her a question. She blinked, wishing it were that easy to cool the spark that seemed to ignite deep inside whenever he got close like this. "Only that no one out there is taking any blame for what happened."

"I doubt anyone would admit that their assassination attempt was thwarted by you." He handed her a clean white T-shirt. "Are you sure this is sufficient? I can order you a new blouse from the gift shop downstairs."

"That isn't necessary. Unlike you, I'm not going anyplace fancy this evening." He took her blouse and tossed it in the trash before crossing to the closet to pull a white dress shirt off the hanger. She gasped when she saw the crosshatched ridges of pink scar tissue peppering his back beside and below the square white bandage that covered the gash he'd gotten from the explosion this afternoon. *I have been hurt worse than this*, he'd said when she'd pulled the shrapnel from his wound. If the view from the front had been stunning, the view from the back squeezed at her heart and made her hurry across the room before he could don his shirt. "Ivan. What happened to you?"

She touched her fingertips to the scars. He shivered as she traced the marks. The scar hidden by his beard was a scratch compared to these injuries. His muscles tensed beneath her hand before he released a deep breath. "Souvenirs from the bombing in St. Feodor. I threw myself over the body of…a friend…to protect him from the shrapnel."

"Just like you did with me today." She splayed her fingers over the longest and most jagged of the scars, indicating he'd suffered burns in addition to the deep wounds. "You are not to do that for me again. Is that understood? You were seriously hurt. How could anyone want to…? I'm so sorry."

With a deep, stuttering breath, he turned to face her. He dipped his face close to hers, his blue eyes focused on her mouth. "Perhaps you had better stop petting me unless you intend to make me late for tonight's festivities."

"How would I…? Oh." Her gaze darted to the bed. "You mean…"

He touched her cheek, smiling as he followed the heat creeping into her face. "If our timing was better and my responsibilities were not so great, I would let you touch me in whatever way you wish. Does it shock you that I want you that way?"

She hugged the T-shirt close to her chest, fighting to assuage the inevitable response that stung the tips of her breasts and tightened the muscles between her thighs. "It shocks me how much I want you, too," she admitted. "I've never had such intense feelings with any man."

He feathered his fingers into her hair and cupped her warm cheek and neck. "Brave, honest, tempting Carly. Do you know how that makes me feel?"

"Not exactly. Most of my experience with men comes from annoying big brothers and taking down bad guys. You're a prince compared to the guys who usually hit on me." Her blush deepened when she heard the double entendre. The heat building inside almost made her light-headed. She needed more than the cooling caress of his hand to right the emotions tumbling inside her. "Thank you for taking the brunt of that explosion and collision with the concrete this afternoon. Those marks on your back should be on me." She leaned into him, winding her arms around his waist in a ferocious hug.

His arms closed around her, securing her against him. "Never. You are becoming important to me." He pressed a kiss to her hair before he leaned back against her arms and framed her head between his hands to study her. "This feels real to me. Perhaps, like two soldiers in the thick of battle together, our bond has formed quickly. Deeply."

She braced her hands against his bare chest, delighting at the discovery of how the crisp, curly hair tickled her palms, and his nipples sprang to attention beneath her curious exploration. "There were never any soldiers like you when I was deployed."

"Like what?" His voice thickened with a husky timbre that danced against her eardrums and quickened her pulse.

"Like I can't keep my eyes and hands off you. Like I already know everything important about you. Like I can tell you anything, ask anything, do…" Her hands stilled on his warm, muscled chest. "Am I foolish for thinking like that?"

"If so, then we are both fools." He leaned in and she stretched up to meet his kiss.

But a sharp knock at the door interrupted the moment. Galina was summoning Ivan to return to his princely duties. "Your Highness? We need you out here to make some decisions."

With a regretful sigh that caressed her skin like a

warm breeze, he rested his forehead against hers. "What was I saying about timing?"

As they pulled apart, Carly rested her hand along his bearded jaw and whispered her regret. "I know you're only in my life for a week, but I don't want this—us—to be a charade."

He sealed his lips over hers, completing the interrupted kiss with a firm stamp that left her feeling wanted and wanting more. "Neither do I."

Ivan stepped back, pulling the T-shirt on over her head. He freed her messy braid from beneath the collar and draped it over her shoulder. How could putting clothes on feel like he was *un*dressing her? The heat that flared between them whenever they dropped their guard and got close felt intimate, she supposed— whether clothes were going on or coming off, whether they kissed, or he simply brushed his calloused fingertip across her cheek as he did now, pulling away. He shrugged into his shirt, looped a tie around his neck, grabbed his suit jacket, then took her hand, opened the door and led her back out to the main room with the others.

Carly pulled her jacket on over the oversize T-shirt. It might be irrational, but she wanted to hide the soft cotton clinging to her skin, as if it were something sensual, protective, private between her and Ivan. Wearing his undershirt instilled her with a symbolic sense of caring that she'd never felt when she'd borrowed clothing from her brothers.

Taking in each of the senior staff gathered around, Ivan buttoned his shirt and tucked it in, running the impromptu meeting even as he prepared for his next command performance. "What needs to be done?"

Aleks handed him a bottle of water and asked, "How are you feeling? The doctor said you required stitches."

Ivan took a long drink before resealing the bottle and handing it to Carly. No one had offered her anything. "My back is a little tender, but I assure you I will make a full recovery."

"Will it leave a scar?"

"A small one." Did Aleks know about the other scars Ivan bore? Marks of survival. Marks of strength and toughness she wondered if Aleks, or anyone else in this room, completely understood. "Miss Valentine's injuries are minor, as well. Thank you for asking." Was it possible she'd just heard a snarky reprimand in Ivan's autocratic tone?

Aleks apparently had. He turned to Carly and gave her a deferential nod. "My apologies. I am pleased to hear that. We owe you greatly for helping our Ivan today."

"I'd hate to lose him." Ivan glanced over the jut of his shoulder at her, giving her a questioning look. *Yes, there was a personal meaning to that statement.* "It definitely helped to have the home field advantage today."

Aleks snapped his fingers. "That is a baseball phrase. I have learned a great deal from your father about American sports. I only wish we had enough time to see a Royals ball game in person."

"Perhaps on another visit, we will make the time," Ivan said.

Another visit? Was it possible she'd have the chance to see Ivan again after this week and her protection assignment was done? As quickly as hope rushed through her veins, it faded. He'd probably be king the next time he came to the US. There would be even more demands on his time, more people surrounding him. She'd still be a commoner who couldn't dance or pick out a proper dress on her own. Suddenly, her entire future shrank down to this week with this man. Ivan Mostek was everything she hadn't even known she wanted in a man. Strong of character. Caring. Brave. Undeniably sexy. Even if they did find the mole and she kept him alive, their time together was destined to end. The finality of that, the ticking clock counting down to the time he would leave her, made every moment together more intense—and too precious to waste on niceties like dating and decorum. If she truly loved this man, as she suspected she did, then she had only a few days to be with him—to love him—before she lost him forever.

Ivan buttoned his cuffs and pulled on his jacket before turning his attention to Galina and the computer tablet she held. "What decisions need to be made?"

Since Galina seemed to be a perpetually put-together woman, Carly guessed that the huff that lifted the other woman's dark bangs indicated annoyance. She gestured to the man sitting on the couch, drinking a bottle of water. "Mr. Decker, for one thing. He refuses to accept any payment for his services. What are we to do with him? He has been most…inquisitive."

Ignoring the dark-eyed daggers she shot his way, Ralph Decker rose and crossed the sitting area to join them. "It's an ingrained habit. I can't help but ask questions." He crushed the empty bottle in his hands and tucked it into the front pocket of his jeans. "Mr. Petrovic and your chief of staff have been regaling me with everything you hope to accomplish for your country while you're here in the US. Sounds admirable and ambitious. Go big or go home, eh?"

Ivan turned to Carly with that frustrated frown that meant he hadn't understood the slang. "You've got big plans for Lukinburg," she explained, "and you won't settle for anything less than what you came here for."

"That is true." He gave his answer to the reporter.

"And you're willing to risk your life to do that?" Decker asked.

"I am." Ivan didn't bat an eye when Decker pressed him for a more informative answer. "Galina, issue this man a press pass for the ball on Saturday. Clear his credentials, of course. The ball is black-tie, Mr. Decker."

"I can find a tux."

"Would you like to cover our visit to the research facility at the university tomorrow? You can see how our raw materials are being put to use in building American technology."

"I'd like to sit down for a one-on-one interview with you. But I'll settle for the invitations." Decker seemed to understand that helping Ivan escape the Plaza and get to the hotel didn't mean he'd earned full access to Lukin politics and conspiracies. "I thought royalty were all figureheads. But you've got a real agenda. You've got some stones, Your Highness."

Ivan looked to Carly again. The lewd colloquialism was something she'd rather explain in private. Or not at all. "It's a compliment. He respects you."

Decker's green eyes smiled as they met hers. "That's the polite translation." He turned his gaze to Galina and winked. "You saving me a dance at the embassy ball, pretty lady?"

Galina arched a regal eyebrow. "I will not be dancing. Certainly not with you. Allow me to show you to the door, Mr. Decker. I will get your contact information to send you the press passes."

Decker laughed. "I like her. She's all business. Kind of makes me want to see what's under that starched collar."

"I beg your pardon?"

"Figuratively, of course." Decker shook Ivan's hand and nodded to Carly before following Galina to the door. "Thanks, Your Highness. Good luck with everything. Officer Valentine. Hey, if a copy of the bomb squad's report on today's incident happens to fall into my hands…"

Not until she read it first. "I'll see what I can do."

Aleks laughed as Galina and Decker disappeared into the foyer. "I think she likes him. At least, she likes being flirted with. I haven't seen her flustered like that since losing Konrad."

After Aleks's matchmaking amusement had been dismissed, and the reporter had been ushered out, Ivan checked his watch. "We have twenty minutes before we are set to leave for the Mayweathers' cocktail reception." He spoke to Filip, who was adding milk to his coffee at the bar. "I assume you have made new arrangements for our transportation? And inspected each vehicle personally?"

Filip set the cup down without ever taking a drink. "There was nothing wrong with that limousine when we left the hotel this morning. I rode with you everywhere today. If I thought there was a bomb on it, would I have done this?"

Carly wanted a better explanation, a better alibi, than the security chief's excuses. "We don't know the details about the bomb yet. It could have been on a timer or remotely detonated."

"A remote detonation would mean someone was watching us to know when we would be in the limousine," Milevski argued.

"Someone *was* watching us today," she pointed out. The hooded man among hundreds of other less obviously suspicious bystanders at the Plaza was her prime suspect. If only she had a name, or even a face, to help identify him. And if she could prove the hooded man was working with any one of these people, she'd close the case and know Ivan was safe.

Ivan buttoned his collar and knotted his tie. "If it was triggered by turning the ignition as it appeared to be, then the bomb was put there sometime after we arrived at the store and went to dinner. That's only a two-hour window."

"One of our people stays with the car always," Filip insisted. "It was Eduard's assignment until we called him for backup to help manage the crowd."

"Eduard was in the store with us," Carly reminded them. "I remember him joking with the clerk who checked us out. Was the limo unattended during that time, too? A skilled bomber wouldn't need more than a few minutes."

Filip stormed across the carpet, his cheeks turning ruddy with temper. "What are you accusing me of? Not doing my job? An attempt on the prince's life? That is treason, Miss Valentine." He thumped his chest, leaning in close enough for her to smell the oily tonic he used in his hair. "*I* am a proud Lukin. If you had not interfered—"

"Are you angry because I got the prince out of a dangerous situation you couldn't control or because Eduard is dead?" Carly wasn't intimidated by Filip's bluster. She had two big brothers she was used to standing up to. She propped her hands on her hips and stood her ground. "Or are you upset because this latest attempt to kill Ivan failed?"

Her challenge left a long silence in the room. Ivan had moved in beside her, no doubt thinking she needed his protection. Now he stood shoulder to shoulder with Carly, awaiting Milevski's answer. Galina returned in time to hear the accusation, hanging back at the edge of the seating area. Aleks cleaned his glasses, either oblivious to or purposely ignoring the tension in the room.

From across the room, Carly heard a grumbling noise that sounded a little bit like laughter. Danya had avoided the whole conversation, but now he moved to the bar to pour himself a cup of coffee. "She knows, Filip. She knows about the threats. This isn't how we ran security in the old days. We should have canceled any royal appearances until we shored up the holes in our security network. Even that day we lost Konrad and the others in St. Feodor, we'd heard chatter about one last hurrah from the Loyalist movement. But you ignored it. Lives were lost that didn't have to be."

"The prince insisted on making that appearance. To show solidarity in the new government."

"The prince relies on us to keep him safe. When there's a threat, what needs to be done shouldn't be up for debate."

"Wait a minute," Ivan calmly interrupted. "What do you mean by holes in security? What is it, Danya? What do you know of today's events?"

Danya turned to his boss, giving him a mocking salute with his coffee cup. "You tell him, or I will."

Filip rubbed his fist in the palm of his other hand before the anger fell away and his face aged with remorse. "There was a security breach sometime last night. A hacker got into my computer files. He has our personal contact information, so it's possible he could be pinging our phones and tracking our movements. He would have known today's schedule, our security assignments." He shrugged his beefy shoulders. "With that information, he or she would have known where the limousine would be parked, and the time frame for your luncheon. He could even have called Eduard's phone to trigger the explosion. I know there were threats made against you in Lukinburg. I fear the Loyalists haven't honored their alliance. They followed you here to the States."

Ivan reflected on the revelation for a moment. Surely, he wasn't about to tell these people that he was the one who'd gotten into Filip's files. Carly reached into the pocket of her jacket and curled her fingers around the flash drive. Still there. Still safe. Still their best lead. Anyone else who had access to those files could have used the information as Filip had suggested—to follow Ivan, to set off the bomb. Ivan wouldn't admit he was conducting his own investigation of these so-called friends and colleagues, would he?

But the prince had a different confession to make. "I have received two threats since we arrived in the US."

Carly's sigh of relief was drowned out by the flurry of concern and protest from the circle of people closing in around Ivan.

Danya cursed. "This is what I mean. It's shabby—"

"Why did you not tell me?" Filip accused. "How can

you expect me to do my job when I do not have all the information I need?"

"Someone has that information," Galina chided. "On all of us. Now we are all in danger. How could you let this happen?"

Filip scoffed at the accusation. "Eduard was our tech man. We'd need an expert in technology to find out where the incursion came from."

From the corner of her eye, Carly glimpsed Ivan adjusting his glasses on his nose and studying Aleks, sending a silent message to the nerdy numbers guy. "This is your area of expertise, my friend."

Aleks blinked once, twice, not understanding any better than she did. "Are you accusing me of—?"

"I am not. But perhaps you could help?"

His adviser's confusion suddenly cleared. "Oh…yes. I am good with a computer. I will look at Filip's program this evening after the party to see what I can find out."

What was that all about? Carly wondered. Ivan had said Aleks was the only member of his delegation he trusted. Was this a regular exchange between the two men? Was he using his friend to cover up his foray into late-night hacking? Had he used his friend to help him keep other secrets before this one?

At first glance, the two men could be brothers, although she'd been spending enough time with Ivan that she noticed the subtle differences in their build and height. She was guessing Aleks didn't carry the scars Ivan did. Both men had blue eyes; both wore glasses, although Aleks had a slightly thicker lens in his. Both men had that rich, raven-black hair, but Ivan kept his hair and beard neatly trimmed while Aleks had embraced his curly locks and grown them out to the point he looked like a turn-of-the-century scientist pictured in one of her schoolbooks.

They couldn't be related, could they? No, their last names were different. Cousins? There were enough lies and secrets in this room that it wasn't completely out of the question. A man would trust his family, wouldn't he? Did the two men share a link beyond friendship? Even as Aleks scrolled through icons on the screen, she wondered if Ivan and Aleks cut their hair the same length and wore the same glasses frame, could they could switch places like twins sometimes did?

But what did their looks or relationship even matter? A man was dead. Multiple attempts had been made on Ivan's life. The threats were real, and as far as Carly could tell, Lukin security sucked. "We have computer specialists at the crime lab if you want me to call them," she offered.

"No," Filip snapped before she finished making the offer. "I want no foreigners looking through my records."

Was that embarrassment? Or did the man truly have something to hide?

Ivan was insistent. He sent her the same silent message he'd given Aleks. *Follow my lead.* "Thank you for the offer, but Aleks can spend some time working on this after our appearance at the Mayweathers' this evening." He dropped a hand onto Aleks's shoulder. "I will expect a report in the morning."

"Roger that, Your Highness."

"Roger that?" Ivan chuckled. "You are picking up many Americanisms." He tapped his watch. "Now go pick out a tie that does not have evidence of your lunch on it so that we may be ready to depart." He turned to

Filip, who was still stewing over the security breach. "Bring the car around, please."

Danya stepped forward. "I will be driving now, sir. Since we are not canceling any appearances, despite the threats. You are giving our enemy an unfair advantage."

Ivan nodded. "Your complaint is noted. Lukinburg is depending on us. On all of us. We shall simply be more careful." He addressed everyone in the room before they all went their separate ways. "We will move forward without Eduard. We will remember him as a brave young man, a Lukin patriot who gave his life for his country. We will not dishonor his memory by failing on our mission to the States. Any questions?"

With a flurry of *thank you*s and *yes, sirs,* Filip, Danya, Galina and Aleks all went in different directions, putting down coffee cups and checking their respective gear before heading out the door to their respective rooms to finish getting ready to depart.

Once the penthouse door had clicked shut behind them, Ivan hurried over to Aleks's computer and sat down at the desk. "Apparently, I need to do a better job of covering my tracks." He pulled down a command from the toolbar, clicked in a few places and typed in a couple of passwords before going back to the home screen and shutting everything down. "There. Filip should not be able to trace the incursion back to this computer now. If he somehow manages to get through these firewalls, and understands IP addresses, all he will find is a dummy account."

Impressive. Ivan seemed to have some skills she wouldn't expect to find in royalty. His penchant for protecting her from threats both physical and emotional? Encryption-breaking hacker skills? What exactly had his job been before being named the crown prince? Would he be on that flash drive, too? Now she really wanted to get to her own computer and dig into the files that were burning a hole in her pocket.

Carly picked up a towel from the wet bar and wiped Ivan's prints off the keyboard and mouse before using the towel to close the laptop. "Now we've really erased your trail."

"Well-done, my lioness." He tipped his face up to hers and smiled. "I sensed you would be a true ally. You have done much for me. You truly have my back. I do not know how I will ever be able to thank you."

Forget Prince Charming. This mysterious puzzle of a man, who made tough guy in a tailored suit and geek with glasses equally hot made her feel soft and feminine and important without having to sacrifice one iota of the tough, working-class cop she was.

"You're welcome." Feeling a connection to him as though they were tethered together at the heart, Carly leaned in and kissed him. She slid her palms against the tickle of his beard and cupped either side of his jaw. Swiveling his chair to face her, Ivan's hands settled at her waist. Then, with a deep-pitched sigh, he skimmed his hands over her hips and cupped her bottom, tugging her between the V of his legs until her knees butted against the edge of the chair and she tumbled into his chest.

Surrendering to the demands of his kiss, Carly parted her lips and sank into his hard, warm body. She made several demands of her own, running her fingers across his short hair and bemoaning the cinched-up layers of clothing between them. Her lips scudded across his. She pulled his firm lower lip between hers, found the point of his chin through his beard and lightly nipped him there, unleashing a feral groan from his chest that spoke to something primitive and needy inside her.

Ivan shifted position again, pushing to his feet and forcing her head back to plunder her mouth with his. He gently touched his lips to the strawberry on her jaw, then nuzzled his way to her earlobe and the sensitive bundle of nerves he discovered underneath that made her jolt with each stroke of his tongue or rasp of his beard against the tender skin there. His sexy, accented voice was a deep purr against her ear. "I will say 'thank you' many more times if this is how you say, 'you are welcome.'" Carly wound her arms around his neck and recaptured his lips. "Thank you," he growled against her mouth. "Thank—"

A sharp rap at the door washed over her like a splash of icy water. Galina's prim, succinct voice intruded. "Your Highness? We are ready. It is time."

Easing her grip around Ivan's neck, Carly dropped onto her heels. "That's…my cue to…to leave." Her lips and fingertips and breasts and blood were still tingling with the electricity that had arced between them, making it difficult to think, much less speak. "You have a party to get to."

"Carly…" His eyes were drowsy pools of deep blue behind his glasses, and she had a hard time looking away. "I wish with everything in me that you and I… that none of this stood in our way." There was another sharp knock. His expression hardened, and he whipped his gaze to the door. "I will be there shortly."

When he turned away, she glimpsed a spike of black hair sticking up from the top of his head and felt a stab of embarrassment. His trim hair spiked up in several places, mussed by her hands. She reached up and smoothed them back into place. "Sorry about that. You have to go out in public. You can't look like you just had sex. Like we… Of course, there wasn't time to… Oh, hell."

While her skin heated with embarrassment, Ivan laughed. He cupped her warm cheek in his cool hand. "My sweet, honest Carly. You are good for me in so many ways. I am filled with regret that I cannot make that wish come true for you."

Right. This relationship couldn't go anywhere. No matter how right it felt, it simply couldn't be. She dredged up a smile. "You are good for me in many ways, too, Your Highness."

She was surprised to see the humor fade from his eyes at her response. A sternness crept into his tone, as if their language difference had created a misunderstanding. "I mean, I regret that I cannot make that wish come true for you *at this time.*"

At this time. Meaning, they were going to finish that kiss at some other time? A light of understanding dawned. She didn't need any translation for what he'd just promised her. He wanted her as much as she wanted him. She pushed onto her toes and traded one sweet, perfunctory kiss. "I hope so."

"I do not suppose we can simply not answer the door and she will go away."

Carly laughed. "You have responsibilities." She pulled the flash drive from her pocket and held it up. "So do I."

He clasped her hand and walked her to the door. "Will you allow one of my men to drive you home?"

Um, bombs? Unknown traitor? Knowing his delegation wasn't especially fond of her involvement with the prince? "Under the circumstances, I believe I'll find my own ride. My brother Jesse won't be at work yet. I'll give him a call."

"Was I right to admit the new threats to my entourage?"

"I think the bomb this afternoon kind of gave it away." They stopped at the door, lowering their voices to a whisper, in case Galina or anyone else was eavesdropping from the other side. "It will certainly stir the pot. Your people will be working even harder to prove their loyalty to you and the crown. Either out of pride or because they want to cover up anything suspicious. That was clever, too, to divert suspicion from you about the stolen files. Aleks won't tell anyone that it was you, will he?"

"He will not. That is why I wanted him to be the one investigating the security breach. He will keep my secret."

"I'm sorry about Eduard. And for his family. He seemed like a nice man."

"Let us hope he is not a martyr for a cause."

She reached up to straighten his tie, but only seemed to be making it worse. Ivan stilled her hands against his chest, "What is it, *dorogoy*?"

"I feel like I'm leaving you alone with the enemy. I can go to the party if you want me to."

He lifted each hand to his mouth and kissed her fingers before releasing them. "I need you to start going over those files. I am tired of people dying and not having any answers to explain who is responsible."

Carly nodded. "I'll get you your own cell phone, too. A disposable one the others don't know about. You can use that one to call or text me. And no one can track you."

"I think that would be a good idea. Thank you for looking out for me."

She ignored the urge to answer his thanks the way she had over in the chair. Instead, she patted his arm. "That's why I'm here, isn't it?"

"It is not the only reason, *dorogoy.*" He drew his fingertip across her uninjured cheek in a familiar caress. "I will see you later?"

A firmer knock rattled the door and Filip's harsh voice called to them. "Your Highness, we will be late. Miss Valentine? You must let him go."

That was prophetic.

Carly ignored the big rock of reality that weighted her down again and reached for the doorknob. "I'll be waiting for you. Be safe."

Chapter Ten

Ivan saluted the trio of men in the Valentines' living room with a forkful of cherry pie before stuffing the sweet, tart bite into his mouth and heading downstairs to Carly's bedroom.

It was strange to see Aleks so enamored with American baseball, and making friends with Carly's father and brother Frank, who was home from the hospital and staying with them for a few days while he recuperated from being poisoned. But then Aleks had always had a knack for socializing. He'd been an asset at the Mayweathers' cocktail party tonight, showing the most charming side of Lukinburg, as well as being a knowledgeable representative to help Ivan discuss their new government policies and trade ambitions with the US. Aleks had covered for him earlier this evening at the hotel, too, allowing him to keep his secrets from Filip and the others. Aleks deserved a break. The three men were spread out across the sectional couch, fixated on the televised game. Filip was in the kitchen, eating a late dinner after trading places with Danya, who sat in the car parked out front and made routine checks around the exterior of the house. The two bodyguards would swap out four-hour shifts, sleeping in Jesse Valentine's old room while the other kept watch. Galina was staying the night at the Lukinburg embassy, handling last-minute details for the ball.

They were all safe for now, the game was an exciting one, judging by their cheers and chatter, and they were all full of Carly's delicious food. Ivan was looking forward to several hours of uninterrupted time with Carly. Maybe to finish that kiss she'd started in his hotel suite, possibly to tell her the truth about how quickly she'd come to mean something to him, certainly to discuss the background records she'd been poring over since dinner, and just to have a few hours where he didn't have to be the prince. For a few hours tonight, he could just be the man who wanted to be with Carly Valentine.

Ivan turned on the lower landing to quietly open and close the door that led down to the finished basement that had been converted into Carly's private space. She had a bedroom area, an office space with a big antique desk and bookshelves, her own bathroom and closet. The ceiling had been soundproofed to give her privacy from her father's loud television and keep whatever noise she made down here from traveling to the upper levels of the house. The windows had been given the proper egress in case of an emergency, yet they were covered with shutters her brother Frank had made.

He turned the lock in the knob before heading down the last few steps. If Carly wasn't already a brave, sexy woman who spoke to everything he truly was, he'd want to be a part of her life just for her cooking. The fancy hors d'oeuvres and champagne cocktails at the Mayweather reception had been tasty, but not filling. Even reheated, the leftover grilled burgers, potato salad and coleslaw Carly had pulled from the fridge had been delicious.

He spotted her over a partition of shoulder-high bookshelves, sitting cross-legged on her bed with the computer in her lap, a pen jammed between her lips, and a yellow legal pad on the quilt beside her. Pausing for a few precious seconds before she looked up from her work, he drank in the sight of her cutoff shorts and long bare legs. Her hair, damp from an earlier shower, hung loose and tumbled around her shoulders. She still wore his T-shirt from earlier, and tremors of a now familiar desire scuttled though him. The decadence of her cherry pie was forgotten as he savored the even sweeter knowledge that that was his shirt on her, and that he didn't have to share himself with anybody but her right now.

The frown of concentration on her face vanished as she reacted to some sound he'd made. She pulled the pen from her mouth and started to shut the laptop.

"Don't worry. I locked the door." He strode around the bookshelves and resumed his place in the blue-striped chair near the foot of her bed where he'd draped his jacket and tie and kicked off his shoes earlier. "Your father, Frank and Aleks are watching the baseball game, Filip is in the kitchen, polishing off the last of your potato salad and Danya is patrolling outside. I warned my staff that unless the house came under attack, we were not to be disturbed. We are safe. We are alone." But she was still frowning. "Is something wrong?"

She hesitated a moment too long before answering. "Maybe. I don't know." She clicked on a file and turned the laptop around to show him the screen. "This is Aleks's file. It's still in Lukin. Except for his name, I can't read any of it. But I think it's been mislabeled."

The dessert suddenly sat like a rock in his gut. "Like I said, I was interrupted before I had the chance to translate all of them. Let me look at it. Trade?" He handed her the pie before pulling the computer onto his lap. "This was the last piece. I noticed you did not eat any at dinner. Sorry, I could not resist taking one more bite. Your cooking reminds me of growing up at my aunt's. Nothing was wasted, and everything was delicious."

"That's a nice compliment. Thanks." She ate a bite of the pie, and he watched her lips close around the fork and slide off. His body reacted with a jolt of need. It felt intimate to do something so simple as sharing food. But Carly quickly reminded him of the job at hand. "Is there a translation program you use? You don't have to read through it word for word and rewrite it in English yourself, do you?"

Mislabeled. A careless mistake for someone with his skills. He should tell her just what she'd find in the file. But she set the pie aside and picked up her legal pad and started going through the suspicious things she'd already found in Filip's records.

"I was surprised to see that Galina served in the army. She seems more like the I-don't-want-to-get-my-hands-dirty type."

Ivan grinned at the surprisingly accurate assessment of the chief of staff and ruler of all things royal protocol. "Every able-bodied Lukin, man or woman, serves two years after schooling. Then they can continue in the army, as I did, or go to university or into the workforce."

"I just don't see her going through basic training. Unless the Lukin version of that isn't as dirty or physical as our army?"

"I will put my training up against yours any day."

"Okay, tough guy. That must explain why you're in such good shape for a guy with a throne job." This time, they laughed together. "I couldn't find in there what she did, though. Medic? That could explain the poisoned apples. Admin?" Ivan pulled up her internet provider and logged into a Lukin public records site. "Please don't tell me she worked with explosives."

Ivan typed in his own access code, following a hunch. "Her fiancé did."

"Her fiancé? I didn't know Galina was engaged."

The familiar weight of guilt settled around Ivan's heart. "Late fiancé. He died in the bombing at St. Feodor."

"Oh. I had no idea." Carly exhaled a sigh. "Now I feel bad for not liking her. She's always so perfect. And feminine. Perfume and high heels all the time? Makes me feel like a slacker. I guess that explains the black she wears." She scooted closer to the foot of the bed. "Did you find what her job was?"

Nothing suspicious here. "Quartermaster's office."

"Supplies. Desk work. Hardly a red flag of suspicion. Manufacturing explosive devices isn't standard training in your army, is it?"

"No."

Carly put a check mark by Galina's name and went on to the next item on her list. "It looks like Filip's most recent search was on Ralph Decker, after he took that picture of us at the hospital. Decker grew up in Kansas City, but he's been gone for years, working mostly with overseas press junkets, reporting for the wire services. He's been embedded with military units all over the world, led a pretty exciting life. He's only been back in KC for a couple of months. He has a job with the *Journal*, but it looks as though he's only been doing fluff pieces."

"Fluff?" Ivan looked up from the screen.

"Human interest stories. Social stuff. Nothing that's hard news."

He pulled up the *Journal*'s website and scrolled through some of Ralph Decker's recent credits. An Honor Flight for veterans, a science fair winner, popular summer day trips around Kansas City, gave him a better understanding of the term Carly had used. "Maybe he is looking to be part of the action again, to break a big story."

"Like who's behind the assassination attempts on a European prince?" Carly wrote a question mark beside the reporter's name. "You don't think he'd create the problem, just so he'd have a story to cover, do you?"

"How would Decker have sent me the threat on the airplane?"

"For the right price, your inside man could have done it for him." Carly dropped her feet off the end of the bed, sliding close enough that her knee brushed his. He really should feel guilty about all the nerve endings that jumped to life at even that casual touch. But he knew the only thing he'd ever regret with Carly was if she got hurt. He blinked away the distracting thoughts, set his glasses on the desk and leaned in to focus on the note she pointed out to him. "Filip's records show Decker's been to Lukinburg. And if he's covered the military, he could have met one of your people then, just like you and I supposedly did."

"Put a star next to his name on your paper. He wants a one-on-one interview. Perhaps he lost someone important in the St. Feodor bombing. I will have this conversation with him at the ball."

"Only if I'm there with you. Saturday is when all hell is supposed to break loose, according to that picture and the date scrawled across it. The last thing you need is to be alone with anyone."

"I am alone with you." She blushed when he lifted his gaze to hers. She wasn't immune to the distractions of working closely together, either. He'd never known a woman so responsive to his voice or touch. He'd never responded to a woman like this, either. It made him want to share many long conversations and put his hands all over her body to discover every place he could touch her and elicit that same rosy heat on her skin. That most male part of him stiffened at the possibilities. But they needed to use this private time wisely. He picked up the legal pad and flipped through the rest of the notes she had written. "What else have you found in Filip's files?"

"A record of threats you've received, minus the two here in the US. Looks like Filip interviewed some of the Loyalist dissidents but didn't reach any conclusions. I called Captain Hendricks and asked him to see if any of the dissident names were in the country now." She wasn't making any effort to put space between them, and neither was he. Ivan liked working with her like this, bouncing their thoughts off each other, sharing her vibrant energy, breathing in her unique scent. "Your appearance schedule is there, right down to parking in the Forty-Seventh Street garage. Changes that were made to coordinate with KCPD, running late, et cetera. Can you tell if anyone else accessed these files before you did?"

Ivan pulled up the data. "Filip, of course. Galina. Eduard."

"Not Danya?"

"He is more of a blunt instrument when it comes to security. He has little faith in technology. But Filip would have shared everything with his team."

"Unless he's hiding something." Carly shot to her feet and hurried around the bed to pick up two cell phones from the bedside table. "I forgot." She opened a text on one phone and handed him the other. "Here's the phone I got for you. I went ahead and programmed in my number and Captain Hendricks's. It's nothing fancy, but it works."

"Thank you."

Ivan set the laptop and new phone on the desk when Carly perched on the arm of the chair and showed him the text. "The captain sent me a copy of the preliminary report on the bomb that killed Eduard. Nothing official yet—it'll take weeks to go through the crime lab. But it doesn't match Filip's report on the St. Feodor bombing. The hooded man, the crowd and the shouted threats are similar, but—"

"It's not the same kind of bomb." Ivan sat back in the chair, recalling what he could from Filip's briefing on the St. Feodor attack. "The St. Feodor bomber used a handheld trigger."

"Today's bomb was detonated by a cell phone. All the bomber had to do was call the number. Either he was watching and knew when you'd be close by, or he called when he thought you'd be riding in the car—according to Filip's schedule. We were late going to lunch and trying to get through the crowd made us even later," she pointed out. "If we were on time, you'd be dead."

"So would you."

"So would a lot of people."

His jaw clenched with the possibility of so many senseless deaths. What if Carly and his team had been with him in the limo? If they'd been in traffic? Or stopped at an intersection with people in the crosswalk? Losing Eduard today wasn't the first time he'd lost a friend. It appeared that whoever wanted to "End Ivan" was intent on destroying many lives before he got around to finally killing him.

"Danya Pavluk's younger brother, Konrad, used to be part of the royal security team. He was killed that day." She'd put a star by Danya's name. He picked up Carly's pen and, with a reluctant sigh, drew a star beside Galina's name.

"What's that for?" Carly asked.

"Galina was engaged to Konrad. Konrad died in her arms in St. Feodor Square."

Carly was silent for a moment, perhaps contemplating Danya's and Galina's grief. "You think one of them wants revenge for Konrad Pavluk's death?"

He'd considered the idea earlier but had dismissed it. The logic didn't make sense. "Why come after me? The Loyalists set off that bomb."

"You're uniting the country. Welcoming the Loyalists into your new regime." Her mouth twisted with an apologetic frown. "Maybe Danya feels like you're rewarding them—instead of punishing them for killing his brother."

"Possibly. Danya would have explosives experience.

He has advanced weapons training. And he came from the same mining region that I did."

"You know how to make a bomb?"

Ivan nodded. "A rudimentary one. It was part of working in the mines."

An uncharacteristic hesitation shadowed her features before she spoke again. "The mines in Moravska? You mentioned it once before—the town where you lived with your aunt and uncle."

"That is correct."

This time she didn't just look away, she got up and walked her phone back to the bedside table. Hesitation wasn't a side of Carly he was used to seeing. Since being forthcoming had never been an issue for her before, he didn't push for an explanation. But it worried him. Surely, there was nothing in these files that made her think that *he* had built and detonated those bombs.

Ivan turned to the last page of her notes. "I see one more entry. Vasily Gordeeva. Mob boss who used to run illegal arms through Lukinburg. Significant influence on the previously corrupt government. His people were the ones responsible for my parents' deaths. He spent his last years in prison and died of cancer." The hate he'd once felt as a younger man had mellowed to a melancholia that hit him when he thought of all that had been taken from him. As a grown man, he replaced the anger and sadness with a good memory from his childhood and then refocused on the tasks at hand—eliminating suspects who wanted him dead and finding out what was bothering Carly. He scratched through Gordeeva's name. "It is rumored that one of Vasily's last acts before his death was to kill the business rival who murdered his daughter. I do not believe there is anyone left with any significant power in either one of those criminal families."

"Unless this terroristic campaign against you is their bid to regain power."

Ivan shook his head. "The new government is too strong for that. They do not have the financial backing they once enjoyed."

"I hope you're right." Carly returned to her perch on the foot of the bed and leaned forward to rest her hand atop his knee. The same nerve impulses that had skittered with delight a few minutes ago now went on alert, bracing him for whatever she was about to tell him. "Speaking of criminals and Vasily Gordeeva... I couldn't find any record of your parents being murdered in your file. No mention of your aunt and uncle raising you in Moravska. That's why I thought the files might be mislabeled. You said they were victims of a mob hit, that the Gordeevas had influence with the government back then. Was the crime not investigated?"

That information was in Aleks's file. The one she couldn't read. The one he couldn't tell her about. He'd given his word to hide the truth.

Even from her.

"Why do you think he was in prison?" Ivan pushed to his feet. He tossed the legal pad onto the bed and paced to the far side of the room before an idea hit him that chased away all the sorrow and guilt. "Enough work." He crossed back to the laptop, found the site he was looking for and clicked on the file he downloaded. He turned up the volume as the melodic strains of a waltz began to play. "You wait on your family, do your job as a police officer, take care of me... It is enough. The rest of the night is about you." He took her hands and pulled her to her feet. "May I have this dance?"

"Touched a sore spot, huh? Okay. I'll stop asking questions." She tossed her hair behind her back and rested one hand on his shoulder as he'd taught her. "You're willing to put your toes through another lesson with me?"

She didn't fight him when he slid his hand to the small of her back and pulled her hips against his. If their knees touching had raised his temperature, feeling her sleek curves nestled against his harder frame nearly made him combust. He rested his forehead against hers, looking down into her upturned eyes. "I am willing to hold you. Always."

Her feet didn't move as he took the first step. Ivan let the music play without dancing until she shared what was keeping her from joining him in the waltz. "We don't have always."

Ivan tightened his hold around her waist and pressed his cheek to hers, wishing he didn't share the same hopelessness about their relationship. "Then I want to make the most of any time I do have with you," he whispered against her ear. "I care about you, my sexy lioness."

"I care about you, too. I want…" Her toes curled into the rug beside his stockinged feet. But her upper body began to sway in time with his.

"What do you want, *dorogoy*?"

"I know it's only been a few days, but I want you." She glanced at the bed and blushed. "There."

"Carly—"

"I know you're attracted to me, too. I mean…" Her thigh slipped between his, brushing against his arousal.

He groaned in helpless pleasure. Her astute powers of observation did indeed make that difficult to hide. "I've had sex. Ages ago, so I know the nuts and bolts."

"Nuts and bolts?"

"But it wasn't great," she hurried on without explanation. "I haven't had a lot of experience, and..." Her cheeks deepened to a rosy hue and she pushed against his chest, ending the dance, though not completely pulling away. "I don't know how to seduce a man."

Her honest confession made him embarrassingly, wonderfully hard. She wasn't the only one who reacted to a suggestive word or familiar touch. Knowing she felt as strongly as he did about how good the two of them could be together triggered an equally strong response in his heart. With all the lies swirling around him these past few weeks, Carly Valentine was one truth he couldn't deny. "Do you want to seduce me?"

"Yes." She broke away to dash into her bathroom and come back with a handful of condoms. That meant she'd been wanting this, hoping for this as much as he had. "I stole these from Jesse's nightstand. I don't know how long they've been there. I don't want to assume anything. But we have all night. And the enemy's at bay right now. No one can get in here." She paused for a moment to catch her breath. "We only have until you leave. Maybe it's crazy, but I don't want to miss out on my chance to be with you. Because I think it might— we might—be really great. Will you please say something, so I stop rambling?"

Ivan took the wrappers from her grip and tossed them onto the bed. He pulled her back into his arms and pressed a kiss to her warm cheek. "It is not crazy. I want you, too." He felt her trembling beneath his touch, but then she wound her arms around his neck and resumed their sensuous dance. They cared about neither the style nor the rhythm, only that they were close enough to feel the heat and shape of each other's bodies. "Tell me what you want."

"I want you to kiss me."

He dipped his mouth to capture hers. He tunneled his fingers into her hair to hold her lips against his as he took his fill of every delicious inch of her beautiful mouth. Her feet stopped moving and she hummed in her throat. Her fingers cupped the back of his head and neck, demanding the same freedom to explore his mouth. The music was drowned out by the pulse throbbing in his ears before he found the strength to end the kiss. Her breathing was as quick and uneven as his own. "What else?"

"I want to put my hands on your skin again."

He'd never truly understood how wickedly seductive true honesty could be. With a nod he stood back to unbutton his shirt, but Carly's hands were there, butting against his as she untucked it from his waistband and pushed the shirt off his shoulders. Her fingers trailed along every inch of skin she uncovered. A sea of goose bumps chased after every caress. His muscles quivered beneath every bold touch. Shoulders, arms, neck, chest, stomach—every part of him craved her touch. He wasn't going to be able to play the patient gentleman for much longer.

Her eager fingers dipped beneath the button of his slacks, yet she hesitated at his belt buckle to lift her gaze to his. "Shouldn't you be telling me what you want, too?"

He curved his fingers over hers, guiding her to undo

the belt and gently unzip his pants. "Trust me, I am enjoying every moment of this seduction."

"I'm doing it right?"

"Yes, my love." The desire that flushed her skin when she freed him nearly undid him. "Yes."

"Will you…undress me?"

Classical music swelled in the background as he peeled the T-shirt over her head and dropped her cutoffs and panties to the floor. As she stepped out of them, he pressed a kiss to her inner thigh. When he felt her shiver, he pressed another kiss to her weepy center, testing her readiness for him. Carly braced her hands against his shoulders, moaning with pleasure. "Your beard…tick…tickles there." He palmed her bottom and kissed her again, loving the grasp of her fingers digging into his shoulders as she came against his mouth. "Ivan. Please. I want…"

Ivan smiled and stood, shucking the rest of his own clothes before unhooking her bra and covering her small, responsive breasts with his hands. He angled one up to his mouth and laved the rigid tip with his tongue. "Tell me what you want, *dorogoy.*"

He was amused that she struggled to speak, but then found himself robbed of words when she tugged him toward the bed. They tumbled onto the quilt, the music long forgotten as this new dance consumed them.

Her hand boldly gripped his arousal and he growled his desire against the curve of her breast.

"Ivan? I don't understand."

Lukin. He'd used Lukin. He paraphrased his need in English. "You have a beautiful body. I want to be inside you. Do you understand what I am saying?" He grabbed the nearest foil packet and tore it open to sheathe himself. "Out loud. Say it. Say you want this, too."

"I want this. I want you. Now."

She swept her arms across the bed, clearing a place for them, tossing aside the legal pad with her notes. A moment of clarity and conscience pierced the haze of wanting Carly that filled his brain. He swung his legs off the bed and sat up. "There is something I need to tell you… You are so honest with me. I must…"

She pressed her fingers to his lips, shushing him. "No more words."

"I am not who you think I am."

"I feel everything I need to know about you. I don't want to waste another moment on anything but this." She climbed into his lap and slid herself over him. The pleasure of their connection robbed him of breath. Her body was magnificent. Tight. Warm. Perfect. "This feels so right, I want to scream. You're sure you locked that door?"

I feel everything I need to know.

"I am sure." Ivan moved inside her. He anchored her with one hand on her sweet, sweet bottom and the other fisted in her hair. He claimed her mouth in a kiss that muffled her scream as she climaxed around him. And while the aftershocks of her release still caressed him, he buried his face in the juncture of her neck and shoulder and squeezed her lithe body tightly to his, hiding the noise of his own completion before collapsing onto the quilt with Carly still snugged in his arms.

He'd never been this satisfied before. He wanted more. He wanted forever to feel like this.

But he was spent, and Carly had fallen, limp, on top of him. They lay there like that for several minutes, his fingers gently stroking up and down her spine until her skin cooled and she rolled onto the quilt beside him. "That was…" Her gaze locked on to his and her lips curved in a drowsy smile. "I knew we'd be great."

He nodded, understanding that there were no words to adequately express the connection they shared. He leaned over to give her swollen lips a quick kiss. "Never doubt your powers of seduction. I will treasure this night always."

"Me, too." She yawned, and her eyes drifted shut, breaking the connection between them.

Ivan slipped out of bed and went into the bathroom to clean up. When he returned, the only light left on was a dim lamp beside the bed. Carly had crawled under the covers and curled up with her pillow. Ivan took a mental snapshot of this serenely tender moment before slipping beneath the covers beside her. He spooned against her back, sliding one arm beneath her cheek and wrapping the other around her waist. He pulled that luscious fall of hair away from her bruised jaw and gently kissed her cheek before settling onto the pillow.

He couldn't remember a time when he hadn't been intrigued by this woman, when he hadn't trusted her to have his back, when he hadn't wanted to be with her like this. He knew Carly Valentine, deep in his soul. He would never know another woman like her. He pressed his lips into her hair and whispered, *"Obicham te, dorogoy."*

There. He'd said it. He'd admitted it to himself. To all the world. To Carly.

Only she was already fast asleep, snoring softly against his biceps, content in the perfection of this moment together.

I love you.

Chapter Eleven

Tonight, Prince Ivan was supposed to die.

The thought of losing the man who could never really be hers made Carly almost physically sick. She'd never really thought about what falling in love would be like for her, or what kind of man would capture her heart. But the moment she'd seen those piercing blue eyes sizing her up at KCPD headquarters, she'd felt a magnetic attraction to Ivan Mostek. From that evening at the house when he'd given her her first dance lesson and then anchored her in the storm of emotions that had buffeted her after Frank had been poisoned, she'd opened her heart to him. Every moment since then, through the danger and the kisses, the laughter and the long conversations, she'd been falling in love. It had happened too fast for her to realize it until last night when she finally understood that whatever was happening between them was completely mutual. She wasn't a convenient fling or a fake girlfriend. Ivan loved her, too. She was as certain of that as her sketchy knowledge of this whole man-woman thing allowed her to be.

She'd fallen in love with a prince. A relationship that could never work.

But even more heartbreaking than knowing he'd be

leaving the country tomorrow was the idea that someone wanted him to leave in a coffin.

That wasn't going to happen. She wouldn't allow that
to happen. They might have to go their separate ways
because of politics and distance. But nobody was going
to *take* him from her.

So Carly smiled and played her part. She'd love Ivan
as hard as she could for the short time they had left before she put him on that plane home to Lukinburg tomorrow.

The music had stopped for now, and Carly stood on
the steps at the edge of the dais, scanning the guests
in sleek black suits and colorful gowns for anything
suspicious.

Waiters moved discreetly through the tables at either end of the massive ballroom carrying trays with
flutes of champagne. Couples and groups of friends
had stopped dancing and chatting to look to the podium
in front of the orchestra. A wall of glass doors framed
in handcrafted wrought iron led onto a wide veranda
of gray marble. Uniformed security guards patrolled
out there, while several more embassy security staff in
black tuxedos and utility shoes stood at each interior
entryway. She recognized two of the waiters as KCPD
officers in disguise, and knew Joe Hendricks, a SWAT
team and more patrol officers watched the gate, parking area and streets beyond the Lukinburg embassy.

The crystal chandeliers had been dimmed to spotlight the handsome man speaking there, thanking their
hosts, the guests and donors, sharing his excitement
over the prosperous future Lukinburg and Kansas City
would share. He looked a little more robust than usual
this evening, since he wore a flak vest underneath his

tuxedo. But only she and the security team who had fitted him with the extra protection would know that. She spotted the Lukin ambassador, the mayor, Chief of Police Mitch Taylor, the university president and numerous other political and society dignitaries around the room.

Their known suspects were there, too. Filip Milevski, standing in front of the podium, his hands folded in front of his bulky chest, his eyes skimming the audience. Galina Honchar stood on the steps on the opposite side of the stage, looking stunning in her glittery black gown, holding her omnipresent computer tablet down in the folds of her skirt. Danya paced at the back of the room, moving from the archway of one wing to the other and back. His barrel chest indicated he was wearing body armor beneath his tux, and his expression indicated he'd rather be anyplace but at this party tonight. It took a bit more searching to locate Aleks in the middle of the crowd, grinning from ear to ear as the blonde on his arm whispered something in his ear that amused him. Ralph Decker had left the gathering of reporters filming and jotting notes about the prince's speech and waited at the base of the far steps near the railing where Galina stood. She could see his lips moving as he whispered something to the dark-haired woman, then he muttered something else when Galina waved him away, no doubt warning him to be quiet and leave her alone while she worked the party and listened to the speech. Interesting. Was Decker hitting on Galina? Probing her for answers to his questions? Or relaying some other bit of information about the danger waiting to strike tonight?

If only she could read lips, Carly thought. No, if only she could read minds. Then she'd be able to tell exactly who wanted Ivan dead. Surely, his enemy was plotting even now—counting down to the grand gesture that could kill countless innocent people, or savoring an intricate plan that was already playing out behind the scenes.

The full, flowy skirt of Carly's turquoise gown had been fun to dance in when Ivan had twirled her across the inlaid walnut floor for the opening waltz. But the fitted body girdle she wore underneath was squeezing the air from her lungs, and the holster strapped to her thigh was chafing. The sparkly heels she wore were beautiful to look at, but the three-inch heels were wreaking havoc on her calf muscles and pinching all sensation out of her little toes.

She pulled her cell phone out of her matching sparkly purse and texted Captain Hendricks.

Nothing suspicious.

He texted back, vibrating her silent phone.

Yet. Keep your eyes open and stay close to Ivan.
At the first sign of trouble, get him to the safety of the SWAT van.
We'll take it from there.

Carly texted back a Yes, sir, and tucked her phone back into the tiny purse she carried.

The ballroom erupted with applause at the end of Ivan's speech.

When she raised her hands to clap, she stopped. Ivan smiled and waved to the guests, but when he looked at her, those piercing blue eyes were sending her a silent message. Oh, hell. This was happening. Right now.

A slight shake of his head kept her from going to him. Instead, he swiped the notes he'd used off the podium and strode across the stage. He took her by the arm and led her down the stairs, pushing the crumpled paper into her hand as he turned his back to the audience to keep anyone from seeing what she was looking at. "It was on the podium when I got there."

"But the ambassador—"

"His notes were sitting on top of mine. Clearly, he did not see it. When I pulled my cards out, it was there."

Carly unfolded what she now realized was a crumpled photograph. It was the same picture of the late king's draped coffin, with a very precise message scrawled across the image. *Ticktock, Ivan. You've failed. Time to pay for your mistakes.*

Carly peeked around Ivan's shoulder, scoping out the room to locate their suspects again. Dr. Lombard from the university was at the podium, sharing a few words about how excited they were to have Lukinburg's support for their research. The ambassador who'd introduced both speakers shook his hand and thanked their guests before inviting everyone to enjoy the rest of the evening, including the special wines and dishes shipped in from Lukinburg for tonight's event.

Ivan stuffed the message in his pocket and faced the crowd, too. "Anyone could have put it there. Aleks helped me write my remarks. Galina put my notes on the podium. Filip and Danya checked the entire stage before the evening began."

The audience was applauding and the orchestra playing again as business was concluded and the festivities resumed. "He's here. He knows you have this. He's probably watching you right now to gauge your reaction."

"I had hoped our killer would lose his nerve."

"Not likely. He's probably getting off on the spectacle an attack would cause tonight."

"And there are too many places where he could hide, even among all these people."

"You've made your speech." Carly squeezed his hand and tugged him toward the nearest archway. "Will you let me take you home now? Or back to the hotel?"

He planted his feet, turning her into his arms and whirling her onto the dance floor instead. Carly put her hands where she was supposed to and kept her eyes peeled for anyone more interested in them than they should be while Ivan whispered into her ear. "I cannot leave. I may be the only one who can prevent everyone from panicking if this goes wrong."

"Goes wrong? Of course, it's going to go wrong." She stumbled over his shoe, silently cursing her strappy sandals. "We should be moving you to a safe location, clearing this building and looking for a bomb."

He tightened his grip at her waist and spun her into the heart of the dance floor. "You are right. We will look for the bomb."

Once they reached the other side of the dance floor, Ivan released her waist and grabbed her hand to lead her through the glass doors onto the veranda. The night air was still sticky with the summer heat, so there were few people outside—only a pair of men smoking near the far end of the surrounding stone wall, and a guard walking through the yard between the veranda and the iron bars that marked the edge of embassy property.

Thinking he'd brought her outside for the relative quiet and privacy, she was surprised when he kept moving across the granite paving stones toward the stairs down into the grass. "Where are we going?"

"The last explosion was a car bomb. We should check the parking lot."

This time, Carly planted her feet, stopping at the top of the stairs. "No." She pulled out her cell phone again. "I'll text Captain Hendricks and have his men begin the search. You need to stay as far away as possible from anything that goes boom."

Ivan closed his hand over hers to stop her. "How many people in there do you think have cell phones?"

The last bomb had been triggered by a cell. Carly looked through the windows to the swaying mass of humanity inside the ballroom. She inhaled a steadying breath at the enormity of what they were up against. "You think there's anyone here who *doesn't* have one?"

"For the last time, leave me alone." Carly and Ivan both turned toward the shrill tone in the woman's whispered voice to see Galina tugging against the grip of Ralph Decker's hand on her wrist as the two hurried out the far door. "I am not going anywhere with you."

Decker released her and put his hands up in surrender. With a noisy harrumph and a nod toward Ivan, she hurried down the steps and disappeared along the walkway around the corner of the building.

Keeping Carly's hand in his, Ivan took a step toward the reporter. "Are you annoying the lady, Mr. Decker?"

The dark-haired man shook his head as if he was baffled by Galina's behavior. "She must have a hot date with somebody. And it isn't me."

"I don't think she's interested in seeing anyone right

now," Carly gently pointed out. "Did you know she was engaged to be married? Her fiancé was killed just three months ago."

Decker swore, his remorse evident as his cocky attitude disappeared. "I didn't know. I thought my charm wasn't working. I'll track her down later to apologize." He tapped the camera hanging around his neck. "Hey, since you're here, how about a picture of the two of you together? Dancing in the moonlight. With your permission, of course."

"Of course." Ivan turned Carly into his arms again and posed for the camera. She realized he was acting as if everything was normal—that there was no threat in his pocket, no bomb to be found—so that Decker wouldn't be suspicious and start asking questions.

He did, anyway. But not the ones Carly had expected. "Did you mean what you said in your speech, Your Highness? The materials Lukinburg is supplying the research team will revolutionize the way our country fights a war? Better technology? Fewer casualties?"

Ivan draped his arm around her shoulders for another shot. "There are also other, nonmilitary applications, but that is my hope."

"Then that's a good thing." With a rueful smile, Decker shook the prince's hand and nodded to Carly. "You two enjoy the rest of your evening. If you'll excuse me. I need to find Ms. Honchar."

"That was a weird conversation."

Ivan agreed. "I have a feeling Mr. Decker is a man of many secrets."

They were still standing at the top of the stairs when the glass door opened and closed, momentarily filling the air with strains of orchestral music. Carly leaned into Ivan's chest. "Is it wrong of me to think of the other nights every time I hear classical music playing?"

He laughed. "I think of it every moment."

"I wish…"

"I know. I wish we had more time."

"There are so many reasons why we would never work."

"And one very important reason why we would." He pressed a kiss to her temple and Carly hugged him around the waist.

Feeling the bulk of his protective vest instead of the warmth of his body reminded Carly how foolish she was to put her heart before the job at hand. She was pulling away when she saw the hooded figure moving near the hedge lining the wrought-iron fence. "Ivan."

Hiking up her skirt, Carly ran down the steps in pursuit. But the moment she stepped off the flagstone walk, her heel sank into the grass and mud, halting her momentum and pitching her forward. "These shoes!"

She would have landed flat on her face, but Ivan was there to catch her. "Carly, wait. We don't know what he's up to."

Leaning on his arm, she sucked the ruined heel out of the mud and stepped back onto the walkway. But when she looked to the hedges again, the cloaked figure had disappeared. She saw the guard several yards farther along the fence, heading in the opposite direction. He'd never even heard the figure to turn around. "Where did he go?" She turned toward the driveway and parking lot beyond that. "The guards will stop him at the gate, right? I didn't imagine him, did I?"

"I saw him, too." Ivan pulled her back up the steps,

hurrying toward the veranda doors and reentering the ballroom. "Where is Aleks?"

She had a more important question. "Where's your security team?"

"There." He pointed out Filip moving through the room toward the front hallway. He was talking to someone on his radio. "Hopefully, the guards outside will have detained the man in the hood and called it in."

She scanned the room for Danya, but he was nowhere to be found. "If the intruder was leaving, that means he's already put his plan into play. A bomb or whatever he intends to do tonight."

"You get to Captain Hendricks." Ivan nudged her toward the exit where Filip had disappeared. "I have to find Aleks."

Carly caught his hand and stopped him. "You aren't going anywhere without me. I'm your last line of defense, remember?"

"Fine. Then walk with me."

They circled the perimeter of the tables and guests, pausing to acknowledge someone when greeted, but otherwise moving as quickly as they could. The music that had sounded like a tender memory a moment ago now seemed inordinately loud, to the point that Carly raised her voice. "How many people do you think are here?"

"Two hundred? Three hundred?"

Galina appeared in the nearby archway, surveying the room until she saw them. She hurried across the dance floor, her dark eyes rimmed by tears, her tone panicked. "Your Highness. Officer Valentine. Please. I must show you something." Turning back several times to make sure they were following, Galina led them back into the quieter private hallway from where she'd appeared. She opened the first door just through the archway into a well-appointed office lined with walnut paneling and gold brocade drapes. "I needed a moment to myself to review the guest list and…"

"It's okay, Galina." Carly reached out and squeezed the other woman's hand. "I could tell Mr. Decker upset you. He didn't know about your late fiancé. I'm sure he didn't mean to dredge up any bad memories. Did you find a tissue?"

Instead of being grateful for the concern, Galina burst into angry tears and crossed to the desk in the center of the room. "I found *this*." She showed them a cube-shaped package wrapped in plain brown paper. *End Ivan!* was written across the top of the brown paper wrapping. "This is the guest office we worked out of this week. Is it…what I think it is?"

Carly caught her breath on a wary gasp and pulled the other woman away from the desk. There was only one thing that package could be. "We need to clear the room. I need to notify the bomb squad. Let's go."

Only Ivan was moving in the other direction. *Toward* the package. He circled the desk, studying it from every direction before he grabbed the letter opener from the blotter beside the package.

"Damn it, Ivan." She watched as he pulled the paper away from the plastic-coated wires wrapped around a brick of plastic explosive. "Careful."

"It is rigged with another cell phone," Ivan announced.

Galina wept beside her. "It's like St. Feodor again. All these people…"

"Galina," Ivan chided, coming around the desk to

take his chief of staff by the shoulders and gently shake her. "Pull yourself together. Do your job."

The dark-haired woman stared at him a moment before wiping away her tears and hugging her tablet to her chest. "What do you need?"

"I need you to find the ambassador. Tell him we have a situation. Have him make an announcement asking everyone to turn off their cell phones—make up some excuse about them interfering with the sound system. Then we need to calmly, without raising too much alarm, evacuate the building."

"Smoke from the kitchen," Carly suggested, rubbing Galina's back, trying to soothe her fear. "Tell them we need everyone outside on the veranda and the parking lot, so we can ventilate the building." She tilted her gaze to Ivan. "I can get to Chief Taylor. He can escort the mayor and some of the other dignitaries out."

Galina nodded. "Cell phones. Smoke. Calm evacuation. I'll have them use different exits so there's not a rush for the doors." Although it probably wasn't protocol for her to do so, she squeezed Ivan's hand before he pulled away. "You're the target, Your Highness. What about you? Shall I send Filip in here?"

"He's outside. He can help keep things organized out there."

"Danya? I haven't seen him, but—"

Carly turned to face her. "Ivan is my responsibility. I'll make sure he gets out safely."

"You don't want me to call anyone to help?"

"No." She walked the other woman out the door. "I want you to start the evacuation."

When she stepped back inside the office, Ivan was holding his glasses close to his temple, bending down to study the bomb again. "We need to get people out of this wing and evacuate the building." He pointed to the phone on the corner of the desk. "Call Joe on that landline. Bomb squad cannot come in with full gear or we'll have chaos. Someone could get trampled or have a heart attack."

Carly called Captain Hendricks and warned him about not using cell phones. She told him to put the SWAT team on alert, that she was bringing the prince out the back way through the veranda doors. She hung up and nodded to the door, expecting Ivan to follow. "Let's go."

"I am not going anywhere."

She tugged on his arm, pulling him away from the desk. "You're not staying here with this bomb."

"I can disarm it. It is not that complicated. Plastique. Wires. The cell phone is not counting down. I can disconnect it—"

"Just because you worked with explosives back in Moravska doesn't mean this is your job. You have a whole country you're responsible for. We need to close off this room and leave."

The music stopped abruptly, and, for a split second, Carly felt as though it was her heart that had stopped. Why was Ivan taking such a stupid risk? "Don't be a hero, Ivan. We have no idea when that bomb will go off."

He glanced up at the grandfather clock standing in the corner of the office. It was barely eleven o'clock. "I am guessing within the next hour. Today was the date on the picture he gave me."

The ambassador's voice coming over the sound system and the rising murmur of the guests responding to the unexpected interruption of their evening echoed the tension twisting through Carly. "Ivan, please."

Ticktock.

"Wait a minute…" Ivan slid the letter opener beneath a trio of wires and lifted them away from the plastique. "The phone is not connected to the explosive. There is no way to remotely detonate it." Blue eyes drilled into hers. "This bomb is a fake."

A fake? After all those threats? Naming the date of Ivan's death? Oh, hell. The hooded man moving through the hedge outside? A bomb inside the embassy? Guests evacuating to the parking lot? "Does that mean…?"

He was already running to the door. "There's another bomb."

They dashed down the hallway and stopped when they saw the orderly mass exodus leaving the building. Just like the scene at the Plaza, when they were being herded toward the parking garage. Toward the bomb.

"A car bomb killed Eduard," Carly said.

"They are taking them out to the parking lot," Ivan muttered at the same time.

Carly ran back to the phone. "I'll tell the captain."

Ivan hovered in the doorway. "We need to find Aleks."

"He's probably on his way outside with the others."

"We have to find him. Priority one is saving Aleks."

"Priority one is saving you." Carly hung up the phone and lifted the hem of her skirt to get to her weapon. She tugged on the lapel of Ivan's jacket and turned him so that she could enter and clear the hallway in front of him. "I have to get you to the SWAT van. That's what we agreed on."

Ivan pulled her hand away and backed into the office. "Go. Stay with Aleks. Get him someplace safe. I need to take this bomb apart."

"You said it wasn't a real bomb."

"Connect it to a trigger and it will take out this wing of the embassy. If we leave it alone, anyone could sneak in and do that."

"Then I'm staying with you."

Ivan pushed her out the door. "Save the prince!"

"But you…" Her back hit the opposite wall and she stood there long enough for confusion to segue into understanding. Then anger sent her charging across the hall. "Damn it, I knew something was off." She swatted his arm. Although, she wasn't sure if her anger was directed at him or toward herself for not guessing the truth. "You're not Prince Ivan. When I read those files… When I see the two of you together, you're so protective of him."

The man of purpose, the man of regal power and supreme confidence suddenly seemed unsure.

"Carly…" He reached for her, but she shrugged off his touch.

Her anger turned into a hurt she felt right down to her bones. "Aleksandr Petrovic?"

He nodded. "I tried to tell you the other night. When we were…in bed."

"But I didn't want to talk." She raked her fingers into her hair, knocking loose some of the upswept curls. She'd been a naive idiot. "I got so carried away."

"*We* got carried away." Ivan's hands were on her shoulders again. His sure, familiar hands. Only, they weren't Ivan's hands. "I should have tried harder. When you said you *felt* the truth about me, I thought—"

"That I knew you were fake? That you were lying

to me?" She pulled away and paced across the room. "I meant I knew what was in your heart."

"You do. I have never lied about that. Not about this chemistry between us. Not about my feelings for you." He caught her by the hand and turned her to face him. "You must have sensed something. You are too good a cop not to have at least suspected."

She nodded. She had suspected something. But she'd been so caught up in her feelings, compounded by the time limit on this affair, that she'd ignored what the clues had tried to tell her. "The scars. Losing your parents. Growing up poor. None of that happened to Ivan. That was *your* story you were sharing. You slipped up."

"Because you were so easy to talk to. You understood me. The real me. We have much in common. I have been living the lie for so long, I did not realize how much I needed someone who cared about me, not the role I was playing."

"If I could read Lukin, I would have discovered the truth. The details in Aleks's file are yours." She pulled away and lifted her skirt to reholster her gun. She didn't have to save this man. "What are you, Ivan's bodyguard? His friend?"

"Both. I am the geeky computer guy, as you say, who runs tech for the prince's security team. We have switched places before—years ago when we realized how much we look alike, covering duty shifts, going to class when one of us overslept, stupid stuff—nothing recent, and never on this grand a stage before. But after the bombing in St. Feodor—"

"You threw yourself over him when that bomb went off. That's how you got those scars—protecting the prince. You're protecting him now."

He nodded. "We switched places seven weeks ago, as soon as the doctor cleared me to return to duty. I'd been away recuperating—it was easy enough to change our hair, our glasses."

She touched the bruise that had been dimmed by makeup on her jaw. "The doctor knew?"

"He was familiar with my injuries—and Ivan and I both thought it was prudent for him to know the truth, in case any health issues cropped up for the real prince while we traveled."

She was silent, not sure what to say. She'd given this man her heart, her body. And he'd lied.

"I did not tell you because I promised Ivan I would not. I wanted to. I wanted you to know the truth. But my sworn duty is to my future king."

"I understand duty. I understand why you lied. The more people who know who an undercover operative is, the harder it becomes to keep it a secret."

"Yes, *dorogoy*. You understand, but do you forgive me?"

Dorogoy. Darling. Did he really love her? She pressed her hands to either side of her head, wishing she could make the hurt and mistrust go away. But she couldn't. Not in this moment. Not when she wasn't even sure what *she* was feeling anymore.

She pointed to the desk. "We have bigger issues to deal with right now. I'll get Aleks…" She shook her head, clearing her thoughts to at least one thing. Duty. "I'll get Prince Ivan out to the van. You see what you can do about that bomb." She paused in the doorway and turned back to those piercing blue eyes. "Do not blow yourself up. We have more to talk about."

Then she ran to join the exiting crowd.

Chapter Twelve

His one fear had been that he would hurt her. He hadn't realized how much seeing that look of betrayal in Carly's beautiful eyes would hurt him.

Aleksandr—had he really gotten so used to thinking of himself as Ivan?—couldn't shake the sense of loss he felt when he saw Carly running away from him. But he could compartmentalize his feelings and deal with the job at hand. The military had trained him to do that. His oath to his future king demanded it.

While the grandfather clock ticked away in the corner, he searched through the desk to find tools he could use. A small pair of scissors. Tweezers. Although this explosive wasn't rigged to blow, he worried that any spark from the cell phone might set off the C-4 accidentally. That meant untangling his way through these wires and removing the phone without building up any kind of static charge as he worked.

He pulled off his glasses that did more to distort his view of the world than correct his slight astigmatism. But they'd been a necessary part of his disguise to pass as the prince, who was nearsighted. He clipped the first few wires and unwound another to pull the phone free of the explosive. Then, he pried the phone apart and removed the battery.

Crisis averted. He breathed in a sigh of momentary relief. Time to make sure the prince was safe.

In that deep breath, Aleksandr caught a whiff of faint perfume lingering in the air. Carly didn't wear perfume—she smelled like the delicious foods she cooked. This was more exotic. Was that Galina's scent? She'd been gone for nearly fifteen minutes. Shouldn't her perfume have dissipated by now?

Sniffing the air, he followed the scent to the drapes at the window and pulled them aside. The window was unlatched, hanging open a fraction of an inch. All the windows on this side of the building had the same floor-to-ceiling design as the veranda doors. Had the bomber come in this way? Or gotten out?

His gaze dropped past the excess folds of the heavy gold brocade to a swatch of dark, dusty material stashed behind the curtain. Aleksandr knelt to grasp what was clearly a sleeve. A collar. A hooded coat. He lifted the coat to his nose, breathed in the overpowering perfume and residue of sweat from a hot summer afternoon, and then he cursed.

Galina had worn this. Tonight. On the Plaza. A replica of the coat worn by the rebel bomber in St. Feodor. Her perfume was expensive and distinct.

Why? Why would the prince's chief of staff want to kill him? Galina Honchar wasn't a political rebel. She had no ties to criminal families. Aleksandr shook his head and pushed to his feet. The whys didn't matter. This was over. He knew who had murdered Eduard Nagy, who had poisoned Frank Valentine, who had tried to kill the prince.

"Carly!" She'd be out of earshot by now, but he called to her, anyway. They were a team. Together, they'd found the answers he needed. "Carly!" He whirled around to see the dark-haired woman standing in the doorway. "Galina."

She held her tablet in one hand and a gun in the other. A gun she pointed squarely at him.

"The building is clear, Your Highness." She eyed the dismantled device on top of the desk. "You took apart my little toy." She strolled toward him. She set the tablet on the corner of the desk and typed in a number on the screen. "But I have another."

He tossed the coat back into its heap, wondering if she had any kind of skill with that gun and just how badly he'd get hurt if he charged her. But more than the gun, he worried about what the numbers and the blinking prompt on her tablet meant. So he stood his ground. For now. "We know about the car bomb, Galina. KCPD and embassy security are searching for it right now."

She trailed her finger around the frame of the tablet. "Yes, but will they find it before I press this button and kill, I don't know, seven innocent people? Just like St. Feodor? Maybe more? All I have to do is send this message."

If she'd been crying earlier, there was no sign of those tears now in her cold, dark eyes. This woman was beyond feeling anything but the rage that consumed her. "You've taken apart many things that were mine. You've destroyed so much."

Aleksandr took a step forward, testing her reflexes. The gun never wavered. He put up his hands in a placating gesture, pretending that understanding made a difference. But he wasn't about to retreat. He had to get that tablet away from her. He had to get past that gun first. "This is about Konrad, the man you loved. This is all about revenge."

Galina nodded. "I simply wanted to poison you—to see you die a painful, horrible death. The Loyalists would have taken the blame for the threats and your death, and all of Lukinburg would understand the pain that I have suffered because of you. But the apples got away from me. You wanted to give them to your girl-friend. Your stupid girlfriend! After that mistake, I real-ized I would have to be more clever. My Konrad taught me many things. How to love. How to build a bomb. How to fire a gun. But he didn't teach me how to live without him. How to live with his senseless death. He died protecting you."

"Konrad's death is no excuse for this." He channeled every imperial syllable of the prince's tone he could. "You will kill many innocent people. Kon would not want that."

"I want that!" She stepped toward him, using the gun to direct him away from the window while she picked up the coat. "My world was perfect until you came along and started changing everything. What was wrong with the old ways? I was happy. In love. Konrad was alive." She tossed the coat onto the desk. "That stupid reporter nearly caught me in here. Otherwise, I'd have cleaned up after myself. Just like I've always cleaned up after your messes. Everything had to be just the way His Royal Highness the Prince of Lukinburg wanted it." Aleksandr countered her position, inching closer to the tablet. She motioned him into the chair beside her and ordered him to sit. Feeling the barrel of the gun press-ing against his skull gave him no choice but to oblige.

"*You* made enemies, and *he* paid the price. Now you're going to pay." She circled the desk again, turning the tablet to face her. "What a tragic, humiliating end to your visit to Kansas City. You will die. Your people will die. Your regime will fail. You can't stop me."

Carly Valentine's kick-ass tone sounded from the doorway behind Galina. "I can."

The color drained from Galina's face before Aleksandr saw the flash of sparkling turquoise behind her. Galina raised both hands, including the gun, as Carly circled around her, her own gun trained on the back of Galina's head as she reached for the weapon to disarm her.

"KCPD. You are under arrest—"

He saw the grim determination flatten Galina's mouth. "Carly!"

Galina ducked and swung around, cracking the gun against Carly's arm, sending Carly's weapon flying. Galina lunged toward the desk.

"Keep her away from that tablet!" Aleksandr shot to his feet, but it really was no contest.

There was a fistful of hair, a kick to the knees and Galina was pinned to the floor. Carly kicked one gun out of reach beside the door and twisted around to locate where her gun had landed. Galina tried to roll away from her, and she was forced to put a knee in Galina's back and hold her in place. "Really, lady? You want to keep fighting me?"

Aleksandr picked up the tablet. "Will turning this off set off the bomb?" he demanded.

"Go to hell," was Galina's answer.

"I will take that as a no." Good thing he knew a little bit about computers. He disabled the tablet's Wi-Fi connection, closed down the screen and pried open the back to remove the battery, just as he'd pulled apart the phone.

He heard footsteps running in the hallway as he set down the tablet. He was pulling off his belt to give Carly something to bind Galina's wrists with when a trio of men burst through the door. He was not a happy man. It didn't matter that Ivan was flanked by both Filip and Danya. He shouldn't be anywhere close to this traitorous witch. "What are you doing here?"

"Are you all right?" Ivan asked. "Carly?"

Filip and Danya must not know they had the real prince with them. "Get him out of here."

The two bodyguards rushed forward, pulling Aleksandr to his feet and flanking him. But Ivan wouldn't listen. "Galina Honchar, I accuse you of treason. Danya, take her into custody."

"Shut up, party boy." Galina was beyond reasoning now. "You're a waste of my time."

The prince stepped forward. "How dare you speak to your future king like that?"

"Future king?" Galina repeated.

"What?" Filip and Danya stood there agape.

Danya released Aleksandr first and moved to stand beside Ivan. "You are the prince?"

Ivan grinned. "Surprise."

Danya turned on Filip. "Did you know this?"

Filip glared at Aleksandr. "I did not."

"What are you saying?" Galina seemed more stunned than either of the men. "You? With all your sightseeing and flirting… I could have killed you a dozen times. Those nights we worked late at the hotel while he was with her?" Galina's roar of frustration was almost feral. "I will kill you!"

Carly hadn't spotted her gun yet, but Galina had. Fueled by whatever grief and anger was driving her, she twisted away from Carly and grabbed the gun from beneath the desk. She rolled, fired.

Aleksandr leaped in front of the prince and felt the bullet strike him in the chest. Pain blossomed on the right side of his rib cage as if he'd been struck by a rocket.

"No!" Carly shouted, her concern followed just as quickly by a curse. And then she switched her focus entirely and took Galina down again. She wrestled control of the gun and jammed it against Galina's neck before the woman finally stilled. "Is he hurt?"

While Filip and Ivan helped him sit up, Danya went to Carly. He picked up the discarded belt and wound it tightly around Galina's arms above her elbows. "This will hold her for now."

Carly shook her head. "She's not getting off another shot. I'm not letting go. Is he hurt?" she demanded.

"I am all right," he reassured her, breathing through the bruising pain. He unbuttoned his shirt and peeled it back to reveal the flattened bullet that had lodged in his protective vest. The shot might not have cracked a rib, but it sure did feel as if it had. He wished he could read the message in Carly's green eyes. Worry? Anger? He still reassured her. "The wind is knocked from my chest. I will be all right."

And then he turned his attention to the prince, who helped him to his feet. "What are you doing here? You're supposed to be safe in the SWAT van."

"Galina wasn't with the rest of the entourage. Neither were you. I was worried. I may be a prince, but I am also your friend. Your very grateful friend."

"Yeah, this is touching," Carly groused. "I need handcuffs." Joe Hendricks and two members of the SWAT team entered the room. She glanced up at him and saw him holding his side. "And a medic."

One of the officers immediately knelt and pulled out his cuffs to take Galina into custody. The other went to the desk to examine the explosive.

"You okay, Valentine?" Joe asked, helping Carly to her feet. That's when Aleksandr noticed that Carly had taken off her shoes—or lost them in the mud outside. "We found the second bomb in the royal limo. Bomb squad is taking it apart now."

Aleksandr moved to the desk. "This one has been dismantled, but they will want to dispose of the components properly." He handed Joe the tablet. "Take this, too. Any good computer tech in your crime lab should be able to trace when she used it to set off the bomb that killed Eduard."

"I'll send someone in to clear the room. SWAT Team Two is doing a full sweep of the building. We'll debrief later." He nodded to the two SWAT officers. "Get her out of here." He turned to the real prince. "Your Highness. If you would kindly stay where we put you this time. It'd be a hell of a lot easier to keep you safe."

Filip agreed. "We will make sure he remains secure. Danya?"

Suddenly, the room was empty except for him and Carly. He got a glimpse of one gorgeous leg as she pulled up her dress to holster her weapon again.

She didn't seem affected by his obvious attraction to her. "You need to be checked by a medic."

When she headed for the door, he blocked her path. "We need to talk."

"Ivan… I mean, Aleksandr. Aleks? What do I call you?"

He took a deep breath. This wouldn't be easy, but he had to make this right. "My friends call me Aleks."

Her lips warped into a frown before she extended her hand to shake his. "Nice to meet you, Aleks. I'm Carly Valentine. I have issues with people who lie to me."

"And you are always honest with me." He tightened his grip and held on when she would have pulled away. "I am sorry I have hurt you. That was never my intent. But I had to keep my word to the prince. I became him to keep him safe."

"You just took a bullet for him. Good job. You're a man of your word. May I have my hand back?"

"No." He pulled her into his arms. She put up a token fight but stopped the moment he winced at a shove against his bruised ribs. "I wanted you to love me. The man whose parents were murdered, the man who served six years in the army." He lifted her hand to his face and held it where she had touched him so many times before. "The man with the scars. Is there any way you would give Aleksandr Petrovic a second chance? One where I do not lie to you?"

The grandfather clock chimed midnight.

Carly rested her hands on his chest for a moment, then busied her fingers rebuttoning his shirt and straightening his tie. When the chimes stopped, she pulled away, as if that was her cue to leave. "You have to go back to Lukinburg. Today. We survived the deadline. Your traitor has been identified. No more bombs.

You have to protect Ivan. I don't even have a passport. We'll probably never see each other again."

"Carly—"

"I'm glad for the time we had. Truly. I felt special. It felt...real."

"Aleksandr." Danya called to him from the doorway. "His Highness would like to speak to you."

"You'd better not keep your boss waiting." Carly put on a brave smile that made him feel as if he'd taken that bullet to the heart. "You said one week. You never lied about that." He retreated to the door but wasn't ready to leave her. "I knew about the time limit on this assignment. I understood I was never going to have a prince of my own—no matter how much I loved him."

Everything inside him went perfectly still, then bloomed with hope. "You love...?"

Danya grumbled a curse. "Petrovic. We must make a statement to the police and then get the prince back to our hotel."

Carly waved him away. "Go. Duty calls. We both know how that is."

Duty. How many times in his life had he chosen duty over love?

How many times had he even been given the choice?

Aleksandr cupped the side of Carly's neck and tipped her face up to cover her mouth in one last hard, passionate kiss. *"Obicham te, dorogoy."*

Then he drew his finger across her cheek and followed Danya down the hallway.

Chapter Thirteen

"Carly! Rise and shine. You have a visitor."

Carly pulled the pillow over her head to muffle the noise of her brother knocking on her bedroom door. When it didn't stop, she threw the pillow across the room and sat up. "I was up late, Frank. Fix your own breakfast for once."

"I ate three hours ago."

She glanced over at the clock. It was nearly noon. Maybe he was looking for lunch. She didn't have much of an appetite herself. Possibly because she was still full of the pint of coffee ice cream she'd eaten when she'd gotten home from the ball. Or maybe because after that self-pity pig-out, she'd cried in the shower until the water had run cold. Then she'd put on her sweats and had run a couple of miles around the neighborhood to clear her head, falling into bed as the sun was coming up. She might have a better grasp on everything that had happened this past week—she might even have a sense of acceptance over the way things had ended with Ivan, no, make that Aleksandr. But she was still too emotionally drained and exhausted to be hungry.

Or social.

Or nice to her brother.

"Go away, Frank!"

"No can do, Carly Barley. It's official police business. He says he needs to talk to Officer Valentine."

Carly tipped her head back and groaned. "Give me five minutes to get presentable."

"Okeydoke."

She was out of bed and freshening up in the bathroom before she heard him head back upstairs. The stack of condoms she'd stolen from Jesse's old room sat on the counter beside the sink, taunting her. Before the memory of that special night overtook her and left her sobbing again, she opened a drawer and dumped them inside. She pulled on a pair of cutoffs and tank top, twisted her hair into a braid and hurried up the stairs, barefoot.

"Who is it, Frank? I'm on vaca..."

"I brought you a present." She froze at the deep, accented voice she found so sexy. Aleksandr Petrovic, once known as His Royal Highness Prince Ivan of Lukinburg, handed her a large, rectangular box with a turquoise ribbon tied around it. He set it in her hands and she nearly dropped it, partly because of the unexpected weight, and partly because she was in shock at seeing him here. He caught the box before it hit the floor and held it out to her again. "I see that you can use a pair of shoes."

Carly couldn't look away from those blue eyes. "What are you doing here? Aren't you supposed to be on a flight to Lukinburg right now? It'll be a long walk home."

"Perhaps not."

"Okay, a long swim."

"I am staying in Kansas City."

Carly blinked. He was staying? She blinked again. "But…" She dropped the box to the floor and closed the distance between them, wrapping her arms around his waist and snuggling in to the place she liked best. "I'm sorry."

His arms folded around her and he whispered against her hair. "For what, *dorogoy*?"

"For getting stuck in my head and not listening to my heart. I felt stupid that I hadn't seen your deception. But then I realized you had to be really good at your job to pull that off, and I admire you for that. You said we would fake a relationship, but every bit of it was real except for your name. I didn't want you to go last night. I don't want you to go now. Wait. Why are you staying?" She pushed against him to see into his eyes and immediately apologized when he grimaced in pain.

"You're hurt?"

"Some bruising and swelling. The doctor says I will be fine."

"Carls, my dear." Her father had gotten off the sofa to join them in the foyer. "The guy's been wounded in action. Ask him in for coffee. Frank? Let's go out back and inspect that work you've been doin' on my deck." He reached out to shake Aleks's hand. "You know she's got two big brothers and me lookin' out for her if you don't treat her right."

"Dad!"

But Aleks grinned. "I would be more scared of her than any of you if I screw this up."

Her father laughed. "Then you do know her. You're okay, Mr. Prince. I like you." He ended the handshake to hug Carly to his side. "Is this what you want?"

She hugged him back. "*He's* what I want."

He kissed the top of her head. "Then go for it. We'll give you two some privacy."

"Thanks, Dad."

Several minutes later, Carly was wearing the burgundy boots she'd admired when she'd been shopping for evening gowns, and she was sitting in Aleks's lap on the couch. "They're beautiful. I love them." She gave him a quick kiss. "Thank you."

Aleks wore another suit and crisp white shirt, but this time without the tie. He looked downright casual and infinitely handsome. He skimmed his hand up and down her leg, from the cuff of her shorts to the top of her new boots and back. The friction of his gentle caress warmed her skin and heated things up deeper inside. "I did not think you would like another pair of those sparkly heels. These make you smile."

"You make me smile." She stroked the fine silk of his beard along his jaw. "You're sure you aren't in any danger from Galina Honchar? Or Lukin rebels? I'd rather not play bodyguard again if I don't have to."

"Galina is being extradited to Lukinburg where she will stand trial. Danya…" Carly tightened her fingers against his skin when he hesitated. "He was not happy to have his brother's death be the excuse she used to assassinate the prince. He is taking some time off. But I advised Ivan to ask him to take over as security chief, and encourage Filip to retire."

"Sounds like a smart plan," Carly agreed. "Now tell me again why you're not going home to St. Feodor with Ivan?"

He pressed a kiss into her palm and smiled. "I asked to be assigned to Kansas City to represent Lukinburg's interests here. There may be a time when I go back to my country. For a visit. But by then, you will have a passport. There is much I would like to show you, just as I have seen much of your beautiful city." He nuzzled the shell of her ear, then kissed his way down her neck until he found the bundle of nerves that made her squiggle in his lap. He smiled against her skin as it heated beneath his touch. "I cannot make you a princess, but perhaps you would be content to be a geeky computer nerd's wife."

"I already said yes." Carly captured his jaw between her hands and kissed him again. "Do you really love me?"

"That is what *obicham te* means."

The guttural expression of his feelings warmed her as thoroughly as his touch. "I want to learn more of your language."

"I will teach you."

"Will you take me dancing?"

"Every night if you wish." He smiled. "Since we are laying down the ground rules of this very real relationship, I know that you wish to continue your work with KCPD. They are very lucky to have you. But you will still have time to bake me a pie?"

"What flavor would you like?"

His smile faded, but the intensity of those blue eyes never dimmed. "Will you love me for who I really am?"

"Aleksandr Petrovic—I didn't fall in love with a prince. I fell in love with a man." She traced the scar that cut through his beard and then touched her lips to the brave, vulnerable spot. "I fell in love with *you*."

* * * * *

THE COLTON SHERIFF

ADDISON FOX

For Allie Burton, Tracy Garrett & Lorraine Heath.

My best memories of Colorado
include the three of you.

Chapter One

Aisha Allen took a slice of piping-hot pizza, folded it in half and bit in. Warm, gooey cheese blended with the tangy bite of tomato sauce, all wrapped up in a doughy pocket that was the very essence of life.

Which made it the perfect antidote to the increasingly gruesome pictures of the dead she'd stared at for the past three hours.

Six bodies. Or seven if you counted the body of Lucy Reese, aka Bianca Rouge, a Vegas prostitute inconveniently called to Roaring Springs, Colorado, the prior January to entertain a high-end client.

And Aisha was counting.

Technically, she didn't have a right to the photos or the background details already collected by law enforcement. Her credentials as a psychologist extended only to the projects she was actually invited to consult on. But Trey needed help and since she was in a position to give it, she wasn't going to back down.

Besides, it gave her an additional opportunity to keep an eye on him. He was her best friend and they hadn't spent many days since the age of eight without talking. Even in the years she spent up in New York getting her "fancy Ivy League degree," as he loved to tease her about, they'd remained close.

And if she'd like to be closer, well, that was on her. The man had his mind on other things, not his moony-eyed best friend. Their current sheriff and all-around most honorable citizen, Trey Colton, was the heartbeat of Bradford County. And he was in the fight of his life:

A serial killer on the loose dubbed by the press as the "Avalanche Killer."

A battle brewing for reelection in November that was going to be horribly tight and already fraught with contention.

And an extended family that was…challenging on the very best of days.

No one would ever accuse the Colton family of being quiet, unobtrusive or unnoticeable. They collectively lived life large, and that would have been true in Roaring Springs even without the family legacy of a former US president who bore the Colton surname.

Having a legendary politician in the family only made the spotlight that much brighter.

Aisha knew Trey wasn't above using the Colton name when he had to, but he hated depending on it. Just like he hated what was going on in his town right now.

Patting her lips with a napkin, she wiped lingering flour dust from her fingers and spread out several of the images. Six bodies, all in various stages of decomposition, from the more recent to practically nothing but bones. The two oldest bodies had also been discovered the farthest down in the shallow grave. Enough depth to hide them and protect them from the elements, but close enough to the surface that they'd been discovered with the impact of a late-spring avalanche.

Although all the victims would need to be identified and ultimately processed as individual crimes, the more recent bodies held Aisha's focus. Especially the characteristics that appeared common. Eerily so, she thought as she pulled one of the photos closer. Sabrina Gilford, twenty-two, was identified as the most recent victim, her long, dyed dark hair and eyes two of her most distinctive features.

Along with the hair color match, she was roughly the same age as the other victims and she had the same physical build. Medium height. Slender. Petite frame. The sort of young woman who turned heads when she walked into a room.

A young woman was supposed to turn heads, Aisha thought, the frustration and anger for these unfortunate six rising up in her chest. You were supposed to be young and free and silly and sometimes a little stupid. You weren't supposed to be dead.

And all these victims would still be missing if it weren't for the overwhelming avalanche that still defied explanation. They'd had late snows before—Mother Nature was always unpredictable if nothing else—but this was something else. A large, prodigious disaster that had killed a ski guest at The Lodge as it did its destructive work.

A while later these six bodies were discovered during the clearing of brush and debris. Although two of the six had been identified, Sabrina Gilford and another young woman who'd gone missing in Roaring Springs the prior winter, April Thomas, Trey was working day and night to identify the others. It was maddeningly slow work and had kept Trey and his best deputy, Daria Bloom, in constant motion for months now.

And then, a few weeks ago, they had a new, potentially disturbing problem fall in their laps. Trey's cousin Skye had gone missing. Marketing director for The Colton Empire—an enterprise that encompassed nearly half of Roaring Springs, including The Lodge, the town's major ski resort—Skye was vivacious and always on the move. Aisha had met her off and on through the years at various events held by Trey's parents and even now she could picture the once small redhead who used to race around Trey's parents' ranch with her quieter twin, Phoebe, in tow.

It was her busy, whirlwind personality that they were all counting on now. Skye rarely sat still and they'd all retained a stubborn hope that she was off on an adventure. Hopefully as far away from Roaring Springs as she could be. Only none of them could ward off the more disturbing idea that Skye had attracted the attention of the Avalanche Killer. Her vivid red hair didn't fit the pattern, but beyond that, her slim frame and age were a direct match.

Thoughts of Skye were inevitably tied to The Lodge and the strange circumstances that had led to the discovery of the bodies. Even with his 24/7 work schedule running down leads, Trey had spoken more than once about the circumstances that caused the avalanche. He was so busy dealing with the voracious press as he tried to investigate the murders that any further investigation into Mother Nature's vagaries had to wait.

Even as the freak incident clearly gnawed away at him.

The ski slopes were groomed regularly, specifically to avoid nature's wrath in the form of an avalanche. Yet here was one, overpowering in scale and scope and late in the season, no less. It was odd. And it was one more thing on Trey's overfull plate that Aisha knew bothered him.

She knew a lot of things about Trey. The broad shoulders that looked as impressive in his sheriff's uniform as in a casual T-shirt while jogging around Roaring Springs. The firm cut of his jaw, lightly stubbled when he wasn't on duty. Which was increasingly rare since he always seemed to be on the job. Or working on behalf of the role he'd sworn to uphold to the best of his abilities, even if that best had his delicious brown eyes bloodshot more often than not lately from lack of sleep.

Trey Colton was a man working off the very edge of his reserves and she was damned if she'd let him come up short. It was why she'd finished up a challenging afternoon session with one of her patients and raced over here. Back to the gruesome files and the endless clues that didn't seem to go anywhere.

"Aw, jeez, Aish, don't look at those."

She turned at the rich, husky tones, unsurprised to see Trey standing just inside the conference room at the Bradford County Sheriff's Office. She hadn't let him know she was coming but had figured the scent of pizza would eventually give him an inkling that she was there. The fact she'd had three other pies delivered along with hers, for distribution around the office, would only smooth her way if anyone was bothered by her taking up space in one of their conference rooms.

"How am I supposed to help you catch a killer if I don't look at the bastard's handiwork?"

"Still." Trey had already dived into the pizza, dragging out the half that was his—pepperoni and sausage with extra cheese. "Looking at that'll make you lose your appetite. Not to mention any belief in humanity and basic decency."

He took a large bite of pizza, momentary relief closing his eyelids to half-mast. "You ordered from Bruno's."

"Of course I did." She reached for another slice of cheese, pleased to turn this time into a shared dinner. "Would I deign to order anywhere else?"

He grinned at that. "No. Of course not. That New York education was good for more than just a psychology degree."

"Damn straight it was."

She'd not only learned the ins and outs of the human psyche, as well as the proper ratio of toppings to sauce, while gathering an education in the Big Apple, but she'd learned a tremendous amount about her own heart, too. Despite what she'd always assumed about herself, it was shockingly fragile.

Breakable, even.

And she'd been unwilling to do much to risk it since. Pining over her best friend was about as far as she was going to go, that lingering hurt keeping her from making any moves to change the status quo between them.

"So what have we got here?" He polished off the end of his first slice and reached for another. "We've all been staring at the same photos for weeks now and nothing's turned up. Other than time of death from the medical examiner and estimated ages and builds on all six women, there are very few lines to tug."

"Sabrina appears to be the only local," Aisha pointed out. "That's a place to start."

"Daria homed in on that, too. It would go a long way toward explaining why we haven't focused on any missing persons in the search for these women at the point they were murdered. But they're also unidentified, so that may be a false assumption."

"But the few missing persons you ran don't match the victims?" Aisha pressed him, well aware his trusty deputy would have been all over those runs in a New York minute.

"No." Trey polished off the last of his crust. "But let's play out your theory. The killer has been stalking victims elsewhere, then dragging them back to Roaring Springs like trophies. Why change patterns with Sabrina?"

"Serial killers do change pattern. It's infrequent but it does happen. Maybe Sabrina was a replacement for the killer's intended victim? Or maybe it's a point of escalation."

"There haven't been any reports anywhere in the state of a young woman escaping a killer's clutches. Isn't it usually an incident like that when a killer scrambles to replace the victim, even if elements aren't perfect?"

She and Trey had been over this already and Aisha knew she was grasping a bit. But everything in the details they'd found so far suggested things were escalating with this killer, who was growing even more dangerous than they had previously envisioned.

"Besides," Trey spoke again, his attention on the photos spread across the table. "If you're doing your dirty work somewhere else, why come back to the scene of your crimes?"

Trey's insight matched hers, but Aisha hadn't had a good answer for it. *Was* her theory about the killer escalating off track? The time between the fifth and sixth victims suggested her hunch was indeed correct, but it was far too big a leap to assume this was the killer's only grave site, too. Colorado was a big, wide-open state and the vast, undeveloped expanses of mountain and forest would offer any number of places to hide bodies.

But… Selecting a local victim *was* still a break in pattern.

"The killer could be growing bolder. Hunting prey closer to home because the need is so great." Aisha sighed and set down her pizza to pull the photo of Sabrina Gilford closer. "Which is the last thing you need the press to get a hold of. They'll have everyone within a five-hundred-mile radius scared out of their minds."

"One more thing Evigan can toss at me for all the ways my county is a public danger."

"Barton Evigan is an idiot who doesn't deserve to have gotten this far."

"But he has." Trey's dark gaze met hers over the scarred office table and the sinister deeds it held. "He's a true opponent for my reelection and I can't afford to dismiss him."

Barton Evigan had seemingly rose up out of the woodwork, a recent entrant into the race for county sheriff. With Trey's stellar reputation and the endorsement of all the local businesses and local law enforcement agencies, it was a surprise—a disheartening one—to see how fast Evigan had amassed support against Trey.

At the heart of it all seemed to be the insistence that, as a Colton, Trey was in the pocket of his wealthy extended family. And on a singular occasion, Evigan had added in a subtly racist slur suggesting Trey didn't have the smarts for the job.

Aisha had tried a few times to point out the man's remark but Trey would have none of it, his only response that he *was* a Colton and they *did* have several unsolved crimes in his county. End of story.

Only it wasn't.

She might be hopelessly infatuated with Trey Colton, but that hadn't blinded her to his talents or his true nature. He was a good and honorable man and Bradford County was lucky to have him as sheriff. Trey ran a tight ship and, until the Avalanche Killer and all the ensuing madness surrounding the missing women, had actually reduced crime in the area. A fact the local tourism industry depended upon.

The Colton family wasn't the only one to run a major resort in the area. The Colton Empire might be home to the largest, but it wasn't the only place to ski or vacation. All local businesses that depended on the patronage of outside visitors had benefited from Trey's steady hand and outstanding leadership.

Her gaze drifted over those horrible photos once more, the truth of the situation stamped in each one of them. No matter how much good Trey had done for the county, if they didn't get a handle on this Avalanche Killer soon, his career was in jeopardy.

She'd be damned if she was going to let that happen.

TREY COLTON RUBBED a hand over the back of his head, the close-cropped hair against his fingers already too long. He'd needed a haircut for three days and hell if he'd had five minutes to breathe to even go get one.

"I wasn't suggesting you dismiss Evigan," Aisha said, her dark gaze serious. "But I think the people who know you and who've admired your work are going to continue to give you the leeway to do that work. If there is a serial killer on the loose, this isn't something that gets solved in a matter of days."

"We live in an on-demand world, Aish. People expect this is as easy as solving a crime in eight binged episodes."

"Fact versus fiction," she shot back.

"Or the skewed reality we all now live with."

"Well, it's a reality that sucks."

A hard laugh escaped his chest. "That it does."

And just like that, his best friend in the world managed to make him laugh and make the whole situation seem a little less dire.

People thought she was so serious, those dark brown eyes always focused a few feet beyond everyone else. He'd heard others call her aloof but he knew her to be anything but. Aisha Allen was an outstanding psychologist and a passionate advocate for her clients, always determined to find treatments to help them cope with their inner pain and struggles.

She was also his oldest friend in the world.

When they were together, he saw her less serious side. Silly, even, when she got going doing an imitation of one of his wacky Colton relatives or teasing him about a long-forgotten memory of one of the millions they'd shared together. And he truly appreciated her support during this whole Avalanche Killer crisis, as well as throughout the subsequent disappearance of his cousin Skye.

However, even with that support, he was in the midst of a firefight. That bastard Barton Evigan was a problem. Trey didn't think himself above an opponent—the exact opposite actually. The people of Bradford County deserved a slate of qualified candidates for the role of sheriff. Just because he wanted the job didn't mean he deserved it on a shoo-in.

But Evigan was something else. The man had little to no actual experience and when questioned on that fact he deflected and diverted the question, immediately going on the offensive on Trey's record. Trey and his team had closed hundreds of cases over the past three and a half years since taking on the role of sheriff. A fact that was increasingly forgotten in the constant attention over a serial killer.

Which meant he had to work harder. Those poor women discovered on the side of a mountain deserved only his best, no matter what it took. Their focused search for his cousin, Skye, required the same.

Turning toward Aisha again, he tapped the closest photo. "Okay. Walk me through it again. What do we know from the bodies?"

"Assuming this was his only burial site, and that's a mighty large *if*, the time between kills was significant. Nearly five years between the first two. Then several years between two, three and four."

"And after?" he prodded.

"That's where things pick up. Either the killer had a trigger of some sort or wasn't able to slake his thirst."

"Him?" Trey homed in.

"Figure of speech. Serial killing is predominantly done by males and should be your prioritization on suspects. But for the purposes of speaking to the press, no gender should be used."

Trey didn't miss the light wash of goose bumps that rose up over her dark skin. He laid a hand there, covering her forearm. "We don't have to do this now. It's late and this is hardly a topic that ensures a good night's sleep."

"We owe it to those women, Trey. And we owe it to Skye."

"But—"

She laid a hand over his. "I'm fine. Let's just push through."

She was fine, of that he had no doubt. The woman

understood the human psyche in ways he couldn't fathom. A few summers back he caught her leisure-reading a biography of Jack the Ripper and when asked about it, she said the man fascinated her. That she enjoyed probing into the mind and trying to understand the mysteries there.

While he enjoyed it in his fiction, he wasn't all that keen on having it in his real life.

Which made his next thought that much harder to say, yet somehow safe when voiced in a room with only his best friend for company. "Would you think less of me if I said I wasn't fine?"

"No."

"Because I'm not." He pushed back his chair, the heavy scrape of metal legs over the linoleum tile a scratchy counterpoint to the drumming in his chest. "I want to be okay but all I can think about are those women. Worse, then I start imagining my cousin and what could have happened to her."

Trey deliberately tamped down on that train of thought. They were all desperate to find Skye, but also determined to stay focused on the positive. She was missing but that didn't mean she'd become the target of a serial killer. They had to believe her disappearance was the work of some other force. Something wild and crazy, just like Skye.

"I know." Aisha nodded. "I know it's hard."

"I look around here and see all the beauty and wild-ness of Colorado. The mountains and the trees and all the wide-open spaces. I see it as a place to breathe. To find myself. And all those women found was death. Quite brutally, too, based on the forensics."

"They did." Aisha picked up the various photos and

turned them over. "Classic serial killer behaviors of dominance and a deep desire to hurt another. To not only kill but to torture before doing so."

"A coward who gets off on causing fear."

"Yes," she confirmed.

"Right here. Under our noses."

He let out a sigh, his gaze drifting once more over the box of pizza. The hunger that had carried him into the room had vanished and now he was left with a strange emptiness roiling in his gut in its place.

All of it had happened right under his nose. And if he didn't get a handle on it, it was going to happen again. Of that he had no doubt.

Chapter Two

Aisha settled herself in the last row of the public meeting room at the back of the Bradford County Community Center. As county seat, Roaring Springs had a number of buildings devoted to local government matters, and this one saw regular use. Public hearings, voting and a host of other issues were considered, discussed and decided inside these four walls.

She'd never been a particularly large joiner, but she'd discovered her interest in public discussion once Trey had taken on his job as sheriff. What had begun as support of her best friend remained that way, but it had given her new perspective into the workings of local government. Sometimes mundane and often quite functional, Aisha had to admit it was never boring. And it gave continued perspective on her life's work: human nature in all its glory.

Tonight's agenda was an open discussion of the Avalanche Killer's crimes and proposed increases in local law enforcement. Which was a bit of a joke since the FBI had already descended en masse to deal with the situation. This was their domain, and even though bodies hadn't been found across multiple states, the Feds weren't leaving this one alone.

Still, Aisha knew this hearing was a prime opportunity for Trey to make his authority clear to their citizenry. She saw several others scattered around the room, there to give him the additional support of friendly faces. His parents, Calvin and Audrey, sat in the middle toward the front. Close enough to be supportive but far enough away to give him space. His trusted deputy, Daria Bloom, was in the front row. She sat tall and straight in her seat, her uniform as immaculately pressed at six o'clock at night as it no doubt had been that morning.

Aisha continued her perusal. She eyed a few more people scattered around the room, including several Coltons, a few resort employees from The Lodge as well as the local hotel and spa, The Chateau, and a guy Trey had already pointed out to her as FBI, Agent Stefan Roberts.

She'd nearly turned her attention back to the front when her gaze alighted on the doorway and the last-minute entrant to the meeting.

Barton Evigan.

He strode in as if he owned the place, a smirk on his face. It was a step up from the perpetual sneer she usually saw there but not by much. He had a few people with him, a guy she recognized as his campaign manager and a slim, mousy woman who had to be his wife. They all took seats in the front row.

So not good.

Aisha pulled out her notes and scanned them once more. Although she and Trey had kept her involvement with the crimes to themselves, she had prepared a few arguments as a Roaring Springs resident who was concerned about the killings and who had a background qualified enough to raise the proper points. Nothing she'd prepared would contradict anything already publicized in the news, but it would put a clinician's spin on the details in hopes of calming some riled nerves. Based on the rumors she'd already heard since walking in, the town's citizens were ready to lock up all young women between the ages of fifteen and thirty in hopes of keeping them safe.

The murmuring that started behind her pulled Aisha from her thoughts, and she finally turned around, curious to what had created the hubbub. The meeting still had about five minutes until things were called to order so it wasn't that slight buzz that swelled just before things started. It was only when a few people still milling around the back parted that Aisha saw the reason for the fuss.

They had a genuine movie star in their midst.

Obviously hoping to sneak in unrecognized, Prescott Reynolds had missed that mark completely. He had Phoebe Colton, one of Trey's younger cousins, on his arm. Although the two of them presented a united front, clearly in love by their connected body language and close heads bent toward each other, their stiff shoulders telegraphed they were both uncomfortable, as well.

Aisha didn't know Phoebe well, but the moment she caught the young woman's eyes, she waved the couple over. The back row still had plenty of room, people anxious for any drips or drabs of gossip having filled in the front. Their voracious appetites now worked in Prescott's and Phoebe's favor.

Phoebe nodded at the invitation and in moments the two of them were seated beside Aisha.

"Thank you for the quick rescue," Phoebe whispered as she settled into her seat.

Aisha didn't miss the way Prescott's arm wrapped around Phoebe's slim shoulders or his clear protectiveness of her.

"Let me introduce you," Phoebe said.

It was the work of a few seconds for Aisha to meet one of the world's most recognizable movie stars. And although her heart had long beat for Trey Colton, she couldn't deny its rapid speed at the heartbreakingly attractive face that stared back at her. Prescott Reynolds was warm and observably kind. Handsome as sin, too. The camera didn't lie when framing his image, but if anything, it failed to truly capture his dazzling blue eyes or thousand-watt smile.

Despite the fanfare that seemed to follow him everywhere, she liked him instantly.

He was also obviously in love with Phoebe.

The two had gone public with their relationship the prior week and it had been the one thing that had given Trey a slight reprieve from the endless barrage of press. While a killer on the loose was and would remain big news, the romance of a major Hollywood heartthrob had added a delicious twist to the endless coverage in Roaring Springs.

Trey had also told her that the couple's willingness to go public wasn't just about their personal happiness. His cousin Skye was Phoebe's twin sister. With her sister missing, Phoebe was desperate for any way to find her, and the constant images on the TV and internet were hopefully a way to draw Skye out. The thought was, if Skye had simply gone away on her own, she would see the news and get in contact. But if she were missing, there was a greater hope the publicity surrounding her twin's happiness would draw out a killer.

A dangerous game, Aisha knew. Sadly, she couldn't find fault in their logic.

The meeting was called to order, and the murmuring at the movie star in their midst died down as the town focused their attention on the front of the room. Trey came out, along with several other county leaders and the mayor of Roaring Springs, who acted as a moderator for these meetings and presented a connection point for the county seat and the broader proceedings in Bradford County.

The mayor set up the purpose of the meeting and in moments turned the mic over to Trey. He'd barely stood and begun to make his arguments for increased patrols, personnel support and the approval of overtime when Barton Evigan started in.

"Great idea. Spend more money on an already mismanaged case. Smart move, Sheriff."

Trey never fumbled but even in the back row Aisha saw the narrowing of his mouth and the steel that filled his deep brown eyes. "We've followed protocol every step of the way."

"This should have been wrapped up weeks ago. You've Keystone-Copped this from the start. *Sheriff.*" Evigan's pointed use of the word *sheriff* clearly wasn't a sign of respect. And while she couldn't see his face from her seat, Aisha had no doubt the man's smirk had vanished and that sneer was firmly back in place.

"We are in the midst of a thorough investigation over the death of six women. I'd hate to shortchange any of their lives or the crimes perpetrated against them out of a concern for poor publicity."

Score! Aisha thought with no small measure of satisfaction. Trey had refused to go on the offensive with Barton but he had every right to defend himself. Pushing on the publicity angle was one of the best blocks he had.

"So in the meantime you put the rest of the town at risk for a serial killer."

Clearly done with Barton and his taunting, Trey stood up. He wore his dress uniform, the starched press of khaki only making his shoulders look broader and more authoritative. "This investigation isn't a TV show, Mr. Evigan. I'm not looking for a daily spot on the evening news. I want the perpetrator of these heinous crimes apprehended and put behind bars as quickly as possible. But I will not put this investigation at risk, making shoddy decisions over protocol, because of uninformed hecklers poking at the work done by the good men and women of my department."

The tide of the meeting turned in Trey's favor, several hoots and hollers swelling up along with the clapping. Evigan had enough sense to sit down but Aisha could still see the hunch of his shoulders. It reminded her of a wounded animal, biding its time as it waited to strike.

"Real charming guy," Prescott said. "I can't believe that clown is running for sheriff against Colton."

His voice was low enough not to carry all the way to the front, but it could be overheard by the people sitting a few rows in front of them. Aisha had already seen their furtive glances back toward Prescott, and their excitement that he was in their presence. Although Aisha wanted Trey to win the reelection fairly and squarely, the clear endorsement in his favor, from an influential celebrity, no less, was a big help.

The meeting continued with little interruption. One of the town's matrons asked about overall public safety with her grandchildren coming in for a two-week visit. Trey assured her they were on high alert and refocused her attention on some upcoming activities sponsored by the local tourism board designed for family-fun days throughout the month of August.

What he didn't mention but Aisha knew was that the risk to children and families was relatively low. Unless cornered, the Avalanche Killer had a specific pattern in victim selection. Small children—thankfully—didn't fit that MO.

It was only when Russ Colton spoke up that the room seemed to take on a new vibe.

"I appreciate all you're doing, Trey. There's no one in town I respect to keep law and order more than my brother's son. But I'd be remiss if I didn't air my concerns about tourism. The film festival last month had a few hitches, as we all know. My daughter Skye is still missing. How are we supposed to rest easy?"

"Oh, boy." Phoebe whispered the words under her breath and reached for Prescott's hand while Aisha raced over her notes once more, hoping to find something to diffuse the situation.

She'd barely stood, hoping to take the mic floating around the room, when Barton beat her to the punch. The obnoxious ass didn't even wait for the mic, he just launched in with his latest round of shouting.

"Even your family's getting worried, *Sheriff* Colton! If the big, bad, rich Colton family is worried, what does that say for the rest of Roaring Springs? For all of Bradford County! What do you have to say to that?"

TREY EMPLOYED EVERY single ounce of self-control he possessed not to lash out at Evigan. The man was a troublemaker, and while Russ had technically started round two, his uncle's concern for Skye was palpable. His cousin had been missing for well over a month and the family was on high alert as to why she'd gone missing and desperate for some way to get her back.

The death of a prostitute earlier in the year had provoked upset, of course. No one wanted any whiff of murder in and around tourists, especially at the height of the ski season. But practicality had also won out at the time. The death of Bianca Rouge was deemed sad and momentarily troubling, but ultimately a blip in the high-stakes life that went on for the wealthy high rollers who stayed at The Lodge.

The death of Sabrina Gilford, however, had changed Russ's tune. He might be willing to overlook a few dismaying events in the life of running a major tourism empire, but the risk to his missing baby girl was something else entirely.

Trey had always tolerated his uncle. His prominent family had given him both a privileged upbringing and a huge albatross around his neck when he decided to run for public office. The change in Russ over the past few weeks had been somewhat refreshing to see. Even if Trey hated the reason for it.

"Mr. Colton, I understand your upset and can assure you we're all working toward the same outcome. A safe return of your daughter. A positive identification for the women discovered on the mountain. And a quick cap-

ture of the Avalanche Killer. The department is working as hard as it can to achieve all of those things as
expediently as possible."

"Yeah, right," Barton shouted back.

Trey ignored the heckles and kept his focus on Russ,
opting at the last minute to take a more personal tack.
"What we need from you, Uncle Russ, from all of
you—" he stopped, allowing his gaze to roam around
the room, settling on all of the assembled townsfolk
who'd come in for the proceedings "—is vigilance. We
get a lot of strangers in and out of town as a tourism
mecca. They come here for a good time and to forget
their own lives for a while. We shouldn't become suspicious of them but we should remain on our guard.
Friendly but focused. Aware of who's visiting us."

"That's your answer to catching a deranged serial
killer?" Barton heckled again, this comment getting
more murmurs and a few more "oh, yeahs" from the
crowd.

Trey ignored Barton and pressed on. "The public's
safety is in our hands. And based on the bodies we're
still trying to identify from the base of that mountain,
someone around here didn't want to let some of the kind
souls who've visited here go home."

As public disclosures went, it was ham-fisted and
clumsy, but Trey had vowed to share what he could,
when he could, with his constituents. Nothing in all
their investigating had turned up a local connection with
the victims and Roaring Springs or, even more broadly,
Bradford County until Sabrina Gilford. Which meant
they had a different issue on their hands.

A local killer who captured—nay, depended upon—

those who came from somewhere else to feed his blood-lust.

A muttered "way to kill the tourism industry" echoed loud enough from the audience to draw Trey's attention, but it was the lone figure who stood in the back who redirected his attention.

Aisha.

She stood there like a warrior goddess, her lithe frame, strong from the kickboxing she loved so much, graceful amid the chaos of the meeting. Trey gestured one of the room's moderators toward her with a microphone. Once she had the mic, she waited a few extra seconds until the room quieted enough.

"Sheriff Colton is correct." Aisha let her words stand and echo from the speakers for an extra few beats before speaking again. "For those of you who don't know me, my name is Aisha Allen and I'm a clinical psychologist with a practice here in Roaring Springs. I've consulted on cases throughout more than a decade of clinical work, and the thoroughness Sheriff Colton and his deputies are using to work this case is by the book."

"We don't have time for by the book!" Evigan shouted. "Not with a killer on the loose!"

To Aisha's credit, she barely looked at the man. Instead, she pressed on, her tone authoritative and her focus absolute. "Identification is crucial to a successful outcome in this case. The care taken to preserve the crime scene and the bodies, in spite of a major natural disaster, is first-rate. The quick identification of Miss Gilford was solid forensics work. And the focus on keeping peace and order while hunting a killer is a testament to the man we elected. I'd suggest we allow

Sheriff Colton and his deputies to do their work without our interference."

Trey's gaze drifted to Daria, sitting proud and tall in the front row, and saw the subtle, barely there smile that ghosted her lips. She rarely smiled but Aisha's endorsement had seemingly struck a nerve. His gaze drifted on to Stefan Roberts a few seats down. The man had played fair with Trey so far, but he had little expectation the FBI wasn't running its own op as quietly as possible, more than prepared to take all the credit for closing the case.

In all honesty, Trey couldn't care less who got the credit—he wanted this done and a killer caught—but he had toyed with asking to collaborate. In the end, however, he'd decided he and his team would get further working their own side of things, bringing the FBI in when they finally had something to collaborate on.

In the meantime, Aisha was his girl and she hadn't failed him once. Her insights were spot-on and even her ability to diffuse the tension filling the room was first-rate.

She maintained that strong posture as she held the microphone, her professionalism more than evident. "This is a difficult time for all of us. I have several patients who've expressed their concerns and the emotional impact of what we face as a community. Furthermore, I've spoken with my fellow medical professionals and we're all focused on extending help and care to those who need it."

The deliberate approach and Aisha's willingness to make the discussion caring and compassionate took the rest of the bluster right out of the room. The murmurs quieted and Trey saw how people turned toward their companions, considering her words in low, quiet voices. The mayor took the opportunity of that lull in the discussion to bring things back on track and read-dress the purpose of the session. Within a half hour, Trey had what he'd come for:

An expanded remit to add on overtime as needed.

Additional deputies sourced from surrounding counties.

And the agreement he'd wanted most of all: the ability to add on a civilian consultant to the work as he saw fit.

AISHA STOOD IN the back of the meeting room with Calvin and Audrey Colton as they all waited for Trey. His parents had found her the moment the session ended, weaving their way through the throngs of people who hurried forward to the elevated dais in front.

She'd loved Trey's parents since she was a small child, their home always a place of warmth and welcome. And animals. Oh, she'd loved the horses that had made their home along with the Colton family on a large spread just outside the Roaring Springs town limits. She'd always been welcomed with open arms, spending her carefree summers playing with Trey and his younger sister, Bree.

Aisha had worked hard to make friends at school as well—and had succeeded over time, still cherishing several friendships she'd had since grade school—but there had always been something special about Trey Colton and his parents.

For one, his mom looked like her. It was a funny thought—one she'd had less and less as she'd grown up—but one that had been important to her as a child.

Attending college in New York had helped expand her social circle wider, but Roaring Springs, Colorado, twenty years ago wasn't a particular hotbed of diversity. To have a woman in her life besides a family member who was also a woman of color had meant a lot to her.

As a result, her own mother had always understood and accepted her bond with Audrey Colton.

Although they'd remained close, Aisha had seen less and less of Trey's parents over the past few years. The busyness of her practice and her ever-growing list of patients had made free time more of a luxury than she'd like, and it was lovely to sink right back into conversation.

"I saw your mother at the market a few weeks ago. She said Tanisha is expecting."

"Late winter," Aisha added. "She's been on my mom to keep quiet about it and let her get to three months but has pretty much accepted that's not going to happen."

"Not if the broad smile and big gleam in your mother's eye was any indication." Audrey pulled her close for a warm hug. "Congratulations on becoming an aunt."

Aisha accepted the affectionate hug and thought about her baby sister, planning the arrival of a new life early next year. They were all so excited, but it was hard to imagine bringing a child into the world when so much of it seemed so out of control. As a psychologist, she knew the desire to hunker down and shelter in place was a fight-or-flight response to the scary reality of a killer on the loose. But as a sister and a soon-to-be aunt…

She'd been struggling with how scary it all was. She could only hope Trey got a handle on the killer before anything else could happen. Or anyone else could be harmed.

"There he is. The star of the show."

Calvin slapped his son on the back and Audrey waited before pulling Trey close for a kiss. Trey went willingly, sinking into the warm acceptance of his parents, and Aisha noticed, not for the first time, what a unit they were.

She had always been lucky to have her mother and her sister. They had struggled for money but never for love, the three of them forging a bond that would never be broken. It had been one of the hardest things ever to leave Roaring Springs and go two thousand miles away to college, but it was her mother who'd encouraged her every step of the way.

And it was her mother who, even now, pushed her to tell Trey how she really felt about him.

Aisha hated that she was so transparent and hoped that it was only a mother's love for her daughter that made her quite so perceptive. She hated to think that Trey knew how she felt. Or worse…that his parents sensed the same and felt sorry for her.

How embarrassing.

Turning away from the threesome, she'd nearly made an excuse to go get something from the refreshment table when a loud, booming voice floated over them all.

"Well, look here."

Barton Evigan had ditched his campaign manager somewhere in the room—or if the manager was smart the man had ditched *his* unworthy candidate—and had only his wife on his arm. The woman had the decency to look slightly embarrassed but it was quickly overshadowed by her reticence to speak or barely move in the man's presence.

Aisha's training kicked in and she was already thinking of a way to speak to the woman when Barton shot out more venom, his lips curled into a snarl. "Someone sure does have a fan."

Sadly, Aisha was no stranger to racist remarks—subtle or otherwise—but the clear vitriol evident in a man running for public office surprised even her.

Before she could say anything, Calvin Colton was in the man's face, his broader shoulders and intimidating height eclipsing Evigan. Even well into his sixties, Calvin's fierce protection was something to behold. "Are you suggesting something untoward against my son, my wife and our dear family friend?"

Evigan eyed them all before gathering himself. "I was simply suggesting you Coltons all stick together."

"Right." Calvin spat the word. "That was your meaning."

Although Trey's dad had the height advantage, Barton still had youth on his side and it was enough to have his worse nature coming through. "You want to suggest otherwise?"

Audrey laid a hand on Calvin's arm. She didn't say anything, but her touch had the calming effect of diffusing her husband. He stepped away, his disdain evident as he presented his back to Barton. "Not worth another moment of our time."

For the briefest moment, Aisha thought Barton was going to cause a physical altercation, hate along with something dark and oily filling his gaze, before he seemed to think better of it. He turned back to his wife, grabbing her by the upper arm and dragging her from the community center, her feet running double time to keep up with him.

"I'm sorry, Mom." Trey turned to Aisha, encompassing her in the apology. "You did nothing but support me in there."

"And I'm going to keep supporting you. There and to anyone who will listen." Aisha moved up into his orbit, wrapping an arm around his waist. The solid warmth of his chest practically knocked every rational thought from her mind, but she hung on, determined to make him understand. "I'm in your corner, Colton. I always have been and always will be. Apologize again and I'm dragging you out back and trying my latest kickboxing moves on you."

Trey hesitated momentarily, a sort of dazed expression filling his dark brown eyes before he blinked out of it. "Okay." He held up a hand. "No ass kicking required."

She held his gaze another moment before nodding. "See that it stays that way."

It was Trey's father who spoke first. "Let's get out of here and go have some ice cream."

"Dad, I've got—"

Audrey shut Trey down before he could make any other excuses. "Come on. We're all entitled to some ice cream and the huckleberry cobbler I made this afternoon."

"You made cobbler?" Trey's voice grew animated, and with it, Aisha heard the tones of their youth. Trey Colton had never been very good at resisting huckleberry cobbler. Or any other kind of cobbler, come to think of it.

Audrey turned toward her. "Aisha, you in?"

"Sure." She thought of the weight bag she'd have to

keep after in the morning but didn't especially mind. "I'll suffer through an extra fifteen minutes of cardio tomorrow."

Trey's mother only shook her head. "You young people and your insistence on all this exercise. It boggles the mind."

"You look great, Mrs. Colton." Aisha eyed the older woman's trim figure and still-slim frame. "You must do something to stay in shape."

"I run a farm with my husband. Never once have I regretted eating ice cream made from the cows I milk or dessert made from the crops I grow."

As Aisha followed Calvin and Audrey out to the parking lot, the two of them walking her to her car while Trey headed for his patrol car, she had to give credit where it was due. She'd never give up her psychology practice, but there was something to be said for daily physical labor and the fruits of that hard work.

An hour later, sitting on the Colton's front porch, full of vanilla ice cream and cobbler, Aisha amended the thought.

There *was* something about enjoying the fruits of one's labor. But it was even sweeter when you shared it with others.

Chapter Three

Trey scanned one of the reports on the discovery of the bodies on the side of the mountain and thanked his lucky stars, once again, for the ever-capable and awesome Daria Bloom. The woman was amazing, her focus and dedication for her job something to behold. He was fortunate for all of his deputies, the individuals currently making up the Bradford County Sheriff's Office staff all strong, capable law officers.

But Daria was a cut above.

The two of them had stayed late the night before, prepping for the visit from local officials that was set to start in another ten minutes. Despite going over the materials until his eyes blurred, Trey had been back at it since six that morning, determined to make the meeting a good one.

And even more determined to make sure they knew he was the right man for the job.

He hated the fact that Barton Evigan had gotten under his skin at Tuesday evening's meeting. From the moment he'd seen the bastard sitting there, all high and mighty and devious in his seat, Trey had known there'd be trouble. He wanted to ignore it. He was good at ignoring bullies and had done so most of his life.

But this was different.

The tone and tenor were the same, but the potential outcome had more far-reaching consequences. If he lost the sheriff's position in the November election to Evigan, his replacement would take Bradford County down a dark road. Trey knew it in his gut and was only reminded of that fact each and every time he laid eyes on his opponent.

Tuesday night had been a perfect example.

"Sheriff Colton." At the knock on his door he looked up to find Winnie Han, their dispatcher and fill-in front desk clerk during the summer months when vacations were in full swing. Although Trey had more than a few deputies offer to give up their vacations until the Avalanche Killer situation closed, Trey wanted to avoid that if possible. Tension was high and the scrutiny on their work was intense. A much-needed and well-deserved vacation was in order for everyone who had one coming their way. "The county supervisor is here."

Winnie waited a beat before continuing. "And the private secretary to the governor."

Well, hell and damn. A surprise attack.

Trey nodded. "Thanks, Winnie. I'll come back with you and greet them myself."

"Bruce Patrillo picked up doughnuts and boxed coffee on his way in."

"Let's make sure he expenses that," Trey added, grateful for the support of his team. Even more grateful they understood the gravitas now that the governor had sent his highest-ranking lackey along for the ride.

Trey adjusted his tie, confirming the Windsor knot was in place just as he'd left it, and followed Winnie out of his office. They'd use the main conference room, transformed after his and Aisha's review of the data on Monday night. He and Daria had used originals of the copies he'd shared with Aisha, posting them all on individual corkboards, lined up in the order each woman was identified by her time of death. Trey had looked at those boards so many times he could see them in his mind's eye.

Could still see Sabrina's face, her eyes staring sightlessly back at him from the photo, a reminder of how poorly he'd failed her.

And how much work there was still to be done.

Although he'd worked blessedly few murders in his career, he'd had a few. Each time, he'd thought the same. What a shameful waste of a life.

He felt the same now, only along with it there was a small ember, growing day by day, burning slow and steady beneath his skin.

Who had done this?

Who felt they had a right to hurt these women, playing with them until fear must have been a frenzy in their blood?

No one had that right. He wouldn't rest until the killer was found, and he'd use every means at his disposal to capture the cowardly bastard.

"Sheriff Colton." The county supervisor Trey knew as Dave Olson extended his hand. "Good to see you again."

"You as well." Trey turned to the governor's senior assistant, Steve Lucas. "Steve. I'm sorry we're not meeting under better circumstances."

"Likewise. I've been following your career. The governor has, too. You have a unique constituent base and you've run it with ease, a deft hand and a fair amount of good humor, if the reports are true."

"I try."

"You do better than try, from all we've heard." Steve waved a hand, but the casual motion was at odds with the tense set of his shoulders beneath an expensive blue suit. "Which only further reinforces why all this Avalanche Killer stuff is a bunch of nonsense."

Trey recognized the campaign trail speech for what it was and decided the front lobby of his station wasn't the best place to talk. His deputies were strong and loyal and avoided overt political sentiment most of the time, but no one wanted to hear their work so readily dismissed. "We've set up coffee in the main conference room. Why don't you both join me there?"

Trey made a show of leading but put himself in front on purpose. He wanted to see both men's faces when they first saw his boards. A few moments later, as they entered the room, he wasn't disappointed. Steve's polished smile fell, his eyes going wide at the prominently displayed photos.

The county supervisor looked no more comfortable, but he schooled his features, already having been present for the handling of the bodies and their removal off the mountain.

Steve spoke first, the initial shock fading as he moved closer to the boards. "These women? All were killed by the same person?"

"We believe so. There's some concern about the sixth victim. Sabrina Gilford." Trey clung to the use of her name, the lack of much else a continued challenge in their investigative work. Using her name, especially when he couldn't for four of the six victims, kept them grounded. Focused.

And constantly reminded of the lives that were snuffed out. Lives belonging to real people with real dreams and real futures.

"Concern how?" Steve surged forward off the table-top where he'd rested a hip.

"While the first four victims haven't been positively identified, we believe the killer's pattern has been to take tourists. The fifth woman, April Thomas, was identified because her mother pressed the issue repeatedly that someone search for her daughter. She believed April had come to Roaring Springs before she disappeared and once she heard of Sabrina Gilford's disappearance she came here herself, seeking answers."

And found a terrible one when the bodies were uncovered off the mountain.

"And the others?" Dave asked.

"We've scoured missing persons, widened the search nationally and have done our level best to collaborate with the FBI where we could. They're not sharing much and we're holding close to the vest as well, but I'm neither so shortsighted nor close-minded enough to ignore their vast resources. When they offered me access to their missing persons database, I jumped at it."

"The Feds do want jurisdiction here. Technically they have it, too," Steve said. Although the governor's aide had regained his composure, nothing visible in his motives playing across his serene face, Trey wasn't willing to take any chances.

He needed support on this and he wasn't going to back down.

"I'm not trying to block them out, but they don't

know Bradford County like I do. Like my deputies do. Kicking us off this case would be a major mistake."

"Whoa there, Sheriff. I'm not suggesting taking you off."

"What are you suggesting?"

Steve leaned in, his focus absolute. "I'm sorry for these women. Deeply sorry. No one except maybe the governor wants the person who did this caught more than I do. But we have a state to run and tourism dollars to protect."

"Yes, sir. I understand," Trey said. He knew the way things worked—he'd run for office himself—but something in the response nagged at him. Was everything political?

At that thought, an image of Barton Evigan's behavior on Tuesday night came flooding back in full force. *Of course* everything was political. Anyone in public office had to understand that. And Trey knew it would be a poor time for him to get amnesia on that subject.

Seemingly satisfied by his answer—or lack of one—Steve resumed his seat on the table. His gaze didn't so much as flick back over multiple boards but instead was firmly focused on Trey.

"You're up for reelection yourself. I understand it's turned messy?"

At Dan's snort, Trey's intended attempt to deflect the question vanished. "I have a verbose opponent."

"The governor has had a few of those in his day." Steve grinned. "I'd offer to help but you're a Colton. I suspect you've got more than your fair share of that."

"Actually—" Trey bit back his answer. He appreciated his family and the influence the Colton name wielded in this part of the country—hell, anywhere in the country—but it wasn't all smooth sailing. Evigan had keyed in on his last name as his very first shot over the political bow.

And the whispers that had grown stronger and stronger since Evigan announced his candidacy had changed, too. They now carried a decided bent toward the idea that the Coltons were *too* powerful in Bradford County. So powerful, in fact, that his name was the reason Trey even had the job in the first place. A puppet in a position of power to turn a blind eye to his family's business empire.

It bugged him. *No*, Trey amended. He was irate. He worked hard for his job and his constituents. If it were only a matter of gossip he'd see past it. He was used to people's small-minded chatter and had long since stopped worrying about it. But when that chatter turned to questions about his job qualification or his integrity, well, damn it, he had a right to be upset. He worked hard at both and it was infuriating to have that questioned.

"My family is large and opinionated, sir. I do my best to ensure those opinions stay at family gatherings and out of my office."

"Wise choice."

Steve glanced around before leaning in. "You're unmarried, too, aren't you?"

Sheesh, what was this guy, his mother?

"I work pretty much 24/7. Not a lot of time for a social life."

"See, here's the thing." Steve scratched at his chin before sticking it out as if he were about to impart serious words of wisdom. "Voters love that idea in theory, a tireless public servant working on their behalf. But what they really love is a good family man. Add in a real sappy love story and they eat that up, too. Your opponent, now, he's married."

"Yes, he is."

Without even trying too hard, an image of Barton Evigan's wife came clearly to mind. The woman was as small and unobtrusive and on the few occasions he'd been in her presence Trey had observed her trying to shrink even more.

Aisha had mentioned the same the other night at his parents' house, when their talk had shifted from the outrageously delicious cobbler his mother had made and beelined straight back to the town hall meeting. Aisha hadn't outright said the words but he didn't miss her concern that the woman was at risk of abuse, if not currently then at some point in the future, and Trey was hard-pressed to disagree.

It was a leap to think the man an abuser—and a mighty large one—but something about Barton Evigan didn't sit well with him.

"You should get yourself a wife. It'd make this whole business easier. Distract attention and give you a solid, upstanding woman by your side each time that blowhard started talking."

"I appreciate your suggestion sir, but—" Trey stilled, the words sinking in. "A *wife*?"

"Sure." Steve shrugged. "You've got the looks and the demeanor for the job. Add in the family man angle and you're golden."

"But I—" Trey glanced over at Dan but the man's gaze had shifted determinedly back to the images posted around the room, as if staring at six dead women was preferable to discussing Trey's love life.

Or lack thereof.

"Look, Steve. I appreciate the advice. Really I do."

The governor's errand boy steamrolled over Trey's comments as if he hadn't spoken. "You're more than qualified. The governor is a smart man and rests easy knowing Bradford County's in your capable hands. Get yourself a wife, or a fiancée at least, and get through the reelection season. After things die down, go back to being footloose and fancy free if you want."

Steve glanced around, despite the closed door, before he lowered his voice. "Hell, keep her and get a side piece. Happens all the time. Just put on the family front for the voters. It'll do a world of good to help your chances."

Trey didn't catch much else, but shifted into autopilot to give his briefing—the presumed reason for the visit. The prep work he and Daria had done the night before worked in his favor and he got through the details on what they knew of the killings, their working theories and the overall progress from the ME's office on the four as-yet-unidentified bodies from the grave site. In less than a half hour it was over and in another ten minutes, after final pleasantries over a doughnut, Trey saw the two men out.

He walked back to his office, still shaking his head as he closed the door. He strolled to the sideboard for another doughnut, then followed the boards, one by one, using the mix of sugar and grease to fortify himself. The terrible images should have cut through his thoughts but he found himself practically staring through them as the unsettling conversation rolled through his mind on a loop.

Married? With a side piece? Putting on the front of a happy, devoted family man? What parallel universe had he walked into that morning? Worse, had it become 1850? Because a huge part of him felt like he'd just been instructed to hunt up a mail-order bride out here in the Wild, Wild West.

Who the hell would he marry anyway?

He hadn't lied about his single status. He'd been working so much the last date he'd had was four—well, hell, it was six—months ago. It hadn't ended very well, either, with him running off to an emergency over at The Lodge. It was a party gone wild and he could have sent out a deputy to handle the matter, but at the chance to escape the date he'd jumped at the chance.

What did that say about him?

Trey walked back to refill his coffee, his phone going off in his pocket.

Aisha's text filled the screen.

How'd it go?

He typed out a quick response. You mean the sneak attack straight from the governor's office?

He saw the three dots for the briefest of moments before Aisha's reply came winging back. No freaking way!

Yep. Gov's head lackey. All neat and refined in his pressed blue suit. He looked like a game show host. Man was a piece of work.

Aisha shot him a few laughing emojis before she added another thought. What did he actually want? An update on the Avalanche Killer?

Trey considered how to play it. Even though it was Aisha and he rarely gave much consideration to anything he typed or talked to her about, it was embarrassing to realize just how long it had been since he'd gone on a date.

Would she think less of him?

She was attractive and successful. Although they avoided the topic for some strange reason, he expected she was out dating and painting the town red every chance she got.

Although…when *was* the last time she'd mentioned a date?

You there?

Sorry. Just busy. Why did he lie? Trey wondered. Since he'd already hit Send, he quickly tried to make up for the unsettling sensation of hiding something from her.

You up for dinner tonight? I have a rare free one and am craving enchiladas. I'll give details then.

She shot back a series of tacos interspersed with more smiley face emojis, which he would have interpreted as a yes for dinner even without her response. Yes!!!!!!

See you at six at Maggie's Tortilla House.

Later, and then she included an alligator emoji.

Once again, Trey was forced to admit the woman the world saw as intense and serious just *wasn't* with him. She used weird smiley faces no one else ever did and had a bizarre fondness for the gator emoji. And she actually ate in front of him.

That woman back in April—no, it was February—
had yelled at their waitress for bringing bread. Who
did that?

Not Aisha. She kicked ass each morning at her kickboxing gym. She continued kicking it all day when it
came to her patients and their welfare. And then she did
it again when it came to enjoying herself.

As if Steve still sat in Trey's office, whispering
from the corner, his unsolicited advice seemed to swirl
through the room.

*You should get yourself a wife. It'd make this whole
business easier.*

Where had that come from?

Especially with his thoughts full of Aisha.

She was a strong, independent woman, not some
small, shy mouse of a human who couldn't stand up for
herself. Or worse, who'd been pushed down so badly she
had no idea which way was up. And she certainly wasn't
the type of woman to agree to a pretend engagement.

Engagement? With Aisha?

That was what he'd taken away from his morning
visitors?

Since Steve's visit had obviously shaken him more
than he realized, Trey figured he was due for a change
of pace. His early arrival to work ensured he had a rare
free hour and he was going to put it to good use downstairs in the gym. A rotation through the speed bag, the
weights and a bit of cardio would go a long way toward
settling his thoughts.

He needed it, Trey thought as he grabbed his gym
bag from the floor beneath his desk. Because for the
briefest of moments, he'd actually considered asking
Aisha Allen if she wanted to be his pretend fiancée.

Chapter Four

Aisha inhaled the warm scents of flour tortillas and gooey cheese and let out her first easy breath of the day. She'd waited all day for this moment and she was going to take a few seconds to enjoy it.

She'd earned it.

A patient she'd been working with for the past five months—and who she'd believed was improving—had a significant setback that morning. It had been a difficult session, followed by a discussion with the man's wife about possible treatment options that went beyond office visits. It had been emotional and painful and the sort of experience she was grateful she didn't have often.

And then her day had gone even further downhill after that.

The press had somehow glommed onto her comments from Tuesday night at the county meeting and had executed a surprise attack with an office visit at lunch. She was so incensed by their arrival and their insistence she give a quote about the state of the investigation that she finally had to have her assistant call the Roaring Springs PD out to help deal with the intruders.

Since that had stretched past lunch, it had interfered

with a patient due into her office, and the sight of the police had sent her into a tailspin. It had taken nearly their entire hour to calm the woman down to the point of coherency, and after that Aisha had been tempted to cancel the rest of her appointments for the day.

So yeah, she thought to herself as Trey handed her the drink menu from the center of the table. She'd earned her sangria swirl margarita. *Maybe even a second.* And the ginormous plate of enchiladas that she'd already selected off the dinner menu, too.

"Tough day?" Trey's question had her eyes popping open but it was the sweet, understanding look that softened the subtle lines around his thick-lashed eyes that caught her off guard.

It was those moments—those quick little shots of intimacy—that never failed to catch her off guard. He *saw* her. It was…well, something she'd do better not to dwell on.

Resolutely ignoring that quick shot of attraction, she shared what she could. "I've had better. But before I bore you with the nonconfidential pieces I can share, I want to hear about your morning. You had a rather impressive visitor."

"The governor's lackey hardly rates as impressive."

"Well," Aisha pointed out as she reached for a chip from the basket at the center of the table, "it wasn't the governor. When he starts showing up, you know you have a real problem."

"That makes a disturbing amount of sense," Trey said as he moved the menus to give the waiter room to set down their drinks.

"Bright-side Allen. That's my name, sunshine's my game."

The joke had him smiling a little bit, but it couldn't penetrate the heavy pall that seemed to weigh over him. They'd met at her office in Roaring Springs, then walked through downtown toward the southern end of the main drag. The upper end was reserved for any number of high-end shops and elite restaurants, but Aisha preferred the hipper and more eclectic choices at the south end. Besides, it was a pretty summer night to walk and she was going to need every step she could find after her enchilada fest wrapped up.

She picked up her margarita and considered a new tack. The lighthearted joking wasn't working. And she knew that stubborn, settled look on his handsome face. Left to his own devices, he'd brood into his beer for the next two hours.

Which meant fixing his mood called for special measures. Time to activate Officer Do-Right.

"The press showed up today."

"What? Where?"

"At my office. Some enterprising reporter read the notes of Tuesday evening's meeting and decided to come grill me on the murders."

"They had no right to do that to you." He slammed his beer on the table, his golden-brown eyes narrowing. "No right at all."

"Which is why I handled it and called for support in the form of the Roaring Springs police."

"You didn't call me. You didn't even tell me."

"I'm telling you now," she murmured.

"It's not the same—"

She lifted a finger, silencing him. "See how it feels?"

Recognition dawned, chasing the lingering anger from those golden depths. "That's not fair."

"It's incredibly not fair. And it's not what friends do. And for the record, I would have told you but I had a few patient emergencies that kept me occupied with necessary paperwork until about five minutes before you showed up. So." She took a sip of her margarita, savoring the cold tartness on her tongue. "Your turn. Tell me about the visit from the chief lackey."

"What do you want me to tell you?"

"What happened? What did they say? Are they going to send the Feds in like you worried about?"

That had become his most recent fear as the situation with the Avalanche Killer spun out. In addition to battling Barton Evigan and the overarching sentiment of the townspeople, Trey was worried about how far the FBI would throw its influence around.

This was his turf. His county and his people to protect. The Feds might want a big score, putting a deranged killer in prison, but she knew that Trey wanted justice for his constituents. He wanted them to feel safe and secure.

Was there anything sexier?

The thought slammed into her, unbidden, and with it Aisha shot a wary glance at her margarita. She'd taken only a few sips and her brain had already shifted to images of Trey in full warrior-protector mode.

It was one of her favorite fantasies and it usually involved the man shirtless, gun in hand, as he patrolled the streets of Roaring Springs like a Wild West sheriff keeping law and order. It was silly and stupid and she felt the blush creeping up her neck at the erotic images that had suddenly taken over her thoughts.

And her body, if the tension curling low in her belly was any indication.

"Aish? You okay?"

"Sure. Fine."

"You don't seem fine."

"It's the margarita. It's strong tonight and I didn't get lunch due to my surprise visitors."

The diversion had its desired impact, his curiosity over her flushed skin taking a back seat to the press intrusion. "I really am sorry about that."

"It's fine. It's over and I lived to tell the tale." She reached for her margarita again and took a tentative sip. "Which is more than I can say for the reporters who were chased off with their tails between their legs."

"You looked positively maniacal when you said that."

"I feel that way. Their presence disrupted my patients. The people who come to me in their quiet moments of need don't deserve that."

"No, they don't." Trey agreed.

And there it was, Aisha thought. They might feel the same way about the situation—even be angry about it—but they'd battle it together. "I told. Now it's your turn. What happened this morning?"

"I don't appreciate being caught off guard and it was a one hundred percent sneak attack."

She nodded as she lifted a small fingertip of salt from the rim of her margarita. "It sounded like it from your texts."

"It wasn't his presence so much as what he said."

Aisha wanted to be supportive but the unexpected ambush was one more example of all the ways Trey's case had gotten out of hand. Did the governor think Trey was hiding something? Or worse, was he convinced the pressure of an in-person visit—from a subordinate, no less—would light a fire under one of the best sheriffs in all the state?

Because if there was ever anyone who had self-motivation down to a T, it was Trey Colton. The man lived and breathed his job and to have a stand-in for the governor just show up... It was insulting.

"You're getting all flushed again."

"This time I'm mad."

"What were you before?"

Caught, Aisha wanted to say. But she bit her tongue at the last minute and pointed toward her drink. "Adjusting to the tequila."

"Oh."

He lifted a lone eyebrow at her, wiggling it before picking up his beer again. "We got off on a weird foot tonight."

"You think?"

"I know. So let's try again." He put down his beer. "Aisha. How was your day?"

"Crummy. Yours?"

"The worst," he said.

"Anything I can do to help?"

She might have left her poker face about three blocks away, but Trey's wasn't very visible, either. That same shell-shocked expression she'd seen off and on since he'd picked her up flashed once more, and for the first time Aisha began to worry.

What *had* happened earlier? Did the governor have information on the killer? Something known only to him?

"Trey. Come on, enough of this. Tell me what's going on."

"I think maybe we should get married."

* * *

As proposals went, it was clumsy and stupid and just all-around bad. He wasn't the smoothest guy on the planet, but he usually had more common sense than blurting out whatever was lodged in his head, drilling at his brain matter like a jackhammer.

The only problem was, he'd thought of little else since the governor's lackey left his office. The gym hadn't helped. Three hours of paperwork hadn't helped. And a jaunt swiping left through his online dating app hadn't helped, either.

All he could think about was asking Aisha to be his fiancée. Or his pretend fiancée, if there actually were such a thing.

Was there?

He knew things like that existed in wacky sex comedies and rom coms, but he had yet to meet anyone in real life who'd felt compelled to enter into a fake engagement to solve a problem. You didn't solve problems by getting married. Or pretending to get married. Or asking someone to pretend to get married.

Only he did.

Or he would if Aisha said yes.

Having his best friend on his arm would solve a ton of problems and would at least smooth out one area of his life for the next few months. Because he was doing a piss-poor job of managing Barton Evigan's full-on attack, finding a serial killer and identifying four dead women discovered in his county. The last two were going to take as long as they'd bloody well take, but the first…

Steve had given him an answer to that one.

"What did you just say?"

"I need you to marry me." Even as mixed up as his day was, Trey knew that wasn't quite the proper framing. "Hold on. Let me start again."

When she didn't say a word, only continued to stare at him across the table, Trey figured he'd better do some tap dancing. Fast.

"The governor's assistant made several good observations today. One of which was that I had an extra vulnerability to Evigan because I wasn't a married man."

"Our governor actually has people on his staff who go around giving out advice like this?" she asked, before adding. "Presumably well-paid people."

"Apparently so."

"And somewhere between this morning's meeting and a round of enchiladas you thought it was a good idea?"

"It's not a bad one."

"Trey!" she scolded. "These are our lives we're talking about. Not some dopey play."

"I know."

"So what has you convinced this is even worth discussing?"

"I need something, Aish. Something to get this problem with Evigan to go away. And I've thought about it. We don't have to be truly engaged. We'd just tell people we are. We've known each other forever. Hell, we know more about each other than most people who are actually married do."

The curious flush he'd seen earlier on her face had faded, replaced with something that looked a lot like anger. Or no, he amended. Disappointment.

Did she think he was a coward, afraid of running against Evigan on his own merits?

Whatever the look, it vanished before Trey could call her on it and she'd already pressed on, ramping up speed with each word. "Just because we know each other well doesn't mean people will suddenly believe we're getting married. We're not even dating."

"What would you call this? Tonight?" He glanced around, the two of them sitting at their table like at least five other couples in his direct line of sight right there in the dining room.

"Thursday night dinner at Maggie's."

"But it could be a date. No one looking at us would think otherwise." He continued to push, curious to see that her initial shock had worn off.

Was his argument working?

Because for reasons that didn't make a single lick of sense, now that he had it in his head to propose to Aisha—even as a temporary solution—he wasn't backing down.

"Even if I buy that, and I'm not saying I do—" she held up a hand to stop him from interrupting "—no one will believe we're engaged. What would your family say? Your sister, who actually is engaged and who knows what that state looks like. Your extended family. Your deputies. They've seen you at work every night for the past six months. How did we magically begin a courtship that's ready for marriage?"

"You're at the office helping me a lot. They'll think something blossomed that way."

"Blossomed?" It was her turn to lift an eyebrow, one she used on him like a deadly weapon. "What actually happened to you today? Because if you don't come clean soon, I'm calling Daria to ask her if you were hit in the head."

"I wasn't hit in the head. I'm fine."

Only he wasn't, which was the weirdest thing. And, oddly enough, he *felt* like he'd been hit in the head. Hard. To the point the world looked entirely different from when he'd woken up that morning.

"Trey. What you're talking about is insanity. We're friends. We spend a lot of time together. How is anyone going to believe we suddenly fell in love and decided on a spring wedding?"

She was right. Empirically, Trey knew that. So why did the image of her in an ivory gown, clad over that slim, graceful frame, suddenly fill his thoughts and tighten his body painfully under the table? He hadn't looked at her in that way for years.

By design. Aisha Allen was a beautiful woman, one who'd grown even more so as she'd aged into herself. She was warm and competent and caring. She ran an amazing psychology practice and she was bright and confident in her work and in her life. And she was gorgeous. He'd figured that out when they were fourteen and had gone diving in the local watering hole. She'd let down her hair, curls springing around her face before coming to rest on her shoulders, and he'd been hooked.

It was that day he'd had thoughts about his best friend that he had no idea what to do with. Over twenty years later, he still didn't know what to do with them so he'd buried them. And he'd left them buried so they couldn't come out and ruin the very best thing in his life.

He'd missed her every single day she'd been away in New York. All that distance had nearly killed him, even as he'd known it was the best thing for her. More than that, it had been the *right* thing. She'd needed to go away and find herself. Find a world bigger than Roaring Springs, so when she came back she'd know she was home.

So she'd stay forever.

He'd dated while she was gone and in the time since and he hoped she did the same. As he'd reminded himself earlier, it was the one area they sort of had an undiscussed truce not to mention. But since they didn't mention those things, he felt he had carte blanche to push his agenda.

Aisha was the key to putting Barton Evigan out of his mind for the next few months. An engagement was the ammunition he needed to squelch the man's shot at winning the election. And it was the path to changing perceptions of Sheriff Trey Colton in Bradford County.

And if he had to keep those thoughts hidden—the ones about his lingering attraction that gripped his insides with a tight, unrelenting fist—then he'd do it.

He'd been doing it for as long as he could remember and he was good at it. A world champion grave digger of emotions. He'd kept his feelings buried this long, and he could do it longer. As long as he needed to, in fact.

Reelection was only three months away.

How hard would it be?

Aisha had finished her plate of enchiladas and her second margarita and she was still as heartsick as the moment Trey had laid his idiotic notion of a fake engagement on her. Only now she could add indigestion into the mix.

A fake engagement? Had she somehow woken up in a Sunday afternoon couch movie? Because who suggested those things? Certainly not by-the-book Trey Colton.

Never him.

Which made the fact she was actually considering his cockamamie suggestion scary as hell.

And wildly exhilarating.

Engaged to Trey? It was like every fantasy she'd ever had, coming true over chips and salsa. She'd sat there, staring at him, and he'd popped out with that proposal. Or sort of one. Which still had her blood pumping and her brain a bit fuzzy two hours later.

What *was* in that margarita?

Only as they walked back up through town, meandering their way toward their cars still parked at her office, she had to admit to herself that her fantasy had holes. Big ones.

For starters, they weren't in love. Or he wasn't. Her long-suppressed feelings weren't the basis for a successful engagement. Or fake engagement. A fauxgagement? Continuing down this path was only going to lead to heartbreak.

But it would help him.

That acknowledgment had swirled in her mind since his proposal and it was the one piece in of all this she couldn't effectively fight. It was actually the only thing.

What would her mother think? Or Tanisha? Or Trey's family. It was all well and good to say the two of them knew the lay of the land, but if they went around telling everyone the situation was fake, somehow the news would leak back to Evigan and all their maneuvering would be lost. Which meant the only alternative was lying to their loved ones.

Her mother wouldn't understand. LaShanna Allen was so supportive over so many things, but when it came to Trey Colton she had a blind spot. Her mother had never made it a secret that she wanted Aisha to end up with Trey and no amount of protests that the two of them weren't meant to be together had deterred LaShanna. Telling her mother she was engaged to Trey would start a veritable storm of emotion the woman might not recover from. And when the inevitable breakup came—*hello*, because it was all fake!—Lord deliver her from the wrath.

Aisha was still so deep in her thoughts she barely registered Trey's motions until he was on top of her. His arms wrapped around her and he half walked beside her, the move looking for all the world like two lovers who couldn't keep their hands off each other as they walked. It was only when he shoved her into the alcove doorway of a small wine bar that was still in high swing for an August evening that she realized he wasn't testing out his fiancée theory.

"Trey?" She tried to protest but he kept moving, pushing her through the door and into the bar. The lighting was subdued but the energy was high, happy conversations echoing all around them.

"Give me a minute," Trey ordered. "Stay right here."

She did as he asked, still stunned at the abrupt duck into the bar. Even more stunned by the warmth in Trey's arms as they came around her like tight bands. Her eyes had barely adjusted to the dim lighting when he strode back in the door. "What's going on?"

"I thought I saw something."

Willing the lingering imprint of his hands against her skin from her mind, Aisha asked, "What sort of something?"

"A guy in a car. I noticed him earlier when I went out

for a sandwich at lunch and then saw him again when we came out of Maggie's. It was weird."

"Do you think he's following you?"

"I don't know. It's no crime to sit in a car on the street."

"Maybe not, but it's also not a crime to trust your gut." Aisha wanted to get out there and see for herself, but something held her back. "You didn't need to shove me in here to go check it out. You could have whispered to me what was going on."

"I had no idea what he'd do."

"Exactly. You're not in uniform right now. Your gun's locked safely away. How did you think you were going to protect yourself?"

A muscle twitched in his jaw. "I'm a trained law officer."

"And I'm a trained psychologist. Someone aiming to do you harm will find a way."

And there—right there—was the heart of the matter. Although she trusted Trey's skills implicitly, the events of the past few months had worried her like no other time since he'd gone into law enforcement. The man put himself in peril every day and now he'd likely caught the eye of a cold-blooded madman. If the Avalanche Killer had grown even more dangerous—and she knew from the photos he had—the risk to Trey had only grown. Standing in the way of an escalating serial killer? One whose need to kill had grown and expanded?

It was lethal work.

Work made even harder by the fact that the killer had honed his skills over many years. He no doubt was eating up the news coverage reporting daily on his crimes. And it was Trey Colton who represented capture if he found a way to end the Avalanche Killer's ride to fame and glory.

Chapter Five

"You look like hell."

Trey looked up from his desk to see his cheerful baby sister, Bree, staring back at him. Her long curly hair was pulled back—a clear sign she was working—but it didn't stop the riot of curls from falling down her back.

"Thanks, Bree."

"Welcome." She practically danced around his office, a fairy sprite of electric happiness, as she took in the surroundings. Her gaze narrowed on an oversize frame on the far wall of his office. "Why is that piece crooked?"

"Earthquake?" Trey offered up, smiling at the way her golden-brown eyes—a match for his own—narrowed.

"I painted that just for you."

Trey's gaze roamed over the wolf that stared out into the broad expanse of Colorado wilderness. "I know you did and I love it. And before you think I don't take care of my things, my deputies were in here this morning for a briefing. There were so many of them a few leaned against the wall and it must have tilted the painting a bit. It doesn't usually look like that."

All censure vanished from her manner and she

whirled back to look at him, the painting forgotten. "All your deputies? Things are that bad?"

"They're not good," Trey confirmed. "The governor's even getting concerned."

Those golden eyes widened in surprise and Bree came around his desk to give him a hug. "I'm sorry for the comment that you look bad. It was insensitive."

"It's true."

She leaned forward and laid a hand over his cheek, the same concern he always saw in his mother's gaze reflected in hers. "It's just rare I ever see my big brother with the slightest bit of scruff on his face and here you have a few days of growth."

"It's only one day." Trey patted her hand. "I'm considering a new look."

The ready snort came winging back in his direction as she dropped her hand. "You haven't had a different look since you were able to grow a beard."

"Maybe it's time to start."

Bree wasn't fooled by his casual dismissal, her gaze once more narrowing in on his face. Although nine years separated them, he rarely was able to pull one over on her. She was perceptive and bright and she cared passionately for her family.

Which nearly had him blurting out his whole misstep with Aisha and the proposal the night before. His best friend had dismissed him outright and it had only made him more determined to get her to see reason and accept his harebrained scheme.

Proposal.

Trey mentally shook his head at all the word implied. Rings. Sex. Forever.

His mind lingered on each in turn and before it could

linger too long on the image of his best friend naked, he shifted gears.

Fast.

"Engagement looks good on you."

"I know." Bree whirled around the desk before plopping down in one of his government-issued office chairs with a hard thunk. She barely gave the slim chair frame and lack of padding a glance, her happiness that great. "And even though there's so much going on and I'm worried about everyone, you most of all, I'm happy. Way-down-deep happy. How weird is that?"

It wasn't weird. Not at all.

Bree might have an open heart and a deep love for her family, but she didn't trust others beyond their core family unit easily. Her creativity had always made her more intuitive than most, and coupled with the challenges of their broader Colton relatives, she didn't let people in easily. Rylan Bennet had somehow found a way past all that and had shown Bree a new path.

"Now. I know you're not here to talk about my decorating skills. What do I owe the pleasure of your company?"

"Mom thinks you're working too hard and wants you to come over for dinner tomorrow night."

What would she think if she found out I had someone following me through Roaring Springs last night?

His mind had been so full of thoughts of Aisha he hadn't given the street-level watch much consideration, but he needed to. Who was following him? Because he'd been in law enforcement long enough to know that was exactly what was going on yesterday.

Mentally vowing to discuss it with Daria, he smiled at his sister, deliberately keeping his tone gentle.

"Mom's right. That still doesn't mean she can order me up or make you do her dirty work."

"Come on, Trey. She worries about you. And she figured if I gave you the doe eyes and the guilt you'd come."

"Both traits you inherited from her." Trey considered his baby sister. Although she had the same lighter skin he did, a perfect blend of their parents, her build and features were practically carbon copies of their mother. "Along with her Machiavellian streak of believing she's entitled to always get what she wants."

Bree shrugged. "Dad spoils her, what can we say?"

"Like Rylan spoils you?"

The mention of her fiancé had the desired impact, and his sister was out of her chair again, roaming the room as if nothing could hold her still. Growing up with an artist, he'd always understood her mercurial personality was a side effect of her creative gifts. And despite the age difference between them, from the moment his parents had brought her home, Trey had seen the ethereal beauty that was Bree. The wide-eyed baby had grown into an active, curious child and then on into a wildly creative young adult. His mother had understood how to channel it, giving Bree space on their ranch that was hers alone. To paint. To dream. To create.

And from that, she'd built her life's work. Her Wise Gal gallery was one of the most popular businesses in Roaring Springs and the vandalism and threats on her business the spring before had been firmly put behind her. She'd even found her future husband from the ashes of that pain. Now she looked forward to her future and Trey couldn't be happier for her.

That happiness dimmed a bit as Bree stopped pacing and turned toward him, the wolf she'd created on high alert over her shoulder. "Has there been any news of Skye?"

"Nothing yet. Phoebe hoped going public with her relationship with Prescott would draw her out but she hasn't made contact yet."

"Mom and Dad have been over at Uncle Russ and Aunt Mara's house quite a bit. Mara's sick over it all. She keeps going back and forth between being sad and upset over Sabrina's death and grateful Skye wasn't a part of the discovery on the mountain." Bree hesitated, the rush of energy she came in with fading in the reality of all their family faced. "It's weird how this all has made Dad and Uncle Russ closer."

"I'd say it's a shame it's taken such horrible crimes for the Coltons to come together as a family."

"I know." She glanced down at her left hand and the ring sparkling there. "There are times I wonder why Rylan wants to marry into it all."

"He wants to marry *you*, Bree." Trey leaned forward, the need to make her understand that suddenly urgent. "Wonderful, awesome you. The rest of us Coltons are just family baggage along for the ride."

"You'd think I'd be used to it by now. But every day he surprises me."

"Isn't that a good thing?"

"It's the best thing." Bree smiled. "I always envied how close you and Aisha are. It's like you can read each other's thoughts. And I never thought I'd meet another person who could do that. But then I'm with Rylan and it's so easy. Natural."

Where had *that* come from?

Trey searched Bree's face, suddenly paranoid that his

sister had read something in his demeanor. Or worse, had somehow heard that Aisha had disregarded his suggestion they couple up to help his election chances.

Careful, he tried to step through the land mine Bree had just set down on the middle of his office floor. "You think Aisha and I are natural? Together, I mean."

"Well, yeah. Anyone who's spent more than five minutes with the two of you knows how much chemistry you have."

"But I'm not marrying Aisha."

"Sure. But I mean…well. She's your bestie."

"She is."

That impulse rose up again, and Trey was tempted to spill his guts to his sister. But something still held him back.

He and Aisha didn't have a relationship like Bree and Rylan. Or like his parents. They were best friends, but that didn't mean they were compatible as a couple.

If they were, wouldn't she have approached his proposal differently? That question had haunted him since he'd introduced the whole idea.

"Trey. You okay?" Bree's gaze searched his face. "You went somewhere there."

"Sure. I'm good. And I will come to Mom and Dad's tomorrow night."

"While we're on the subject, bring Aisha with you. I haven't seen her in a while and I miss her."

"I'll ask her if she's free. It is Saturday night. She might have a date."

"Well, yeah, sure." Bree hesitated for a moment, the carefree attitude she'd breezed in with fading. "That doesn't bother you?"

"No."

Even as the denial left his lips, Trey knew otherwise. The idea of Aisha on a date with some strange guy did bother him. He'd always sort of accepted she dated, but now that he was faced with accepting that and actually acknowledging it out loud, he realized he didn't want to.

Only what was he supposed to do about it?

No matter how he twisted or turned it, he'd asked the woman to be his fiancée and she'd said no. Even as a practical, slightly devious way to fix a problem, she wasn't interested in getting on that train with him.

Why would she ever want to do it for real?

And why, after nearly thirty years in each other's lives, did that suddenly seem like a tragedy?

It HAD BEEN a full day since her conversation with Trey and Aisha still hadn't quite recovered. Even now, more than twenty-four hours later, she was still dazed and confused. A state that had been reinforced by how often she caught herself staring into the distance.

Like now.

Her focus returned to the cream-colored walls of her kitchen and her pinging oven timer. She opened the door and checked the brownies—his favorites—with a toothpick. At the confirmation that dessert was done, she pulled it out, her thoughts already back on their discussion the night before.

"Engaged?" she wondered aloud.

Fake engaged, her conscience quickly taunted back.

Still, real or fake, it would be announced to the world. Had the man gone out of his mind?

She understood the pressure he was under. A murder in Bradford County would be stressful enough, but he was dealing with seven of them. His family had been seemingly under attack since the new year and he now also faced a threat to his job. Putting her more romantic feelings aside, Trey Colton had been her best friend since they were eight. She *knew* him. And she knew the current situation was eating him up.

But was an engagement really the answer?

Leaving the brownies to cool, she crossed back to her kitchen table and the photos that had consumed her off-hours. Or that *had* consumed her off-hours until Trey's bombshell.

Seven women.

It was alarming how often that thought kept going round and round in her mind. Although her primary concentration was slanted toward patient work and positive outcomes with therapy, she'd done plenty of study in her undergraduate and graduate degrees on psychopathic personalities. The unique mix of raging need and lack of remorse or empathy was a hallmark of the disorder.

And disturbingly evident in each photo she reviewed.

Who would do this? Was it someone who walked among them here in Roaring Springs? And if it was a person they all knew, how scary was it to think they'd hid such violent behavior for so many years?

Aisha had every confidence Trey would find the culprit. He had determination on his side and a commitment to his job that was unparalleled. But what if it took a while to catch the killer? The man—and professionally she knew that was the most likely choice—had eluded capture this long. He might be on a downward spiral but he wasn't to be underestimated.

What if it took so long Trey was voted out of office in the meantime?

The thought of that alternative—a world where Trey wasn't able to do the job that mattered so much to him—was difficult to imagine. She could still remember the night of the last election and how they all sat around his parents' house, waiting for the voting results to be tallied. The call had come in around ten and they'd all celebrated until the middle of the night. The happiness had been palpable, each of them excited for Trey, for his future and for the people of Bradford County who'd just elected a man who would always put their safety and well-being above all else.

Now he had to defend his reputation and his position against a man who appeared to have the disposition of a rattlesnake. And a rather disturbing racist streak.

She hadn't missed Evigan's dig the other night at the town hall, nor had she missed it the last few times he'd made public comments about Trey. After all these years, it still hurt. A wild slap in the moment, and then a sting that lingered in a constant state of frustrated sadness.

But that was also part of what had made her and Trey so close.

Growing up, there hadn't been many children of color at school. That had changed over the past few years as Roaring Springs had—thankfully—become more diverse, but a quarter century ago things were different. She wasn't shunned outright but she wasn't the first kid chosen for sports or the one with a circle of friends out at the playground. To compensate, she'd taken to reading during those periods and had her nose shoved in her latest obsession, Trixie Belden's adventures with her best friends and fellow mystery solvers, the Bob-Whites.

Then one day, it all changed. The boy with the

golden-brown eyes she'd noticed in the hallways had sat down next to her. She had a favorite spot on the far side of the playground, off by herself and away from the teams she was never selected first for. Her own self-appointed haven on the steps of a small slide someone in her class had declared was for babies and which forevermore remained untouched.

Then, that one day, she'd felt a tap on her shoulder and looked up into those serious eyes.

And she saw a friend.

"What are you reading?"

"A mystery."

"Is it a good one?"

It was her favorite one. A mystery involving emeralds missing since the Civil War and a race to find them against a rather unpleasant bad guy. She'd read it three times now and each time she understood how the author had layered in clues along the way.

"I like it."

"That's a big book. No one else in our class reads books that big."

Aisha knew she was ahead of everyone on that count but didn't know what to say. The statement was matter-of-fact and it didn't sound like he was making fun of her, but you never knew. People liked to act like they were saying nice things to you but there was really something not nice underneath. It happened to her mom a lot and it bothered her.

She was still trying to assess his motives when he spoke again, wedging himself in next to her on the step. "I think it's cool. I tried one but I'm not ready to read it yet. So my mom got me a heap of comic books and said we'd read them together. She's pregnant."

"Really?"

*Aisha had a younger sister and still vaguely remem-
bered her mom pregnant, but it had been a long time
ago. And after her dad took off to have his new life with
his new wife, her mom didn't seem interested in getting
married again. She was always hugging Tanisha and
her and saying how they were the Three Musketeers.*

"Is it a boy or a girl?"

"Don't know yet."

"Which do you want?"

*"I don't care. A baby brother would be cool but a
baby sister would be special. I'd be a good big brother
to her. I'd have to protect her and watch out for her."*

"Babies are small. You'd look out for a brother, too."

*"Yeah." He shrugged but she saw a subtle determi-
nation in him. "People need watching out for."*

"Do you?"

*"Sure, but I have my mom and dad. Not everyone's
so lucky."*

*She wasn't sure what he meant by that, but for some
reason it seemed too personal to ask him.*

*Especially because she knew people talked about
him. A girl in her class called him a "Colton" in a voice
that made her think his last name was important. She
even talked about going up to the big ski resort in town
and said that it belonged to his family.*

*"You want to come play? I know your book is inter-
esting and all but we're going to get in one more game
of kickball before recess finishes."*

*Aisha glanced at Trixie on the cover and was filled
with happiness at the fact that the race to the emeralds
could wait until later. "Sure."*

"Come on!"

The heavy knock on her door was followed by a call out, muffled through the door. "Pizza's here!"

Both pulled her from the memory she hadn't thought about in a long time. She still had that book, though. Nestled in her wall-to-wall bookshelves in the living room. Each time she glanced at it, whether it was to dust or to do an occasional quick reread to channel the comforts of an easier time, she remembered that day on the playground.

The day she'd met Trey Colton.

Aisha usually just hollered back for him to come in but even she'd given in to the collective concern about the Avalanche Killer. She hadn't left her door unlocked in several months. "Coming!"

Trey stood on the other side of the door, a large cardboard pizza box in hand giving off the most delicious scents. He'd changed out of his work uniform and Aisha had to mentally stop herself from staring at the low-slung jeans and broad shoulders beneath his T-shirt. "Hey."

"Hey." The nerves that had been constant company for the last twenty-four hours grabbed at her with frantic hands. "Thanks for picking up pizza."

"Would I fail you on a Friday night?" Trey came in, his back straight as he walked to her kitchen. "Friday nights were made for pizza."

It was banal conversation, the sort of meaningless words that floated between people all the time. As a psychologist, she understood it. The ways people communicated and made themselves comfortable with one another. Only now, this was anything but comfortable. It felt stilted and awkward.

This was her best friend, damn it. She wasn't nervous around Trey. She might be wildly besotted and aware of his every move, but she wasn't awkward. She'd left awkward behind on those slide steps years ago and hadn't looked back. That day had changed her life. It had proved to her that the world always looked better with a friend.

And from that day forward, she'd always had Trey.

WHAT HAD HE done?

That thought kept Trey steady company as he walked the piping-hot pizza back to Aisha's kitchen. Her apartment was a nice size—two bedrooms with plenty of room for her and her cat—and Trey had always felt comfortable there.

But right now?

It was like they stood on the edge of a cliff at fourteen thousand feet and the only way to navigate was some ginger sidestepping while the altitude stole your breath.

Of course, who needed a cliff when Aisha was around? She had her hair pulled up in some sort of haphazard bundle beneath a clip, loose, wispy curls falling around her face, and she wore some of the yoga pants she favored in her off-hours. The damn pants always drove him crazy, the way they hugged her hips and clung to her very attractive curves.

Seizing on a topic and *off* thoughts of her very fine derriere, he focused on the cat she'd rescued as a small kitten five years ago.

"Where's Fitz?"

"Hiding. He's in one of his moods today."

Trey busied himself getting plates. "Why? He has nothing to complain about."

"I don't know," Aisha said as Trey opened the pizza box. "But he's in a mood. He'll come running once he decides pizza is better than pouting."

"Let's eat before then." The heavy scent of pizza was no match for the pan sitting on top of the stove. "Or we can skip dinner and go straight to dessert."

"Just like a man."

Unbidden, one of those stubborn images of Aisha naked dive-bombed his brain and he nearly bobbled his plate. Ignoring it and the need to reply with some smart remark, he took a seat at the kitchen table. The photos from the stack he'd shared with her were still spread out at the end, and he set down his plate, determined to stack them up.

Hell, he'd burn them if he could.

"We started our week like this and now we're ending it the same." Trey quickly gathered them together, then turned them over to avoid even one image staring back at them through dinner. "Not one damn thing's changed."

"It's only been a few days, Trey," she reminded him.

"And a few weeks since the discovery. The lab's no closer to identifying the other women and the FBI's starting to throw their weight around a bit more."

"They want the case?"

"Oh, if you ask them, there's no wanting anything. They *have* the case. I'm just the county schmo they're keeping in their confidence in hopes they can get something out of me when they need it."

She arched a brow. "I thought Agent Roberts was a good guy?"

"Daria keeps telling me he is and I trust her judgment, but he's gone quiet these past few days. Makes me think he's getting orders not to be quite so cooperative with the locals."

Trey knew his role. His job—the one he was elected to—was to protect his constituents. They were his priority and he didn't want to lose focus. He'd also been in law enforcement long enough to know that the Feds could take over jurisdiction as they saw fit.

But that didn't mean he had to sit idly by, twiddling his thumbs. A killer had targeted his town. His *home*. And based on recent events, there was every indication the killer's sights had turned firmly toward the Coltons. Skye's disappearance weighed heavily on them all.

His fears may not be as acute as those of Russ and Mara, but he worried for his younger cousin and her safety. Or for any other woman unlucky enough to capture the eye of a killer.

Those photos he'd turned over indicated a ruthless predator with little intention of releasing a selected victim. There couldn't be another.

He was determined to catch him before the unthinkable happened.

Chapter Six

Aisha wasn't sure how it happened, but somewhere between their awkward moments when Trey arrived and the curative properties of pizza, the two of them got back on track. He'd shared his concerns over the case—and his fear they wouldn't get to a new victim in time—and she did her best to help him focus on what they could control.

The autopsies. The hunts through any and all missing persons databases they could access. Even the basic investigative work digging into Sabrina Gilford's and April Thomas's last days were essential steps in finding a killer.

And then there was his proposal. It still hovered between them as distinctly as the lingering scent of pepperoni, but at least they were laughing again.

Even as both of them resolutely avoided the topic of an engagement, fake or otherwise.

"Did you make the dark chocolate brownies?"

"With the caramel filling."

"Why'd I eat so much pizza?" Trey patted his stomach, his gaze already drifting to the pan on the stove.

Aisha nodded. "Go get 'em."

He leaped out of his chair and nearly stumbled over

a squalling Fitz, who'd taken up a corner of the rug beneath the kitchen table where he could pray for any discarded pepperoni.

"Keep dreaming, little man." Aisha glanced down at him and when she was met with only his soulful green eyes, she snuck a small piece off her unfinished second slice. "Oh, fine."

The cat lapped up the offering before slinking off. They'd lived together long enough that Fitz knew there wasn't a second bite coming. If he skulked off he could at least get in the final word of waving his tail, that demonstrative appendage stuck straight up in the air.

"Is that the cat equivalent of a middle finger?" Trey asked as he took his seat.

"I'm pretty sure it is."

"You'd think he'd be more grateful."

"Aw, I don't know. If I was forced to eat dry niblets, specially formulated to ensure I don't get hairballs, I might be grumpy, too."

"No cat equivalent to pizza?"

"Not if he hopes to see his senior years."

"Spoken like a true health professional."

Aisha winked at Trey before reaching for the photos he'd set aside earlier. In one of her attempts earlier that day to avoid thinking about him, she'd forced herself to look at the murders from a new angle. Although her notes still felt way too sparse to do any good, she was anxious to run a few things past him.

"Do we have to keep looking at those?" He plated one of the brownies and handed it over. "Those images are stuck in my head and aren't going anywhere."

Trey had worked in law enforcement a long time and she'd probed off and on through the years to make sure he was taking care of himself and not burning out. His distaste for the pictures suggested the time might have come to look a bit closer.

"You doing okay? With all this?"

"These women are dead. Have been dead for years, right there on that mountain."

"Because of a deranged mind."

"And it all happened right under my nose. How good am I as Bradford County sheriff if this was going on and I had no idea?"

"But a serial killer acts in shadows. Many of them go years before their crimes are discovered. These are crafty individuals who know how to hide their sickness."

"That shouldn't matter. This is a resort area. We get visitors from all over the world who come here to ski and enjoy the Rockies. I'm supposed to look out for them, yet somehow it's never even hit my radar we've had a number of women missing here for over a decade."

While she could understand his frustration, the sudden guilt was unexpected.

"What were you supposed to do?"

"Protect these people. Look out for them. Like my cousin Skye!" Trey pushed back from the table on those words and paced the kitchen. Agony rode his hard body, tightening the already impressive shoulders with tension and bending his spine with a sadness she'd never seen in him before.

That same agony painted him in dark lines when he turned to face her from across the kitchen. "I keep seeing those women, Aisha. And all I can picture is a call coming in that someone's found my cousin. Battered and broken and violated beyond anything a human being should endure."

"Oh, Trey."

The urge to comfort overrode all else. The tension that had gripped them since dinner the night before. The fantasies she carried for him that somehow they were more than friends. Even the walls she'd erected around herself after the crash-and-burn that was her grand romance in graduate school softened at the pain she saw in her friend.

Without thinking, she went to him. She wrapped her arms around him and pulled him close. Although he was a little over six feet, her five-foot-six-inch height was tall enough to get a solid grip around him.

And she held tight.

"We'll find her."

A hard, empty laugh echoed at her ear as he leaned into the hug. "I'm not doubting that. I'm just scared to death of what we're going to find."

While she hated the reason for his upset, she couldn't deny how good it felt to be wrapped in his arms. To wrap hers around him in return. The part of her—the one that knew it was an ongoing form of self-torture to want what you couldn't have—knew she should pull away.

Yet she stayed.

Wrapped in those strong arms, pressed against that broad chest. Held. Cherished. Loved.

Aisha squeezed just a bit tighter before pushing her personal thoughts away to focus on Trey's concerns. Although she didn't want to believe his cousin was yet another victim—didn't want to even put that sort of mental energy into the universe—Trey wasn't wrong. All signs pointed toward an escalating killer, operating in their small corner of the world.

And it was entirely possible Skye Colton had unintentionally put herself in his crosshairs.

They stood like that for several minutes. There were a million questions Aisha wanted to ask, but she held them back. There'd be time to press and probe, gathering a clinical stance on his mental state as he battled all the forces swirling around him.

For now, she had something she could do—fully in her power—to address one of those forces.

"If the offer still stands, I'll be your fake fiancée."

THE HUSKY TIMBRE of her voice still echoed against his neck where she'd whispered the words. Trey lifted his head, hardly daring to believe he'd heard her right.

"You'll what?"

"I'll take part in the ruse. You need all the time you can to focus on the Avalanche Killer and battling Barton Evigan shouldn't take a single moment of that. I have a way to help and I want to do it."

"But Aish—" He broke off as the truth of her offer sank in.

Although he'd initially asked as some sort of weird, fix-it-in-the-moment sort of solution to his problem, the reality was that having a chance to ignore the force that was his opponent for Bradford County sheriff would go a long way toward easing his mind.

And if the increasingly inappropriate thoughts about his best friend were the price he had to pay to gain that upper hand against Evigan, then he'd deal with it.

"You're really sure?"

"Yes, I'm really sure." Her gaze roamed over his face as if she searched for something. Seemingly satisfied, even though he had no idea what she'd found, she stepped back from their embrace. "But we have to set a few ground rules."

"Like what?"

"Well, for starters, I want to make sure the ruse doesn't hurt other people."

"Like who?"

"First and foremost, our families." She held up a hand before he could get into the issue of the size of his family. "Our immediate families. Your parents and sister. My mother and sister. That's it."

Once again, his smart, practical and—damn, yes, incredibly attractive—best friend had it right.

"What do you want to tell them?"

"The truth. We'll be lying to everyone else, it's the least we can do for them. Besides, they can help spread the word. If they're in on it, they'll help make sure as many people as possible know Barton Evigan is not only running against the solid, upstanding, experienced Sheriff Trey Colton, but he's also running against a soon-to-be-devoted family man."

"You've given this some thought."

That gaze was back, only this time instead of mystery, he saw cold, hard fact along with a wry little light deep in that dark chocolate gaze. "Can you honestly tell me you've thought of much else since yesterday when you brought this whole thing up?"

"No."

"Well, neither have I."

"It's just for show, Aish. We know the truth."

"Which is why we're going to put some ground rules in place. No dating other people while this is going on. It will fly against all you're trying to accomplish in looking like a family man until November."

"Fair enough." Not like he'd been doing all that much dating lately, but her point was valid. What he didn't expect was the gratifying shot of satisfaction at the idea she wouldn't date anyone between now and November, either.

"I have an old ring from my grandmother we can use as the engagement ring," Aisha continued on, oblivious to his thoughts. "And no kissing."

"What?"

"We're not actually engaged. We're not going to start making out around town."

Since his brain had fallen straight out of his head and was currently rolling around somewhere on her kitchen floor, Trey fought to keep hold of what stray thoughts he could manage. Especially since his hardened body and the brain that sat below his belt had taken over anyway at the thought of kissing Aisha. "But that's what people expect. Grand gestures and hand-holding and canoodling."

"Canoodling?"

"You know what I mean."

She shook her head. "Honestly, I'm not sure I do. But we'll do the bare minimum so no one gets suspicious. That's all."

Since he was at dangerous risk of overplaying his hand, he nodded and kept his comments to a minimum. "Sure. Right. No kissing."

"I'll call my mom later. What about your parents?"

His afternoon conversation with Bree came winging back. "They're actually having a small picnic tomorrow. Bree and Rylan are going over and I was asked to invite you. We'll do it then."

"Good." Aisha nodded, apparently satisfied they'd

worked out all the particulars. "I'll go get the ring now. It's in my jewelry box."

As he watched her go, Trey had to admit his fly-by-night scheme the evening before wasn't well thought out. It fixed his immediate situation, but he hadn't actually reduced the number of problems currently in his life.

He might have traded in battling Barton Evigan for sheriff but he'd just gotten sexy, tempting Aisha Allen in his place.

Life was not going to get any easier.

THE COLTON FARM just outside the city limits of Roaring Springs welcomed them as they drove through the gates to the property. Aisha had always loved coming here, the sprawling property like a second home.

Shortly after their first meeting on the slide stairs, Trey's mother, Audrey, had called Aisha's mother with a playdate invitation. Her mother had heard her talk nearly nonstop for two weeks over this nice boy who played with her at recess and nearly jumped at the chance to see her daughter make a new friend. LaShanna Allen had envisioned the two of them living happily ever after and, best as Aisha could tell, had been doing it ever since.

Which was why Aisha had barely gotten out of her mother's kitchen, the woman had kept her talking so long about the fake engagement. One, Aisha knew with absolute certainty, her mother wished would become real.

And now they'd go through it again with Trey's family.

He drove down the long, rolling drive, pulling into a space near the stables. The horses at Trey's family farm had always held a special place in her heart. She'd been a "horse girl," loving the animals since she could identify one in a photograph. While her mother had always done her best to support her girls' interests, horse riding lessons had simply been out of reach.

Which had made the amazing animals at Trey's family farm like a dream come true. One that had sprouted wings and taken flight from her very first visit when Trey's parents had taken her out on one of the mares. Aisha was hooked and Audrey had struck up a friendship with her mother that ensured she and her sister, Tanisha, had become permanent fixtures at the Colton farm each and every summer.

"Like a dream."

"Hmm?" Trey asked, glancing over from the driver's seat.

"Your home. This farm. It's always been like a dream come true to me."

"My father's often said the same thing. He's fond of saying the air out here is different." Trey shrugged as he cut the engine. "I don't know. I think maybe it's the people out here who are different."

Although she didn't understand it when she was younger, as an adult Aisha had learned that Trey's father, Calvin, had gone a different direction from the rest of his family. While his older brother, Russ, was busy building The Colton Empire, and his younger brother, Whit, was busy running after anything in a short skirt, Calvin had met and married Audrey Douglas and had settled down to raise a family.

"No Colton Manor for your dad?"

"Nope." Trey smiled. "Not for Dad. He loves it out here and always has. Give the man a horse and my mother, not in that order, and he's content to while away his days."

"I think that contentment is what makes him so special. He knows who he is. Your mom, too. Once you have that, it's a heck of a lot easier to accept others for who they are and where they're at."

"That's a nice way to put it."

"It's true." Aisha stared out at the horses beyond the windshield. "Do you think they'll accept what we're doing here?"

Although she had insisted they tell Calvin and Audrey the truth, now that the moment was upon them, Aisha's feet had grown rather cold.

"They'll understand."

"Maybe. But I can't help feeling they're going to think we're making a bad choice."

"I don't know." Trey turned to stare at her, his gaze dropping to the slim band of emeralds she'd slipped on her left hand last night. "Do you think we're making a mistake?"

"I didn't think so last night."

"And now?"

"I'm not sure. People don't like being deceived. And while we'll remain friends after this all goes down, someone's going to get upset if they realize we lied."

Trey's hand snaked out and covered hers. "Then no one has to know the reason. We'll simply say we ended the engagement. Not that we stopped being friends."

"Do you think it's that simple?"

"We're going to make it that simple."

She wanted to believe him. More than that, she wanted to believe in her own conviction that she'd do this, support Trey during this time and then they'd go back to the way things were.

Before.

Before she'd had a taste of telling the whole world she was in love with him.

TREY SETTLED INTO one of the comfy deck chairs on his parents' back porch and watched his dad work his magic with the grill. Although *magic* was probably a stretch.

Meals at the Colton farm were nearly always better in winter—when he was assured of a meal crafted by his mother's deft hand—but his father was passable on the grill.

Usually because his mother made enough sides to fill them up *and* had figured out a few tricks with marinades that could offset his father's insistence that anything formerly living was thoroughly cooked.

The man had never eaten a raw steak in his life and was determined no one else should, either.

"I'm glad you're here, son. It's been too long since we had a family dinner."

"I know."

"It's my duty to stand out here and tell you that your mother's worried about you." Calvin set the large tongs he used to turn the steaks and burgers over beside the grill, picked up his beer and took the seat next to Trey. "That's all true. But I'm worried, too."

"I'm good, Dad. Honest."

"Don't mistake my meaning. You're solid as a rock. Always have been. But this is unlike anything any of us have ever seen."

"I know."

"Russ and Mara—" Calvin broke off, Trey's normally steady dad crumbling under the weight of the burden they carried as a family. "They're sick over Skye."

"We all are, Dad."

"And those women. The news reports have quieted a bit now that there are not updates coming every day. I haven't decided if that's good or bad."

Although the press coverage that had descended on Roaring Springs had been oppressive during the height of the discovery, the quiet over the past week or two had grown frustrating. Less active news coverage meant less time for the killer to see his crimes glamorized on TV. And less TV time meant he had the mental bandwidth to plot and plan for his next strike.

"We're working as fast as we can," Trey finally said, determined not to assume the worst over his missing cousin. "And the news media will be back when we have something to update them on. I'm not going to complain about the quiet in the meantime."

"It wasn't quiet the other night."

"You mean Evigan?"

"Your mother's run up against him a few times. He's not big on any of the local activist groups. He's made trouble, throwing his weight around at a few of the marches she's done in town over the past few years."

At the idea anyone had even looked sideways at his mother, Trey stiffened. "He do anything?"

Calvin's eyebrows shot up. "You think he'd still be standing if he had?"

Trey couldn't hold back the smile. "Course not."

"All I'm saying is the man's a troublemaker. Watch your back and keep your guard up."

"Yeah, Dad. So about that…"

As the idea of sharing the news of his fake engagement materialized in more solid form, Trey realized he and Aisha hadn't exactly discussed how they were going to handle things. Since it wasn't an *actual* engagement, he had to assume it was okay to tell his father without her. In fact, Trey amended to himself, it was probably for the best. He could gauge his dad's reaction and then figure out how to break it to his mother.

"What's going on?"

"The governor sent one of his aides to visit me the other day."

"Oh." His father's exhale suggested the news wasn't lost on him.

"Yeah. I'm not surprised they're keeping tabs on what's going on here with the Avalanche Killer investigation, but I was surprised when the aide pushed the conversation in a new direction."

"He's not questioning your judgment, is he?"

That same fierce pride Trey had seen in his father's defense of his wife was as equally rabid for his son. It warmed Trey and was a visceral reminder of all the reasons he worked so hard. He'd rather cut off an arm than disappoint Calvin and Audrey Colton.

"No, but he suggested my status as a bachelor sheriff might contribute to Evigan's arguments against me."

"You're joking."

"No. And neither was the aide. Which got me thinking."

His father's eyes narrowed but he remained silent as Trey dived into the details. "I mean, I want to get married but there hasn't been a lot of time lately to form romantic attachments. Or to even go on dates, for that matter."

"You're a young man. You should be out enjoying yourself."

"I'll enjoy myself later. After—" Trey stopped himself, the reality of what remained unsolved looming as large as ever. "The point is, I'm not currently married and don't exactly have a quick way of fixing that. Or, I thought I didn't."

"What's going on?"

"I talked to Aisha and she's going to go in on it with me."

"In on what?"

"She's going to play my fiancée. From now until the election. We'll make a show of being engaged, planning a wedding, all that. It should ease people's minds that somehow I'm not as solid a choice for reelection because I'm not a family man."

"That is ridiculous."

"Is it?" Trey waited until his father's initial shock wore off and took a sip of his beer to let the news settle in.

It did seem ridiculous on the surface and for all the reasons Aisha listed for him the night before. Yet even knowing all that, he'd been unable to come up with an alternative that would settle public sentiment until the election.

"Look at it from the voters' perspective. I'm the one in an elected position and I haven't gotten the job done."

"You've kept law and order in this county for nearly four years. A serial killer is uncovered, one who the Feds can't even get a bead on, and somehow you're chopped liver?" Calvin shook his head. "I'm not buying it, Trey."

"People need a scapegoat when they're scared."

"But you're above reproach. You've handled this by the book every damn step of the way."

"And there's still a killer at large."

His father opened his mouth, then shut it again. He seemed to weigh his words before finally speaking. "I love Aisha. Your mother and I both do. But is this really a good thing for the two of you?"

And wasn't that the heart of it all?

Although he could think of no one better to fake his way through the next three months with, he was misguided if he didn't think there'd be some consequence to their actions.

He believed their friendship was strong enough to withstand it. *Knew it*, really. And still, he worried. "She knows me."

"And you know her."

"We've been friends since childhood."

Calvin nodded. "That, too."

"We'll figure it out. It's not like we're going to do anything different in private."

The thought was out before he could contain it and his father didn't miss the slip. "You'd like to be doing something in private?"

"With Aish? Come on."

"I don't know, son. She's a beautiful woman. Sharp, too. Any man would be lucky to have her."

His father was right. Any man *would* be lucky to have her. And someday, he was going to have to accept the moment when another guy did. But that wasn't today, and for now, he had to focus on the present. "I know."

"So maybe you should make the most of these three months. You two might surprise yourselves."

"Calvin Colton, are you burning those burgers?" Audrey's voice floated out to meet them as she marched onto the back porch. "I know you like a well-done burger but quit jawing with your son and get those off the grill."

A lifetime of farming had kept his father in prime shape, but he moved even faster than Trey would have given him credit for. Calvin leaped out of his seat and rushed back to the grill, lifting the lid to remove the burgers.

"Whew! Just in time." His mother shook her head before sidling up next to her husband. "I'll finish those. Go on in and say hi to Bree and Rylan. They just got here. And I think Aisha needs a fresh drink." She softened the instructions with a kiss on the lips, then patted his butt. "Get."

Trey waited until his father was out of earshot before stating the obvious. "I think he's grateful."

"Of course he is. If he cooked these much longer we'd be eating bricks." His mother carefully lifted each burger off the grill, transferring them to a fresh plate beside the silver monstrosity that still couldn't magically correct his father's cooking. "As it was, I put dinner at risk by giving the two of you five extra minutes."

"You gave us time?"

"He's wanted to talk to you. I had to talk him out of driving into town yesterday."

Although both his parents were observant and involved in his and Bree's lives, Trey tread carefully as he tried to navigate around his mother's sixth sense when it came to her kids. "It's been a difficult time, of course. But I can handle it. I'm doing fine, Mom."

"You are handling it but you're *not* fine. We'll argue that subject at a different time."

Trey sighed. "I knew what I was getting into when I signed on for the job."

"I did, too. That's why we're not getting into it."

He moved up next to his mother and pulled her close. "I love you for that."

She turned into his hug and the no-nonsense demeanor and tough attitude faded as her arms came around his waist. "Don't mistake our worry for questions about your ability. You make us proud every single day."

"Thanks for that."

"Now tell me something else."

He tightened his hold and pressed a kiss to his mom's head. "Sure."

"Why is Aisha wearing a ring on her left hand?"

Chapter Seven

Trey stepped back from his tight hold on his mother and dropped his arms. Damn, the woman was scary. She took the concept of "a mother's intuition" to new heights.

"Uh…you noticed that?"

"I'm not the artist your sister is, but I usually observe the world around me. And I notice new jewelry. I'd have gotten around to the question eventually but I saw her glancing down at it more than once while we talked. It got me wondering."

"It was her grandmother's."

"Oh."

Trey took the briefest moment of satisfaction at stymieing Audrey into thinking the ring was a simple fashion choice before he fessed up. "But your superscary intuition is still right."

"About?"

"Some rather powerful government officials think I would be harder to beat in November if the voters saw me as a family man."

"You are a family man."

"No. I'm a Colton and there's a difference."

Where he might have expected argument, all he got

was a heavy sigh. "Yes. A fact no one around here likes to forget."

"Also a fact my opponent has been using to his advantage. Evigan hasn't exactly been subtle about using the Colton name as a target. Or punching bag," Trey added.

"What does this have to do with Aisha?"

It's like pulling off a bandage, he thought, before diving in. "She's agreed to pretend to be my fiancée for the next few months. Just to get past the election."

"Trey Douglas Colton. You're going to lie to everyone?"

His mother didn't pull out his middle name often, so the fact that she did only added to the lingering questions he hadn't quite answered satisfactorily in his own mind.

"Aisha and I are good friends. It's no one's business just how close we are, or how we choose to spend our time."

"But you're using the ruse to ensure votes."

"I'm using the ruse to ensure a thoroughly unqualified ass doesn't get into office."

Audrey's battle stance wavered before the arms at her hips fell to her side. "I want to stay on my soap box over this, but I'm having a hard time. That man is awful. And while I'd believe no one was a worthy opponent against you, I'm not so bewitched by own son not to recognize there are other qualified people in the world."

"So you understand?"

"I understand. I don't have to like it."

"I don't like it, either," he confessed. "But I really don't see any other way. And if this will take the pressure off the election I can focus all my attention on catching a killer."

"And you really think this is the only way?"

"Can you think of another?"

His mother's formidable stare stayed firmly in place, the rich brown eyes he loved so much never faltering. Until something obviously clicked and she nodded. "No."

"Aish and I are strong. We'll get through this and go back to normal in no time."

Whatever conclusions his mother had satisfied herself with shifted at his words. "You think it's that simple?"

"Sure it is. We've been friends for nearly my entire life. We know each other. And we spend enough time together. She's the obvious choice."

"Hmm," Audrey whispered. "Obvious, you say?"

"Yeah. Everyone knows we're friends. How big a leap is it to say something more developed?"

And how hollow did it seem to think that people would actually believe their ruse and then they'd go back to normal, like nothing had happened?

Even if something had happened.

A fake something, but *something* all the same.

"Do you think you can do this? Without your heart getting involved."

"My cold heart's the problem here. And my lack of a wife."

"You're sure about that?"

Was he? Especially because he felt neither cold nor sure when he was around Aisha. Swallowing back the prevarication, he projected a calm he absolutely did not feel. "Of course."

"Then what about Aisha's?"

"She's fine. You know Aish, she's solid."

His mom reached out, laying a hand against his cheek. "Oh, baby. Do you hear yourself?"

"It's an op, Mom. It'll be fine."

Her dark eyes searched his and even with the fading summer light, he saw her skepticism. But it was her quietly voiced question when she finally spoke that pulled him up short. "What if it isn't?"

"Why wouldn't it be fine? Why would you think that?"

"You two are close. You always have been. It would be unfair to parade her around town, telling people how much you care for her."

"I do care for her."

His mother's hand dropped away. "Like a man loves a woman, Trey."

Once again, his mother's intuition twisted the kaleidoscope, shifting the landscape seemingly before his eyes. "But we're friends."

"What if one of you develops feelings?"

The unsettled thoughts that had accompanied him since his engagement idea first came to light returned once more. Only this time, instead of assessing his own emotions, he had to wonder about Aisha's. "You think she'll do that?"

"How often does she date?"

"I don't know. Often, I suppose."

His mother zeroed in on that one. "You *suppose*? Don't friends talk about those things?"

"We don't."

"Why not?"

He shrugged against the scrutiny. "I don't know,

Mom. We're friends but she's entitled to a private life. I don't ask her about hers and she doesn't ask me about mine."

"Just promise me you'll be careful with each other."

"Sure we will." When the frown on her face didn't fade at his words, he pulled her close again. "I will be careful. She's my best friend. I'm not going to mess that up. For anything."

"I hope not, baby." Audrey sighed, the light sound drifting into the evening light. "I really hope not."

HE'D HAD HIS eye on the woman since she'd flounced out of the nail salon in downtown Roaring Springs that afternoon. It hadn't been hard to keep tabs on her—she'd seemed to enjoy the attention her high, tight ass and doctor's office boobs received as she paraded up and down the main street of the resort town.

He'd seen many women come and go over the years. Even in winter, the ones with good bodies found a way to accentuate their figures in tight ski outfits and winter ski jackets that nipped in at the waist. But in the summer...

Well, it was easy to show off.

And this one was perfect. She had the same look and build he needed and if he played his cards right, she'd be relatively easy to lure.

He had a job to do.

The wad of cash he'd refitted before heading out bulged in his pocket. It was so easy to look impressive when you slung a few Benjis outside a stack of singles. He'd been doing it for years and was amazed the ruse never got old.

Or failed.

The dark-haired beauty didn't disappoint as she continued her trek toward the entertainment district of Roaring Springs. The row of bars and nightclubs were ramping up for a busy Saturday night and she was clearly out on the prowl. He waited, watching which bar she selected and was pleased when she chose one of the ones with a darker interior.

Perfect.

He waited until she slipped through the door, confident she had found her destination for the evening, and got out of the car.

It was time to go to work.

AISHA UNLOCKED HER front door and stepped inside her apartment. Trey followed, his presence both welcome and unwelcome. Which was a departure from every other time in her life she'd been in his company.

Had things already changed that much between them?

Although she'd resigned herself to the ruse they were going to perpetuate on nearly everyone they knew, the reality of actually voicing their plans to Trey's family had worn her out.

"You want some coffee?" Aisha flipped on the lights before reaching down to pick up Fitz where he wove in and out of the space between her calves.

"Sure."

She headed for the single-cup brewer on her counter and selected a pod she knew Trey liked. In moments the coffeemaker was going and the cat had grown bored with the attention, scampering off to his favorite spot under the bed in her spare room.

"My parents enjoyed seeing you tonight." Trey stood

at the entrance to the kitchen, one shoulder pressed against the door frame.

"And I enjoyed seeing them. But then again, I always do." The welcome was always warm at the Colton farm. "It was good to see Bree. She and Rylan look really happy."

"I know I'm failing in my job as big brother, but I really can't find a reason to kick the guy out."

She smiled at that, remembrances of the day Tanisha brought her husband home still vivid in Aisha's mind. "I felt the same about Randall. I wanted to dislike him on sight but there's something special when you see a person so besotted with your baby sister. I almost felt bad for the guy."

"Why's that?"

"Because I knew what he was getting into." The coffeemaker finished gurgling, and she handed Trey his mug, then turned back to select her own pod.

"That sounds devious."

"Nope. It's honest." She set her mug in place and pressed the button for her own cup of coffee. "Fortunately, Randall might have been wildly in love, but he had his eyes open. An important combination to make it to happy-ever-after."

"You think that's what it takes?"

"I think so." She shrugged, well aware she hadn't made it to happy-ever-after. "Or I figure it has to be a big part. You can't put your spouse on a pedestal yet you have to believe there's something extra special about them. It's a balance."

"Why no pedestal? Trey asked.

"Humans don't live on pedestals. It's a lot to ask

someone to live up to. An ideal instead of learning to love a real live human being."

He considered her words. "But that extra special part? That's important, too."

"Ah," she said, snagging her own mug off the brewer. "That's the real trick, I suppose. Thinking someone's still special after you've gone on a vacation together or cooked a holiday meal or shared a bathroom. That's when the hard part starts."

"When it's abundantly clear there's no pedestal?"

"Exactly."

Trey took a seat at the table and she took one opposite. The Avalanche Killer photos were still in a stack and she shifted them so as not to spill her drink.

"What about that?" Trey nodded toward the pile. "Those photos. The evidence someone lives in the shadows."

"I'm not sure."

While she understood marriage and other relationships had their challenges, what made someone so sick and twisted? Way down deep inside so that there was no evidence—or hope—of humanity. Or of ever living a life that anyone would consider sane or normal.

"I think that's the hardest part. Knowing how those women suffered is awful. Knowing it happened here in Roaring Springs, right alongside of all of us? I can't shake it." Trey dropped his head. "Or the sense that I've failed them."

"How can you think that? You didn't do this, Trey. None of this is your fault."

"Yes, but keeping people safe. That is my job."

"It's your job to deal with it when someone does bad. But you're not omniscient. You can't know what's coming before it happens." Aisha stared at the overturned photos, not needing to look at them to know exactly what they contained. "You can't know the sickness that lives inside someone."

"So what's the alternative? Stop worrying? Stop caring?" His last question came out on an agonized cry as Trey leaped up from the table. "I don't know who I am if I'm not a protector. Yet everything around me suggests I'm doing a piss-poor job of it!"

Aisha had never seen him like this before. While she'd never considered him an arrogant man, Trey Colton oozed self-confidence and purpose. His by-the-book attitude to his job had always made him a ready leader and his staff followed suit. He lived in a way as to be above self-reproach.

And while she firmly did *not* believe humans lived on pedestals, he was the closest to real-deal perfect as she'd ever met. He was kind and caring. He treated others with the utmost respect, regardless of how they'd treated him in return. And he was loyal. Trustworthy. Real.

And oh, how she loved him.

She'd argued to herself for years that it would be a mistake to act on her feelings. Hell, she'd told *him* as much the day before, setting strict ground rules for behavior. She knew attempting anything with him was a mistake that could—and likely would—ruin their friendship.

Yet in that moment, his pain roaring through every part of him, she couldn't stay away. And she couldn't leave him to stand on that precipice alone. Unable to fight temptation a second longer, Aisha stood and walked toward Trey. She waited a heartbeat—one lone beat—to stare into his golden eyes before she acted.

And then she leaped, pressing forward until their bodies collided. Until her lips met his in one hot, searing kiss.

TREY WASN'T SURE how it happened. One moment he was roiling inside, the panic and guilt and fear that someone else would be hurt on his watch consuming him, and then Aisha was in his arms.

And they were consuming each other.

Her long, lithe form filled his arms, her mouth covered his and all rational thought had vanished.

All he could feel or taste or *want* was her.

Over and over, the kiss spun out, growing by the moment, pulsing with a need he hadn't even realized was there. Yet… Now that she was in his arms, her mouth on his, Trey couldn't deny how right it felt. How good.

How perfect?

He ran his hands over her biceps, warm flesh unable to hide the strength she'd honed beneath that expanse of softness. Still, he was unable to drag his mouth away, the feel of her plump lips beneath his the warmest welcome of his life. Her tongue met his, a warm, coffee-flavored duel both seemed determined to master, and he sucked her into his mouth, memorizing her taste. Attempting to brand her in return.

This was Aisha.

His Aisha.

Just like she'd always been. And just as she'd never been.

Unbidden, his mother's voice filled his head, their earlier conversation echoing in his mind with all the power of a nuclear blast. *What if one of you develops feelings?*

Feelings?

Dazed, he lifted his head and stared down at her. The high curves of her cheekbones were flushed, as visibly warm as the woman in his arms. "Aish?"

"Hmm?" Her eyes popped open at the sudden realization they'd stopped kissing.

"Um."

"Oh." Slim brows rose over those eyes, dark as a midnight sky. "Oh, wow."

She pushed back, out of his arms before crossing her own. "Okay, right. That didn't take long."

He felt as dazed as she looked, but the quickly clearing haze that filled those midnight depths should have clued him in. "Long for what?"

"For me to break the ground rules."

"What ground rules?"

She tossed up her hands. "The ones we agreed to yesterday!"

"Don't get mad at me."

"I'm not mad, I'm—"

"Because I didn't do...*that*."

Whatever slight hope he had that she wouldn't get angry vanished at his accusation.

"I sure as hell didn't do it myself."

"You started it."

"I—" The bluster immediately went out of her, a balloon deflating in the middle of her kitchen as if popped. "You're right. I did."

"It was nice." Nice? If transcendent experiences could be called *nice*. Was he really that boring? That ridiculously straitlaced?

Kissing Aisha Allen wasn't nice.

Or simple.

And in that moment, Trey realized nothing about this situation was easy.

And he had no one to blame but himself.

"I'm going to ignore the *nice* comment and ask you to leave."

"It's probably for the best."

"I think it is."

Trey stood and walked his mug to the sink, watching the liquid wash down the drain. He turned on the tap to erase the lingering stain, wishing it was as easy to erase the last few minutes. Hell, the last few days. Since the arrival of the governor's aide and the ridiculous notion that had consumed his waking hours from the moment the man had walked out of the nondescript county building.

"You can leave the mug in the sink."

Job done, he did as she asked and turned to face her. The flush had vanished from her cheeks but the aftermath of what they'd done—how they'd ravished each other—still held her body in tight, quivering lines of tension.

He wanted to go to her. Wanted to resume the anything-but-nice passion that had flared between them and see how fast they could generate it again.

He'd give himself even odds it would take less than ten seconds.

Only he didn't do that. Because good cop Trey Colton didn't do things like that.

He didn't pretend to be engaged.

He didn't do a single thing not by the book.

And he didn't kiss his best friend until both of them had lost every functioning brain cell between them.

"I'll talk to you tomorrow?" Since he'd known her, he had asked that question a million times, always firmly assured of the answer.

When she said nothing, just let him pass through the kitchen, Trey understood something else.

Just how shocking it was to realize a kiss could change even the simplest of things.

Chapter Eight

Monday morning dawned crisp and clear, the cool Rocky Mountain breeze washing over Aisha's face as she ran through Roaring Springs. She'd already left downtown far beyond and had nearly reached The Chateau as the summer morning sun rose high in the sky. She'd momentarily considered stopping in to check on Phoebe but figured even Trey's hardworking cousin was still asleep in bed at 6:00 a.m.

Or was putting the early hour to even better use and making love with her handsome fiancé. If she were smart. And Aisha didn't know the woman to be anything else.

Which was way more than she could say for herself.

She'd always believed herself to be a smart, savvy woman who had her crap together, but after Saturday night, she was forced to reconsider that assessment. Thirty-five years of thinking one way about yourself didn't go down very well when you realized, instead, that you'd been a delusional fool.

How the mighty fall.

It was one of her mother's favorite sayings, each time she watched a celebrity self-destruct or as she shook her head over a news article transcribing the downfall of one politician or another. Aisha had always felt the thought rang with an air of disdain, like the folly of her fellow humans was a foregone conclusion.

Even after the heartbreak of her relationship in grad school, she had wanted to believe the best in others.

As a clinical psychologist, Aisha was well aware she couldn't help everyone. She wouldn't have gotten past her first year of practice without accepting that reality. But she still retained the hope that people *could* be better. That they always had the ability to rise above themselves.

Yep, she thought, disgust still clogging her breath in ways that had nothing to do with the exertion or the altitude. *Delusions.*

She was full of them.

She'd beaten herself up repeatedly since Saturday night, the consequences of going with impulse not lost on her.

It was nice.

Nice?

The woman seated next to her in church was nice. The scent of her new laundry detergent was nice. The wildflowers blooming in her backyard were nice.

But kissing Trey Colton. That was…

Exceptional.

Only he clearly hadn't thought so. He'd been polite and kind and had hotfooted it out of her kitchen as fast as he could.

And he hadn't called yesterday.

They didn't talk every day, but they talked most days. Or at minimum, they texted. But he hadn't done either yesterday and she'd stayed diligently away from her phone, going so far as to bury it in her purse around lunchtime.

As a distraction, she'd spread the Avalanche Killer paperwork out on her living room floor, sitting in the midst of it as she attempted to decipher patterns within the data. Patterns she knew were there if she'd only look hard enough.

It was only after eight hours with the images and becoming increasingly depressed at the lack of any real connection that she'd finally given up. She'd swept up the photos, tucked them in her work bag and headed for bed. Burying herself beneath the covers didn't do much for her mind-set but it had given her time to think through how to reset her relationship with Trey.

They couldn't put the genie back in the bottle, so all they could do now was damage control.

This wasn't their first bump in the road. Although Trey likely didn't know the reason why, she had pulled away from their relationship during the Year of Kenneth. At the time, she'd used the stress and pressure of grad school as her excuse for the limited conversations, missed trips home and less-than-newsy emails. It had seemed to work because Trey was there for her when she came back to the land of the living and hadn't seemed wise to her heartbreak.

Not that she'd been all that forthcoming once the sharp pain faded into something more manageable.

Kenneth was a grand love story, a dramatic heartbreak and an enormous life lesson, all rolled into one. Even now, she could think back on that time and feel the twin emotions of exhilaration and embarrassment as if they'd happened yesterday instead of over a decade ago.

Which made her decision to push Trey toward the physical on Saturday night an even bigger mistake.

What had come over her?

Trey was what had come over her. The sheer torture of watching him struggle over the discovered bodies and his missing cousin, Skye, had been too much to bear. He was such a good man. And she was still willing to give him that credit, despite the "nice" comment.

This wasn't Trey's first difficult case. Although Bradford County hadn't seen anything like a serial killer before—thankfully—his tenure hadn't been crime-free. The region had considerable money, and with that, power inevitably followed. In his nearly four years in office, Trey had brought down a gun smuggling ring and a drug gang operating up near Vail and had solved two separate murders.

But watching him struggle through the Avalanche Killer case? Observing the forces that acted around him—the Feds, the pressure of his family and the overwhelming anxiety of Barton Evigan's mounting campaign against him. It was all much harder than she could have imagined.

The property for the stately spa resort known as The Chateau rose up in front of her, the impressive facade home to one of the most decadent places in all of Roaring Springs. Although she didn't go often, there were occasional professional events held there that she'd attended. A few years back she and Tanisha had treated their mother to a day of pampering for her birthday, and Aisha had held Tan's bridal shower there, as well.

Stopping now to catch her breath, she stared at the large property known as "a little piece of France," nestled in the heart of Roaring Springs Valley. Like the rest of their resort town, The Chateau was a playground for those with money. Its status as a private enterprise meant it could—and did—decline press attention and reporters on the property. And its dedication to maintaining that privacy ensured its high-end clientele returned again and again.

Money. Wealth. Privilege.

Why did the image of riches suddenly stick in her thoughts?

Aisha considered all the photos she'd spent so many waking hours studying, then bumped them up against the crime scene photos of the murdered prostitute discovered on Wyatt Colton's ranch back in January. Bianca Rouge had been flown into town specially for a high-end client, there to entertain the man while he was vacationing. She wasn't common or unobtrusive and as terrible as it was, her murder had seemed like one of opportunity, not careful intent.

Add on, while she made her living as a prostitute, the woman who regularly assumed the role of Bianca Rouge had money. Investigators had turned up very nice digs in her hometown of Las Vegas and a sizable bank account. She wasn't lost or lonely and she certainly hadn't run away to Roaring Springs.

Sabrina Gilford didn't fit the lost-and-lonely bill, either. She was a party girl with a little too much in her bank account. The Gilford family wasn't "Colton rich," but who was? Their history in Roaring Springs was entwined with the Coltons and went back nearly as far. They might not play in the rarified air of the wealthy visitors who came to town to enjoy themselves, but they did well for themselves.

The other woman identified from the mountain—the

victim whose mother had insisted she was missing—
wasn't wealthy. Far from it.

Was there something in that?

An angle they'd overlooked up to now?

Aisha considered the little they did know and felt
it was important enough to tell Trey and gauge his
thoughts. Turning on her heel, she left The Chateau in
her wake as she headed for town.

It was time to face Sheriff Colton.

"ARE YOU EVEN listening to me?" Daria Bloom asked
Trey as she handed over a full mug of coffee.

"Of course I am."

Serious dark eyes stared at him over the rim of her
own coffee mug. "Tell me what I just said."

"You think the Feds are holding out on us and Agent
Roberts is an ass."

"I didn't call him that."

"You were thinking it."

"You're right, I was." Daria smiled. "And how do
you do that?"

"Do what?"

"Look like you're not paying attention when you
really are. It's freaky," Daria added as almost an af-
terthought.

"It's called multitasking. And I paired you up with
him for a reason. He might irritate you but you're good
with people. You read them and respond accordingly."

Since he'd spent two sleepless nights tossing and
turning over Aisha and was now using every remaining
firing neuron to focus on his job, he opted not to waste
any of them arguing with his favorite deputy.

"So Roberts is playing it close to the vest?"

"Yeah. He clammed up good and tight. So much for making nice with the locals. That seems to have vanished."

"He's in a tough position," Trey mused.

"You're excusing him?"

"No." He took a sip of his coffee. "I just figure the less time they spend with us the less time we have to spend with them."

"It also means we don't have their latest thinking."

"And ours isn't worth the sum total of a sheet of paper to write it all down on."

"I didn't say that," Daria added.

It was Trey's turn to smile. "But you were thinking it."

"Damn it."

Before he could say anything, a heavy knock came at his door, followed by Aisha rushing through it, her gorgeous long legs shown off to perfection in running shorts. "Hi."

"Hi."

She looked around, a halfhearted wave for Daria. "Am I interrupting?"

"It's hard to interrupt nothing," Daria groused. "The Avalanche Killer is a big fat dead end."

"Well, I think I may have something."

"What?" Trey and Daria asked nearly in unison.

Aisha tilted her head toward the door. "Let's go in the conference room. To your boards."

In collective agreement, they all filed out of his office, heading down the small hallway to the main conference room that had been taken over with images of murder.

"I'm going to get a coffee refill. Can I get you one?" Daria asked.

"Do you have a water?"

"Sure thing."

Daria's small detour gave Trey a few minutes to himself and he turned to Aisha the moment they cleared the doorway to the conference room. "You doing okay?"

"I'm good."

"Because you look—" He broke off, the sight of her in her workout attire still interrupting his ability to think clearly.

"Nice?" Aisha asked.

Allen, score one. Colton, score zero.

But the joke hit its mark. He smiled in spite of the fact that she clearly wasn't over his careless comment. "I promise I'll make that up to you."

"How?"

Before he could respond to the simple question, Daria walked back in and handed Aisha a bottle of water. "What's going on?"

"I was running this morning, out past The Chateau."

"When?" Trey leaned forward from where he was perched on the edge of the conference table. "In the dark?"

"The sun was coming up."

"So it was dark when you left home? Aisha, that's dangerous in the best of times, but especially with a killer on the loose."

"Trey—"

Daria interrupted before they could fall into a full-fledged argument. "Whatever this is you two can bicker about it afterward. And for the record, Aisha, I'm with Trey on the running in the dark. Now. What was your idea?"

Aisha shot him one last look—evidence that she was

most certainly *not* over the *nice* line—and turned to Daria. "Money. Wealth. Sabrina Gilford came from a bit of money but April Thomas didn't. She was a loner who came here to disappear."

"So?"

"So Sabrina's a break in pattern. Just like the woman murdered back in January. Bianca Rouge wasn't a poor, lonely woman off on her own. First she's a set-up on Wyatt Colton's property, but now we've associated her with the Avalanche Killer. What if she isn't?"

Trey considered all his cousin had been through, with the discovery of a body on his property and the subsequent investigation that ultimately cleared his name. "What does that have to do with the killer we're hunting?"

"It's a break in pattern. We've been looking at Sabrina as the sixth victim because she was discovered with the other bodies. But what if she wasn't one of them? Just like Bianca Rouge wasn't one of them."

"A different killer?" Daria set down her mug and walked over to the board set up specifically for Sabrina Gilford. "How would that killer know where the other bodies were? Sabrina was found with the others."

"I don't know." Aisha tugged on the curls that spilled out of her ponytail. "But I do know something's not right."

"And—" Daria added, on a roll "—if it weren't for the avalanche we wouldn't have even found the bodies. We can't discount the element of opportunity that favored the discovery."

Undeterred by the pushback, Aisha added, "Trey's said from the beginning something about the avalanche bugged him. The fact it came so late in the season. The level of destruction on a run that is regularly groomed."

She was right. He *had* been saying that from the start. Things had gotten so busy after the discovery of the bodies that he'd had to put the natural aspects on the back burner, but something about the impact of Mother Nature's wrath had bugged him from the onset.

"You are onto something, Aish. You've been saying Sabrina was a break in pattern." Trey thought once more about the avalanche. "Maybe it's more than a break."

Daria took another sip of her coffee, her attention still focused on the murder board. "I think we need to make a visit out to The Lodge. Take a look at that run again."

"The late spring rains probably haven't left much," Trey speculated.

"Only one way to find out," Aisha countered.

TREY PLODDED THROUGH the grass at the base of Wicked Mountain and tried not to wince at the large volume of mountain bike tracks crisscrossing the earth. Although the area where the bodies were discovered was still roped off, they hadn't been successful in shutting down the entire mountain.

Which meant the likelihood of finding anything of value was slim to none.

"Damn it." He dropped to his knees to look at the depth of the tracks. "It's been too long since the bodies were discovered. We're not going to find a thing."

Aisha moved up next to him. "Let's keep looking. This part of the mountain gets a lot of bikers who come down off that nearby green run. Maybe we just need to go up a bit higher. Get away from the heavy tracks."

Trey didn't have much hope they'd find anything farther up but knew she was right. They had to look. He'd had a few deputies who had canvassed the area the day after the bodies were found. They hadn't discovered anything and he'd left it at that, but now that he considered the vast area, he should have taken this task himself.

Or ordered more time spent looking.

Wicked Run was one of the most challenging in all of Bradford County. Vacationers came to The Lodge specifically to ski or snowboard the run, its double black diamond status an irresistible challenge.

It was well used. And it was groomed regularly to avoid disasters. Yet there had been one all the same.

"You find something?" Aisha's question broke into his thoughts.

"No."

"What are you shaking your head for?"

"It's bugged me from the start. They keep this run in pristine shape. Where did an avalanche come from in the first place?"

"Nature can be unpredictable."

"Yeah, but it's predictable, too. That was a late-season storm but the run was constantly looked after. My family may make me crazy but they run a solid resort here. They take care that their visitors are safe."

"What are you saying?"

"I don't know." Trey threw up his hands. "But I do know it's bothered me from the start. Even if the weather was unpredictable enough to cause an avalanche, what we had was a mess."

Aisha looked toward the peak of the mountain and

pressed a hand over her forehead to shield her eyes from the sun. "How would you tamper with a mountain?"

"What do you mean?"

"If you wanted to recreate a natural disaster, how would you do it?"

Trey shrugged. "Same way the grounds crew grooms the mountain. Set off charges. Manage the clearing of the snow."

"And The Lodge keeps the equipment to do that?"

"Sure. All of the local resorts do." Trey saw where she was going as all his lingering frustration over the situation faded. "Let's go talk to the groundskeepers."

"TREY, I CAN'T let you go out there scaring the grounds team."

"Then go with me. Either way, I need to talk to your crew."

Aisha watched the byplay as Trey negotiated with his cousin Decker. The tall, attractive man had always been one of her favorite Colton cousins, even though his workaholic devotion to The Lodge had prevented him from coming to every Colton event. A state that had changed since the prior spring when he fell in love with Kendall Hadley, a conservationist working for her father's company, Hadley Forestry.

Trey had kept her up to date on the specifics at the time, including Kendall's near abduction in March, and then Aisha had personally witnessed the worst event of all. She'd watched in horror, along with several Colton family members, including Trey's parents, when Kendall was targeted at an event at Bree's gallery. A huge rock tossed through the wide, front glass windows resulted in falling glass and a serious injury to Kendall's face. The necessary surgery to save her eye and the plastic surgery needed to mend the injury to her face had been extensive, Decker at her side every step of the way.

Aisha was as happy as the family to hear the news of their engagement, and their wedding had been one of the most beautiful she'd ever attended.

Even with the positive changes in his life, Decker was all business as he negotiated with Trey. "Your deputies asked questions after the avalanche. Damn Feds have been poking around, too."

"Anyone find anything?"

"No. Of course not," Decker shot back, his chest puffing out slightly.

"Any of those pokers ask to speak to the grounds crew?"

"No." That note of triumph was noticeably absent this time around.

"Look, Decker." Trey's tone quieted as he shifted to a new tack. "I'm not going to scare anyone and I'm not trying to suggest they don't know how to do their jobs. But we need to talk to them."

"Fine," Decker finally acquiesced. "But I'm going with you."

"Of course you are. Solid front. That's what we need."

Although Decker wasn't unkind, he was puzzled when he shifted his attention to her. "Aisha, it's good to see you as always. Maybe I can set you up here? I can get you a cup of coffee. Some breakfast."

"She's coming with me." Trey nearly growled the words. "This was her idea. She deserves to see it through."

"You want to question my grounds crew like they're criminals?"

"I want to talk to them like people. People who have eyes and expertise and might be able to use both to help us." Trey put an arm around Aisha's shoulders. "My fiancée has the same skills and she's going to put them to use watching your crew."

"You're engaged?" Decker's eyes widened. "Hot damn, congratulations!"

As announcements of their "joyous news" went, Aisha had expected she'd be a bit more prepared, but no time like the present. She went into Decker's open arms and was surprised to feel his genuine happiness for her in the warm hug.

"Welcome to the family." Decker pulled back, staring down at her. "Or should I say, finally?"

Before she could think up a response to that one, Decker had turned and pulled Trey into a hard hug. "This is awesome news, man. Congratulations."

The surprise of their engagement was enough to shift the tense tenor of the room. Decker talked to them a few more minutes about their upcoming nuptials as he waited for his admin to get the grounds crew pulled together outside for questioning.

"Mr. Colton." The discreet knock at the door pulled them off the discussion of weddings. "The team's outside and ready for you."

"Thanks, Maris." Decker had dropped into a more casual pose as he spoke of wedding plans, leaning against his desk, but that vanished at what was still to come. "Why don't we get this over with?"

Trey nodded. "Let's go."

Both men gestured Aisha to go first, and as she left the rarified air of Decker Colton's office, she had to wonder what they'd find.

Knowledge and transparency?

Or more of the runaround that had seemed to be the hallmark of this case?

THE WOMAN'S SOULLESS stare gazed toward the sky. Her pretty, made up face had long since vanished, her anguish stamped in the way makeup smudged around her eyes from crying and the corners of her lips had chapped after so many hours attempting to get free.

None of which was his fault. He wasn't a sicko and he hadn't abused her. She was the one who went crazy on him, her eyes wide the moment she'd come to with the gag in her mouth. He'd tried to talk to her, but the moment the gag had come down around her neck, she'd started screaming, unwilling to listen to him. He'd finally backhanded her to get her to shut the hell up.

Damn, women could scream.

She'd gone unconscious for a while, giving him some silence. *Finally.* And then he did what he needed to do before she regained consciousness again.

"Ends to a mean," he muttered to himself as he turned her to her side. He needed the blood and hair sample and he needed to do it fast. He was expected in town in a half hour and he had to finish his staging and get the call made.

After all, "The Avalanche Killer" had a reputation to maintain.

Chapter Nine

Aisha replayed the discussion with Decker as they approached the groundskeepers, all dressed in green golf shirts and khaki shorts and lined up in military precision. The Lodge was several large buildings and they were outside the main business office, the majesty of the Rockies rising up behind them.

She tried to remain unobtrusive—like she looked all that professional still clad in her running clothes—and observed the line of groundskeepers. It was heavily weighted to men, but there were three women scattered throughout the line. All appeared as competent as their male counterparts, their bodies strong with their outdoor labor.

None of them appeared nervous, just curious. It was a state she'd apply to everyone in line. Certainly, getting called to the offices by the big boss was reason for some curiosity, but no one seemed anxious or uneasy. And all remained that way, even when Trey came out of the business office like they'd rehearsed, the khaki of his uniform starched and pressed where it stretched across his shoulders.

Decker turned toward Trey. "This is Sheriff Colton.

He has a few questions. I'd like you to answer anything he asks."

Aisha kept up her close watch. A few nervous laughs and shuffling feet began after Decker's announcement, but other than that, no one had the trapped-animal look so often associated with panic and fear.

"I have a few questions about the avalanche that came so late this past spring."

"The big one?" A man who wore a different-colored shirt and that further identified him as the head grounds-keeper with a small badge over his chest pocket spoke up. "That helped them find the bodies?"

Decker nodded. "That's the one, Rick."

"Bad business that." Rick shook his head. "We've been trying to figure it out ever since, but it doesn't make sense. We keep up with that run. We keep up with all of 'em."

"You find it strange?" Trey asked. "That there was an avalanche."

The groundskeeper shrugged at that. "The nature part's always unpredictable. That's almost always true with a late snow like that. But the size of that one? It's not how she behaves."

"She?" Trey probed. "She who?"

Rick hiked a thumb over his shoulder. "Her. The mountain. Wicked. She's a bitch but she's too big to hide her secrets, you know?"

Fascinated, Aisha moved a bit closer. Rick talked of the mountain like it was a person. Which, she considered, for those who made their living on her, perhaps it was.

"You were surprised by the avalanche?" Trey queried.

"Don't mistake my meaning, sir. The danger on the mountain is real and no matter how much work we do, she can get a mind of her own. But the severity and the absolute destruction? It's not usual. Not at all. We're still finding areas we need to clean up."

Decker finally spoke. "Why haven't you said anything, Rick?"

"Not my place. Sheriff's deputies came up and asked questions. Federal guy did, too, flashing his badge good and solid, like it was some sort of diamond." Rick spat on the ground. "Yet when we tried to explain how she works, everyone's eyes glazed over. Figured once no one came back it was done."

Aisha knew Trey well enough to know a few of his deputies were going to get a drubbing back at the station, but Trey kept his tone level with Rick. "I'd like to understand it. And I can promise you, my eyes won't glaze over."

"Okay." Rick pointed once more toward the mountain. "Let's go up on her."

Trey was still struggling with the news that his deputies had fallen down on the job but he'd worry about that later. After he was done kicking his own ass for not pushing harder on this angle.

The grizzled groundskeeper might think mountains had a gender and mutter about them like they were pissed-off people, but the man knew his stuff. He'd already pointed out several key attributes of the land that helped explain how they set the charges to groom the runs, shifting and moving snow to make the mountain as safe and passable as possible.

Or as safe as a mountain identified as a double black and regularly used for ski competitions could be.

Trey had left the rest of Rick's team to go back to their job and now tromped up the side of the mountain with Decker and Aisha. She'd been a trouper, following quietly. She had even gone along with the engagement announcement that he'd sprung on his cousin to change the subject a bit.

It had felt strange to do it—and his motives hadn't been entirely pure—but it had also felt good.

And truth be told, Decker's warm response—and hearty welcome to the family—had filled him with pride.

Welcome to the family... Or should I say, finally?

Was that how everyone saw Aisha? He knew she was a fixture in his life, but he'd had little understanding of how his extended family perceived her. It made sense, though. She'd attended pretty much every picnic or holiday party his parents had hosted in the last twenty-five years. He'd brought her to several family events hosted by other family members and she'd regularly acted as his plus-one to the obligatory Colton Empire events held by his uncle Russ and aunt Mara.

She belonged with him.

Didn't she?

And wasn't that the heart of it all? Faking the engagement with her was an easy ask because it wasn't all that fake. Put aside the fact they weren't dating, they had every other attribute of a couple on the brink of marriage. Affection. Shared confidences. Friendship. Love.

As friends, he quickly amended. He loved Aisha and

had since he was young. He made no secret of that, nor did the idea scare him.

That didn't make him *in* love with her. Decker and Kendall were in love. His sister and Rylan were in love. Hell, his parents were in love, the great, golden shining example of *in love* as a permanent state.

He and Aisha weren't there.

"You see this here?" Rick's voice pulled Trey from thoughts that had no business meandering through his mind, let alone settling in and taking up space, and he tried to focus on the head groundskeeper.

"The divots in the mud?"

"Yep. Those. The charges were dropped there. When they detonated it left that small depression from the blast."

"I see it."

"We place 'em strategically when we need to remove unstable snowpack."

"Makes sense." Trey had a mental image of Rick and his crew moving around on the side of the mountain like ants on a mound and suspected the work was a bit more scientific than that.

"How do you know where to detonate?"

"An experienced team gets a sense when they're out working with the grooming equipment. Areas that feel loose. Anything they experience out skiing. The patrol and the teachers are instructed to report in anything suspicious, as well."

"But no one reported anything on Wicked?"

Rick shook his head, deep grooves forming around his squint as he stared up the face of the mountain. "Nope. She was on the list for the next night's runs but nothing seemed off."

Trey glanced over at Aisha, but she didn't say anything, just nodded toward Rick as the man continued on up the steady slope of the mountain.

"Where did the teams who came out to visit with you look?"

"Base of the mountain. A few thousand feet up."

"Where did the avalanche start?" Aisha piped up from behind him.

"Higher up." Rick gestured with his hand as he kept trudging up the slope. "Around four thousand feet."

"And no one looked there?" Trey asked, the team meeting he was going to have back in his office already taking shape in his mind.

"It was a freak accident, Sheriff. Mountain's unpredictable and like I said earlier, the late snows are the worst. Never know what you're going to get. There's a lot of ice and heavy wetness mixed in. It doesn't take much for gravity to take hold."

"How much force is needed to dislodge the snow?" Aisha moved up the slope, her breathing steady and even as she kept pace with the apparently indefatigable Rick.

"That's the hard part. There are lots of scientists who come up here and try to run computer models. Simulations." Rick tugged his hat that proudly displayed The Lodge logo off his head and scratched at his temple. "It's all well and good and helpful sometimes. But it can't model everything. Nature has its own rules. A simulation might be right ninety-nine percent of the time and then something isn't accounted for. A large rock in the way. A portion of snowpack that's extra tight so the snow has to work around it. You name it."

Trey followed behind them, intrigued by the ques-

tions Aisha asked. Gravity. Slope. Wind velocity. He
was fascinated by the way she used her limited knowledge of each as a method to pull out Rick's expertise
and natural understanding of the land. Where the man's
prior experiences with the police had obviously left him
cold and feeling dismissed, Aisha used the simple gift
of interest to bring the man's talents to the forefront.

Amazing.

That lone thought drifted through his mind, over and
over, as she slowly shifted the conversation from one of
modest distrust to potentially game changing.

"It's far more simple than I could have imagined,"
Aisha said, laying a hand on Rick's offered arm to get
over a particularly wide gully. "Inclines and gravity."

"That's all there is." Rick helped her another few
steps before he pointed toward a line of snow that still
sat at the very top of the mountain. "Old skiers warning.
If the slope is steep enough to ski, it's steep enough to
get an avalanche. Visitors don't want to hear that. They
want to come out and have fun and not worry about it.
Mr. Colton feels the same way. So we take as many precautions as we can to manage the land. We also have
emergency response in place when something comes up
that we haven't controlled for or couldn't control for."

"How do you—" Trey's words vanished on the summer breeze as he fell forward, barely catching himself.
Although he narrowly avoided falling flat on his face,
the momentum was enough to trip him forward and he
tumbled straight for Aisha and Rick. Her arms came
around him and Rick's reactions were steadier than his
grizzled features might have indicated, steadying both
of them with a loud, "Whoa."

"Are you alright?" Trey had already gained his balance, his hands reaching for Aisha's waist to hold her still.

"I'm good." Her hands came over his, still gripping her waist. "Fine. I'm okay."

Satisfied his clumsy oaf routine hadn't hurt anyone, Trey reluctantly dropped his hands from Aisha's waist. Not, however, before noticing the soft skin that peeked out over her shorts and tantalized his fingertips.

"What *was* that?" He turned quickly, his embarrassment at his slip and the lingering heat of her body churning through him with its own force of nature.

Rick's broad smile faded as he took in the ground where Trey had stumbled. "I'm not sure." The groundskeeper dropped to his knees, his focus on the deep divot that Trey had stumbled through.

"Rick?" Aisha asked softly, moving up beside the man. "What do you see?"

"This. Here." Rick pointed toward the edge of a deep depression in the earth. "See how this craters like this?"

Trey dropped into a squat, his gaze tracing the area Rick pointed out. "It looks like the divots before. The ones you showed us farther down the mountain."

"It does. Only see how deep this one is? And how there are two craters seeming on top of each other."

Trey watched how the man traced the outlines, two circles forming half-moons on top of one another from the way their shape indented the ground. "Yeah, I see it."

"That's two charges, set off on top of each other. Like they had to compete for space."

"Do you drop two at a time?"

"Sure. But not one on top of the other. Too much is moving for that to work."

Trey leaned in closer, the twin outlines like mirrors of each other. "Why would anyone even drop two so perfectly close together?"

"They don't." Rick sat back on his heels. "These were set. Likely put in place and detonated remotely."

Trey narrowed his eyes. "You know that for sure?"

"Yes, I do. And we didn't set any charges before that avalanche."

The certainty of Rick's words left little room for questions, but still Trey did his job. "You keep a record of that?"

"Sure do. Lodge policy. All detonations are posted on the schedule and counted off. If something comes up and is unplanned while out managing runs it gets reported after. We have to keep track of the ammo and make sure nothing gets left on the mountain that doesn't detonate."

With The Lodge being one of the premier ski resorts in all of Colorado, Trey knew his family ran a tight ship. And the level of security was equally impressive. A proper accounting of their work was essential to guest safety and it was clear Decker and the entire staff took that seriously.

Rick had radioed in his discovery, quickly gaining confirmation back from one of his staff members that the charts were up to date, all logged and filed against The Lodge's safety protocols.

"Trey." Aisha moved up close to them, her hand wrapping around his in support. "If The Lodge didn't do this, that means the charges were deliberately set."

Since she'd voiced what already concerned him, he only nodded and squeezed her hand.

"Rick. I want to close off this area and search it. We need to see if there are any more."

Rick nodded. "Yes, sir."

Then he radioed for more help.

AISHA STARED AT the photos spread out on the conference room table and mapped it to images of Wicked Mountain still fresh in her mind. Trey's team's search had, unfortunately, produced fruit and they'd discovered three other charge sites after spending all day on the mountain. Each had that same overlapping pattern of charge detonation and the combined impact of two charges going off at once.

And it was all because Trey tripped.

What were the odds?

That thought had kept her steady company since leaving The Lodge. She needed to get back to work, and Decker's wife, Kendall, had offered her a ride. Kendall's own recent brush with danger had clearly left the woman ruffled, and Aisha was glad to have a few minutes with her.

Although she couldn't take credit for fully calming her, Kendall did seem less scared when she'd dropped Aisha off at her apartment and headed back out to her animal sanctuary. Kendall had even secured a promise from Aisha to come out that weekend for a bit of time caring for the animals and Aisha was glad to see that talking about Kendall's life's work had gone a long way toward calming the woman down and restoring her equilibrium.

"What about your own?" Aisha murmured to herself, tracing the detonation pattern on the photos with her fingertip. "What about Trey?"

He'd gathered his team in his office for an update on the findings, then asked two of his deputies to stay after. Although she hadn't been present for either, Daria had given her the update on the team meeting and the tersely worded order to stay at the end for Tom and Jeff when she'd dropped off the copies of the photos.

Aisha didn't envy the deputies the tongue-lashing they were no doubt receiving. And she really didn't want to think about the renewed attacks from Barton Evigan when it came out that the deputies had fallen down on their jobs.

Even if it had been dumb luck that had Trey tripping over the charge site, the news that the team hadn't looked very hard shortly after the avalanche occurred was a dark mark on the department. The fact that the Feds missed it—Daria's parting shot at their competition when she brought the photos—wouldn't slow down Evigan.

"No pizza?" Trey's face was grim, his mouth a firm slash beneath a day's growth of beard. "I figured you'd be all over Bruno's by now."

"We've had a lot of pizza this week. I ordered in salads instead. That new place downtown delivers and I got a few spring mixes."

"Great. Rabbit food." Trey tossed a slim folder onto the table, his motions stiff with irritation. "Just what I was hoping for."

Aisha had been more than prepared to give him a wide lead after the day he'd had. It had been long and tedious and full of potential embarrassment—whether deserved or not—to his campaign. But last time she checked, she wasn't his dinner lackey. "I think your fingers work just fine. Dial up Bruno's if you want pizza."

"I don't want any damn pizza."

"You look like you don't want help, either. I'll get out of your way."

"Aish—" A hand snaked out and snagged her elbow, just as she was working up her own head of steam to walk out of the room. "Come on."

Although his hold was gentle—a plea to stay more than force—she was shaken enough for both of them. The killer's work was disturbing enough. But the deliberate charges set on the mountain?

What had been dubbed an accident of Mother Nature now had taken a sinister turn, and Aisha couldn't hide her fear at what Trey was dealing with.

At what their small town faced.

What was someone up to? Was it possible there were two killers on the loose? One who targeted women and another who was determined to mimic that behavior or hide behind it for gains of their own.

"Leave me be, Trey."

"Why? So you can go home and brood over what an ass I'm being?"

"Yes."

He dropped his hand. "Not that I can blame you, then."

The events of the past few days hung heavy between them and somewhere deep inside, even as she knew it was a bad idea, a small ember began to burn.

She might not be his real fiancée, but for all the rest of Roaring Springs knew, she was right now.

Maybe it was time she began acting like it.

"Don't shut me out on this."

"I'm not," he retorted.

"Yes, you are. I can see it in your eyes. In the bad

mood you walked in with. You're not unkind and you rarely show your anger to others. So the fact that it's so close to the surface suggests something."

"Come on, Aish. Don't analyze me."

"Then don't give me something to analyze."

Trey pulled out a chair and dropped into it. "What do you expect? This is all on me. The Feds can swoop in and say it's their case, but this is my jurisdiction."

"Then you need to stay two steps ahead of them. They missed the clues up on Wicked, too, Trey. That mountain's face is huge. You can't assume you're at fault because you didn't find anything before today. A few divots in the mud. Who could expect to find that?"

"It nagged at me, you know?" He started in as if he hadn't heard her. "The late-season avalanche. And the severity of it. I might not know that mountain like Rick or even Decker, but I know Colorado. I know where I live. We don't get destruction like that so late in the season."

He shook his head. "I *knew* it, Aish. But I ignored the signs. I made fighting for my job and pushing off the Feds more important than doing good, solid investigative work. How much further along would we be if we found this six weeks ago after the bodies were found?"

"But you found it now." She took the seat beside him and laid a hand over his. "You know what you're dealing with now. That has to be your focus."

"And if I'm too late? For Skye? For some other poor woman we don't even know about yet?"

Once again, the weight Trey carried struck Aisha as a visceral, living thing. A mountain of worry that sat on his back as if he were the proverbial Atlas, carrying it all alone.

Only he wasn't.

"You're not in this by yourself." She offered up the support, even as the risk of rejection in the form of his stubborn refusal to share the load posed a threat.

But she was made of sterner stuff.

A harsh laugh escaped his throat, at odds with the stillness that surrounded them. The office had quieted after Trey's staff meeting and while Aisha knew there were still team members in the building, everyone had hunkered down at their computers or headed out to do some evening fieldwork.

It felt like just the two of them.

Was it wrong she wished it *was* just the two of them?

"You're not, Trey. I'm here. Daria is as loyal as they come. And despite today's bump in the road, your deputies are good and loyal. To you. You've trained them well and they're good at their jobs."

"What if we don't make it in time?" He shook his head, the golden-brown depths of his eyes cloudy with worry and what she now realized was fear. "What if there are more?"

The temptation to brush it off was strong, but she knew that wasn't the answer. Ignoring a threat didn't make it disappear, nor did it dissuade the one who worried over it. Trey might be struggling in a moment of doubt, but she knew the man could—and would—walk through fire for his job.

"If there are more, then we'll deal with it. Together."

"What would I do without you?"

"You're not going to need to find out." Her gaze remained firmly on his, but she couldn't resist a small poke. "Unless you keep criticizing me for my dinner choices."

"Oh. Well. When you put it that way." He turned the hand still beneath hers over so their palms met. "What *would* I do without you?"

He asked the question again, his tone shifting as if the words truly registered in ways they hadn't before. They'd been a part of each other's lives for so long, it was easy to assume the other would always be there.

But what if that changed?

Or what if the circumstances between them shifted so irrevocably they could never get back what they had?

"You're not going to have to find out."

She said the words as much to convince herself as to reassure him. And then, as if in a dream, his other hand came up and brushed at a few of her curls that had come loose from where she'd clipped back her hair.

With his fingertips, he traced the curve of her cheek, a light, teasing smile playing over his lips. "Unless I refuse the salad."

"Right. Then," she said, her voice breathy under the softness of his touch. "A girl's got to hold the line on something."

"As I remember, you laid down a pretty firm line on something else."

Aisha understood his meaning. And even though they'd shared that one kiss, she'd believed herself able to maintain a firm hold on not doing it again.

Oh, how delusional she'd been.

"You think I can't?"

"I don't know." He tilted his head, moving closer, yet staying far enough away his lips hovered just out of reach from hers. "First dinner. Then kissing. I'm asking you to give up an awful lot."

"Do you hear me arguing?"

He stilled, his dark eyes searching hers. "No."

The moment seemed to stretch out, a second in time yet an eternity as she waited for him to finally decide. The quiet of the room was broken by the ringing of an office phone at the corner of the conference room table, but it might have been a million miles away for all she heard it.

Or for all the effort either one of them made to reach for it.

And then his lips met hers and the ringing faded. The quiet disappeared. All she heard was Trey. The light groan that echoed from his throat. The soft, matched moan that came from her own. And the lightly delicious sound of skin against skin that whispered between them from the rub of his beard stubble.

The kiss was as wonderful as the first, only this time there was something different. What had seemed like impulse the first time was noticeably absent this go-round. Kissing Trey this time felt purposeful. *Determined.* And oh so amazing.

Aisha allowed herself to sink into him, meeting his tongue thrust for thrust as his mouth moved over hers, devouring her and any hint of resistance. This was right.

Real.

And so damn tempting she was ready to…

"Trey!"

The heavy slam of the door hitting the wall along with the harsh bark of his name had them pulling apart as if burned. Daria stood in the doorway, her neatly pressed uniform still starched against her stiff frame. Not a hair was out of place and she looked as she always did—cool and competent.

Except for the urgency that nearly had her dancing from foot to foot.

"Sheriff. I'm sorry to interrupt. I—"

Trey stood to his full height, the move enough to stop her. "What is it?"

"The Avalanche Killer. He's on line one."

Chapter Ten

Trey picked up the phone and pressed the button for line one. He'd already instructed Daria to capture the call on the station's recording system but his trusty deputy had already put the details in motion before telling him of the call.

And now he'd face the man who'd been terrorizing Roaring Springs for who knew how long.

"This is Colton."

"Mr. Colton. Or should I call you Sheriff?"

Trey knew the taunt was nothing more than a ploy for the upper hand and he kept his tone even. Firm. "Sheriff'll do."

"Yeah, you enjoy that title while you still have it."

The voice was muffled by a technology overlay, but the intent was more than clear. Trey recognized the gambit for what it was and fought to ignore the personal jab. Instead, he filed away the fact the killer knew of local politics. "My deputy says you have something you want to talk to me about."

"You've been so far off the mark lately I decided to throw you a leash."

A leash?

Although Trey knew the FBI had profiled the Avalanche Killer as highly dangerous, the man on the other side of the line could just as easily be a crackpot. He needed to get through the call, but the conversation wasn't what he'd expected.

"Why don't you and I set up some time to talk? You can tell me about it. All of it."

"How stupid do you think I am?"

Since the guy had made a phone call to a law enforcement agency, Trey opted to leave that one alone. "This is about what drives you. I want to understand that."

"You want to get reelected. Plain and simple."

Before Trey could react to that, the man pressed on. "Out front. Just beyond the cameras. I left you a package. Have fun."

The line went dead and Trey hollered into it, even as he knew it was useless. He'd had no chance to ask about Skye. Or to even probe for clues to where his cousin might be.

"Trey!" Daria shouted down the hall. "Team's on it."

Not without him, he thought as he raced out of the room. Aisha still sat in the same seat she'd taken opposite him, but the heat and need that had driven them both only moments before had vanished.

A killer had been within close range of the precinct and they'd all missed it.

Daria had already cleared the front door of the station, her gun drawn with three of his deputies bringing up the rear behind her. All swept the space before them, clearing the perimeter just as their training indicated, in arcs that increased yard by yard.

He followed behind, his own weapon drawn, more than ready to lay down fire should it be needed.

But nothing came.

In moments, another shout went up at the discovery of the package. Trey was prepared to have them call out SWAT to ensure the package wasn't rigged, but as he narrowed the gap between him and Daria, he saw that there was no need.

The "package" was a plastic bag, full of blood and hair. There was no need to worry about a bomb.

But the evidence suggested he did need to put out an APB for another missing person.

AISHA STARED DOWN at the contents of the envelope, the thickened blood pooled on the hair sample already in an evidence bag. She had pressed Trey to be allowed to stay, her civilian status a risk now that they'd received the call and the new piece of evidence.

But he'd brushed off any concern and told her from that moment on she was a civilian consultant.

Trey's team had already photographed the evidence, well aware they couldn't hold off the FBI for much longer. A call of this nature—and the deliberate taunt that came with it—had to be handled by the authorities in charge. And whether Trey liked it or not, that jurisdiction was now owned by the Feds.

Which had only added to the urgency with which Trey's team went into motion.

The photos, copies of the recording and a transcript had already been generated. Daria was running scenarios through a computer while Trey ordered various hunts for missing persons, widening the search to all of Colorado as well as Wyoming and Utah.

And Aisha sat there, staring at her notes and wondering why she was so bothered by the outreach.

The break in pattern was concerning, but that wasn't what had her sideways. Nor was it the gruesome package, delivered as casually as a sack of groceries.

It was *how* the killer had broken pattern.

If there hadn't been an avalanche, they wouldn't have even known about the six other women. Suddenly, the killer was seeking attention and taunting the cops?

"I'd say penny for your thoughts, but those look like silver dollars, easy." Trey sat down next to her, his gaze going unerringly toward the package.

"It doesn't make sense," Aisha murmured, struggling to see through the hazy veil that seemed to have covered a part of her thoughts.

She *knew* something was off, but she was damned if she could find it.

"Why don't I move that?" Trey gently picked up the sample and moved it to a small box at the end of the table. "Agent Roberts will be here soon to pick it up anyway."

Aisha waited until Trey resumed his seat, her voice low when she spoke. Several of his deputies still moved in and out of the conference room and there was no use riling up anyone further. "Do you think he'll shut you out?"

"Probably." Trey ran a hand over his short hair, cupping the back of his head before massaging his neck.

The desire to move in right then and rub away the tension was palpable, but Aisha held back. The news of their "engagement" might have raced through the station like wildfire but this wasn't the place to advertise.

Besides, they *weren't* engaged. It didn't matter if she'd shifted a ring to her left hand or answered questions as if she were a glowing bride-to-be—she wasn't one.

And Trey had spoken to a killer.

Bone-deep fear rattled through her and for the first time, the severe magnitude of what he was up against hit her. Oh, she'd understood the problem. The photos of the dead women had already tainted her dreams and, she well knew, would for years to come.

But even as real as those details were, something had struck her about that phone call. The taunting voice. The bloody package. And the fact the killer had been in plain view of the station at some point that day.

How easy would it have been for him to stand at a distance, a gun trained on Trey or Daria or any member of his team?

"Trey. I need you to promise me you'll be careful."

He looked over at her. "Of course I will."

"No, I mean you have to *promise* me." Aisha heard the desperation in her voice and prayed she was getting through. That he understood the gravity of the situation.

"Aish." Trey moved closer and tugged on the arm of her rolling chair, pulling her close. "I am careful."

"I just can't lose you."

"You're not going to lose me."

"Just promise—"

Before she could finish the words, he'd leaned in and pressed a soft kiss to her lips. It was gentle and full of promise and she wanted to cling to him right there. Maybe would have if not for the audience in close proximity.

For several long moments they stayed just like that. Although she could feel heat behind the kiss, it was more designed to comfort and ease her fear than it was some sort of carnal feast.

And while she had enjoyed every moment of that kiss, it was humbling to realize how something so simple as their touch of lips could so quickly calm her roiling thoughts.

Trey lifted his head. "We're going to find him. Take him down."

"But he's out there. And so close." Her gaze drifted of its own volition toward the end of the table and what she knew still lay there. "He got so close."

"Which is why we'll catch him. I have to believe that." He ran his fingertips over her cheek. "So do you."

Aisha nodded. Fear could be overwhelming if you allowed it room to breathe and grow, taking shape and form. She saw it in her patients and understood how debilitating it would become if left unchecked.

While she'd never diminish her patients' needs or consider them less for accepting the help she could provide, Aisha also knew that much of what consumed them were fears that overtook their better judgment. Whether it was unchecked anxiety or the unfortunate consequences of mental illness, as a professional she could help them find coping mechanisms and ways of managing.

This was different.

There *was* a killer on the loose. Not a figment of her imagination, but a man who'd stolen the lives of at least six women, now a seventh. A deranged killer who now had Trey Colton in his sights. No matter how hard she tried to find a bright spot, there wasn't one.

And she had no idea how to ensure the safety of the man she loved.

TREY WATCHED THE emotions play across Aisha's beautiful face, each thought she battled taking shape and form. In her eyes, pressed upon her lips, setting firm in her chin. He watched each one—fear, determination, even a subtle thread of resignation—before her gaze returned to his.

"You will catch him." Conviction lay beneath her words and once again, that determination returned to her gaze.

"We will."

Trey wanted to stay like that a bit longer, but the quiet buzz of activity that had hummed through his station since they'd all returned from the parking lot had shifted. Trey stood, turning to find Agent Stefan Roberts at the door.

"Colton." Agent Roberts nodded.

"Roberts."

Trey was more than willing to give the man his due, but he wasn't a pushover. And he was still the sheriff of Bradford County. He deserved to be spoken to as such.

"Guy's got some brass balls." Roberts's gaze softened. "Deputy Bloom said you and your team handled it like champs."

Trey's gaze shifted to Daria, who sat quietly at the edge of the table, her bearing proud and tall. He'd deliberately put her as the liaison with the Feds, hoping her stoic nature and apparent by-the-book approach would win them over.

Or at least make the way between them smooth and even.

For all her seeming agreement, Trey had the additional knowledge of how good Daria was. The woman was indefatigable, digging until she found answers. And she had a way of doing it that was complementary to the situation instead of intrusive. Hell, Trey acknowledged to himself, Daria would solve the crime and still make the FBI think they'd won the round.

"As soon as Deputy Bloom knew who we were dealing with, she had the team moving. We got a full recording."

Agent Roberts gestured to the room at large. "Why don't you walk me through it after you make introductions."

Although Aisha spent a fair amount of time around the station, she'd been absent each time he'd interfaced with the Feds. Clearly, that time was at an end.

"Agent Stefan Roberts. Let me introduce you to Aisha Allen, civilian consultant."

"Consultant?" Roberts's eyebrows rose.

"Ms. Allen is a clinical psychologist. Her insights have been invaluable to us." Trey nearly held his tongue but decided it would seem more conspicuous should Roberts find out later. "She's also my fiancée."

Those eyebrows rose a few more notches, but other than that the agent conveyed little else. "When did you get engaged?"

"This past weekend."

Aisha moved in, extending her hand. "It's a pleasure to meet you, Agent Roberts."

Although she stopped short of flirting, Trey didn't miss the subtle thread of deference she showed. A very un-Aisha-like trait, but one that served her well when Roberts's features relaxed a fraction.

Trey also didn't miss the agent's appreciative gaze as he considered Aisha. He remained a perfect gentleman, but Trey didn't miss the warming in the other man's dark brown eyes.

Which pissed him the hell off.

But it was Daria's hard cough as she stepped up to the table that distracted Trey. "Agent Roberts. Perhaps you'd like to look over the evidence."

While there was nothing overt in her tone, Trey couldn't help but think his trusty deputy was irritated. Mad, even, though he had nothing to go on.

Roberts snapped to attention at Daria's suggestion, his smile growing broader as he took in those stiff shoulders. "Let's take a look, then, Deputy Bloom."

Daria snagged two rubber gloves from a nearby box, then handed it off. Her movements were stiff and efficient and again, Trey couldn't hide the sense that she was pissed off about something.

"I think she likes him."

Aisha's voice was a whisper in his ear, low enough that no one could hear, but she might as well have shouted it for how startled he was by the news.

"What?"

Aisha tilted her head ever so slightly. "Watch."

Trey did just that, but saw no further evidence that anyone liked anyone else. And what was this anyway? The fifth grade? Were they all jockeying for one another's affections on the playground?

Since his own feelings for Aisha hovered a bit too close to the surface—especially that shot of He-Man testosterone when Roberts shook her hand—Trey had to admit that the playground analogy was a bit too close for comfort.

"This is a distinct break in behavior." Roberts turned

the evidence bag over in his hands. "An escalation of sorts, even though it doesn't have that feel, either."

"The pattern is not only different, but so distinct as to suggest a new player," Aisha added. "A copycat maybe?"

Although skepticism had painted Stefan Roberts's features when he'd been introduced to Aisha, Trey saw the tenor of the conversation shift. "You do much work with serial killers, Ms. Allen?"

"Not much. My work is primarily clinical in nature, but I know enough to understand the underlying psychoses involved."

"And your take on this?"

"The abrupt change in pattern is concerning. It's possible that the discovery of his crimes with the avalanche triggered something in him, but still." She shook her head. "The abrupt change and the taunting of law enforcement… It's as concerning as it is puzzling."

"My colleagues need time to go over this, but I believe their conclusions will mirror yours."

"Thank you."

Roberts tapped the table. "Do you have the envelope this was delivered in?"

"No envelope," Daria said. "The sample was in that plastic bag. All we did was add the evidence bag."

"No notes?"

"Nope," Trey's deputy confirmed. "Team did take photos of the scene. I'll go get copies of those for you."

Aisha caught Trey's eye before she tilted her head toward the door. "I'm going to give you time to discuss the case. I'll be heading out."

"Wait for me?" Trey said, the words more command

than request. When he got a lone raised eyebrow for his trouble, he added a hasty, "Please."

"Of course."

Roberts waited until both women left before he shifted his focus. "You've gotten some attention here. Make sure you watch your back."

"I will."

"We're here for you, Colton. We're on the same side."

"Are we?"

Although he knew it was tantamount to a challenge, Trey was suddenly tired of the politics and the need for diplomacy. They were in crisis and had a killer roaming free in Roaring Springs.

The time for diplomacy was at an end.

"You think we're not?" the agent asked. The modestly congenial air he walked in with had vanished and all Trey saw in its place was a hard-ass.

Again, those warning bells went off in his head, but he didn't care. "I think you all want to nab a madman. Your profilers want to make a fuss and show how all the investment in the Bureau pays off now that you have a target."

"You don't want to catch a killer?"

"I want a very serious threat out of my town. Off my streets and away from my people. I'm not interested in patterns or escalations or questions about his mental state."

"So why the civilian consultant?" Roberts grinned. "Or should I call her your fiancée consultant?"

Trey ignored the dig, unwilling to discuss his relationship Aisha with this man. "She knows Roaring Springs and she knows human nature and I need both to solve this."

"We want that, too, Colton. Anyone who suggests otherwise doesn't know me."

Trey wasn't convinced the Bureau's attitude was quite the same as Agent Roberts's, but he had to work with what was in front of him. Right now, that was with an earnest agent with a job to do.

"Six women, Agent Roberts. Now a seventh. And my cousin still missing, as well." Trey never broke his gaze. "I want it done."

"You know the governor sent his lackey to see me a few days ago?"

"Steve Lucas pay you a visit, too?" Roberts mused. "I wonder who he hit up first."

"He's making the rounds, then?" Trey wondered if Agent Roberts had gotten the same push for a walk down the aisle but somehow figured Lucas knew a bit better than to overstep with the Feds.

"Sure is. The governor's very concerned with the discovery of the bodies. Wanted to ensure this case is the Bureau's highest priority. All that usual desperation when reelection is staring you in the face."

Once again, Trey was forced to acknowledge the reality of the situation. He wanted to catch a killer. And everyone he came in contact with seemed to want a political win.

Six women discovered on the side of a mountain weren't political. A woman lying dead somewhere in Roaring Springs wasn't a pawn in the midst of some powerful people's chess moves. And he'd be damned if his cousin Skye was going to be left to the rabid wolves, hungry for power and prestige, as the bright, shining example of how a dangerous killer was finally taken down.

They were running out of time.

What Trey couldn't understand was why he seemed to be the only one staring at his watch.

Chapter Eleven

Aisha slipped into the vibrant wrap dress and considered how she was going to play the evening. Although the Colton family was still deeply upset over Skye, the hair samples sent to Trey's office on Monday evening had been definitively proved as belonging to someone else. It hadn't lessened the tension everyone felt, but it had gone a long way toward giving the Colton family hope.

Elated that the evidence wasn't linked to her twin, Phoebe insisted they have a celebratory family dinner at The Chateau to officially toast Trey and Aisha's engagement.

Which meant Aisha had spent the past hour in and out of her closet, trying on any number of outfits. The normal slacks-and-blouse routine she wore for work was too casual. A few of her more elegant cocktail dresses seemed way too formal, even with The Chateau's perpetual air of elegance. Still, she'd admonished herself as she'd twirled in front of the floor-length mirror in her bedroom. People thought she was getting married, not going to an awards ceremony.

She'd finally stumbled upon the wrap dress she'd purchased last year for a date that had gone terribly, and in some sort of weird mental retribution, she'd shoved the outfit to the back of the closet. So now here she was, the body-hugging silk clinging to her frame in a pretty drape of lavender.

"Bad omen, Allen?" She turned to the side, checking the lines of the dress as the date resurrected itself in her mind's eye. "Or an inspired choice to keep firmly in mind that there is no engagement?"

Her date had vacillated between a weird sort of pride because he'd "asked a black woman out," and some strange sort of self-flagellation over the fact that he rarely dated. By the end of the appetizer, she'd given up on any hope the date would produce romantic prospects and began giving him free psychological advice.

A girl had to entertain herself somehow.

Fortunately, the evening was unlikely to bear a repeat, but she still had to put on a happy face and pretend to be someone she wasn't. The Colton family had always welcomed her and now she had to smile and act as if she was going to become one of them.

The knock on her door interrupted the sudden souring in her stomach, and she snatched a small clutch from her dresser and left the bedroom, hitting the light with a firm snap. She could continue these bouts of guilt every time the subject of the engagement came up or she could do what she said she would and grin and bear it.

Trey deserved a partner who was all in on this.

A fact that had grown more insistent throughout the week when the press got hold of the news that the department received a package. A situation that had puzzled them all—Agent Roberts included—since the detail was on lockdown as they all hunted for the victim.

That hadn't stopped the press from camping out in

front of the sheriff's station or Barton Evigan from running his mouth for any camera that'd capture his ugly mug, spouting off on what a terrible job Sheriff Colton was doing in his post.

A second note had come in late Wednesday and she'd stared at her copy of it so many times her eyes had nearly crossed. Despite having memorized every word, she still couldn't puzzle out the meaning.

Slow like the fox.
You'd better watch out.
Evidence in a box.
Another victim, no doubt.

Aisha had spent every spare minute at the station, trying to decipher the meaning and getting nowhere. The rhyming was juvenile and the language was clumsy, as if the goal of the note was to simply put words together that made a rhyme.

And when were foxes slow? The animals were known for their stealth and burst of speed, weren't they?

It had frustrated her and she was safe and cozy in the station house conference room. Trey and his deputies were another story. All had been out canvassing from one end of Bradford County to the other, all to no avail. Now that it was Friday, spirits had definitely dimmed that they were no closer to finding a killer or his victim.

Pushing that dismal thought from her mind, she pulled open the door. And found Trey, dressed in a sharp gray suit and red tie, standing before her.

Wow.

The word—and a sigh to match the sentiment—nearly escaped her mouth before she caught herself at the last minute.

But wow, did the man look good.

"Hi, Sheriff."

"Hi, yourself." He stepped through the door and pressed a chaste kiss to her cheek. "You look beautiful."

"Thank you."

Trey's appreciative gaze looked her over once more. "Isn't that the dress you wore to that awful date last year?"

The hazy shimmer of attraction winked out as Trey hit on the memory she'd tried to bury along with the dress in the closet. "Great. You remember that?"

"Only because you called the man a semibigoted asshat and bitched about how much you spent on a purple dress." He smiled, rubbing his hands. "Lucky me."

"What? Why?"

Trey moved in close and settled his hands at her waist. "I can't give you a worse evening. Maybe I can give you a better one."

"You're not starting off very well."

The smile fell from his face. "Why?"

"You remembered that conversation. And the bad date. One of the ones I told you about, anyway."

"You've had other bad dates?"

That one stopped her. "Haven't you?"

His face had fallen, but his broad palms remained firmly planted on her waist. Aisha knew she should ignore the heat that seemed to radiate from that very spot along with the increasing urge to lean into his body.

"Well, yeah. But it's always been the one subject we didn't talk to each other about. I was surprised when you mentioned it last year but figured it was because you were so mad."

As conversations went it wasn't what she'd expected, but now that Trey had given her the opening, she was going to take it. "Why do you think that is? That we don't talk about dating with each other."

"Not sure. A man-woman thing. Or maybe just the one area of our lives where we felt we deserved a bit of privacy."

She considered that. Even when she had been dating Kenneth she'd told Trey very little. For as happy as she'd believed herself to be while she was with Kenneth, something had always felt like a slight betrayal of Trey. She hadn't actively thought about it while she was dating, but each time there was an opportunity to tell her best friend about her boyfriend, she'd chickened out.

And when the bastard had gone on to break her heart, she was secretly glad she hadn't informed Trey about him. It was embarrassing enough to break up when you were crazy in love and you found out the man was just playing at the same. When the insult that he was married, too, got layered on top, it was a blessing to say nothing.

Not one damn word.

To this day, the only two people who knew were her sister and her grad school roommate. To anyone else who asked, she and Kenneth had simply gone their separate ways. She back to Colorado. He to a wife and, as she'd later heard, two children with a third on the way.

"Aish? You in there?"

"Yeah. Sorry." She shook her head and tried to play it all off. "You're probably right. It's a man-woman thing. And just because you're my best friend doesn't mean you don't have a right to your privacy."

"Sure. You're right." He dropped his hands and stepped back. "Privacy is a good thing."

It might be a good thing, but now that she thought

about it, privacy had also given them both an impenetrable wall neither was willing to scale. She'd known him practically her whole life and had no idea if he'd ever been in love. Or if he had a heartbreak. And he had no idea about hers.

As that idea sunk in, she pointed the door. "You ready to go?"

"Let's do it." He extended an arm. "Fiancée?"

Aisha threaded her arm through the crook of his. "Fiancée. *And* friend," she added for good measure.

The week had been a stressful one and they were now going to what would hopefully be an evening of light-hearted fun. That was her last thought as she flipped off her apartment lights and pulled the front door closed.

TREY TOOK A seat at the long table in The Chateau's main dining room and looked at his assembled family seated up and down the length. His ninety-four-year-old grandfather, Earl, had been given a place of honor at the opposite head of the table, and his uncle Russ and aunt Mara given the center on one side, his parents the center on the other. Everyone had turned out, the family filling in all the spaces around them along with Aisha's mother, sister and brother-in-law.

Which left the head of the table for him and Aisha. He leaned over and squeezed her hand. "You doing okay?"

"I'm good." She settled a hand over the back of his chair and leaned in close. For anyone watching them, they looked as cozy and comfortable and in love as the rest of his newly married or newly engaged cousins around the table.

Only they both knew the truth.

Their conversation at her apartment still nagged at him. Why had they kept personal details from each other? She was right, of course. Being best friends didn't mean they weren't entitled to private thoughts or straight-up privacy.

But both of them had deliberately omitted details of their personal lives from one another. He knew she'd had a big, bad relationship while she was in New York, but she'd never spoken of it and he'd avoided asking. In return, she knew very little, if anything, of the women he'd dated in his past. And while he might have been in a recent slump due to the pressures of his job and his increasing indifference to spending his time with women who didn't interest him, for a long time he'd seen dating differently.

Yet they'd kept those details from each other and, as a result, had each seen that part of their lives as off-limits.

Had there been another reason?

He'd brushed it off to her as a "man-woman thing," but maybe it *was* something more.

Maybe it was a "Trey-Aisha thing."

With that thought lingering in his mind, he watched as his cousin Phoebe stood up. Her hand lingered on her fiancé's shoulder, and Prescott's gaze heated as he stared up at her.

"I'm so happy we could all be together tonight. We've had our challenges, but we've had our joys, as well. And tonight we have another one to celebrate." She lifted her glass and turned to where Trey and Aisha sat. "To Trey and Aisha. The news of your engagement is the happiest of news. Aisha has always been a member of our family, but now my cousin's going to make that official and I know I speak for all of us when I say we couldn't be happier."

"To Trey and Aisha!" The cheers went up, glasses clinking as each of his family members toasted their impending "marriage."

The toasts continued throughout dinner and Trey held Aisha's hand, the two of them smiling through each and every one. Faking their way through it all.

He'd diligently avoided looking at his mother. While she'd kept a broad smile on her face, her talk of the up-coming wedding with various family members by all appearances happy and excited, he hadn't missed the dark looks she'd shot him. Nor had he forgotten her words of caution the prior week at their family barbecue about one of them developing feelings for each other.

At the time, he'd believed his mother was talking about Aisha. Now…

As he glanced over at her, talking with Decker and Kendall to her left, luminescent in the form-fitting lav-ender dress, he had to wonder if he was the sucker in all this. When this charade was over, was he actually going to go back as if nothing had happened? Now that he knew what it was like to kiss her? To pick her up at her home to go out as a couple, dressed like a vision. To work with her, seeing that scary-smart brain in full gear over pizza and crime scene photos.

He'd done this to himself, of course. All his cousins had found partners this year and he'd instead defaulted to work mode, taking an easy out with his best friend in order to get reelected. His gaze caught on the various faces assembled around the table, each smiling, happy couple reinforcing that truth.

Wyatt and Bailey had the seats nearest Earl. Bailey's

gentle nature had Trey's grandfather clearly charmed, his broad smile all lit up for Wyatt's new wife. On Earl's other side were Blaine and Tilda. His cousin Blaine had rediscovered his high school girlfriend and, in even more life-altering news, had discovered their young teenage son, Joshua. Trey had watched Blaine, an extreme sports enthusiast, put himself in harm's way for years. It was awesome to see now how he'd changed. That daredevil spirit still lived inside him, but he'd put his energy into rebuilding his family from the ground up and Trey couldn't help but envy the way fate had given all three of them a path to their future.

Which was awfully self-centered and had absolutely nothing to do with his happiness for his cousin. But still, that envy coursed through him like an angry wind blowing through the trees.

Had he given up the opportunity for all of that for his job? For that sense of duty that drove him to work the hardest and focus on doing every damn thing by the book.

What if one of you develops feelings?

Ignoring his mother's lingering voice—or the reality that there wasn't a happy-ever-after in his future after this ruse ended—Trey kept his gaze on the table.

Next came his cousin Sloane and her new husband, Liam Kastor. A detective with the Roaring Springs PD, Liam had been a valuable link to what was going on with the Avalanche Killer and he, Trey and Daria had regularly shared information. The Feds might have taken over the majority of the case, but Liam came from the same school of thought as Trey: the Avalanche Killer had targeted *their* town and they had a vested interest in catching the bastard.

He'd already spent a few minutes over a beer catching Liam up on the latest note that had come in, Aisha filling in her impressions of the clumsy writing and poorly articulated clues. If they even *were* clues, she'd added. Liam's light green eyes had sharpened at Aisha's description and he'd obviously wanted to know more before Trey's sister, Bree, had admonished them to stop the shop talk, then pulled him and Aisha away to sit down for dinner.

"Enjoying yourself?" Aisha leaned in close once more and, again, Trey imagined that all anyone saw was a happy couple, speaking in intimate tones meant only for one another.

"Yes. Why?"

Her gaze was direct when she whispered the words meant only for him. "You're smiling, but I can see the sadness in your eyes."

"I'm happy for my family. It's been a difficult year for the Coltons and they've all come through it." He tilted his head slightly, gesturing to the table at large. "Every one of them has faced down some of the worst days of their lives and come out the other side stronger for it."

"You don't think you can do the same?"

"I don't know anymore."

Before he could consider the move, he leaned in and captured her lips with his. He *didn't* know anymore. In fact, he was shocked to realize how little he had a grasp on. His job. The killer haunting Roaring Springs. Even the upcoming election. All of it was out of control, rocketing through his life with all the destruction of an erupting volcano.

Yet somehow, Aisha sat in the center of it all, a calming force that never ceased to amaze him. She was *there.* Present. Involved and engaged in every way that mattered.

Not only was he not ready to give it up, but he couldn't stop himself from taking a taste of what was so close.

Their lips met, hot and hungry. Even as he remained conscious of their audience, he couldn't quite stem the tide of need and desire that whipped through him.

Her lips were plump but firm, a soft place to land yet strong enough to carry the passion that built and expanded between them. Her tongue met his, neither tentative nor shy, hesitant or cautious. Although they'd kissed only a few times, she was a woman who knew her own mind and who kissed like it.

Who met him as an equal.

He reveled in the exchange, the heady attraction intensifying even as he knew he needed to keep a firm hold on his emotions. More, that he couldn't have what his body so obviously desired. She'd made that abundantly clear when they'd entered into this arrangement. This kiss—hell, this evening—was for show only.

But what was it about this woman? And why, after so many years having her in his life, had something changed?

His suggestion had been so simple. Pretend for a few months to be engaged. They already spent considerable time together. All they needed to do was put on a public front for others and leave the rest of their life as it was. Settled. Comfortable. Normal.

Only now, nothing was normal. He wanted his best friend with a need that increasingly bordered on manic. And for as unsettled as Aisha Allen made him feel, he couldn't twist the situation in any way that it didn't feel right.

Overwhelmingly, satisfyingly right.

"Well, well." The slow clap of hands interrupted the moment, growing louder as the joyous laughing around the table fell silent.

"You're not welcome here, Evigan!" Someone, Trey thought maybe Rylan, growled in warning.

Undeterred, Barton Evigan moved closer to the table. "I'm just stopping by to congratulate the happy couple."

As his hulking form towered over Aisha, Trey didn't even think. He stood, moving into Evigan's physical space as a way to shift the man away from Aisha. In the distance Barton's wife stood, wringing her hands as she stood next to a man who could have been her husband's carbon copy.

"You've said your piece. Now move on."

"Oh, come now, Sheriff." Evigan's bloodshot blue eyes lit up. "Is that any way to talk to one of your constituents?"

"Is that what you're calling yourself now?"

"I'm a taxpaying resident of Bradford County. What else would I be?"

"A public nuisance." Aisha shot out the insult, standing and moving to Trey's side.

While Trey wanted nothing more than to shield her from his opponent, he wasn't going to get another chance like this one. Especially as all talk had quieted in The Chateau dining room.

Evigan's brows rose as his gaze roamed over Aisha, something dark flashing in those bloodshot depths.

"I suggest you have a little more respect for the woman .who is going to be my wife"

"A real man doesn't need to throw his weight around." Aisha's gaze shifted meaningfully to Evigan's wife, standing a few feet away, her eyes on the floor. "He's more than confident to walk beside his wife."

"You're a little spitfire, aren't you? Uppity with your degree like that makes you someone." Evigan lashed out the words, meting them out in a quiet voice that stung with all the force of pelting ice. To anyone watching, the byplay appeared physical and tense, but even straining to hear, they'd likely have missed the exchange.

Or the repeated evidence Evigan bore a distinct streak of bigotry.

His disdain was practically a living, breathing entity between them. Trey had known from the first that Barton Evigan would be a poor choice for Bradford County. It was disheartening to see, once again, just how correct he'd been from the start.

"Come on, Bart." The man who was clearly his brother moved up behind them, slapping Barton on the back. "People are starting to notice. You catch more honey with flies, you know that."

A dark grin spread across Barton's lips, as equally cold as the sneer it replaced. "How right you are, Trace. We should let this family get back to their celebration."

The two men backed away, their twin forms matched in width and girth. Trey never moved, nor was he willing to sit down until they'd left the room. He'd learned early in life not to turn his back on a feral animal, and the two jerks leaving The Chateau's dining room certainly qualified.

He did, however, want to reassure Aisha. With his gaze on the retreating forms of the Evigan brothers, he reached for her hand. "Are you all right?"

She linked her fingers with his, squeezing gently. "I'm fine."

"He's not worth our time."

"Maybe not, but he is worth our fight." Once the two men exited the room with Barton's wife, Trey finally turned to face her.

What had he brought her into? "I'm so sorry for that. For what he said to you."

"I can stand up to a bigot and a bully. I've had some practice."

He clenched his jaw. "You shouldn't have to. Not here. And certainly not from a man seeking public office."

"That's why you're going to beat him. I'm in this with you, Trey. And I'm going to help you do it."

He pulled her close for a hug, not caring what his family saw or what they assumed. Barton Evigan had lashed out at Aisha and while there was no law against being a jerk, Trey was going to protect her all the same.

Whatever else had happened tonight, his opponent for office had shown his hand. His true nature had trickled through before, but tonight the raw ambition and barely leashed ferocity was on full display. He'd come to the table to taunt them, arrogance personified.

But it had backfired.

Whatever lingering doubts Trey had about the rightness of his and Aisha's deception had vanished. Evigan needed to go down and Trey was just the man for the job. He hadn't been afraid of the school bully as a kid and he'd be damned if he was going to be afraid of the town bully now.

Only one thing was different.

This time, Aisha had put herself in the crosshairs.

Chapter Twelve

Daria stared at her computer screen, search results falling in a cascade beneath the query box. She scanned each of them quickly, disappointed when nothing bore fruit. Not a single Bloom.

Anywhere.

She fought the small pain that arrowed through her heart and shut down the search program. She was always on the lookout for new tools available to the sheriff's office and when she'd heard about the updated missing persons database she'd hoped it might give her what she needed to find her birth mother.

But nothing.

Another strikeout, and on a Saturday night, no less.

She was a workaholic so the Saturday night wasn't anything new—especially not with all that needed to be done at the moment—but still… She'd hoped the twenty-minute carve out for herself would be a bit more successful. Even if she hadn't found immediate evidence of her mother, a small kernel of information she hadn't uncovered before would have been a victory.

She picked up the nameplate that identified her from the edge of her desk.

Daria Bloom.

A change from the name she'd carried most of her life before coming to Roaring Springs.

Daria Colton.

Bloom had been her birth name and the one she'd returned to when she'd decided to look for her birth mother in earnest. It connected her—or so she'd believed—and she had embraced the change. How disappointing to realize that the name change hadn't put her any closer to answering the question that had haunted her for most of her life.

Why had her mother given her up?

Even with the steady love of her adoptive parents, nothing had erased the desperate need to find out where she came from. Joe Colton had been a model father and he wanted what was best for her—he still wanted that—but he hadn't been able to give her the one thing she needed.

Answers.

So she'd come here. Of the few clues she had, one was that her life had begun in the West, likely Colorado. When she'd realized she could be near her extended adoptive family by coming to Roaring Springs, she'd taken the opportunity. Although the branch of the Coltons that lived in Colorado was rather distant from former President Joe Colton, she'd still loved the idea of being near family.

Telling them who she was, however, was an entirely different matter. When she finally declared herself a Colton, she wanted it to be because she knew who Daria Bloom was.

Unfortunately, she'd been in Roaring Springs for nearly a year and still had no answers.

And now everyone she knew, including her distant cousin Trey, had no idea who she really was.

What would they do when they found out? A year of deception didn't exactly sit in her favor. Even as her conscience kept nagging at her to just come clean. They were family. Somehow, they'd understand. Or would eventually. But still, she held back. She loved working for Trey and knew him to be a fair and honorable man. In her quieter moments, she'd nearly convinced herself to tell him everything, confessing her secret.

Then an opportunity would present itself and she'd chicken out.

Which was silly since he might even be able to help her. The Avalanche Killer currently occupied their minds 24/7, but she'd seen his work style over the past year. He was methodical and careful, by-the-book yet able to toss that book when he needed to act on gut instinct. It was a rare gift—a leader who could balance both—and Trey Colton had her undying devotion and respect.

So tell him.

That small voice whispered again and she pushed back from her desk, willing it to quiet. She'd grab a fresh cup of coffee and head back to the conference room and review the murder boards. That would give her something to focus on and temper the disappointment of another dead end.

It had to.

Ten minutes later, her coffee full of a small dab of cream, just the way she liked it, she stared at the evidence they'd accumulated on the latest potential victim. The hair and blood sample didn't necessarily mean death, but since the killer's call on Monday night and the delivery of the package, they'd operated under the assumption there was a body to be found. The second note and the use of the word *victim* had further solidified the assumption.

"But what if?" She murmured the words out loud, nearly bobbling her coffee when an answer came winging back at her.

"What if she's still alive?"

Daria whirled around to find FBI Agent Stefan Roberts standing in the doorway. "What are you doing here?"

"I could ask you the same."

"I work here," she huffed.

"That's why I came to find you."

"Me?"

He pointed to one of the rolling chairs, neatly pushed in around the conference room table. "Mind if I sit?"

"Sure."

His dark gaze drifted to the boards, and she used that moment to consider him. He had the prettiest skin she'd ever seen, and that wasn't a term she usually used when she considered a man. His skin was dark brown, his complexion smooth and unblemished. Every time she saw him, she had this crazy urge to reach out and trace the tip of her finger over his cheek, convinced she'd feel nothing but the lightest scratch of his beard.

He was delicious.

It was all she kept coming back to, as images of replacing her finger with her lips would immediately shift the image from curiosity to urgent need.

Which was why she avoided thinking about how Stefan Roberts looked. Or possibly tasted. Or sounded.

Even if that deep, resonant voice had invaded her

dreams more than a few times since they'd met over the Avalanche Killer case.

"How can I help you, Agent Roberts?"

"The latest note. The one that came in on Wednesday. We've been over it and over it and feel there's something to the use of the word *box*."

"We agree."

"We?" He leaned forward, his gaze holding hers for a moment. "Not *I*?"

"We're a team here."

"So I've noticed."

She heard the dry notes and wasn't going to let them lie. "You have a problem with that?"

"No."

"Because you sound like you do."

"You heard wrong."

"My hearing's quite good," she shot back.

"Then listen well. I don't have a problem."

Daria wasn't ready to change her mind but she had no interest in arguing the point. "So. The note?"

"Slow like the fox. You'd better watch out. Evidence in a box. Another victim, no doubt." He recited the words she'd already committed to memory, the message as puzzling out loud as it was on the page.

"It makes no sense beyond the rhyme," she said after he'd finished.

"You think that's important?" he asked, curiosity glimmering in his gaze.

"You don't?"

"It's meaningless crap. All of it."

Aisha couldn't resist the smile, so she attempted to hide it behind her coffee mug. She spoke just before taking a sip. "Is that your professional opinion?"

"Mine and the profilers." He didn't hold back a grin of his own. It was subtle and started slow, but once it spread across his face, it positively electrified his features. The man went from incredibly handsome to mind-blowingly hot in the matter of a smile.

The intense and immediate reaction was enough to quell her own smile and Daria shifted gears, determined to focus on the ramblings of a killer. "What do they think about it? I have my opinions, but profiling isn't my expertise."

"The bodies discovered after the avalanche suggest all the classic patterns of a serial killer. Meticulous and methodical behavior. Careful management of the bodies. Even with the destruction of the avalanche the depressions in situ showed they were all buried with the same precision. The same body position from what we could find. That indicates a level of awareness and preparation."

"The note doesn't say the same?"

"That rhyming mess?" When she only nodded, he continued on. "It's hasty and dumb."

"Maybe it's a break in pattern?"

"Or someone else entirely."

Aisha had hit on the copycat idea earlier in the week, sharing her thoughts with Daria and Trey only, so it was fascinating to get the hypothesis backed up by Agent Roberts and his profilers.

"A copycat?" she asked.

"Yes."

"So where's the real killer?"

"Out there and on the loose. Which is why I'm here."

Not for a Saturday night flirt session.

Which empirically Daria knew, but still, she couldn't

stop the shot of disappointment that settled down around the same area in her chest as the earlier setback regarding her birth mother.

Burying all of it way down deep, she put on her most professional face, her voice all business. "What do you need?"

"Trey suggested the other day that the governor has taken an interest in this case."

"Of course he has. And I'd wager whatever pressure Trey is getting, your office is getting double."

"You'd win that bet."

She quirked a brow. "How does that affect me?"

"You're smart and you're competent. I know we agreed that we'd work together but so far we've grudgingly helped each other. I'm willing to show my cards. All of them."

"Why?"

"Because I want to apprehend the real killer," he replied. "Catching a fake might make politicians sleep easier, but it won't help me. Not one bit."

Daria considered what the agent was saying. And also what he wasn't. The pressure on all of them to close the Avalanche Killer case was extreme. But if the governor caught wind of a copycat, it would be all too easy, for political reasons, to push to close the case over a fake.

And then they'd all be out of luck, the citizens of Bradford County most of all.

The Avalanche Killer had operated under the radar for well over a decade. If the blame ended up being pinned on some sick copycat and not the one truly responsible, the killer could be in the wind before any of them blinked. Serial killers might have patterns, but they were also smart. Eluding capture for as long as he had, it would be easy enough for the killer to pack up shop and resume his evil machinations somewhere else. As far as the public knew, the Avalanche Killer would be caught, rotting in jail.

And the real killer would be free to wreak havoc all over again.

"I'll have to check with my boss."

"Of course. I want Colton's agreement, fair and square." Stefan looked around. "Where is he, by the way?"

"At his engagement party. His cousin threw him and Aisha a dinner tonight." A dinner she wasn't part of, even though she was a Colton, too.

And whose fault is that, Daria Colton Bloom?

Whatever—or whoever—she was, Daria was honest with herself. She'd been that way always, but had doubled down on the trait with the decision to find her mother. If she didn't keep a steady grip on her emotions and her motivations, she'd never get the answers she sought.

It was with that understanding that a new idea took root. If she and Agent Roberts did work more closely together, perhaps he could be a conduit to her search for her mother. The level of information and data she had as a county employee was vast, but it was still nothing compared with what the Feds possessed.

Could she trust him to help her?

Did she dare ask?

She'd nearly decided to take the bull by the horns when Stefan smiled again, distracting her from her question. "Good for them. It's important to take the good where you can find it."

"Always."

That vibrant smile fell once more, replaced with a sadness she could actually feel. "It's too rare not to."

"Not a lot of good in your life right now?"

"No." His brown eyes were direct on hers when he spoke. "Not one single bit."

AISHA STILL FUMED inwardly as she thought about the sheer malevolence that had spewed off Trey's opponent for sheriff. Where she'd initially believed Barton Evigan was just a troublemaker, the events at the town hall last week and tonight's little display in The Chateau's main dining room had forced her to rethink that opinion.

Yes, he'd come over to their table to make trouble, but the resulting exchange of words had held a dark danger she'd not expected.

Who did that bastard think he was? Trey had hung close after it happened. Her mother and sister had moved in as well, followed by Calvin and Audrey, all of them closing ranks around her. She was in the midst of the people she cared about most in the world, and still, nothing had managed to calm her.

That was what the good people of Bradford County were going to get on their ballots come November?

His brother was a piece of work, too. A big, hulking brute who looked as ready to do harm as Barton did. Maybe even more. She hadn't missed how he'd hung back with Barton's wife, almost as if he were the guard dog waiting to attack anyone who dared to get in the way.

"I know that look." Audrey Colton sat down beside Aisha, her voice soft and low. "My husband tells me that's the look I get each and every time I head out for a rally."

Audrey had been an activist since Aisha was eight. She'd fought for everything from the safety of Colorado land to protections for the Native people of their area to basic rights for women and minorities. It was in her blood to raise her voice and use it, and Aisha considered it the highest compliment that Trey's mom might see even a glimmer of that coming from her.

"I'll consider that the highest compliment, but one I can't accept."

"You had the warrior look on before. You stand up when you need to and that's all that really matters."

"You stand up for everything."

Audrey shrugged, those slim shoulders still elegant into her sixties. "I formed my opinions and my actions in my own time. You'll do the same in yours."

"He's a monster." Aisha willed the overwhelming frustration aside, hoping by doing so she could find some semblance of balance again. "Trey should have an opponent. It's not good to have a shoo-in election. Or no real opposition for people to vote on. But Evigan is not that person."

"No, he's not." A definitive snort was added to the comment as Trey's grandfather Earl came up to stand beside her and Audrey. Although he needed the aid of his cane, his movements slow, he had that Colton determination in spades. Aisha knew Earl had been declining over the past few years, but that night it felt like they had the old Earl Colton with them.

"Mr. Colton." Aisha leaned down to give him a kiss on the cheek. "I'm so glad you could make it tonight."

Audrey followed, a soft kiss to the older man's cheek. "Pops."

"My girls." Earl smiled, his gaze drifting to where his sons and grandsons assembled in a small conversation circle. "I love my boys, but I'm damn happy there are more girls in this family. More and more every month!"

"There are a lot of weddings going around," Aisha agreed, ignoring the guilt that reminded her there wouldn't be one for her and Trey. That the evening was all for show.

If Audrey felt the same, she didn't show it, instead turning on the full wattage of her smile for Earl. "Isn't it wonderful, Pops? Everyone happy and settled."

"Sure is."

The old man slapped a hand on his thigh. "We'll have a lot to look forward to in the fall. Trey's going to beat that ass, Evigan, and then we'll have Aisha here joining our family."

Aisha's gaze snapped to Audrey's over Earl's bent frame, but all she saw was that continued smile. One that had veered decidedly toward mischief. *Well*, Aisha thought. *No help from that quarter.*

"Thank you, Mr. Colton."

"About damn time, too. I've seen you two running around since you were little ones. Peas in a pod, you both were. That's what I always told my Alice, may she rest in peace."

Earl inclined his head on the last, and Aisha had a memory of Earl before age and time had riddled his body. He'd been a strong, proud man and his wife, Alice, had matched him in her love for their family and for the land. She'd been gone several years, but it was easy to see there was a bond that would never leave him.

Wasn't that what she had with Trey? They might not have the romantic elements, but in all other ways they were boon companions. And they had been from the start.

Was that why the lack of a true romance and love hurt so much?

"Mama Alice loved watching the kids run around," Audrey added. "She told me years ago that Trey and Aisha were going to end up together someday."

Aisha nearly tumbled in her heels, despite standing still beside Earl and Audrey.

End up together?

Had she entered a parallel universe? She'd heard the same nonsense from her mother for years, but Audrey knew the truth. She knew that there was nothing truly going on between Trey and Aisha.

Except for those kisses...

Aisha had no idea what to say to any of it. With her mother, it was easy enough to brush it off with an "Oh, Mom" or a "Be serious." However, with Trey's family—and a pretend engagement ring on her finger—it wasn't quite so easy to dismiss. "That's so sweet to hear. And proof that everybody loves a happy ending."

"Especially when two good people find each other." Earl turned to her and pressed a soft kiss to her cheek. "That makes the best sort of happy ending, darlin'. When someone deserves it."

Earl moved on, headed for the circle of men who'd moved to the end of the table. Aisha watched him go, his words still echoing in her mind.

Oh, how she wanted to deserve it.

All of it.

TREY WALKED AISHA to her door, the lingering frustration over Evigan's visit during dinner nearly erasing what was a great time with their families. While he hated the reason for it, he'd seen how hardship and danger had brought his extended family closer over the past several months, and he couldn't find fault with the outcome.

His cousins had proved that. Each had given their unwavering support as they'd stood in the dining room, the aftermath of Evigan's visit still lingering in the air. And each was equally determined to help him in any way they could.

Even his grandfather had been in fine form. They'd all watched with sadness as age had done its inevitable work, but it was great to have had a few hours where remnants of a younger man still shone through.

"You doing okay?" Aisha finished opening her lock and turned to him as her front door swung open.

"I'm good. And remembering all the things I have to be grateful for."

He saw the immediate question in her gaze but gestured her in. "My family. I've been so focused on Evigan I nearly forgot what a nice evening it was. Or how much I enjoy their company."

She smiled, her natural warmth immediately lighting her features. "It was that."

"Everyone loves you."

"And I love them. Your family is quirky and intense but they care deeply for each other. It's nice to see."

They also cared deeply for Aisha. That had been a continuous theme through the evening. Every bit of congratulations he'd received had quickly been followed by admonitions of "It's about time," "What took you so long?" and "I knew it all along."

His grandfather had been even more vocal, telling him he'd begun to suspect Trey was a damn fool for making the woman wait so long.

How had he missed what each and every one of them had seen?

And was it even remotely possible it was the governor's lackey who'd put it all into perspective? Or at least pushed him in the right direction.

Since Trey was increasingly coming to the conclusion it was *exactly* like that, he wasn't quite sure what to do with it.

Nor was he sure if Aisha felt the same way.

He knew there was attraction. The heat that generated each time they'd kissed had proved that beyond a shadow of a doubt. But physical attraction wasn't love. And whatever else they had, the two of them had an extraordinary foundation of love, respect and friendship. Did he dare put any of that at risk?

Yet as he looked over at her, at that beautiful face he knew as well as his own, backlit by the soft lights of the living room lamp, Trey wondered how he could resist her.

"My family thinks you and I are a good idea."

The smile that still lingered over talk of his family faded. "They all said similar things to me."

"Do you think it's a good idea?"

"This engagement?" She let out a small sigh before tossing her small evening purse onto a nearby chair. "We both had our eyes open going in. This is a means to an end, and based on Barton's intrusion into our dinner this evening, I'd say we made the right decision."

Logical. Quantifiable. Tangible.

All the reasons they'd entered into this sham engagement in the first place.

But now he wanted more. A *lot* more, and he wanted it all with her. "My family seems to think so."

"It's in the air. They've all begun to see love everywhere. From Wyatt and Bailey to Liam and Sloane and all the rest of your cousins who've coupled up this year. Even your sister, Bree, and her fiancé, Rylan, have stars in their eyes."

"What if they're right?"

"About what?"

Trey hovered there for the briefest of moments. A nanosecond, really, before he closed the gap between them. "Us, Aish. You and me."

His hands settled at her waist, but that was as far as he went. The urgent need to kiss her—to take her in his arms and brand her as his—pounded through him in intense waves. But he held back, his hands at her hips and the nearness of their bodies the closest he'd come.

He needed her to do the rest.

Needed to know that she not only felt the same way, but that she wanted to take that last step, too.

"Oh, Trey." The dark depths of her eyes seemed to gleam in the room's soft light. "Do you know how long I've wanted that?"

"You have?"

"Yeah. But it will change us." She stilled, her hands settling over his. "It will change everything."

"Maybe I want to change everything."

"Just so long as you understand we can't go back."

Somewhere, deep inside, Trey knew what she meant. They couldn't go backward. He'd suspected as much, as soon as the suggestion of an engagement left his lips, but now, it was so much more.

And in reality, there was no going back. So he'd do what felt so perfect between them.

He'd push forward.

"I want that, Aish. You. Me. I want things to change."

She nodded, the lightest sheen of tears filling her gaze before she leaned in and pressed a soft kiss to his lips. But it was the words she murmured after that confirmed she felt as he did.

"I want that, too, Trey. You and me."

Chapter Thirteen

Aisha wondered if she was in a dream.

It felt like it, she thought, as she reveled in the long, languorous strokes of Trey's fingertips over her body. They'd drifted into her bedroom, the lamp from the living room spilling far enough to provide plenty of ambient light to observe him.

This was Trey.

And while she'd always felt rather proprietary toward him, something changed inside.

This was *her* Trey.

Whatever happened tonight would be between just the two of them. She wasn't without apprehension, fully aware they would never go back to where they'd been. Their friendship was rock solid, but making love would irrevocably change them.

Both of them.

She knew she should be more worried about that. That somehow, she should shield her heart from breaking wide-open. Hadn't she learned that lesson once before? And hadn't she lived with that heartbreak ever since? She'd loved Kenneth, but their relationship had been nowhere near as deep or intense or *essential* as her friendship with Trey.

And still, Aisha pressed forward.

She accepted his lips against her own, their mouths fusing together with the heat and need and sheer desperation that now drove their bodies. And when his fingers went to the zipper at the back of her dress, she could only wait in delicious anticipation of what was to come.

The zipper slid lightly over her skin and Trey ran the fingertips of his free hand down her spine, trailing just behind the freed material. His lips continued to play over hers, a mix of hot and urgent that kept her body at the edge of something.

Need.

Want.

Desire.

And underneath it all, love. It was an impractical emotion and one that came with more risks than she could count, but she loved Trey. She hadn't made love to that many men in her life, but she wasn't inexperienced. Only in the past, sex was the next step in the relationship. A pathway to love, not something that came after.

But with Trey?

The love had been there, ever since that day on the slide stairs when a girl became friends with a boy. The best boy in school who'd grown into the very best man in the county.

Once again, those few tears she'd felt in the living room pricked the corners of her eyes. Trey Colton was a good man. And the reason they were in this situation was because others were not only unwilling to believe that, but were determined to drag his name through the mud.

"Aish? You okay?" His voice was husky in the room.

Even with the need that pulsed in his words, she heard the concern, as well.

"I'm good."

Although he didn't move away, his hands shifted to settle on her shoulders. "Do you want to do this?"

"Yes."

Dark eyebrows lifted over those golden irises. "Then why are you crying?"

"For you."

"Why?"

"You're a good man, Trey. One of the very best I've ever known or will know. And the reason we're here is because someone has made it their business to make people think otherwise."

"Do you think that's why we're here?"

Although she hadn't given that much thought, now that the idea had dug in, she couldn't think of anything else.

If it weren't for Barton Evigan—and wasn't that a depressing person to think about while in the midst of sex?—she and Trey would never have even considered the need for a fake engagement. If there was no fake engagement there'd be no forced intimacy. No forced intimacy, no barriers dropped to have sex.

It was that simple.

Even as it was complicated as hell.

"Isn't it?"

"It's not why I'm here." He trailed the tip of one finger over her cheek, tracing the line of her jaw. "Are you?"

It wasn't but how did she tell him she'd wanted to be here for years? That despite all her apprehension and terror they'd ruin what they have, that she wanted him all the same?

"I suppose not."

"Suppose?" Trey's hand fell. "I've known you nearly a lifetime, Aish. You don't suppose anything. You know."

And there it was, once again. He *knew* her. "Yes. I want to be here."

"Me, too."

"What if we ruin everything?" Her fear spilled out, oozing between them.

"You think I don't worry about the same? You're my best friend. You're my port in the storm and you know me better than anyone. I don't want to lose that."

"Me, either."

"But then I realized something." Before she could answer, he kept on. "I *won't* lose you. I will never lose you, Aish. You matter to me and nothing, no force on earth, is going to change that."

They wanted each other—of that Aisha was beyond certain—but the sincerity in Trey's entire manner had changed. He wanted what was between them, yes, but he hadn't dismissed her questions.

Or how much their friendship mattered to him, too.

And in the end, it was that sincerity that calmed her fears.

Trey Colton was a part of her life and nothing was going to change that. They might be changing the dynamic between them, but in the end, they couldn't change the fundamentals of who they were.

Of what they'd always seen in one another.

But they might find a path to something more.

TREY PRACTICALLY HELD his breath, waiting for Aisha's response. He ached for her, and his body was strung out on a very thin cord because of it. But nothing—not the physical needs that had exploded between them or the tension that came with sexual attraction—had a damn thing on how desperately he wanted to reassure her.

Nothing would ever change how he felt about her. She was all the things he'd said and so much more. And he wanted her to believe him because he'd meant every word.

But was it enough?

The thought had barely crossed his mind when her arms came around his neck again, her lips soft against his. But it was her whisper that came next, a subtle movement of lips, that confirmed it.

"Please, Trey. Make love to me."

Need exploded through him once more, cratering his self-control and the tight leash he'd kept on his body. On the desperate need to join with her.

How had they ignored it for so long?

Because here, now, with Aisha in his arms, that was the only qualifier Trey could put on their relationship. Both of them had been so determined to ignore what was there, as if it were some sort of self-defense mechanism to protect their friendship.

Only now, he saw what that restraint had also done. Kept them apart for so very long.

Still in awe, Trey resumed his exploration of her womanly curves, the warm flesh of her back nearly singeing his fingers as he slipped the dress from her body. The silky material floated to the floor, pooling at her feet, and he shifted her lightly so she wouldn't get tangled up in the material.

That shift in position was enough to press them both against the bed, their thighs flush with the mattress. Aisha sat down, clad in nothing but her bra and panties. A small smile flirted with the corners of her lips as Aisha stared up at him. "I think you're wearing too many clothes."

"Your sound, responsible sheriff to the bitter end."

Although he'd meant it in jest, he didn't miss the narrowing of her eyes or her understanding of what each day cost him. He was Mr. By-the-Book because he couldn't afford to be otherwise. He needed people to know he was responsible and worthy of their trust. Worthy of their vote.

Funny how it was Aisha who'd always understood that. While his cousins and friends and fellow deputies always urged him to cut loose, it was Aisha who knew his reasons for walking the straight and narrow.

She reached up and tugged on his tie, pulling him down for a kiss, murmuring as she closed that distance. "You don't have to be responsible in here."

"I'm always responsible."

"I think you've just laid down a challenge. A very sexy one." She stood once more, her hands going to the buttons of his shirt. He'd shed his sport coat and tie when they'd gotten into the car earlier and he was suddenly grateful for the foresight. It took mere moments for her to slip each button from its mooring until the shirt lay open down the front. She ran her hands over his chest and up over his shoulders, slipping the dress shirt from his body before those clever fingers returned to the hem of his T-shirt, slipping that up and over his torso. He grabbed the material, dragging the soft cotton off the rest of the way before wrapping his arms around her, desperate for the skin-to-skin contact of their bodies.

Anxious to *feel* her.

"You've been working out."

Although he'd always kept in shape, both as a matter of personal pride and as a function of his job, the Avalanche Killer case had him spending even more time in the gym. Their facility on-site at work helped fill random hours when he needed to be alone with his thoughts, puzzling through one aspect or another of what they'd already investigated.

The weights or run on the treadmill had given him time to collect his thoughts, using the physical test to his body as a chance to free his mind. To give himself time to take the random and process it into some form of order and understanding.

It was only now, the admiration shining in Aisha's dark gaze, that Trey realized there had been another benefit. One far more personal and exhilarating.

"You keep feeding me pizza. What else could I do?"

"Very impressive, Sheriff Colton."

She leaned in and pressed a kiss to the rounded curve of his shoulder, following the line of muscle to his collarbone and then on down over his chest. Little darts of heat followed the skim of her lips, the heat of her tongue, as she erotically traced his skin. It was sexy and tantalizing, and need pushed up another notch as her lips created a firestorm.

His body pressed insistently against his slacks, his erection straining for freedom. Despite their current situation—and how far things had already gone—Trey sensed a momentous shift in the air as her fingers slipped to the clasp of his slacks. Aisha freed the closure and pressed her hand to thick flesh, and Trey was lost.

And, he humbly realized, pressing his forehead to hers, found.

In the physical, yes, but the emotional, as well. The tight rein he'd always kept on his attraction for her lifted, freed at last to explore all of the woman he knew and loved.

A lifetime of need and want suddenly exploded like a fireball. He laid gentle fingers around her wrist, stilling her movements as they grew nearly unbearable. "I want you so damn bad, Aish."

Her chocolate-brown eyes flashed in the soft light, so deep he wondered he didn't drown. "I want you, too."

Easing her hand into his, he linked their fingers together as he pressed his mouth to hers once more. The simple act of kissing, their tongues meeting and mating in the moonlight, was one more example of how good things were between them. How they moved in sync, each understanding the other, from their matched breath to the easy way they sank into each other.

Choosing to savor, even as his body clamored for him to rush, Trey walked a sharp edge. And knew this tightrope hovered over a soft, warm landing.

Suddenly conscious of too much clothing, he made quick work of it all, dropping each remaining piece into a careless pile. Aisha reached for the clasp of her bra before he stopped her, anxious to remove the last few pieces himself. And when her breasts spilled into his hands moments later, Trey knew a bone-deep satisfaction. She was warm. Willing.

And his.

IT WASN'T SUPPOSED to be like this. Not this good and fulfilling and necessary. Those silly thoughts kept filling her mind, a sort of disbelief that pulsed in counterpoint to the truth.

It *was* this good.

They'd barely begun and she was more fulfilled than any intimacy she'd ever shared before.

Holding her tight in his arms as he moved them both to the bed, Aisha knew a new definition to the word *necessary*. She'd always assumed breath, food and water were the only elements to fit that category, but it looked like there was a fourth.

Trey Colton.

They'd both slipped off the last barrier of underwear and now lay nestled against each other naked. It was the most erotic sensation of her life as the heat of his skin seemed to paint every inch of hers. Their breaths met and mingled in the small cocoon of intimacy that wrapped them together. Although she'd had sex since her breakup with Kenneth, Aisha was forced in that moment to admit the truth to herself.

She hadn't made love.

"Aisha?"

He so often called her Aish that the use of her full name, quietly spoken, pulled at her.

"You okay?"

"I'm good." She nodded.

"You went somewhere there."

"Just thinking."

His eyes widened as his mouth formed an exaggerated O. "I'm doing it wrong."

"You're doing everything exactly right. Which was

suddenly apparent to me, hence the moment of quiet awe."

"Quiet awe?" The slightest edge of concern that had teased the edges of his gaze vanished. "That's quite a compliment."

"I meant it."

"Then let me say, without any reservation, ditto."

"Copying my paper, Trey Colton?" The words spilled out in a tease, made that much sillier by the fact he'd never so much as borrowed her homework notes.

And reinforced by the fact that she'd known him long enough that he could have.

In the end, Aisha realized it was that truth that drove them both forward. Roots, long planted, gave them the base for the change in their relationship. And the strength of them—the sheer, solid depth—would see them through this new dimension.

Buoyed by the knowledge and more than willing to push the last bit of fear aside, she ran a hand over his cheek. "I have protection in the end table. I think it's time to put all this quiet awe to very good use."

He did as she asked, pulling the new box of condoms she'd picked up the week before on a mix of intuition and insight.

"They're new," she said, her voice low.

"Which only proves how much of a wavelength you and I operate on."

"Oh?"

"There's a matched box, brand-spanking-new, in my end table."

It was silly and not at all surprising as they were two healthy adults, but it was all completely wonderful. And at his words, something inside her heart cracked wide-open at the idea he'd anticipated this, too.

"I think we'd better get busy."

The double entendre wasn't lost on him and he wasted no time in proving her right.

The words that always formed the basis of their friendship—the water to those deep, strong roots—faded as they forged a new path. One based on friendship, yes, but on something more.

A new sort of bond that would live between them forever more.

Trey shifted her to her back, his weight settling over her. He mouth was hot on her skin, the heady combination of lips and teeth and tongue tracking a path from neck to chest before he stopped, taking time with her breasts.

Light exploded before her eyes, pleasure curling low and deep in her belly as his mouth explored first one breast, then the other. Luxurious strokes of his tongue hardened her nipples to tight points, that crater of need rocketing through her nerve endings in one continuous roll of sensation.

The quiet man she knew—the one who'd teased about living by the book—clearly had a well of sensuality that he kept firmly tamped down. After a generous and thorough exploration of her breasts, he moved on, his lips teasing the sensitized skin of her lower stomach.

But it was when he moved lower still that Aisha knew a sense of wonder that humbled even as it exhilarated, a steady, insistent pulse beat that grew with mounting force.

Her fingers sank into his short-cropped hair as he pleasured her with his mouth. Wave after wave of mindless sensation took over the moment, pushing away her ability to think.

This was feeling. Raw. Emotional. *Essential.*

He kept up a steady rhythm, driving her body higher and higher to the point of breaking.

Only when the world finally exploded, it was the opposite of destruction.

It was life. Glorious and wild. Free and open to all that was still to come.

Aisha wanted to lie in that beautiful glow, his arms already cradling her as he lay back beside her. Yet even as her body still rocketed with aftershocks, she wanted more.

Craved it.

Reaching for one of the condoms he'd laid on the end table after opening the box, her fingers closed over the slim foil and she made quick work of the package, shifting her attention to his straining erection. A hard groan escaped his lips as she fitted the condom, and Aisha knew a sense of power that filled her once more with wonder.

He was hers.

And this moment was theirs.

Whatever had come before or would come after had no bearing on the now. On the steady hum of desire that drove them both.

She straddled his hips, moving over him so that she could guide him into her body, then sinking to take him in fully. That glorious sensation of being stretched added sparks to the aftershocks of her first orgasm, pressing on with the greedy intention of having more.

Of *taking* more.

Trey's large hands came over her hips to both steady

and guide as they set a rhythm between them. Pleasure became the only goal once more, as together they pushed one another on toward a peak.

Toward a summit they'd scale and share together.

She'd expected to feel a little sad, that the relationship they had was passing away. But as the heat and need and sheer demands of her body pushed her toward another orgasm, Aisha realized how wrong she'd been and how misplaced her fears.

As he pushed one final time, filling her completely, she knew a rare moment of perfection.

And the absolute knowledge that their relationship hadn't faded away. Instead, it had grown to make them both more. To make friends, lovers.

And to cement the love they had for one another into an unbreakable bond.

THE CALL CAME in at 3:00 a.m. Trey and Aisha had just finished another bout of lovemaking, their bodies sated as both were nearly asleep, when his phone rumbled on her bedside table.

An hour later, Trey stood over the dead woman, a steaming disposable cup of coffee in hand as the August breeze swirled around him.

Hell, if he wasn't staring down at a body, he'd have enjoyed sitting out on his back porch, a beer in hand as the cool mountain breezes kept him company, Aisha at his side.

Aisha…

He tamped down on that, his emotions still raw and wild from the power of making love with her. Of making love with his best friend.

Instead, he focused on the corpse before him.

It's not Skye.

That thought had kept him company along with the breeze, floating as steady and insistent through his mind as his deputies worked around him, photographing and cataloging the site while they waited for the medical examiner.

The hair and blood sample analysis that had come in earlier in the week on the package they'd received at the station had definitely proved Skye wasn't the victim. Now, looking down at the woman who'd died, Trey had another quiet moment of relief. He had no doubt the ME would confirm the blood and hair samples received were a match for the poor young woman who lay before them.

It did little to battle the ongoing fear that something had happened to Skye, but there was comfort in knowing she hadn't been left discarded in the woods like this unfortunate soul.

Aisha had wanted to come with him, but he'd encouraged her to stay warm and in bed. There'd be enough time later to analyze everything. But was it selfish that he wanted her to stay home, untouched by this evil? Even if it were only for a few hours more.

She was his partner in this. She'd proved it, day in and day out since they'd found the bodies on the side of the mountain, and she'd been there for him ever since. He wanted her take on this latest terrifying discovery made by a couple of newlyweds who'd stumbled out of their camping tent. Even now, the duo sat huddled together on the far side of the discovery site, wrapped in light blankets, despite the warm temperatures. A purported late-night craving that required another package of chocolate bars in their SUV parked offsite had sent them out of their tent.

That chocolate was long forgotten for the body they'd practically stumbled over, laid out in plain sight.

In plain sight.

"It's another break in pattern." Daria sidled up beside him, her own cup of coffee steaming in her hand.

"A dump site in the woods?" Trey asked.

"Yes. Added to the taunts we received this past week, it's not like the other murders."

Trey had already assessed the same and was going to get Aisha's take on it all when they spoke later. Daria continued on. "Agent Roberts thinks we have a copycat on our hands."

Trey had asked Daria to stay close to the agent. He'd sensed from the start they'd get more cooperation and collaboration if he appeared separate from the investigation.

But this was new.

"When did he say this?"

"Last night."

"Last night was Saturday."

Although he couldn't see any evidence of a blush in the darkened light, he did see her shoulders stiffen slightly. "I was working late."

"Daria. I know we're under a lot of pressure but I don't expect that."

And he didn't. They worked like fiends during the week, and while he appreciated the additional time everyone was putting in over the weekends, that didn't mean more evenings were required. "You're entitled to a life."

"If you hadn't been at your engagement dinner, you'd have been there right along with me."

Could he honestly argue with her?

Before the whole engagement charade with Aisha, he absolutely would have been there. He hadn't taken more than about three days off since the discovery on Wicked Mountain. But even knowing that about himself, he didn't expect it of his deputies. No matter how talented and gifted they were.

"I still think you could find better ways to spend your weekends." He held up a hand before she could say anything. "But we'll argue that another day. What did Roberts want?"

"His visit was unexpected. I've done my best to get close to him, like we discussed. Up to now I've felt like he's doled out a few dribs and drabs." Daria took a sip of her coffee. "Enough to make it look like he's being collaborative but really just a front, you know?"

Trey did know. It was why he'd hoped Daria would get more than he had, but it remained clear the Feds wanted this case. Sharing information was on their agenda only if they could get something in return.

"He just showed up?"

"Yep. Surprised the hell out of me. Surprised me even more when he not only shared information, but seemed like he needed to get a second opinion."

Trey considered Agent Stefan Roberts for a moment. The guy had come off as entirely aboveboard. Although Trey's experience with the Feds was limited, he had worked with a few throughout his career. Most were fundamentally decent, but they operated at an entirely different level.

And expected to be alpha in every single situation.

While he wouldn't say Roberts hadn't come in to mark his territory, he had been respectful and fair and it had gone a long way toward easing Trey's attitude. If the man had shifted to cooperative and in need of help, it suggested the Avalanche Killer case was more of a challenge than any of them had anticipated.

"What did he have to say?" Trey finally asked.

"They're puzzling over the killer's note, same as us."

"Their profilers haven't figured it out?"

"Nope. Not only that, but they can't get a handle on any of the words or the cadence of the note." Daria turned to face him, her eyes glittering in the glare of the halogens his deputies had set up. "It's why they think it's a copycat."

As ideas went, it made sense. Everything about the murder, from the killer's taunting to the hair and note to the discovery out in the open, broke pattern. Neither was it a big mystery that a killer was on the loose. The press had descended into Bradford County over the past few months with all the finesse of locusts. Anyone looking for an angle would need to look no further than their morning, noon and evening news.

And someone looking to commit a crime could easily position their work as the killer's, in hopes they'd get away scot-free when the Avalanche Killer was eventually caught.

"Sheriff!"

One of his deputies hollered from the clearing where the body still lay. They'd covered the woman as best they could while waiting for the ME but the sheet did nothing to hide the reality of what was beneath. Someone, acting in cold blood, had taken another woman's life. In the end, that was what stung.

Trey didn't really care if it was a copycat or the original killer. Another woman had died on his watch. Another innocent life placed in the tally column.

A bit of coffee spilled over onto his palm, and Trey quickly eased his grip on his cup. He'd deal with this like he dealt with everything else.

By the book.

With dedication and focus.

And he hoped like hell he'd get there in time before the killer struck again.

THE MAN STOOD back in the clearing, his attention fully focused on the grisly tableau that played out before him. Another kill.

And he wasn't behind it.

What were the odds?

Had someone else decided they could use the bumbling police to their advantage?

He'd definitely taken advantage of pulling the strings from a distance. Having a killer in their midst had been a stroke of good fortune and he had never been one to turn down a bit of luck. Or a chance to capitalize on the misfortune of others.

But this was concerning, too. He'd used the Avalanche Killer to his advantage, keeping an eye on the man's every move. Hell, he'd taken pride in the fact that he was the only one in town who knew the man's identity. But a new player in the game meant he now had a blind spot.

The police continued working over the site, like ants scurrying over a mound, and he considered Sheriff Trey Colton. The man's reputation preceded him, just as every other damn Colton in town. Was it at all possible he was the target?

It seemed like a long shot, but a serial killer on the loose was bad news for local law enforcement. He'd watched as Sheriff Colton had grown more haggard and worn as the hunt for the killer continued on over these past few months. His use of several well-placed charges had set off the avalanche in the first place, and it had been their trusty sheriff who'd borne the brunt of the cleanup work.

His maneuvering behind the scenes ever since had only added to the sheriff's busywork. He'd had such fun poking at Phoebe and Prescott, ensuring last month's film festival was full of unpleasant moments for both of them. And even before the killer's crimes were discovered, he'd ensured the Coltons remained in danger. Hadn't he put the gun in David Swanson's possession in hopes the man would use it on Bree Colton? And wasn't he the one who'd knocked Sloane Colton out before setting fire to her barn?

He was careful and methodical, no one even close to figuring out he was responsible. Yet because of his work, everything he'd ever wanted was falling into place.

Which meant he had to get ahead of this copycat. Vengeance on the Colton family was his to take, not some nameless, faceless stranger.

He'd come this far. There was no way he was giving it all up now.

Chapter Fourteen

Aisha struggled to balance the bursts of happiness that even now still coursed through her with the reality of what was discovered in the wooded area just outside Roaring Springs.

Another body.

Although just as with the taunting letters and the blood and hair samples, this crime appeared different from the work of the Avalanche Killer. Colder, somehow.

Or no, Aisha admonished herself as she stared at the crime scene photos. Functional. The bullets to the body, the way the woman had been dumped in the woods, even the way the hair had been cut from her head, all indicated a functional treatment of the body.

A definite break in pattern.

Aisha hadn't been at the station long, careful not to look as if she were rushing over, but it hadn't taken long for the whispers to reach her. A copycat killer was the running theory on the unidentified woman.

While there was an odd comfort in not feeling as if the young woman had been targeted and toyed with, the raging disgust was no different. A human being had lost their life due to the will of another. Not natural causes. Or Mother Nature's wrath. Or even the horrible ravages of disease.

No.

Another had preyed on her and, for whatever sick reason, had deemed her no longer able to live.

What right did she have to be happy? Aisha wondered. Not when it was evident what was going on mere miles from her. The violence that had befallen Roaring Springs for the past eight months was horrifying.

As a mental health professional, she knew that was her internal response to such horrors. But as a woman, she couldn't quite veer the course. Whatever else might be going on, the violence that had befallen Roaring Springs for the past eight months was horrifying.

And terribly sad.

"Aisha?" Before she could register his arrival, Trey had her in his arms, pulled snug against his chest. "What's wrong?"

It wasn't until his arms came around her that Aisha realized the depth of her sorrow. "I'm sad, Trey. And sick over what's happening."

"I know. I know how you feel. And I'm sick over it, too."

"Why does this keep happening?" she finally asked.

"I don't know. This is a quiet place. I wouldn't go quite as far as bucolic, especially because of the high-end crowd that we get here, but this is fundamentally a quiet place."

"You're going to catch him. I know you are."

Trey's arms tightened around her, and she felt the strength there. She'd felt it in different ways just the night before. The powerful strength of his body as they had sex. The even more powerful feeling of rightness that had taken over once they both got past the initial nervousness of taking the large leap into intimacy.

It had been wonderful. And if she'd woken up alone in her bed with the momentary concern that things had changed, well, that was normal, wasn't it?

And just like that, she was back in her head, obsessed with whatever it was spinning out of control between her and Trey. They both had bigger things to deal with, yet here she was, thinking about the night they'd spent together.

But how could she think of anything else?

"You don't have to be here. It is Sunday."

The solid strength of his arms that remained wrapped around her belied his casual words.

"I do need to be here. And I want to be here. I want to help."

Trey shifted, pulling back from the embrace. "The FBI thinks it may be a copycat. A conclusion you came to last week."

"It makes sense. More and more when you consider the breaks in pattern. The call and the taunting with the hair samples. The body left in plain sight." Her voice trailed off as her gaze caught, her attention on the table.

He pointed to the photos. "Do you see something?"

Aisha reached for one of the crime scene photos that had particularly caught her attention. "Did you notice this one? The fingernails."

Trey caught on immediately. "It doesn't look like she struggled very much."

"No. And I don't see how that could be. Clearly, this woman was abducted, yet she didn't fight him off. Who wouldn't do that? Or maybe a better question is *why*.

The bodies discovered on the mountain all showed signs of struggle and acute distress before death."

In her own mind, Aisha was helpless not to imagine the absolute fear that would descend upon her if she were in the same situation. Fear. Panic. And a desperate need to escape.

Trey traced the hands in the photo. "She did fight. A little bit. There's some bruising on her face and you can see struggle around her mouth. Likely from a gag."

"There is that. But you think she would be manic to escape. Yet that's not evident around the fingers, the nails. There's not any blood or even any bruising. Look here." Aisha pointed to what had really caught her attention. "Her nails are painted and you don't even see any chips or stress points in the paint on any fingers other than those two. This woman didn't really struggle before she was killed."

If she wasn't a civilian, she'd directly pose the question to the FBI. Although Trey had given her the title of civilian consultant, she didn't want to draw attention to herself. But Trey and Daria could. This was an area they needed to press.

"The ME has her now. If there were drugs in her system, the tox records will show it."

Aisha's gaze drifted over the victim's nails once more. "I don't see how there can't be."

"Me, either."

A new idea struck her. "If this is a copycat, does it become your jurisdiction or the Feds'?"

"If they definitively rule out the work of the Avalanche Killer it will shift back to us. As it is, the Feds are keeping close tabs but giving us a bit more deference than I've seen so far."

"That's good." She hesitated, taking in the grim slash of his mouth. "Isn't it?"

"I don't know anymore, Aish. We need all the help we can get. And copycat or real thing, we're sitting on another body."

He picked up one of the photos, studying it before throwing it back on the table in disgust. "Another woman. Another life."

Aisha struggled to find a reply that didn't sound as empty as she felt when Daria rushed into the room. "Trey! Come quick."

Daria waved them over to one of the TVs mounted in the corner of the conference room. She flipped it on and in moments had them on a local news station. An image of the sheriff's building came into view, a yelling, posturing Barton Evigan visible in front of it.

"How long will the good citizens of Bradford County put up with this? Another woman has been brutally murdered!"

TREY MARCHED THROUGH the station and toward the front door. He'd purposely kept the death of the young woman on lockdown, anxious to determine her name and notify next of kin before alerting the news media. Clearly, it had been too much to hope the news would hold for a few hours as they did their work.

How the hell did Evigan find out so fast?

Although he'd struggled with Evigan from the start, Trey had believed his opponent to have some shred of decency. Using the latest death to his own political advantage proved once again just how low the man would sink.

The ranting that had been muted in two dimensions

on the TV came into full, 3-D effect as Trey left the building. A wall of cameras swung his way, drawing momentary attention off Evigan as the various reporters assembled caught sight of the county sheriff. Although he'd been willing to take the high ground, the attack on Aisha the night before at dinner had reset his perspective. "What's the meaning of this?"

A flurry of reporters screamed questions, ignoring Trey's.

"Sheriff! Can you confirm there's another body?"

"Has the Avalanche Killer struck again?"

"What are you doing to keep Bradford County safe?"

Trey lifted his hands to both calm the questions as well as indicate he was prepared to speak, determined to keep the spotlight off Evigan. The man's eyes had already narrowed into slits at the interruption and Trey knew he didn't have long.

"My office is working with all available law enforcement personnel and agencies to find the perpetrator."

Another round of questions echoed back toward him in a wail of sound, variations on a theme and all tied to the premise that the Avalanche Killer had struck again.

"One at a time." Trey pointed toward a reporter from Denver who'd been somewhat sympathetic to him so far.

"Sheriff, where was she found?"

Trey wasn't sure if the victim's sex was a guess, and again he wondered at the knowledge the media already had. "A female victim was found in the copse of woods outside Roaring Springs. My office was contacted early this morning and we've been doing our very best for her ever since."

The reporter attempted a follow-up, but Trey pointed toward another waving notebook.

"Sheriff. Is this the work of the Avalanche Killer?"

Trey knew the question was coming and sought to position the crime in a way that didn't immediately incite panic. "While we recognize the legacy of those crimes has been front and center, the body was only recently discovered. It's premature to assume the perpetrator is the Avalanche Killer."

"Assume! What else are we supposed to do!" Evigan shouted into the crowd.

Trey maintained a level, even demeanor, channeling every bit of composure and confidence he'd gained since taking on the role of sheriff nearly four years ago. "What you need to do is allow the police to do their work."

"Work! Bah!" Evigan puffed up his chest. "Like you've done any work so far. Six women, pulled dead off the side of a mountain. A visitor to town back in January, dead with no leads. Another woman, dead in our town. You're useless, Sheriff."

Trey refused to back down. It didn't matter that every word Evigan screamed matched all the emotion and frustration Trey carried in his heart. He would not let this man win.

"I recognize there is little comfort while this is happening, but these women deserve a thorough investigation. We have not yet found evidence against any one individual. And I'm not interested in making a false arrest against a potentially innocent person simply to satisfy a ten-second sound bite."

"Sound bite? Are you suggesting this is a ploy for the media?"

"No, Mr. Evigan. I'm suggesting *you* are using this opportunity to garner ammunition for your campaign."

Trey turned to the assembled reporters. "My focus right now is on finding the perpetrator who killed an innocent woman. We will share information as we have it and as we are able. I will plan on convening a press conference this afternoon at four o'clock to provide an update on where we are."

Without waiting for more questions, Trey headed back into the sheriff's station. Evigan continued to rant and rail behind him, but the reporters were decidedly less interested, a few of them already scattering at the idea Evigan was using them for political gain. Trey had no doubt it was a temporary victory, but he'd take what he could get.

And now he had to figure out how to address this situation by late afternoon.

AFTER A MORNING spent holed up in the conference room, Aisha was pleased to get out and stretch her legs a bit. Ever since the press conference, Trey had been distracted. She'd seen little of him as he was either embroiled in back-to-back meetings with various deputies or hunkered down over his computer in his office poring over the case.

Every available resource had been called in. And each deputy was stretched like a very thin wire. Which had made her lunchtime walk a double benefit. She'd get out and pick up lunch so everyone would get food.

A win-win.

Unlike the poor woman who even now lay in the morgue.

Aisha had turned it over and over in her mind throughout the morning. Why the break in pattern? It was the question she kept coming back to and simply could not let go of.

April Thomas, the sixth victim discovered on the mountain, had been the same. Although Aisha hadn't fully identified it at the time, now when she compared that death with the other five she saw what she'd missed at first. Thomas's death felt more like opportunity rather than the woman being specifically targeted because she fit a profile.

Was the copycat angle the right one to pursue?

And if it was, did that mean the killer and his crimes were being ignored?

Goodness, it was overwhelming. She knew Trey was under enormous stress—had known it for months and had sympathized with his situation—but now seeing it up close she realized just how maddening it all was. It was as if each thread you attempted to tug came up with both a knot and a dead end.

The sign for Bruno's Pizzeria came up ahead of her, and Aisha's attention was so focused on lunch she missed the man loitering in front of a nearby shop.

"If it isn't the little woman." The man she recognized as Barton Evigan's brother spoke up.

Her pulse sped up, but Aisha kept her voice even, her tone as full of disdain as she could project. "I don't believe we've met."

"You know we did. Last night. At your fancy dinner. But I'll remind you again for good measure. I'm Trace Evigan."

"What do you want?"

"A little respect." The man's eyes were dark and dangerous, a combination she'd seen before. He thought himself above her, whether because she was a woman, or worse because she was a black woman.

"I give respect where it's earned."

"Like your precious sheriff?"

"Trey Colton is a good man. Unlike your brother, who is an opportunist and a snake."

The man took a few steps forward before he clearly thought better of himself. "You'll be talking a different tune before you know it."

Talking a tune? She ignored his odd response in the more urgent need to get away from him. "Don't count on it."

"You're the one who needs to stop counting things. You and your boyfriend have been counting roosters that haven't even hatched yet."

Aisha knew a fruitless argument when she saw one, but the urge to go another round with the ass was great. But why? Every exchange between Trey and Barton Evigan had been fraught with drama and a not-so-subtle sense of danger. Like an undercurrent, the threat from both men was hard to pin down, but there all the same.

She was prevented from making a choice she'd regret when Trace backed up, his attention still pinned on her. "My brother's going to make a hell of a better sheriff for the good people of this county. You can count on that." He cocked his finger in the shape of a gun and mimed pulling the trigger. "It's only a matter of time."

"And an election," Aisha muttered to herself after she was satisfied he'd gotten into his car.

The rich scents of Bruno's Pizzeria welcomed her as she ducked into the shop. A stack of pizzas already rose up at the edge of the counter, and Aisha did a quick scan and figured the six boxes were her order. She walked over to pay, more relieved than she'd have expected by Rosa Bravo's broad smile.

"Hello, my girl. How are you doing?"

"I'm good, Rosa." Aisha thought about the swirling morass of feelings that currently occupied her life and pressed on with the lie. "How about you?"

Rosa shook her head and clucked. "I heard about what's going on down at the station," she whispered and bowed her head. "Another poor dead girl."

Aisha sighed. Between the media coverage and the speed with which news flew around a town the size of Roaring Springs, it wasn't a surprise Rosa knew. But still...

How was Trey supposed to keep a lock on this? The dead woman might be big news but law enforcement needed time to do their jobs.

Although Rosa's concern was genuine, Aisha was hesitant to say much. Her loyalty was to Trey and she didn't want to come off as if another death in town was gossip fodder. "It's very sad."

"And in the midst of so much happiness." Rosa reached over and laid a hand over Aisha's where it lay on the counter. "An engagement. It's all your mother could talk about the other day."

While the death of an innocent might not be fit gossip, conversation about an upcoming wedding was straight up the line of small-town conversation. Although she knew she and Trey had technically "gone public" with their dinner the prior evening, her mother knew better. She'd have to have a conversation with LaShanna about her eagerness to spread the word.

Even if she'd had every intention of avoiding her mother for a few days until she'd internally settled a bit over having sex with Trey. Her mother knew her better than anyone and Aisha had serious doubts she could keep her joy under tight enough wraps. It already felt like excitement oozed out of her pores. Wasn't a mother trained to know when stuff like that happened?

And hell and damn, what had she gotten herself into?

"Trey Colton is such a good man." Rosa's broad smile punched through the confusion over how to handle LaShanna Allen. "I've been pulling for you two."

"Thank you."

Shades of Earl's comments the night before seemed to echo through the pizzeria. *About damn time, too. I've seen you two running around since you were little ones. Peas in a pod, you both were.*

Were Rosa and Earl in this together? And what was it with everyone telling her and Trey that they'd always expected them to get together?

Vowing to puzzle through it later, Aisha opened her wallet to pay for the pizzas before Rosa waved her off. "My treat today. You tell everyone down at the station house I'm grateful for them."

"Rosa. You don't have to—"

The older woman waved a hand. "It's my pleasure. And you give them my thanks."

"I certainly will."

Aisha snagged the pizzas and headed back out to the street. The walk to the station house was a short distance away and the time passed quickly as she considered all that had happened since she'd walked out twenty minutes ago.

All of Roaring Springs knew there was another dead body.

Those in the know in Roaring Springs knew she was engaged.

And her mother had clearly taken great joy in spreading the word far and wide about her daughter's fake engagement.

When had her life gone so sideways? And why did it increasingly feel as if things would never go back to the way they used to be?

HE WATCHED AISHA Allen hotfoot it through downtown Roaring Springs, lunch clearly in hand. Did he call her the little woman? Or a pain-in-the-ass busybody?

Or even more likely, a complication?

He'd heard the rumors, of course. Roaring Springs was small and he was well connected. She was engaged to the sheriff. It seemed sudden but the two of them were thick as thieves. Always had been. It wasn't too big a leap to see them suddenly figure out there was something sparking there all along.

Besides, she was hot. Truth be told, Trey Colton should have been tapping that a lot sooner if the man had half a brain in his head.

The real question was how did he use the information to his advantage? Aisha Allen was smart and she was well respected. He'd always had a healthy disdain for shrinks, but also knew to keep his distance. There was nothing they loved more than digging into someone else's backstory and deep, dark history, dredging up whatever they could.

He'd buried his past a long time ago and had no interest in seeing that change.

Not one bit.

Perhaps it was time to create a little distraction.

He wanted his vengeance but he wanted it on his own timetable. A sheriff up for reelection would be damned focused on hunting down clues to catch a killer.

Since he didn't know yet who'd killed the woman, he needed time to figure it out. The only way he could do that was if he changed the game.

Aisha's form had grown smaller as she'd walked toward the sheriff's station, disappearing altogether when she turned into the parking lot. It didn't matter. She'd make a nice diversion for Trey Colton but deep down he sensed he needed a bigger play.

Something even more distracting than putting the sheriff's woman in the hospital.

Something a little more personal.

Chapter Fifteen

Trey heard the commotion just before he smelled the distinct aroma of meat, cheese and doughy goodness. The damn-near stampede down the hall from the bull-pen to the front entrance paraded past his office with all the finesse of a herd of rhinos and, as his stomach let out a trumpeting roar of its own, Trey got up and quickly followed behind.

Aisha was back.

Since his heart did a weird little flip at that thought, he slowed his walk and tried for a few extra beats to gather his thoughts. Despite the craziness of the early-morning phone call and all that had come since—including a call from their esteemed governor—the night they'd spent together hadn't been far from his mind. He knew he should be focusing all his effort and attention on catching a killer—copycat or otherwise—but his brain was determined to dissect every single second of making love with his best friend.

Who knew it could be so incredible? Or maybe a better question was how had the two of them taken so long to get to that place.

Together.

Mental images had assailed him all morning,

matched by the sizzling-hot memories of how her skin felt beneath his palms. The weight of her breasts as he'd held each in his hands. The light moans that tore from her throat as her orgasm took her under.

All of it was as vivid as if she were still in his arms and seared in his mind with a mental branding iron.

The hallway from his office to the front entrance of the station wasn't that long, and in a matter of steps he'd closed the distance. Aisha stood in the middle of his team, her curly hair spilling out of her ponytail holder and her fit frame shown off to perfection in a sleeveless tank and shorts.

She was perfect. Not only strong and beautiful and lovely on the outside but just as amazing—even more, really—on the inside. She'd keyed in so quickly on the crime scene photos, her unerring cleverness hitting on the fact that the latest victim didn't put up much of a struggle. She'd been equally quick to entertain the copycat notion, already settling in to work up some scenarios of what that might look like. The woman wasn't a profiler, but she was good at her job and she understood human nature.

And she understood him.

What he needed. What made him tick. Even the quick run to get pizzas was as much of a gift to his team as it was to him. She understood how hard they all worked and was determined to make them feel encouraged. Supported.

Believed in.

Oh, God, how was he going to give her up?

He'd flirted with that thought off and on since they'd started the whole fake engagement thing, but something about making love to her had made the reality of that sharper, somehow.

And much starker.

"I saved you a few slices of pepperoni from the ravening beasts," Aisha said as he moved closer, setting her own slice down on the counter.

"Thanks." One of his deputies made kissing noises and Trey shot him a side eye. "Nice, Brooks."

Nathan Brooks was a jokester and the subtle encouragement was all he needed. "Some fiancé you are. You two should be out interviewing DJs and tasting wedding cake and instead you're stuck here. It's a wonder she sticks around, Sheriff."

"Lucky for us she did."

Nathan wiggled his eyebrows at Aisha while clutching a hand to his heart. Trey didn't miss the small dab of pizza sauce that stuck itself just over the B on Brooks's Bradford County T-shirt and suspected Aisha didn't, either. "Drop this one, Aisha, and say you'll be mine forever. I avoid working most weekends and I'm loyal."

"You may be loyal but you're barely house-trained, Brooks," Aisha shot back. "But you are cute. I've got a cousin I can fix you up with."

All joking left Nathan's face. "You serious?"

"Sure." Aisha nodded before reaching over and wiping off the sauce with a napkin. "I'll give you her number."

Trey knew the exchange for the joke that it was, but something still stuck hard in his throat at the idea of Nathan Brooks asking Aisha out on a date. The quick shift in focus to her cousin didn't do much to assuage the tension that knotted his shoulders. "Remember you owe her one."

Nathan's eyes already danced in anticipation. "I sure do."

With their immediate hunger satisfied, people headed back to their desks with paper plates full of second and third slices. "Thanks for running out. I'll get that expensed for you."

"No need."

"Sure there is. You don't need to feed us."

"In this case, that was a delivery only. The pizzas were on Rosa."

"Really?"

"Yep. And for the record, she's pulling for you."

Without checking the impulse, Trey bent down and pressed a kiss to her mouth. He took his time and lingered, the warm garlicky taste of pizza and sauce still on her lips a delicious counterpoint to the soft warmth of her mouth and the memories of what they'd shared only a few hours earlier. "I'm pulling for us, too."

"That's not what I meant."

"It is what I meant." Trey leaned in for another kiss, but unlike the first he felt the slightest reluctance emanating from her.

"Aish? You okay?"

"Sure." She smiled but he saw the truth beneath the warm veneer. She wasn't okay. The question was why? Was it the discovery of a dead body? Or the realization that there was a deep, abiding attraction between the two of them?

"I'm just tired is all. It's been a busy day and I'm not sure this is the right place to be—" she hesitated before adding quietly "—carrying on."

"We're alone." Trey glanced around the office. Although there wasn't anyone in the immediate vicinity, his team was all over the building. There wasn't any reason to think someone wouldn't walk back, either for more pizza or simply in the normal course of their work. "Besides, we're engaged."

"Is that what we're calling it?" She lowered her voice. "I thought it was a ruse designed to cover any manner of sins."

While they'd made a pact at the start to minimize displays of affection, hadn't things changed last night? "Is that how you see what's going on?"

"It certainly isn't the truth."

Trey wasn't sure when or how things had gone sideways, but he wasn't about to be cavalier about it.

Not one bit.

"Last night was the truth," he finally said.

"Was it?"

SHE HADN'T INTENDED to pick a fight. Not at all.

But now that the first few licks of fire were out there, Aisha realized it had been building for quite some time. Since the fake engagement. Since the endless feelings she had for Trey that she'd struggled to make sense of.

This was neither the time nor place for it to all come tumbling out, but she couldn't stand there and pretend to be all nicey-nicey. Or kissy-kissy, as the young officer had indicated.

Nor could she pretend she wasn't affected by Trey. By all of it.

She'd believed herself able to handle what they were doing, but increasingly, it looked like she had deluded herself. Her heart wasn't nearly as well armed as she'd thought and it was only now beginning to become obvious what a risk she'd taken by agreeing to this ridiculous ruse.

He'd kissed her. Over pizza and in plain view of his deputies. Like she belonged there.

Like they belonged together.

She wanted to believe it, but she'd thought something similar once before and she'd been wrong. She'd had a relationship once built on a mirage and now here she was, doing it all over again.

Weren't people supposed to get smarter? Wasn't a person meant to learn from their mistakes and make different choices? Wasn't that what she strived to tell her patients, helping them past the blocks in their life to move on to something better?

Only the joke was on her.

They said doctors made the worst patients, and here she was proving the adage right.

"You think last night was a lie?" Trey finally asked, all hint of his teasing sexy smile vanished.

"That's a loaded word."

"You put it out there, Aish. You questioned if last night was the truth." Trey quieted for a moment before he spoke, something tight and pinched in his tone. "It was to me."

Did he really believe that?

"This isn't the place for this conversation."

"No, it's not. But it doesn't mean we're not having it. Let's go to my office."

The heavy scent of pizza still lingered on the air. It was a smell she always associated with happy things—Friday nights and eating with your hands and friends—and now she'd have another memory to add to the list.

Breakup with best friend.

Even with the truth that loomed large before them,

she followed Trey to his office. She was an equal participant in this charade and it was hardly fair to run out. And wasn't she always fair? Always willing to listen to both sides. Willing and able to hear where the other person was coming from.

Hadn't she done that for Kenneth?

Of course I love you, Aisha. I think you may be the love of my life. I just had the bad luck of meeting Grace first.

That memory had always loomed the largest for her.

Wasn't that just so sad for him? Yes, it was sad for her. The reality of their circumstances meant she couldn't be with him, but it also meant Kenneth couldn't be with her.

The love of his life.

Which was a big steaming pile of BS but it hadn't seemed like it at the time.

At the time she'd been heartbroken, desperately searching for answers to why it all hurt so bad. Deliberate in her need to believe that he'd be with her *if only*.

Trey stopped at his office door, gesturing her in and then closing the door behind them. The office was government grade, which meant it was functional and way too gray, but Trey had still made it his own. A few pillows she knew his mother had sewn herself rested on a couch that had likely come off the line when Clinton was president. And one of his sister's paintings hung on a side wall, a lone wolf staring out of the image with startling eyes.

It was all vintage Trey.

That mix of family and function defined him, just as much as the wolf did.

Bree had chosen well when she'd painted the picture. She understood her brother as much as anyone and innately recognized that the representation of a hunter who could stand alone yet be fiercely protective of those he called his own was the perfect match for her brother.

"Why'd you pull away out there?"

"I didn't pull away."

Trey dropped his head before those penetrating golden-brown eyes lifted to hers. "Whatever else is going on between us, I deserve the truth."

He did and Aisha was embarrassed at how quickly the words had tripped out instead of the real work that needed to be done. The confession she had to tackle head-on. The words that stuck in her throat like hardening concrete.

"I loved someone. When I lived in New York."

"I know."

That quick acknowledgment brought surprise and a bit of heat as she wondered why he'd never said anything. Unwilling to examine *that* reaction too closely, she pressed on. "I thought he loved me, as well. That I was going to marry him."

A hard and, sadly, still-bitter laugh rumbled from her throat. "Which is incredibly hard to do when the person you expect to make a lifetime vow to is married to someone else."

Something flickered in his eyes—anger? Remorse?—before he tamped it down. "I can see how that would be true."

"He played me well, I'll give him that. We even looked at engagement rings one Sunday out strolling the city hand in hand."

Trey winced, but his voice never wavered above that level calm he seemed to channel. "A bastard of the first degree."

"In the end, yeah, I guess he was."

"I'm sorry you went through that."

While it hurt, she wasn't sure she could say the same. Whatever else Kenneth's role in her life, he was the single biggest reminder that she had to be humble and fair when she dealt with her patients. The dynamics between human beings was rarely rational and it had taken her a long time to come to the realization that Kenneth had likely believed every word he'd said to her.

His tortured longing to be together. The "bad timing" of their romance. Even the whole "love of his life" thing had come out with a level of anxious sincerity that he likely believed.

Yet none of it made a life. Nor was it able to drive a relationship forward, built on trust and commitment and forever.

Not to her and certainly not to his wife.

"Have you ever wondered why you didn't tell me about him?" Trey's quiet voice carried all the power of a hurricane. "Why you felt you couldn't share something that made you happy?"

"It didn't feel right."

"But you loved him. You were happy."

She had been happy. For nearly a year she'd been blissful, floating on the sea of passion and adrenaline and the certainty that she'd found "The One."

And still, she'd not told her best friend.

"I was."

"For a long time I kept telling myself you'd come around. You'd tell me about him and your life together. You'd share this great relationship. But you never did."

Whatever emotions she'd carried over Kenneth, both while they were dating and since, faded in the face of his hurt. Not only hadn't she told Trey about Kenneth, but she'd also spent the time avoiding her friend, coming up with any number of excuses to duck having to tell him.

Only she couldn't avoid the issue any longer. "How'd you find out?"

"Your mom mentioned it to mine at the market. It was a casual comment, how she hoped you'd bring him home for a family function. My mom brought it up in passing, assuming I already knew."

Aisha remembered that time. Her mother had planned a picnic to celebrate Tanisha's graduation from high school and had been so excited to meet Kenneth. Aisha had been equally excited for the moment she'd introduce him to her family.

She'd booked her plane tickets, offering to put her and Kenneth on the same reservation, only he'd said he would handle his own. His secretary was also booking his work travel that week, he'd told her as they lay in her bed on a lazy Saturday afternoon, and he'd have to fly in from business up in Seattle. Oh, how perfect it all was. Her successful business-traveling boyfriend, flying in to meet her family after a week of meetings.

Until she'd driven to the Denver International Airport, receiving a text as she was pulling into a parking spot that he wasn't coming. That he'd been stuck in meetings and had to work on a project for a demanding client that would occupy him all weekend.

Just perfect.

Only in her haze and desperate desire to believe in him, she'd soldiered through, rationalizing his behavior as a matter of course when you dated an older, successful man. She could hardly be mad when he was stuck on the other side of the country, working all weekend.

Later, she'd accepted there'd likely been no trip to Seattle. Or any of the numerous other places he told her he was often heading out to. They'd been excuses to cover up when he was really spending the time with his family.

"I'm sorry you found out that way."

"Are you?" Trey asked, his hands going to his hips. "Even after all this time, when you've still never said anything. Are you sorry or are you really just relieved you didn't have to tell me?"

"I don't owe you an explanation for something that happened in my personal life."

That calm, cool visage broke wide-open. Anger pressed deep grooves into his face, his mouth a solid slash that set his jaw. "Like hell you don't."

"I don't, Trey. We're friends."

"We're more than friends. We always have been and this weekend's proved that."

"Don't mix up the two."

"It's all mixed up, Aish. All of it. How I feel about you now. How I felt about you then."

"What's that supposed to mean?"

"It means I cared about you! And you didn't think to tell me about the most important thing in your life. You hid it from me and you went away, too. Other than text messages I don't think I talked to you more than three times that entire year."

"It was never the right time to tell you." As excuses went it was a lame one, especially when she really owed him an apology. But it was all she could handle at the moment. "And then it was over and there wasn't anything to tell you other than what a clueless idiot I'd been."

"You can tell me anything."

"I know you think that, but I couldn't tell you. Every time I thought to I found another reason to put it off."

"Why?"

The heavy rap on his door was followed by the briefest pause when Daria pushed her head through. "I'm sorry to bother you."

"What is it?" Trey rarely lost his temper or his patience, but the strained response indicated he was close to losing both.

"Agent Roberts is here. He's got backup."

"Backup?"

"It looks like his supervisor has joined in on today's fun."

"I'll be right there."

Daria ducked out as fast as she'd come in but it was enough to give Aisha her window of escape. "I'll leave you to it."

"We're not done talking about this."

"Probably not."

Trey moved in closer and reached for her hand. She felt the warmth of his fingers closing around hers. The way his thumb rubbed lightly over the back of her hand. "I'm here for you. Always."

"Just like I am for you."

"We can't lose that." His gaze bore into hers, and she saw all the years that spanned between them, starting way back to that day on the playground. "Ever."

"I know."

He squeezed once before striding from his office. She watched the door a few moments before her gaze drifted to the image of the wolf on the wall. Although Bree had painted the animal alone, Aisha knew how wolves worked. In the wild, there'd be a pack nearby.

She was part of Trey's emotional pack, just as he was to her. And still, it was hard to talk to him about Kenneth. Hard to talk to him of her naïveté and her embarrassment. Harder still to explain why she'd never told him about Kenneth from the start.

Things to think about and question, but she'd save all of it for the privacy of her own home. A Sunday afternoon curled up with Fitz on the couch over a weepy movie might be just what she needed.

It was only as the credits rolled on a good weeper with Julia Roberts a few hours later that she allowed her conversation with Trey to replay in her mind.

He'd said she could tell him anything.

But could she?

Kenneth had ruined enough of her life and shattered her self-confidence to the point she still had moments when she was reminded of just how badly she'd been hurt.

Like today.

If she told Trey, she'd make it real. Tangible. And possibly create a barrier neither of them could ever fully get past.

She stroked Fitz's soft fur and stared at the rolling credits on her TV screen.

And acknowledged to herself that she'd never felt more alone.

TREY HAD DEALT with the Feds over the years. You didn't get to spend long in the role of sheriff without bumping up against federal agencies from time to time. He'd also had a few run-ins when he'd worked in local law enforcement before becoming sheriff. Each time, he'd accepted there were a pecking order and a hierarchy. It was less acquiescence and more the understanding of chain of command and, to some degree, just how the world worked.

But he had zero interest in placating Agent Stefan Roberts and the man who, it had quickly become apparent, was the agent's "big boss."

"These incidents are concerning, Sheriff." Deputy Director Jared Wright rubbed at his goatee. "Very concerning."

"I agree."

"Yet they continue to happen." Wright's gaze narrowed. "Have you connected with local law enforcement?"

He and his team had connected with everyone, from local law enforcement to the various private security firms that provided protection for businesses in Roaring Springs and beyond. Although all of Bradford County was affected, Roaring Springs had been the epicenter of the problems and had retained the majority of Trey and his team's focus.

"My team and I are in regular communication with the Roaring Springs PD."

He was going to give a list of all the organizations they'd been in contact with but decided at the last minute to hold back. Whatever interrogation Wright felt he was entitled to, Trey was determined not to make it easy.

"So lots of eyes on the town."

"I'd say so, yes," Trey said.

"And still a killer continues to find a way." Wright stroked that goatee again. "Even coming as close as this sheriff's station to drop off a package of a victim's remains."

That reality had stuck in Trey's chest since the mysterious phone call earlier in the week, and while it frustrated him to have it tossed in his face, he knew his own anger on the matter was a fuse just waiting for a spark.

"The killer knew the exact distance to keep away

from the station's security cameras. The package was just out of range."

"And no one else on the street caught a glimpse of a man with a package?"

"We've checked all the footage up and down the town. Nothing is a match."

Nothing was.

Each and every video feed they'd reviewed had turned up a shocking lack of detail. No one with a package. No one moving in a furtive manner. He'd looked at the feeds himself and nothing had indicated a killer on the loose. Hell, nothing had even indicated a person of interest for him and his deputies to bring in and question.

"Then you find a match, Sheriff."

Trey's gaze drifted from Wright to Agent Roberts, who'd sat quietly at the table while his boss delivered his thoughts. "I thought good old-fashioned police work meant you hunted for the truth. Not a convenient way to wrap up a case."

"I'm not talking convenience."

Trey was done playing nice. "Then what are you saying?"

"A killer has walked these streets without punishment for nearly three months. Who knows how much longer before that? Yet *your* department's been unsuccessful in even coming up with a few viable leads to tug."

It was the matter of a simple inflection when Trey heard the real problem. The slight note of frustration that proved the killer had not only stymied all of them, but that the Feds were as frustrated as he was.

"It sounds like my problem is yours, as well. Isn't that what you're really trying to say, Director?"

"This is your county, Sheriff."

"And you've made it clear this is your investigation. Maybe if we did a bit more work together instead of in separate streams we'd get farther."

Wright glanced toward Agent Roberts. "We've kept you informed."

Trey had no interest in throwing the agent under the bus. His assessment from the first was that Agent Stefan Roberts was a good guy. That didn't mean he needed to give him any leeway for carrying out the Machiavellian practices of his leadership.

"Agent Roberts has done what he can, but I've no doubt your resources are far vaster than my own. What sort of detail have you gotten out of national databases? Any like crimes? Any missing persons who match the feminine description of what the killer seems fixated on."

"We've found a few hits but nothing that's panned out." Agent Roberts stepped in, taking effective control of the conversation. "What I'm more concerned about is the seeming change in direction. The sixth victim off the mountain, Sabrina Gilford, didn't match pattern. The woman lying in your morgue doesn't, either."

"I've read the reports," Wright snapped. "But why a copycat?"

"That's what we don't know, sir," Roberts continued. "But Sheriff Colton has had several family members who have also been targeted this year in various ways. Something seems to be seething under the surface."

It was the most accurate description Trey had heard yet and verified what had bothered him. Each attack on his family, each strange occurrence from the murder setup in January on Wyatt's ranch to the way Bree had been targeted the prior spring to the lurking danger they'd faced at the film festival in July. All of it had seemed under some sort of external control that didn't match the way each case wrapped up, neat and clean.

He'd been satisfied the cases were closed yet couldn't help but feel something lingered just out of his reach, like a flash in his peripheral vision. But each and every time he tried to look at it, he couldn't quite see it.

Even as he knew it was there.

Was he looking in the wrong place? Or had he been lulled into a false sense of security when each case had wrapped, thinking the danger was over only to be masterminded from afar?

"Do you agree with that assessment, Sheriff?"

"Yes. I've tried not to go this direction, but there is something decidedly personal about what's going on. But I don't say that to take our focus or attention off a killer. There is a psychopath on the loose and none of us can forget that."

"No." Despite the bluster he'd rode in on, Wright had calmed during the discussion, his respect for Roberts clear. His equal respect for the frustration facing all of them coming clearer, as well. "We are here to help, Sheriff. You have my word on that."

"Thank you."

The men lingered a bit longer and Daria even managed to push a few slices of pizza on them before they left. It was only after they'd gone that the weight of the day made itself known. His shoulders knotted in tension, and he debated his next step.

Go down to the gym and work some of it off or head straight over to Aisha's? The fact that the latter held nearly his entire focus was more than enough reason to head to the gym but he was sick of doing what he was supposed to.

Of following some internal protocol that didn't rile up a bigoted opponent campaigning for his job and didn't intrude on the Feds and most certainly didn't ask his best friend why she was happily dating someone and not telling him.

All of it weighted heavily on him. His deep-seated desire to do what was right instead of acting in the heat of the moment. He was in law enforcement and he knew what happened when people acted in haste. Only…

Weren't there times to act in the heat of the moment?

He marched back to his office and snagged his workbag off the chair. He'd come back if he had to, but he needed to get to Aisha. Needed to finish out their discussion from earlier, even if it meant they were going to butt heads a bit more.

Maybe they'd even make up.

The hope of that carried him from the building and back into town. He would have taken his car but it was quick enough to walk to her place. And it would give him a few extra minutes of early evening fresh air as he worked out his approach.

As he considered all he wanted to say.

The sun settled low over the mountains that rimmed Roaring Springs, a bright light that had his eyes squinting even as his soul soaked up the rays and the glorious reds and golds in the sky. It gave him hope and the innate belief that he and Aisha would get through this. They'd find their way and they'd come out the other side, even better than where they'd started.

An explosive night together indicated there had to be a good outcome for them. And he had to believe a lifetime of friendship further ensured it.

It was that thought—no, *belief*—that put the extra spring in his step, speeding up his pace.

And it was likely the thing that saved him as a car came whipping out of nowhere, clipping him from behind and driving his body into the air with the force of a tornado.

Chapter Sixteen

Aisha took the call from Daria. Her hands trembled as she heard the words. The room swam before her eyes. And the world disintegrated into a clanging whirl as she registered the roaring sirens that screamed outside her window, clearly in answer to the call made by the sheriff's office.

Someone had run Trey over.

Or tried to.

Or did.

It was all jumbled as she fought for breath and struggled to take in Daria's instructions.

"Do you need me to call his parents?"

"I'm calling them next." Daria's voice was strained but steady, projecting a calm Aisha was nowhere near feeling. "Do you need me to send someone for you?"

"No. I'm okay."

She wasn't, but she didn't need to pull a single member of Trey's team away from where they needed to put their full focus. Going after the bastard who dared to hurt him.

"I'll be there in ten."

Aisha disconnected and sat down hard on the couch, the phone falling from her hand.

Trey had been run down. The details were fuzzy as

to the why or how, but that fact was 100 percent clear. He'd left the station and had apparently been walking, his car still parked in the station lot. His prone body found out on the main drag through Roaring Springs.

Which meant he'd been coming for her. He left his car only when he walked to her place. His own apartment was too far away and his parents' ranch on the edge of town meant their home wasn't his destination, either.

Why had she left?

Or why couldn't he take their fight at face value and leave her alone to cool off for the night?

Instead, his choice to walk had put him in prime view of a killer.

She considered calling Audrey and Calvin to see if she should drive out and pick them up, but the need to get to Trey overrode the thought. Daria would make the same offer to them—she could send out a cruiser to pick them up—but if Aisha knew Trey's parents, they'd arrive at the hospital within minutes of her.

And then they'd wait.

She'd tried to suss out how badly he was hurt, but Daria had little information beyond the fact that Trey was unconscious when the ambulance took off for the emergency room at Roaring Springs Memorial.

Ever since the Avalanche Killer's crimes had been uncovered on the side of the mountain, Aisha had battled a subtle sense of dread. The idea crimes of such magnitude had taken place, roiling beneath the surface of their small town, had shaken her. She'd done everything she could to keep the fear at bay. From working out to focusing on her job to helping Trey, each action had been designed to give herself some measure of control over the fear.

Yet where had any of it gotten her? Gotten any of them?

Trey lay in an ambulance, likely fighting for his life.

THE DREAM WAS fuzzy, too hazy to grasp any images as it hovered just out of reach. Aisha standing in his office, clad in a summer tank the color of a tangerine and khaki shorts that showed off her long, sexy legs. Her face was angry and her mouth set in hard lines, but he couldn't figure out why.

Was she mad? Sad?

It nagged at him, even as something else tugged at him. He kept looking out the window of his office, trying to see what lay beyond. Was he looking for something? And why did he have to call the governor?

Someone took his hand. Was it Aisha? Or was that his mom's voice? All of it mixed up in his mind in a hazy whirl. It was only when that voice spoke again that a weird humming started in his mind.

"Wake up, baby. We're here." Definitely his mom.

"Trey? Please come back to us." Okay. That was Aisha.

Come back?

Where was he?

Before he could ask, a low, steady beep sank in, a counterpoint to their gentle voices. That beep was subtle but insistent, keeping him from truly sinking back into the hazy fog that wanted to wrap his mind in a warm blanket.

He'd nearly given in to the fog and ignored the beeping anyway when he caught the sound of tears. It was light—just a sniffle and a small gasp for air—but he knew that sound. He hadn't been raised with a sister not to know what tears were.

Was his mom crying? Or Aisha?

His eyelids were stuck closed, and that added a subtle sense of panic. Why was someone crying and he couldn't see them? Focusing on the task, he ignored the beeping that seemed to grow louder and pushed harder, desperate to surface.

To wake *up*.

And then his eyes popped open and Trey realized three things. His mom was crying. So were Aisha and Bree. And there was a weird beeping.

Because he was in a hospital.

"Hi." That lone word croaked from his throat. Everyone began talking at once so his mind just kept on whirling, trying to take it all in.

He fought the subtle disorientation as his mind shifted directions, anxious to understand what had put him in the hospital. He mentally cycled through the past few days—it had been only a few days?—cataloging memories as he went.

A picnic at his parents' house on a pretty summer evening. A dinner with his extended family over at The Chateau. Making love with Aisha.

Aisha.

"What happened?" he finally asked.

"Shh," his mother whispered. "You were hurt, baby."

"How?"

"Someone tried to run you down." His father spoke up, his voice husky. His eyes were shiny, just like Audrey's.

That welcoming haze that insistently tugged at his mind, willing him to drop back into darkness—back into the dreams—beckoned, but the intense looks on everyone's face kept him focused.

They were all there. His parents. Bree as well as Rylan, who was hovering behind her, his hand on her shoulder. And Aisha. She had taken up a spot at the foot of the bed, her hand resting on his foot as she kept watch. She'd tell him what was going on.

"What happened to me? Aisha?"

"Someone came after you in their car. When you walked out of the parking lot at work."

He remembered walking. He was going to see Aisha, their fight still lingering in his mind like an open wound. He needed to make up with her. Needed to make it right, even if he wasn't sure at that moment what had been wrong.

All he did know—and could remember clearly even now—was that he had to fix it somehow.

"You were ambushed, son." His father spoke up. "Best your deputies can tell, someone lay in wait for you to come out of the office. You were hit from behind and left in the middle of the street as the bastard drove off."

His father's careful words, simple and direct, were enough to ground him. He'd been hit from behind, and *ambush* was the right word.

"When?" Trey asked.

"Around six o'clock." His father continued to provide answers. "It's about ten thirty now."

Trey didn't remember much of the hit, the car coming out of nowhere, just as Calvin had described, but vague memories of what had come since drifted through his mind. The heavy whirl of sirens that screamed, seemingly outside him even as they clanged in his head. That must have been the ambulance ride, he realized now.

He'd been so cold, only made worse by the fact that they'd ripped open his shirt to check his vitals.

He also remembered questions. Requests to move his body or wiggle his fingers. A doctor asking him to rotate his feet and then running something over his heel that had made Trey push against whatever it was tickling his skin.

And then he'd slept.

It was the constant drowsiness, that thick, heavy exhaustion that kept tugging at him, even now. So he pushed on, pressing against the promise of sleep to understand what had happened.

He struggled to sit up, grunting through the pain as the movements sent a new wave of agony coursing through him. The pain had been dull and vague when he'd first opened his eyes, but now that he'd moved it seemed to take over. Everything hurt, including the fiery pain that ran up and down his back.

A nurse bustled in and Trey vaguely recognized the guy. He and his deputies knew most of the staff at the hospital and Trey was still struggling for a name when he caught sight of Dan's name tag.

"How you feeling, Sheriff?"

"Like I was run over."

"That's good." Dan went to work, his gaze scanning a monitor as he tapped on the keyboard beneath. "It hurts but the pain means you can feel everything."

Dan's attention shifted from the monitor, his bright green eyes direct. "That means you have movement."

Trey didn't miss the underlying message and knew his family hadn't, either. Since Dan's arrival, they'd made varying mentions of leaving and it was only as his mother squeezed his hand, telling him they'd wait outside, that he keyed back in and focused on Aisha.

"Stay. Please."

She nodded but moved to the side of the room as Dan bustled around, taking various readings, tapping more notes into the keyboard and even adding something to an erasable board at the foot of the bed. It was only when Dan left with a wink and a promise to snag Trey some extra dessert that Aisha moved closer.

Before he could say a word, she'd leaned forward, her lips fervent against his.

"I'm sorry. I'm so very sorry."

Even though it hurt to move, the pain faded to manageable as he settled his hands on her shoulders, his thumb tracing lightly over the side of her neck. "I'm sorry, too."

"It was me. I was overwhelmed from last night. From us. And I shouldn't have said what I did."

"Yes, Aish. You should have. You can say anything to me. Always."

The tears he'd sensed earlier as he'd heard sniffles came back in full force, filling up her eyes and spilling over her cheeks. "I was so worried. And then I kept thinking those were the last words we were going to say to each other. I can't lose you." She laid her hands over his, her palms cold from the cool air of the hospital and something else… Fear?

He tried to reassure her, but as he struggled to find the words he realized he had none.

Someone had deliberately come after him. As a member of the law enforcement community, he recognized he put his life on the line for his job. He'd understood that from the start and knew it was a requirement for the job.

But this?

A deliberate act, perpetrated against him?

This was a warning. There was someone who lurked, roaming the streets of Roaring Springs, who wanted him dead.

They'd made that abundantly clear.

HE HEARD THE commotion coursing through town, like a steady heartbeat. That morning while picking up doughnuts for the team. Later that day after he got to work. Even at the gas station between the pumps as he and a few others filled their tanks.

Everyone was talking about Trey Colton.

The sheriff's near miss in the center of town as someone tried to run him over was all anyone in Roaring Springs could talk about. That topic was followed quickly by another. Those poor, poor Coltons and all they'd endured this year. The pain and suffering that *poor* family dealt with, evidenced by this latest mishap and the still-missing Skye Colton.

The poor Coltons, his ass.

As far as he was concerned, that family had made this bed themselves. But he didn't tell anyone else that.

Oh, no.

Instead, he'd listened to it all, seemingly rapt with attention as he selected a few glazed, a few chocolate filled and a cruller he knew a coworker loved. He'd nodded sagely as he topped off his tank, offering up the subtle note of affirmation that he hoped the traffic cameras downtown could see who was at fault. And he'd listened to all of the gossip, disguised as well-meaning words, as he ate his own Boston cream.

There would be no traffic cameras capturing anything worth noting. He'd seen to that as well as the blurring of the license plate with fresh mud on the car he'd "borrowed" from a few towns over to do the deed. He'd subsequently returned it where he'd found it, parked just outside town with a large dent in the front.

It was a damn shame Trey Colton had sped up there at the end.

He'd deliberately selected a hybrid, their quiet motors ensuring he'd get closer before his victim knew the direction of his intention. But even with that, Colton had seemed oblivious to the impending danger.

Like they all were.

Wasn't that the real joy in all of it?

Everyone talked about the *poor* Coltons, which he knew was a steaming load of crap. He knew better than anyone that they'd earned every bit of trouble they were now facing, after a lifetime of lording their name and their money over everyone.

But even as he'd stared down this path, determined to have his vengeance, he had to admit that he'd expected them to be more aware. Clearer, somehow, on the danger they all faced and the fact that their time was up.

So freaking up.

Ah, well. He took another bite of doughnut—the one he'd allow himself this week—and focused on the day in front of him.

It was time to shift attention back where it belonged. He had Trey Colton in the hospital, a sitting duck for whomever else meant him harm.

He had a sense of who'd committed the murder of

the woman in the woods. It had come to him late last night and he just needed to tug a few lines there to make sure. Shame the cops were too dumb to figure it out, but that wasn't his problem.

He dealt in information and careful calculation and vengeance.

He understood what the cops didn't: those were the qualities that made the world go round.

AISHA HAD RARELY, if ever, regretted her decision not to go to medical school. She'd chosen clinical work because she wanted to interact with patients day in and day out and hadn't wanted to delay that work by the demands and time required to earn her MD.

It was only now, as she watched the steady stream of medical professionals who came in and out of Trey's room, that she'd like to better understand what they were looking at.

He'd been told several times now how lucky he was that he'd rather miraculously avoided a concussion. But he hadn't avoided the equivalent of two tons of steel bearing down and clipping him from behind and putting his entire body in a world of hurt.

What had to be at least a hundred Coltons had come through his room or called or texted over the past twenty-four hours. The network was strong and family members from as far-flung places like South Dakota and Texas had called to check in and see how he was doing. He'd handled all of it with steady equanimity, even as she saw the strains around the edges.

Which meant now, Monday night, he was still cooped up in his hospital bed and loaded for bear.

Even Bree and Rylan's arrival hadn't done much to

calm Trey's ire. Although he did put on a good show. It wasn't fooling Aisha and it certainly wasn't fooling his sister, but they'd both used the time to verbally tap dance over Trey's frustration.

"I'd love for you both to come out to the animal sanctuary this weekend. Rylan's adding a few emus soon and we're fixing up an area for them." Bree's gaze darted to the machines that surrounded Trey's bed. She hesitated slightly before seeming to come to some decision. "We'd love the help in getting set up."

"We'll let you know," Trey grumbled.

Aisha knew all he didn't say—they all did—but she pressed on, cheerful and happy. "That sounds great. A few days outside and out of town would be good. An emu? Really?"

"They need good homes." Bree's gaze dimmed. "And their former owner should be strung up and shot."

Aisha sat quietly as the conversation spun out. She and Bree ultimately decided to walk down to the cafeteria to get coffee, leaving Trey to talk through the hit-and-run with Rylan. Although Bree's fiancé wasn't law enforcement, he'd spent several years in the army and his tactical knowledge was what Trey needed to puzzle through the latest.

"He's in a mood." Bree rolled her eyes the moment the elevator doors closed before them. "Not that I blame him."

"That he is. He hates being cooped up here and nearly exploded when they told him they wanted him to stay one more night for observation."

"Do you think he's okay?" Despite her sisterly frustration at Trey's surly attitude, Bree's fear was unmistakable in the closed space.

"He seems to be. I don't understand all the medical nuances but I know enough to get the gist of what's going on. He doesn't have a concussion and he hasn't broken anything. However, he did take a serious hit to the middle of his body and between that and being tossed to the ground they want to keep an eye on his circulation."

"Good. That's good they're being cautious."

Aisha thought it was but Trey clearly had other ideas. His grumbling had reached a fever pitch after the last attending had visited and he'd grown somewhat unbearable since. Even his parents had decided to take their leave, giving him some space and promising to come back the next morning.

In moments, Aisha had led them both to the cafeteria. She'd spent more time there over the past twenty-four hours than she'd ever expected to—or wanted to—but at least the coffee was decent. As she and Bree moved to the small service area to doctor their coffees, Aisha asked, "Did you mean it about us coming out to the animal sanctuary?"

"Oh, yeah. We'd love the help. And I'm so proud of what Rylan has built there."

Aisha hadn't been out yet to the sprawling property on the edge of Roaring Springs but had heard about Rylan Bennet's work to rescue various animals that belonged in the wild.

"Can I ask you something?" Bree's tone was serious and an immediate departure from discussion of Rylan's ranch.

"Of course." Aisha tossed her stir stick and gestured toward a nearby table. "Let's sit down."

They'd barely taken their seats when Bree launched

in. "I don't want to burden Trey with this or make him think I don't support him. And I know everyone's focused on the newly discovered body."

"But?" Aisha pressed.

"Is anyone looking for Skye? I hate that my mind keeps going to the same place but I'm worried about her."

"Trey is, too. We all are. And I know all his deputies were briefed on her disappearance." Aisha didn't want to make excuses for Trey or his staff, but she knew just how stretched they were. "It's all coming at them at once."

"I know. It's been like this all year but the discovery on the mountain has made it all worse."

"You doing okay with it?" Although she rarely pushed her clinical work on her loved ones, she was conscious others might think that and quickly added, "And I'm asking as a friend."

A quick smile filled Bree's pretty features. "And a sister."

"That, too." Aisha couldn't bring herself to say the word *sister*. She and Trey might have made tentative steps to making up, but none of it changed the fact that their engagement was still a fake. A night of amazing sex didn't change that.

Or it shouldn't.

They'd made a pact and she was determined to keep her head above water. It would be so simple to lose herself over how easily things had clicked for them in the physical sense. Which was the exact reason she had to guard against it.

"Lookee here. Two string beans in a pod."

The dark words had her and Bree going silent. Aisha didn't even need to turn around to know who it was.

She recognized that voice and, worse, the disdain and hostility beneath. "Do I need to call security?"

Barton Evigan's brother stood before her, looming over their small table. "I haven't done anything wrong. This is a public place."

"Yet you keep showing up in my space and you never have anything nice to say. I'm beginning to think you're a stalker."

Although he'd made a pest of himself, he was right that all his encounters had been public. She'd received no threats anywhere near her home and Aisha knew her pushback was flimsy.

And yet...

She didn't miss the way his eyes narrowed or the belligerent hunch of his shoulders. "Trace Evigan isn't a stalker and I sure as hell ain't stalking you."

"Then what do you want?" Bree asked.

"I came to pay my respects. Heard the news about the sheriff. Sure would be a shame if he died before my brother could beat him in November."

Respect? The man didn't know the meaning of the word!

"Counting chickens again?" Aisha shot back.

"Hee-hee." His guffaw was loud and obnoxious, echoing through the vast, nearly empty room. "Them roosters are looking pretty good right about now."

With that he let out another harsh laugh and headed off. Aisha was still staring at the empty doorway to the cafeteria when Bree spoke. "What roosters?"

"He's a weirdo." Aisha shook a hand, the vague memory of their run-in the day before at Bruno's still fresh in her mind. "The man doesn't know how to deliver an idiom to save his life. Yesterday he told me Trey was counting his roosters before they hatched."

"He's a problem."

"I know he is. But since there are others that are bigger today, we'll worry about him later."

Aisha meant it and had nearly put Evigan out of her mind. She did mention it to Trey after Bree and Rylan had left—he was mad and grumpy enough, keeping him out of the loop was tantamount to starting another fight—but she was determined not to let Trace Evigan get her goat.

Which was not only the proper animal, but the proper way to say it, she thought with no small measure of satisfaction as she settled in for the night in a small chaise in the corner of Trey's room. She'd intended to go home—Trey had pressed her to get some sleep in her own bed—but despite her desire not to give the man head space, something about the run-in with Evigan had her restless and seeking the solace of Trey's company. The TV was on low but she kept keying in and out of the news stories that droned on and on.

The discovery of the body was still front and center, and over the past day Trey's deputies, working with the Roaring Springs PD, had identified the woman as Wendy Sinclair. She'd been a visitor to the area and, according to the front desk clerk at the hotel she was staying at, had spent little time in her room, anxious to be out and enjoying the waning days of summer.

Some enjoyment now, Aisha thought, her mind drifting as she faded toward sleep. The poor woman was dead, a trip to Colorado the last vacation she'd ever take.

Sleep had nearly taken her under when Aisha sat straight up, all of it coalescing at once.

The dead woman.

Evigan's stupid comment about chickens.

And the note.

"What is it?" Trey was still awake, his attention sharp and focused and not at all stilted by sleep.

"The note. The one that came in last week. After the hair sample was left outside."

"It's on my phone." Trey snagged his cell off the small tray beside his bed. He swiped a few times before handing it to her. "Here."

She scanned the image of the letter, the nonsense words rearranging themselves in her mind as she read the note through a new lens.

Slow like the fox.

You'd better watch out.

Evidence in a box.

Another victim, no doubt.

Slow like the fox.

They'd been so focused on the nonsense of the rhymes that they'd missed the bigger piece. Foxes weren't slow, they were *sly.* A person who understood idioms would know that. Yet Trace Evigan consistently confused his.

"What's going on, Aish?"

She walked Trey through her concerns. The strange comments and the consistently confused statements Trace Evigan used in his everyday speech. "He did it at dinner last week at the Chateau. Remember? He said, 'You catch more honey with flies.'" Aisha pushed on, "And he did it to me yesterday when I was getting the pizza at Bruno's."

"You think it's him?"

"I think it's a line to tug."

"And he's got more to gain than most." Trey extended his hand. "May I have my phone?"

She handed it back not surprised when he called Daria. What she hadn't expected was what came next. "Call Roberts and get him over to the station with his profilers. I'm getting out of here and I'll meet you there."

Chapter Seventeen

Trey fought the pain that coursed through his back muscles and pushed on. He'd surprised the hell out of the nurses' station when he'd started pushing his call button. But it was his near attempt to remove his IV that finally had one of them moving into action instead of trying to quietly convince him to stay in bed.

He'd checked out of Roaring Springs Memorial in what he figured was record time and knew he'd have hell to pay with his mother and with Aisha once this was all said and done.

But he needed to get to work.

Daria had already begun pulling background and whatever information she could find on Trace Evigan and had it all spread out on the conference room table when he walked in. Agent Roberts was already with her, wide-awake even for the late hour.

"Okay, Colton." Roberts pointed toward the files. "Take us through it."

"Ms. Allen will." Trey turned to Aisha, pride at her insight and quick connections racing through him. She was so damn smart and this only proved, in yet another of a myriad ways, why he loved her so much.

Love.

All-the-way love. The sort that took the base of their friendship and added to it, layer by layer, facet by facet.

Hell and damn, why'd he think of it here? Now? When they had an audience and a potential killer to catch.

Oblivious to the direction of his thoughts, Aisha pulled the note they'd received the prior week to the top of the pile. "All along, we've been concerned about two key pieces. The change in pattern of this most recent murder and the seeming nonsense of the letter that was delivered here after the initial hair sample."

She tapped the photo, a match to what he'd shared with her on his phone. "It was the fox reference that got me. All along it seemed like the jumble of words was a way to make the letter rhyme, but that first sentence matches other patterns."

"What patterns?" Roberts sat forward, his already watchful pose shifting into high alert.

Aisha walked Roberts and Daria through the same details she'd shared with Trey in the hospital. She outlined Trace Evigan's comments from the dinner at The Chateau and the interaction they'd had in Bruno's, culminating in the insults he'd tossed at her that afternoon in the hospital cafeteria.

"He's pushing for his brother to become sheriff. Clearly, he's got something to gain." Roberts was thoughtful as he considered the folders Daria laid out. "But it seems like something more."

"A real boon to his business," Daria added. "There have only been whispers. Nothing that's pinned on him. But rumor has it he's moved from some small-time stuff into running guns."

"Define small-time?" Trey asked, curious to how they'd missed any of Evigan's activities.

"Nothing sticks to this guy other than whispers, but now that I've asked some things are popping. Apparently he's been rumored for years to be a local bookie as well as an arranger for when the big-money high rollers come to town. He knows where to get recreational drugs and high-class hookers and has made a fair business doing both."

"And the guns?" Roberts probed.

"Looks like Evigan's gotten into a new line of work." Daria pulled out a slim folder. "The details are really vague but a shipment was intercepted at the New Mexico border about four months ago."

"I remember that," Roberts said. "Our office got a big notice on it and then the murders were discovered and all attention shifted."

Although Trey had assumed the Feds had unlimited resources, the recognition they struggled with manpower, too, was strangely comforting. "Well, we now have a lot of suspicion and speculation but not enough for a warrant."

"We can try to push down the bookie angle. See if we can get something for a warrant," Daria said.

Trey had watched his deputy work through it all, along with Roberts, and was proud of how far she'd come. But it was time to step in and help get this one over the finish line. "We don't need a warrant."

"Why not?" Daria asked.

"The man loves attention. Craves it. I'll pick a fight with his brother and we'll use it as the jumping-off point."

Aisha spoke first. "You were in a hospital bed up until an hour ago."

"Now I'm not."

"Trey, come on."

"She's right, Colton." Agent Roberts stepped in. "This guy's not to be underestimated, horrendous rhyming skills aside."

Trey appreciated the concern but he wasn't going to let a few bruises stop this train. For the first time in what felt like forever they had a lead. A direction that had real merit for pursuit. He'd be damned if he was going to waste it.

"If Evigan is looking to expand his offerings by putting his brother in a local position of power, we need to stop it. It's bothered me all along that my opponent for the job comes off like a belligerent fool. I'm not missing my chance to prove why."

AISHA KNEW IT was useless to argue but she wasn't giving up without trying. Daria had taken Agent Roberts to an empty office so he could make a private call and it had given Aisha a few precious minutes to make her case.

"Trey, tell me again why you won't let this go for a few days. Evigan's clearly not going to evaporate into the wind. He's backing his brother and making a nuisance of himself. Where's he going?"

"He might jump if word gets out we've connected him to the murder."

"Which is a stretch." She wanted him to succeed—truly she did—but the damn stubborn man needed some time to heal. "We don't know if he's a murderer. It's an awfully big leap from running numbers and local hookers and guns to murder."

"He's obviously leveled up. Has more to risk." Trey paced his office, ticking the man's possible crimes off on his fingers. "Murder isn't as big a stretch as you think it is."

"But he's a local guy no one's even truly pinned a crime on. He wasn't on your radar and now here—" Aisha knew it the moment she overstepped.

The moment all his pain and frustration and anger over the current state of the investigation flared up into one raging fireball.

"I'm well aware the bastard hasn't been on my radar. Which is why he's not going to get away with anything else."

"That's not your fault."

"Yes, it is!" All that pain bubbled up and needed somewhere to go. She knew it and understood its root cause, so she settled in to do what she could to help him through it.

"His brother is my bigoted, bigmouthed opponent. He's been a thorn from the very first. I should have made it my business to understand who these people are and why they've targeted the sheriff's office seemingly out of nowhere."

"You're not omniscient, Trey. No one is."

"It's my job to understand! To know!"

Her mental insistence on staying calm and listening vanished in a heartbeat. "Right. Because while in the midst of dealing with a serial killer on the loose and a bunch of Feds breathing down your neck, you should have known somehow. Big, bad Sheriff Colton!"

"Yes."

"Bull!"

The heat burning off Trey in waves bumped up against her and she decided then and there that she was done. "I've watched you. For the past few months, I've watched you take this on. You've convinced yourself, somewhere way down deep inside, that you have to carry the entire burden."

"Because it's mine."

"It's ours. It's your family's. It's your deputies'. All of us are here for you. Have been here for you." Aisha hesitated before pressing on. "Would have been here for you, with or without a fake engagement."

"That's separate from this."

"Is it? You get a visit from the governor's lackey and suddenly decide you need a charade for the whole damn town?"

"It's not a charade."

Panic flooded her veins. Oh, goodness, she had to be careful here. She didn't want any of it to be a pretense—hadn't wanted that from the start—but if she was going to shift gears now and start believing that what they had was not only real but had a chance for a future, she was done for.

She'd done that once before. She'd believed a charade and been deluded by pretty lies and had paid a terrible price. It had taken years to rebuild her confidence, and in the end, that was after realizing that Kenneth was nowhere near the man Trey Colton was.

Nor would he ever be.

It was only now that she knew the deepest truth. The one her conscious mind had whispered over and over, even as she refused to listen. Her feelings for Trey weren't fleeting.

And heaven help her, there was no way she was getting out of this unscathed.

But she needed to believe she could hold on to some semblance of control. With that foremost in her thoughts, Aisha pressed back. "Yes, Trey, it is."

He moved, whip quick and surprisingly agile for having been in a hospital bed less two hours earlier. His arms came around her, hard and fast, and his mouth met hers. Harsh. Demanding. And absolutely in the moment.

Oh, how she wanted this. Wanted to believe they could sink into the heat and need between them and everything would be okay.

Because it *felt* okay. More than okay, actually.

It felt glorious.

That was her last coherent thought as his mouth took her under, his tongue urgent and insistent as he branded her. Unwilling to hold back, she gave him the same in turn, willing all her feelings to somehow manifest in the physical what she knew she couldn't have in the emotional.

They were friends. Better than friends, really. But that didn't mean they were destined for forever.

She'd convinced herself they could be better. Bigger than what they'd already been. That making love and pretending their way through a fake engagement was something their friendship could withstand.

Only now she knew the truth of it all.

There was no going back.

Ever.

There was only one way forward and she feared once the dust settled they'd realize that path was one they'd each walk alone.

"Trey." She pressed her hands to his shoulders, holding him still.

He stopped immediately, his dark gaze sharp with awareness. Of her. Of what beat between them. "Oh, Aish. Please don't walk away."

"It's not real."

"Yes, it is." He pressed his forehead to hers. "It's the most real thing I've ever experienced."

"It's a mirage." She whispered the words, afraid of their power. As afraid to deny what was between them as to accept it.

"No, damn it, it isn't! I love you!"

Whatever she'd been expecting—hoping for, even— was contained in those three simple words.

It would be so easy to give in. So easy to fall. But she'd done that once before and she had to stay strong.

Lifting her head, she pressed her lips to his, whisper soft, before she pulled back for fear she'd lose her nerve. "I love you, too. I always have. But it's not enough."

TRACE EVIGAN IGNORED the third ping from his cell phone and settled in with his laptop. He and Barton had always had a limited relationship and over the past month he'd remembered why.

Damn, his kid brother could whine. He'd done it as a kid, chasing behind him on the ball fields and as they rode bikes and even as they got older, battling each other for some of the prettiest girls in high school. His brother was a grade A pain in the ass and the last thirty years hadn't done much to change that.

So yeah, he was going to ignore his texts and focus on his own business. The whole reason he'd taken such an interest in Barton's sudden deep-seated desire to serve the public.

What Trace really needed was for Barton to get the job so he'd have an ally in the sheriff's office, ready to look a blind eye toward his expanding business.

The guns had been a lucky thing. He'd been looking for a few expansion opportunities and the high rollers who filtered in and out of Roaring Springs had finally paid dividends. Trace always kept an ear to the ground and when he'd caught wind through one of his enforcers that a player in the drug and gun trade was giving up his beautiful Miami winter to do a bit of skiing in his great state, he'd made it his business to charm his way into an introduction.

He'd worried in those first few minutes. Victor Espirito hadn't seemed all that interested in expanding and seemed more than a little pissed he was being asked to give up any part of his vacation to talk business. His dark eyes were cold—way too cold for someone who spent the majority of his time in the heat—but Trace had pressed on. He'd explained his connections in the western part of the United States and how he could help build an expansion plan for Espirito's business. Yeah, sure, it had been a bit of tap dancing, but he'd pushed his way through.

And had a contract to run a few shipments of drugs and guns by mid-May.

The discovery on the mountain of all those women had nearly done him in. Espirito had spooked, concerned that the "federal scrutiny" suddenly bearing down on Roaring Springs would be too much, even though the first few runs had gone perfectly. But again, Trace had pressed on.

That was when he'd gotten the idea to drag baby Bart in on the whole thing.

Barton thought all Trace did was run numbers and that was fine. The less his brother knew, the better. But putting Big Bad B, as he'd begun calling him, into the sheriff's office would go a long way toward calming down any fears there was too much interference in his business.

If only there was someone other than a Colton in the sheriff's spot. And Trey Colton was the worst of the bunch. Trace had analyzed how he might make inroads, planting something at the dude's house or making up false accusations, but the man's reputation was ironclad. Add on the new fiancée he was parading around town, and Trace was stuck.

He needed something, and time was running out. He'd believed Barton had the upper hand, especially as they spread rumors about Trey Colton's incompetence in dealing with the Avalanche Killer, but based on the rumors around town, the winds might be changing. People loved the guy, and the woman he'd left for dead at the edge of the woods had people concerned but possibly thinking a copycat was on the loose.

Which was the last thing he needed.

He'd been careful but he didn't need Espirito catching wind of the news up here. Nor did he need someone who suddenly decided they needed to look for someone else other than the Avalanche Killer.

Damn, what a freaking mess.

His phone went off and he answered it by rote, forgetting he was screening Barton's insistent messages. "Evigan."

"Hello, Mr. Evigan. I'm glad you've answered."

Trace pulled the phone back, curious to see the number was blocked. Was it Espirito?

He didn't dare ask, so he pushed as much snarl into his tone as he could. "Who is this?"

"A friend."

"I have plenty of friends. And I know all their names."

"You don't need to know mine."

"Then I should hang up."

"Do and it will be all too easy to share your name with the authorities. They're rather desperate to close the case on the death of that poor Wendy Sinclair."

Panic, raw and edgy, coated his stomach, and Trace stood as nerves pushed him into motion. "I don't know who you mean."

"Of course you do. She's the poor tourist, traveling here alone, who ended up dead at the edge of the woods. You did a good job of hiding your identity, but not quite good enough."

Trace had learned the lesson early that you never gave in or gave up too much. He had been careful, and other than those few taunts to the cops to poke at Colton and make his deputies think less of their sheriff, he'd been careful with the kill. It wasn't his favorite chore, but he knew how to do it and he knew how to keep his hands clean.

"As I said, I don't need any more friends."

"I think you're going to want to get to know me. Why don't we aim for that copse in the woods you're so fond of? The one now covered in police tape? I'm an early riser so I'll see you at five."

The line went dead before Trace could protest or even attempt to keep up the pretense of innocence. The back of his neck prickled—had done so since the start of the call—but there was nothing for it. He needed to see this one through.

Too much was riding on his new work with Espirito. He was standing with the big dogs now. And big dogs didn't leave any stray leashes hanging around.

IT'S NOT ENOUGH.

Trey stared at his computer screen, refusing to give in to sleep even as the words and images blurred and his eyes burned with fatigue. But Aisha's words burned in his mind, far hotter than sleep burned his eyes.

They were enough. He knew they were enough. It might have taken them a long time to get to this point— and their path was far from logical or orthodox—but they were *here*, damn it.

They'd found their way.

Why couldn't she see that? Or worse, why was she so determined to paint him with the same brush as that ass she'd dated in college? Yes, their fake engagement was a ruse they'd conjured up, but that didn't mean it was totally a lie. They'd been honest with each other. With their immediate families, too.

What had happened to her in New York had been something else entirely.

Damn, the man had a whole family he'd hidden from her, blithely leading her down a path of pretend happiness when all along he'd played her.

This wasn't the same.

Since his thoughts kept circling around that same thought, he tried to shift gears. He was tired already, might as well keep going. Besides, there was no way he could risk losing another day while a killer loomed large.

Besides, Aisha wasn't with him so what did any of it matter?

He'd downed another round of aspirin around 2:00 a.m. and settled in with the files Daria had pulled. They were classic Daria—thorough and detailed— and still he'd had to read several of them over, fighting through the exhaustion.

The ring of his phone startled him, pulling him from the lull of putting one mental foot in front of the other. Trey glanced at his mobile phone, the screen face lit up and the caller identified as *Unknown* immediately piquing his interest.

Unknown?

To the county sheriff's personal number?

"This is Colton."

"I thought you'd be up."

The voice was slightly muffled, as if the caller wanted to hide his voice, but there was no mistaking the menace or an odd, underlying glee.

The Avalanche Killer?

"What do you want?"

"Oh, it's not what I want. It's what *you* want."

"I don't want anything." Which wasn't true, but Trey opted to go for it, curious to the possible reply.

"Sure you do, Sheriff. We all want something. Respect. Understanding. Reelection. Human beings have any number of reasons for why they do things." A low rumble of laughter came through the line. "You should know that better than most. Your pretty fiancée studies the human mind, doesn't she?"

At the mention of Aisha, Trey's blood ran cold, fear

ratcheting his pulse through the roof. "What do you want?"

"I told you, friend. It's what you want."

"What do I want?"

"The man who killed Wendy Sinclair. You can find him at the dump site. Be there around five. You'll catch your man and watch the sun come up."

The phone clicked off and Trey hardly dared to believe what he'd heard, let alone the meaning behind any of it. Who made a phone call and offered up the location of a killer?

Trey glanced at his watch, mentally calculating the time he had and how quickly he could call in reinforcements. He wanted to catch a killer—desperately wanted to put something right in his world—but he wasn't stupid.

Nor was he interested in going into battle without any backup.

"I DON'T LIKE it, Trey." Daria sat beside him in one of the two unmarked vehicles they had for the office.

"I don't either, but what am I supposed to do? I can't ignore it."

"No."

He'd called Daria first, then toyed with phoning Aisha. In the end, he'd opted for a text, telling her that he loved her and didn't like the way they'd ended things. It wasn't quite a final declaration in the event things went south at the dump site, but it was something.

And it gave him a place to build upon once this was over.

Whatever this was.

"I don't know why you won't call Agent Roberts."

While Trey was pleased Daria had developed a better working relationship with the federal agent, he wasn't ready to let the man fully in on their turf.

"This case is ours. Wendy Sinclair is ours."

"Yeah." Daria finally nodded. "She is. She has been from the start."

"So we'll end this."

They'd roused six other deputies, setting people into motion as quickly as they could for roughly ninety minutes of op prep from the moment the call came in until Trey had to approach the dump site. Two followed behind in the other unmarked vehicle and the other four were partnered, one in a patrol car and the other pair embedded in the woods.

"You ready?" Trey adjusted his vest, well aware his torso might be protected but his head wasn't. The same went for Daria.

"Yeah."

He stepped from the car, his gun in hand as he walked toward the dump site. He had no illusions holding a gun was going to make his visitor happy, but he refused to put even a single extra second at risk.

The clearing was empty and he could still see a few stray pieces of police tape lying on the ground. This was the spot.

He didn't question Daria had taken up her position out of sight, and he moved farther into the clearing, determined to see this through. The call hadn't sat well with him from the start, but risking losing out on a killer wasn't an option.

The real question was, who had made the call?

The real Avalanche Killer, irritated that he had a copycat?

Or someone else?

It hadn't escaped his notice it felt like there was something beneath all that had happened this year. The attacks on his family. The strange occurrences at the various Colton Empire properties. Even the arrival of Barton Evigan, seemingly from out of the woodwork, had been a surprise. Unpleasant, but out of place, as well.

"Colton!"

Trey whirled at the shout, various pieces falling into place as he registered the tableau spread out before him. Trace Evigan stood in the clearing, a gun of his own in hand.

But he had one distinct advantage.

Daria stood beneath the crook of his arm, held flush against his body as a gun lay pressed to her skull.

AISHA READ THE text from Trey, the early-morning missive a surprise. She was used to waking up to one of his texts—something he'd thought of during the night or even something goofy he'd seen on TV or read online winging its way to her—but nothing like this.

Our conversation isn't over.
I'm not giving us up.
I love you.

There was a weird finality to it all, even as she wanted to believe the words. Did he think she was giving up?

Hadn't she?

The question flew through her mind so quickly she couldn't hide from it.

Wasn't that exactly what she had done?

She'd painted him with the "Kenneth Brush" and let that color her view of everything happening between them. It wasn't that they didn't have things to work out—people went from friends to lovers in a flash in fairy tales, not real life—but she was being unfair to both of them to say they didn't have their heads on straight.

Or not know what they wanted.

The ringing of her phone startled her, and she saw Bree's name cover the face. An unnatural feeling of dread filled her throat as she struggled to sit up. "Hey."

"Aisha. You have to come. Meet me at the gallery."

"What's wrong?"

"It's Trey. Rylan got a call from Liam. He's down at the park and his deputies have called in backup."

If she hadn't been sitting, Aisha knew she'd have fallen to her knees.

Suddenly it all came clear. That was the reason for the text. The weird sense of apology and finality.

He'd gone out to confront a killer.

TREY KEPT HIS focus on Trace and Daria, cursing himself every step of the way. He'd done this.

Pushed this.

Insisted on this.

"What are you doing here, Evigan?"

"What are *you* doing here?" the man shot back. "How'd you intercept me? Are you the caller?"

"What caller?"

Evigan tightened his hold on Daria when she attempted to speak, his body shaking as he stood behind her. "Don't lie to me! It was you who made the call."

"I didn't. But I got a call, too. That wasn't you?"

"Hell, no!" the man screamed back, and Trey kept his gaze on Daria. He knew she was trained in crisis management and knew she'd take whatever opportunity presented itself to get loose.

Which meant he had to be prepared.

He'd already turned off the safety on his weapon and wouldn't hesitate to shoot Trace Evigan. Even if it meant they knew less than when they'd arrived and would miss the opportunity to learn more.

Or even why both of them had been called there in the first place.

"Let her go, Evigan."

"Are you crazy? What other protection do I have?"

"The protection of the law if you lower your weapon and let Deputy Bloom go."

Trace snorted. "Right. Like you're going to protect me."

"I am. Because it's my job and because it's the right thing to do."

"That's a load of crap," Evigan snarled.

"Don't you believe your brother would do the same if he wins in November?"

"Barton is too stupid to know any better."

Trey had figured as much but now wasn't the time to get into it. "He's running for the job. He should be prepared for it."

Another snort echoed through the early-morning hour. The faintest twinges of light had begun in the east, adding to the purple color that filled the air. And still, the man held Daria in a solid grip, his hold unwavering.

"Why did you come here? Did you kill Wendy Sinclair?"

"I'm not telling you anything."

"So you're the Avalanche Killer?" Daria asked.

"Hell, no! I didn't kill those women and I certainly haven't been at it for a decade."

Trey heard the vague slip—and the possible indicators that the man did kill Wendy Sinclair—but he didn't want to agitate him. "Then let the deputy go and we'll talk about it. You can tell us what you do know so we can cross you off the list."

"I'm not stupid, Colton!" Evigan screamed, the suggestion to turn himself in going no better than Trey's first attempt.

Which meant they were at a standoff and each moment they stood still, the more risk there was to Daria that Trace would shift into rasher behavior. Desperate men did desperate things.

"Come on, Evigan." Daria pushed and probed, her voice harsher than he usually heard. "You can tell us. It's not like any of us are going anywhere anytime soon. How'd you do it? Lure your victims in. And then how'd you find that place on the side of the mountain to put them all?"

Trace's eyes grew large, the taunting clearly getting to him. It was just the break she was obviously waiting for, and the moment the man's arm trembled, Daria made her move.

With a high-pitched scream, she shoved her arms skyward, fully dislodging him even as she dropped down, out of his grip. Evigan caught on quick—faster than Trey would have expected—and was already aiming his weapon at Daria as she crawled over the grass to get away.

The backup waiting in the woods moved in, but Trey was already in motion, the kickback of his weapon registering as Trace's form fell to the ground.

It was over in moments, the echo of his weapon still

flooding his senses as Trey took in the downed form of Trace Evigan. His deputies moved in and Trey followed close behind, determined to see this through.

Determined to be the leader they all deserved.

Trey knelt to the ground, searching for a pulse. It was only when he found none that he sat back on his heels. Although the sound of gunfire still rumbled in his ears, turning the morning air quiet, Trey felt the first stirrings of relief.

They hadn't caught the Avalanche Killer. He'd bet nearly anything on it. But they had caught the man who targeted and killed Wendy Sinclair. With careful police work he knew they'd finalize that case, connecting each and every dot between Trace Evigan and the young tourist.

For now, it would have to be enough.

AISHA FOUND HIM like that, kneeling beside the body of Trace Evigan. She wanted to race toward him, but Trey's deputies stood in a protective circle around him, blocking her way.

So she gave it a minute, letting it all sink in. And allowing the fresh morning breeze to blow the last vestiges of doubt from her mind.

They belonged together.

Everyone they knew had seen it but the two of them, and it was high time she and Trey caught up.

Daria finally saw her there beyond the edge of the circle, and beckoned her forward. At the same time, she laid a hand on Trey's shoulder, urging him up.

He turned, holstering his weapon as he did, and Aisha knew she'd chosen wisely. The able protector, determined to do right by all.

It was time she did right by him.

Unwilling to get too close to the scene, she waited for Trey to come to her. A million thoughts of all she wanted to say flooded her mind, but the moment he was close enough to touch, she wrapped her arms around him and pulled him close.

There would be words later. Apologies, too. But for now it was the two of them.

"I love you, Trey. I'm sorry it had to come to this for me to say it. And I'm sorry I left last night with so many things lingering between us."

"I love you, too." He pressed his lips to hers in a hard kiss before pulling back. "I want to make a life with you. For real. Nothing fake or pretend or for show. I want it for us."

"I want that, too."

"When can we start planning it?" His eyes clouded and he glanced over his shoulder. "I'm going to have to take some mandatory leave after this morning. Protocol."

"That will give us time to plan." It would also give her time to keep an eye on him, making sure the emotional aftermath of killing Evigan could be managed and dealt with. "Oh, and help with the emus."

"What emus?"

"The ones your sister and Rylan are welcoming at the ranch. They told us about them, but you were grumpy and not paying attention."

"That doesn't sound very relaxing."

"I've known you since you were eight. I've never seen you relax."

"You're right." He smiled and pressed his lips to hers

once more. Despite the pall that hung over the clearing, there was joy.

So much joy.

And emus.

Epilogue

It had all gone according to plan. A few well-placed phone calls and every idiot member of this little play fell into line. That moron Evigan had been a boon but hey, he knew how to take advantage of an opportunity when it presented itself.

And Evigan had qualified in spades.

How could it be that easy? Even as he asked himself the question, he knew the answer.

The Coltons had no idea what lived and breathed, right there in their midst, just beneath their collective noses. They'd spent their precious little lives living in a bubble of luxury and pride and greed and it was all going to come crashing down.

Every brick in The Chateau. Every tree at The Lodge. Every single portion of The Colton Empire was going down.

He'd already laid the groundwork.

All that was left was to pull the trigger.

* * * * *

COMING SOON!

We really hope you enjoyed reading this book. If you're looking for more romance, be sure to head to the shops when new books are available on

Thursday 8th August

To see which titles are coming soon, please visit

millsandboon.co.uk/nextmonth

MILLS & BOON

HEROES

At Your Service

Experience all the excitement of a
gripping thriller, with an intense romance
at its heart. Resourceful, true-to-life
women and strong, fearless men face
danger and desire - a killer combination!

LET'S TALK
Romance

For exclusive extracts, competitions and special offers, find us online:

f facebook.com/millsandboon

🐦 @MillsandBoon

📷 @MillsandBoonUK

Get in touch on 01413 063232

For all the latest titles coming soon, visit
millsandboon.co.uk/nextmonth

JOIN US ON SOCIAL MEDIA!

Stay up to date with our latest releases, author
news and gossip, special offers and discounts, and
all the behind-the-scenes action
from Mills & Boon...

 millsandboon

 millsandboonuk

 millsandboon

It might just be true love...

GET YOUR ROMANCE FIX!

MILLS & BOON
— *blog* —

Get the latest romance news, exclusive author interviews, story extracts and much more!

blog.millsandboon.co.uk